Festung Europa

Festung Europa

The Anglo-American Nazi War

Jon Kacer

SEA LION PRESS

First published by Sea Lion Press, 2017

ISBN: 1976423236
ISBN-13: 978-1976423239

The following is a work of alternate history. For narrative purposes, everything except the Afterword is written 'in-universe,' as if the events herein took place.

Up until October 1942, they did.
After that date, with some exceptions, they did not.

Preface

Before examining the actual final conflict between the Western democracies – chiefly Canada, Great Britain, and the United States – and Nazi Germany, it is worth reviewing the circumstances that brought the world to that critical juncture.

In 1939, Nazi Germany, then also called the Third Reich or simply the Reich, had initiated the European Phase of the Second World War with the invasion of Poland. At the time of the invasion, Germany was in a state of near-alliance with the Soviet Union with Soviet oil and agriculture providing much of Reich's fuel and food. Poland was supported by both France and Great Britain, and the two Western states had made clear that an attack on Poland would lead to war. It has long been debated why the Democracies waited until the Polish crisis to confront the still-developing German war machine, but the decisions made in both London and Paris in late summer of 1939 were resolute, and both nations believed that their combined power would be sufficient to deter Adolph Hitler's Germany from aggression against Poland. On September 1, 1939, Hitler demonstrated his contempt for, and disbelief in, the Democracies' statements and warnings when the German military (or, as it was known at the time, the Wehrmacht) crossed the international frontier separating Germany and Poland and unleashed an early version of mechanized warfare against the Polish Army. Shortly after the Reich's invasion of Poland, its quasi-ally the Soviet Union entered Poland and annexed a significant portion of the country's eastern provinces. Strangely, this action caused no reaction by either the British or French governments while those of the Reich were responded to with declarations of war.

Despite these declarations, and the fact that Hitler had focused well over 80% of his total military strength against the Poles, neither France nor Britain made any serious attempt to attack Germany at this point of greatest vulnerability. Much like the decisions made as early as 1936, this failure to act has been the subject of enormous debate among military professionals for almost three generations, with no consensus having been reached beyond a general agreement that the period from September through mid-November 1939 represents one of the great missed opportunities in military history. Considering the results, this failure must also be considered to be one of the starkest tragedies in human memory.

Following a period of time dubbed the Phony War by the era's media, German forces invaded Norway in March and then attacked France and the Low Countries in May of 1940, achieving strategic surprise despite the existing state of war between the Germans and the Democracies of the West. Much as had been the case in Poland in 1939, German mobile tactics, built around armored formations supported by air power, proved to be insoluble by Allied commanders. While the failure of the Poles to contain and defeat German spearheads can be at least partially explained by lack of proper equipment, the same can not be said for the inexplicable collapse of both the British and French armies which had equal, if not superior, equipment, especially in the area of tanks and motorization. Whatever the cause, the Reich's invasion of Western Europe was a stunning and rapid success. By the end of June 1940, Germany and her Italian ally controlled all of Western Europe save the British Isles, Iberian Peninsula, and Switzerland.

While Germany was demonstrating a stunning efficiency, their Fascist Italy partner was showing nearly the exact opposite. Whether the result of poor civilian leadership or a case of Military General Staff incompetence on a grand scale, the independent Italian war effort proved to be a disaster for the Italian people. An ill-advised adventure into Greece was retrieved from defeat solely by the intervention of Wehrmacht forces sent by Hitler to save his Italian ally. Unfortunately for Rome, Hitler proved to be unwilling to send German forces to Africa when Italian forces found themselves overmatched by British Commonwealth forces in the North African Desert. When the British, with the support of "Free French" political leaders, used Italy's attacks into the Middle East as a pretext to seize French colonies in the region and depose the pro-Axis Shah of Iran, Hitler presented Mussolini with an ultimatum demanding that Italy take no further actions outside of Europe until the Bolsheviks had been defeated or face the loss of all German support. Faced with the prospect of losing his gains in Greece and the portion of France that had been ceded to Rome by Hitler as spoils, Mussolini relented. The resulting low-level naval war in the Mediterranean persisted until the end of active hostilities in Europe without causing any significant impact on the war's outcome. The end of German activity in the Mediterranean Theater also marked the effective end of active combat with Commonwealth Forces in all areas except the North Atlantic, where Germany waged a serious and quite nearly successful submarine warfare campaign against shipping headed to Great Britain.

In June of 1941, after nearly a full year of preparation, Germany launched Operation Barbarossa, the invasion of its erstwhile ally the Soviet Union. Thanks, in large part, to the remarkable failure of Josef Stalin to react in any reasonable manner to pre-attack intelligence reports regarding German build-ups on the frontier pre-invasion, and Stalin's post-invasion ham-handed intervention in the actual conduct of Red Army operations, German forces made huge gains in the war's opening months before the first year's campaign was brought to a close by the Russian winter. The winter of 1941-42 was where the Reich's yearlong preparation for Barbarossa first bore fruit. Having anticipated defeating the Soviets in the war's first few months, the Germans had amassed a large amount of winter uniforms and equipment for the expected occupation forces (and, unknown to most of the Wehrmacht's planning staff, Einsatzgruppen detachments) that allowed German ground forces to endure the very poor conditions better than the shattered elements of the Red Army.

In December of 1941, following the Japanese attack on Pearl Harbor (covered in detail in Volume II), Germany declared War on the United States. While this put Germany into a state of war with the UK, USSR and US, the situation was not nearly as severe as first glance would indicate. The Reich had begun construction of massive defensive fortifications along the entire French coast. Foreshadowing the horrors to come, more than 80% of the labor engaged in construction of the so-called "Atlantic Wall" and other German military facilities in the Occupied Territories was provided by what can only be described as slaves. These unfortunate souls were brought in to do this manual labor from Poland and culled from among Russian PoWs (in direct violation of the Hague Agreements). By early 1942 these fortifications already made any thought of attacking into France via the capture of a port virtual suicide. Combined with the general lack of preparedness of American ground forces in the winter of 1941/42, Germany did not face a true two-front war danger for at least a year and a half from the time of America's entry into the war. It was time the Reich spent very well.

In the spring of 1942 the Germans resumed their offensive in the USSR. This offensive met with nearly the same successes as in the previous year. In the early summer, a drive toward the Caucasus was undertaken, including a serious drive to the Volga. The key position in this southern section of the Soviet Union was centered on the city of Stalingrad. For reasons both practical and symbolic the engagement here was determined to be one that neither side could lose. Losses on both sides were dramatic, beyond anything seen to that point in the European Phase. It was not until October 12 that German forces completed their isolation of the city's defenders when they took what both sides had come to call "The Crossing", the only location on the western side of the Volga where Soviet reinforcements could land in support of the city. Loss of the Crossing meant the inevitable loss of Stalingrad. While small units of Red Army forces fought until early January, the inability of the Soviets to resupply the forces in the city made the heroic stand of these small units all the more tragic. Moreover, the capture of the Crossing released better than

240,000 troops of the German 6th Army for duty along the rest of the Volga line before winter fell.

Stalin, never the most forgiving of leaders, reacted violently to the loss of his namesake city. Most of Stavka (the Soviet High command), including Marshall Georgy Zhukov, perhaps the most forward-thinking Soviet commander at the time, along with Marshall Timoshenko, the head of the General Staff, as well as virtually every surviving general officer and Commissar on the Southwest Front, were given six-minute trials followed by a bullet between the eyes. These actions, even more than the actual loss of the city and use of the Volga, were to prove a disaster to the Red Army, one from which it was never to recover fully.

Shorn of most of its planners and leadership by Stalin's fit of pique, Operations Jupiter and Mars, the Soviet attempts to counterattack in March of 1943, were unmitigated disasters, with Red Army losses totaling over 850,000 men killed, wounded, and captured. When Stalin died on March 23rd 1943 – reputedly of a heart attack, although persistent rumors exist to this day that his death was anything but natural – the power vacuum atop the USSR led to a general collapse of Soviet resistance as NKVD and Red Army units fought for position and personal survival. When Beria's NKVD faction was defeated by a group that had Foreign Minister Molotov as a figurehead, the situation had deteriorated to the point where the USSR was forced to seek terms from the Reich.

Unsurprisingly, these terms were well beyond harsh, and both eviscerated the USSR and greatly enhanced the German state. The bounty received by the Reich was staggering, ranging from Soviet gold reserves to fully operational munitions factories to thousands of tons of raw material and supplies that had been produced in American factories and sent to the Soviets as part of Lend-Lease. The remarkable amount and quality of the Lend-Lease materials is reputed to have caused Grand Admiral Raeder of the Kriegsmarine (as the German Navy was known at the time) to state "maybe we shouldn't have sunk so many of those Murmansk convoys!" While the accuracy of this legend will never be known, it would have been an accurate statement.

The State of the War in the West 1942-43

While the US and Great Britain had agreed to a "Europe First" strategy before the war had even begun, for the United States the circumstances in January of 1942 presented problems for the policy. Even at this early date the Reich's fortification efforts along the Channel were enough to give the Combined Chiefs-of-Staff pause. While American planners wanted to close with the Germans at the first opportunity, the where of that encounter was difficult to find. American troops were not trained or combat tested yet, and the British, after their disastrous encounters with the Reich's ground forces, were more than slightly hesitant to invade 'Fortress Europe' until the Soviets had, hopefully, cut the 200+ division German ground force down to a more manageable size. Until then, the Allies would have to find ways to nibble at the Germans without exposing themselves to potential disaster on the beaches of France.

Perhaps the most frustrated members of the American and British militaries were the Air Force commanders. While British Bomber Command was making regular attacks against European targets, they were having almost no impact on German war production while exacting a serious toll among Bomber Command aircrews and aircraft inventories. American commanders were eager to make their debut, but the number of available aircraft was low both in bombers and in escort fighters. While American commanders were certain that the B-17 and B-24 heavy bombers could fight through any opposition, the experiences of Bomber Command indicated that this confidence was somewhat misplaced. In any case, the American bomber forces would not have enough of the "D" model B-17 bombers to begin any sort of offensive until early summer, if not later. Long range bombers were also in great demand in the Pacific, as well as along the American Atlantic coast, where German submarines, the famed U-boats, were causing havoc.

Anglo-American plans for taking offensive action in Europe before mid-1943 were dealt a stunning series of blows by the German successes in Russia, with the Stalingrad disaster causing the Allies to come to a fork in the road regarding war planning. With the sudden possibility of a Soviet collapse, the Allies attempted several large-scale raids into France in hopes of relieving pressure on the Soviets, all of which resulted in failure, or at best pyrrhic victories. The recapture of Guernsey Island, along with the smaller Herm and Sark Islands and several of the nearby islets, from German forces, while providing a morale boost for the British public, was hardly worth the better part of a British parachute division lost in the failed assault on Jersey, or the loss of HMS *Sheffield* and three destroyers, along with the crippling of the cruiser USS *Savannah*, in the Force Jersey rescue effort. Worst of all, these efforts diverted neither German attention nor forces from the main struggle in the East while costing the Allies highly-trained men and much-needed shipping.

As the Eastern Front collapsed, the best the Western Allies could come up with was a rather pointless, if ego-boosting, invasion of Vichy Africa, a move which resulted in the German reoccupation of the previously "independent" portions of European France but no other German reaction. The only significant damage inflicted on Axis fortunes was the destruction of most of the Italian fleet in a series of sharp actions mostly involving Royal Navy forces with only minor USN participation. Even by November of 1942, the USN, led by the relentless efforts of Chief of Naval Operations King, had shifted its gaze to what it saw as the main field of battle in the Pacific.

When Molotov agreed to the German terms for peace, he left the Western Allies in a quandary. There was little doubt that the German Army, with well over 200 battle-hardened divisions, was an overmatch for the currently available Anglo-American ground forces, even if the number of divisions needed to police the freshly conquered territories were taken into account. A significant disagreement broke out between the American and British chiefs regarding the course of the war. The British, strongly supported by Churchill, wanted to invade Sicily as the first step of a Balkan Strategy that would allow access to Europe via the "soft underbelly of the continent". The Americans saw anything but a soft underbelly in the mountains of Italy and the Balkans and believed that they saw a British strategy designed to maintain its Imperial holdings, something that the British stoutly denied. In the end there was no agreement on the next offensive step, simply a decision to ensure that the Reich would not be able to further expand into the Middle East or, now that it was freed of the Eastern Front, invade the British Isles.

Shortly thereafter, American and British divisions deployed into Iran and Iraq, while intense diplomatic pressure was applied to Istanbul to keep Turkey out of the Axis and bring it into the Allied camp. Often the Allied diplomats found themselves competing for calendar space with their Reich counterparts, who were pushing equally hard for Turkey to join the Axis. The Turks, for their part, remembered well the disaster that had befallen them the last time they had allowed themselves to be drawn into a Northern European conflict. They accepted all visitors and kept their options open, hoping for nothing more than to be left alone.

As part of the Allied determination to prevent any invasion of the British Isles, tens of thousands of American ground troops and what rapidly became a stunningly large US air armada settled onto what seemed to be every flat surface in Britain. While regular daylight precision bombing began by the USAAF 8th Air Force, RAF fighter squadrons received reinforcements in the form of American P-38 night fighter squadrons. Soon Luftwaffe bomber pilots learned to dread the silhouette of the "fork-tailed devil" in the night sky as the heavily armed and exceptionally fast Lightning took to the skies against their missions.

Still, even with the diversion of so many soldiers and aircraft, the Allies found their naval forces at loose ends as the U-boat threat was defeated by improved tactics and decoded messages (for details on the decisive impact of allied code breakers against both Germany and Japan, see Chapter 5 of Volume II). These naval units were not left without work for long.

The Third Reich and the creation of Greater Germany

The goal of Nazi Germany in beginning the European Phase of the Second World War was to achieve, it claimed, "living space". This was alongside a desire to unite all the German peoples into a single nation. Both of these claims were, even at the time, viewed with more than some skepticism outside of the Reich's borders. While there were legitimate issues involving the treatment of minorities in various European states (including German speakers in a number of nations), the extreme measures taken by Nazi Party officials as early as 1933 indicate that the desire was far darker than that stated publicly. Reading Hitler's own published works makes clear that a primary driver of the author, and later of his associates, was an overt racism of both remarkable virulence and wide scope. While the Nazi Party had established even before gaining power via the ballot box that it was anti-Semitic, this was far from unusual in 1930s Europe. Such prejudices were widespread and surprisingly accepted across much of society. What were very different were the additional hatreds that were part of the Nazi manifesto, with groups ranging from Slavs to Asians to Roma (Gypsies), along with homosexuals, Communists, intellectuals, the handicapped, and followers of several religions all being marked as "different" and hence dangerous to the "Volk" (German for people, it was commonly used in place of "citizen" or "residents" in the Reich). These beliefs were to produce remarkable results during the acquisition phase of the Reich's attacks across the European continent and in the following years.

An additional element nearly unique to the Reich was that Party ideology, rather than economic or even military considerations, controlled policy making on what quickly became a continental scale. Many studies have been made of the economic damage Nazi racial policies caused to Greater Germany, and they are well beyond the scope of this work. However, it would be remiss not to provide an overview of the Nazi policies and activities that had such a dramatic impact on the eventual outcome of the conflict between the West and Germany.

Well before the invasion of the Soviet Union, the Reich had begun to clear Germany, followed by Austria and Czechoslovakia, of Jews and other undesirables. Initially there appears to have been some question of exactly where the displaced Jews were to be sent, with numerous schemes considered (including a rather bizarre study conducted following the defeat and occupation of France involving moving all the Jews in Europe, along with certain other undesirables, to the island of Madagascar), but with the occupation of much of Poland, with its substantial native Jewish population, it seems that all half measures were considered to be insufficient. This resulted in the infamous "Final Solution to the Jewish Question".

A plan to do nothing less than murder every Jew in Europe (presumably as a first step in ridding the entire planet of them), the Final Solution was a plan of unprecedented scope, involving the extermination of some eleven million people. That even this number was to eventually become just the tip of the exterminations conducted by the Nazis speaks to the power of Hitler himself and the dedication of his subordinates. Headed by Heinrich Himmler, the head of the Nazi Party Internal Security forces, the exterminations of such a massive number of persons became a ghastly testament to the power of the industrialized state. After several false starts involving firing squads, trucks designed to vent exhaust gases into a passenger compartment filled with victims, and simply forcing victims off of cliffs or from bridges of acceptable height – all of which proved to be inadequate given the number of deaths required – Himmler's SS department (a force of troops with unique uniforms who made a personal pledge to Hitler and were outside of the Wehrmacht's command structure) came up with the concept of extermination camps. These camps, designed to kill and "process" as many 115,000 people per month, were established in the region known to the Reich as the General Government (formerly central Poland). The camps were operated as a combination of simple murder sites and slave labor camps where products, many but not all, meant for use by the military were produced. Inmates of the camps were also used to work within the camps, build roads and rail lines, and even construct more camps. These tasks were all done under starvation conditions until an inmate was too weak to work, at which point they were murdered. A common method of determining if an inmate could still perform labor tasks was to punch them in the face. Those who did not fall over, or were able to regain their feet, were deemed capable of continued labor. Had the Nazi government simply committed these acts, it would have been as evil a regime as had ever existed. Of course, the Reich went far beyond even that level of effort.

With the defeat of the USSR, Germany found itself with millions of new subjects, many of which the Party preached as being less than fully human. While there was a need for many of these new subjects as workers, there were far too many to keep around simply laboring for the glory of Greater Germany. Other actions would be needed. Himmler found the most popular answers in the practices of "re-Germanization" and the self-descriptive "extermination through labor".

Re-Germanization was a practice built on the demented racial views of the Nazi Party elite of "The Aryan Ideal". In its most simple form, this meant a native-born German without physical defect. However, as the war continued, this view was gradually expanded, first to German speakers born outside the Reich to "good German stock" and then to individuals and families with blond hair and/or blue eyes. Individuals were offered the opportunity to become "honorary Germans" who would eventually become fully accepted members of the Reich Volk – or, if very young, were simply stripped away from the families and sent to Germany to be raised by Party families (this was especially common with very young infants whose parents had the misfortune not to look German enough to be offered a place in Greater Germany). Individuals who turned down this offer were frequently selected for extermination through labor, where they joined a long list of undesirables including Polish and Soviet PoWs, Roma, Slavs, and especially Communists and other political prisoners. The extermination through labor policy was so effective that SS forces effectively emptied most of the non-critical urban population of the conquered eastern regions through the practice (rural populations were, after a few false starts, mainly left alive to produce food for the Reich). These forced laborers were the engine that built up the famed Atlantic Wall to its eventual fortification depth of 10 kilometers along the French Channel coast and to narrower, but still impressive, size along the rest of the occupied territories. The human toll of completing these defenses is still a subject of considerable debate, mainly centered on the exact definition of a direct casualty of the construction, but is generally agreed to exceed thirteen million in France alone.

Remarkably, the Reich was so confident of its re-Germanization policy that the probationary members of the Volk were soon given jobs in even the most sensitive portions of the Reich's production facilities. Here they often encountered other foreign workers who had nearly as little reason to love Germany as the dispossessed Germans-to-be. The Party was foolishly overconfident that its secret police, especially the dreaded Gestapo, would be able to maintain order and security in every case.

Of course, this level of construction would have been impossible had it not been for the tribute (or "reparations" as the Reich described it) that Germany extracted on a daily basis from the Molotov Government. This tribute, initially filled by stripping the Soviet Union of machine tools, raw materials supplied by the Allies under Lend Lease, and eventually entire factories (Göring is on record as having said "well, if they could move them behind the Urals, they can surely move them back" when an aide questioned the ability of the Molotov government to supply sufficient machine tools to fill its quotas) and later supplied from the immense mineral wealth of the Siberian Steppe and the labor of millions of Russians. When combined with the "contributions" from Axis allies like Vichy France, Denmark, Norway, Croatia, Bulgaria, Hungary, and Italy, and materials purchased from the few unconquered European states, sufficient materials were accumulated to construct the Atlantic Wall and still be able to maintain the German military machine. The steady stream of materials coming out of Siberia, along with the availability of almost no-cost labor, also encouraged German planners to build many of the Reich's new factories in what had once been the Ukraine despite the ongoing low level partisan war that was an ever-present fact in the territories that had once been part of the USSR.

With the addition of Belgian, French, Danish, Dutch, and Ukrainian shipyards, the Reich was also able to begin a serious naval building program with the goal of being able to meet and defeat any Western invasion fleet. While many of Hitler's advisors suggested that it was impossible to catch up to the Royal Navy, much less the USN, Hitler was set in his vision of a Kriegsmarine equal to anything the West could produce.

The re-organization of the Greater German military and its allies

In understanding the eventual events of the final Western Allies-Reich clash it is important to have an overview of the evolution of the Greater German military structure and how its allies and client states fit into the overall European defense network.

With the defeat of the Soviet field armies and the apparent Allied inability to make an immediate entry into occupied Europe, Berlin gradually altered the structure of its own forces and began to make increasing use of the military organizations and/or available manpower of their conquests. In this structure, two different types of non-Reich forces existed: National forces and "Pan-European" units.

National forces were fielded by nations that had more or less joined the German wars voluntarily. These were chiefly forces from Bulgaria, Croatia, Denmark, Italy, Hungary, Norway, Romania, and Slovakia, with France joining these early allied states in late 1945. The National forces had nominal independent command under their respective governments, but all were obligated to follow Berlin's specific directions in military matters. All of the National forces were able to, if they desired, manufacture their own weapons and other equipment, including, in the case of Italy and France, their own aircraft and warship designs. Overall, the National forces, and their home countries, gave many of the appearances of independent states, at least on the surface. In actual fact, each of these countries was utterly dominated politically by Germany, with political leaders selected by Nazi Party leaders in each country with the final approval of Berlin necessary before any changes were made. Each independent European ally also had its own secret police force, based on the SS Gestapo, and staffed by fanatical fascists who often were more radical than their German counterparts. These units crushed any signs of dissent and generally maintained a reign of terror under the oversight of SS Headquarters in Berlin. National military forces were also generally deployed outside their home country (French troops, as an example, were the most numerous garrison forces in southern Italy and Sicily) which reduced the chances of any sort of unfortunate Nationalist uprisings. Although these did occasionally occur, they were crushed with swift brutality. While the overall quality and morale of the National forces was uneven, all were more than sufficient to work as fortress troops with some units being equal to any pure "Old German" formation.

Countries that had not been found to be sufficiently politically reliable to be granted the independence of the Reich client states were not spared from supporting the Reich. In these countries, there were three different levels of conscription all lasting 12 years. The first level was effectively voluntary, as soldiers in SS battalions. These volunteers were limited to those who met the Reich's Aryan ideals in appearance and were, for the most part, fascists and/or dedicated anti-communists.

The second level of conscripts formed the "Pan-European" units. These conscripts were subjected to brutal discipline, required to learn German and subject to ongoing "political education". Discipline in these units was maintained by a combination of fear and blackmail; officers in these units were not required to even file reports if they executed any enlisted man below the rank of Sergeant and desertion was punished, not by execution, but by the liquidation of the deserter's entire family out to first cousins (to remove the "family's taint" from the population). Generally these forces were used against partisans in the East or, if conscripted from eastern populations, as Fortress troops or common laborers.

The third level of conscription was effectively a death sentence as members of labor battalions. This level was reserved for deserters (including those from National forces), those suspected of political activity, criminal acts, individuals with physical or mental deformity (if able to work; those unable to work were sent to extermination camps), and those of "questionable blood". Those unfortunate enough to be assigned to these battalions were used to clear booby traps, mining, agricultural labor, and in many cases medical or scientific experimentation. The 12-year term of service for these conscripts was purely for show. Their actual fate was extermination through labor.

With the organization of the rest of occupied Europe and Reich client state manpower into military formations, the Nazi Party proceeded to remake its own forces. In this, it was again guided as much by ideology as by common sense or tradition. The German Army, despite its great successes in the European Pulse, was nearly dismantled in the immediate aftermath of its victory and replaced by a military wing of the Party, the Waffen-SS. The dismantling of the Heer (as the German Army was then known) had long been a goal of Hitler and his advisors, one that was confirmed as necessary when Heer troops and officers, from the most junior platoon leaders to some of the General Staff's senior members, protested when the Heer was used to round up and, in some cases, execute Jews, Roma, and other undesirables in what the traditional Heer members found to be dishonorable conditions. Many of these troops, including senior officers, were either demoted or placed under the authority of SS commanders who found the professional military to be "squeamish" when it came to achieving the goals of Greater Germany. With the introduction of National forces and Pan-European units into garrison duties, the Waffen-SS became a mainly armored/mechanized formation, with much of its complement assigned to oversee loyalty of the client militaries and act as mobile reserves to reinforce the defenses of the Atlantic Wall. A separate group of SS troops, these mainly comprised of former Heer enlisted men who had committed some minor offense with long-time Party and SS officials as commanders and senior NCOs, were organized into Einsatzgruppen with the mission of hunting down and liquidating fugitive Jews, Roma, partisans, and escaped Soviet PoWs. This was a difficult assignment, with removal to a penal battalion becoming the fate of troops who failed to show proper commitment to the task at hand.

The traditions of both the Luftwaffe (the German Air Force) and Kriegsmarine were altered less than that of the Heer, but both were heavily influenced by the Nazi Party leadership. The Luftwaffe was under the direct command of Hermann Göring, a WWI fighter pilot of some considerable skill who was an early part of the Nazi movement. In addition to his role as Air Force commander, he was also the Deputy Führer of the Reich. Göring was remarkably jealous of the Luftwaffe's privileges and position. Anything having to do with combat in the air, from ground-based anti-aircraft artillery to paratroopers were, in Göring's opinion, property of the Luftwaffe. This led to the unique circumstance of the Air Force being a military inside the military, with light infantry units and even a heavy armor division sharing the Table of Organization with anti-aircraft battalions, fighter, bomber, and observation aircraft squadrons, who all reported to the same command staff. So protective was the Luftwaffe's Chief of his position that the Naval Air Arm took orders not from the Kriegsmarine, but from the Luftwaffe, with the aircraft being the property of Göring's branch, not of the service that owned the ships off which the planes operated. The Luftwaffe also was the true commander of the various National air forces that were supposedly under the command of their independent states.

The Kriegsmarine, of all the German service branches, maintained its long-held traditions. Alone among the armed forces of Europe, the Kriegsmarine maintained the traditional military salute common among the world's militaries, as well as retaining many of the same rituals that would have been recognizable to naval officers from the turn of the century. It was the least political of the Branches, although Party membership was nearly as important as actual skill when promotions were announced. Nearly destroyed in the first two years of the war, the German surface fleet was rebuilt and expanded by Hitler, as much as a symbol of equality with the Allies as with any specific mission in mind, with surprising speed thanks to the resources of the occupied territories and client states. This was especially true after the de facto 1946 cease-fire when the end of regular bombing allowed construction to proceed in an orderly fashion.

The Allied Pacific Campaign and the shaping of the Western Forces

With the collapse of the USSR, the Western Allies suddenly found themselves in a quandary. They had agreed that the Nazi state was the more serious threat, and to follow a "Europe First" strategy despite the loud protests of the Chief Naval Officer, Admiral Ernest King, who believed that Japan needed to be brought to book for its attack on Pearl Harbor and other Western Allied state colonies and bases across most of the Pacific. With the loss of their Soviet ally, London and Washington found themselves suddenly facing a ground force exceeding 200 divisions, meaning that any assault on Fortress Europe would require 600 divisions (using the accepted 3-1 attacker/defender ratio in use at the time). Even with the combined strength of the entire British Commonwealth and the United States of America there was little hope of gathering that level of troops in the foreseeable future; the Allies would need to reduce the Heer's force size prior to any invasion to make the liberation of Europe possible.

The only reasonable option for the Allies was an air offensive using heavy and medium bombers with the goal of damaging German civilian morale and the German industrial base sufficiently to allow a lower number of ground forces to make a successful attack. This approach ignored the fact that bombing had not broken the will of the German population despite regular attacks since 1940 and had done nothing but set the resolve of the British people as they faced ongoing attacks by the Luftwaffe. What followed was a massive war, involving armies totaling well over a million men, where almost no one on either side ever touched the ground of the enemy's territory except after being shot down. When viewed on a percentage basis the losses of the aircrews on both sides exceeded those of infantry forces in 1917 France. Even the addition of American 8th Air Force bomber wings in daylight precision attacks to the long-established RAF

Bomber Command night area bombing did little to deter the German war effort. Whether this strategic bombing campaign would have, as it was claimed, worn down the German ability to wage war (as did happen to Japan) if the USSR had not fallen will never be known. However, then came the release of the huge number of aircraft from activity in the East, combined with the unplanned, but very real, benefits from the decision to establish major factory sites in the General Government and western Ukrainian areas of occupation. These factories were out of range of even the longest range Allied single-engine escort fighter available, the P-51 Mustang, ensuring that the Allied efforts would be no more successful than the Luftwaffe's against Great Britain (at least until the late introduction of the F8B). By late 1944 both sides were nearly exhausted from the continuous poundings when the Reich upped the ante with the A-4 guided missile. The destruction of the A-4 sites by USMC Corsairs carrying Tiny Tim unguided rockets on September 22nd 1945 was one of the few true successes of the air war despite the heavy losses experienced by the attacking squadrons. Operation Bulldog also featured the first jet vs. jet combat when USAAF Shooting Star fighters operating out of Scotland in support of the operation tangled with Luftwaffe Me-262 fighters attacking the withdrawing Marine F4Us.

Had it not been for the European Pulse, the Allied war in the Pacific against Japan would have been recalled as the most vicious since the introduction of gunpowder. Almost from the opening moments, it represented as much a clash of cultures as of arms. Imperial Japanese forces, steeped in a highly-distilled version of *bushido* (the traditional Japanese Way of the Warrior) viewed prisoners and surrender in a vastly different manner than their Anglo-American opponents. These differences rapidly turned the war into one fought with remarkable intensity, mistrust, and outright hatred on both sides. Japanese troops were found to feign surrender, making it less likely that their Western foes would accept surrenders. This in turn meant that fewer Japanese tried to surrender, in an escalating loop that ended with Japanese civilians throwing themselves and their children from cliff tops on Saipan and Okinawa. By the same token, Japanese forces, especially in the case of junior officers, treated Allied prisoners in what can only be described as a savage fashion that would have been very familiar to observers of SS troops in the General Government area or Ukraine. This brutality was magnified by the theater of operation, where nearly all combat took place in either jungle environments or on small islands which offered no opportunity for retreat or even reasonable withdrawal. Most Japanese island garrisons suffered 95% or greater casualties with almost all survivors being conscripted Korean laborers. Jungle combat was little better, with wounded on both sides suffering horribly, what little evacuation resources available used for one's own troops with the predictable outcome for those who were left in the septic conditions of the front lines.

The savage warfare on land was closely mirrored at sea and in the air. Japanese pilots, even early in the war, demonstrated a great willingness to conduct ramming attacks against enemy aircraft in addition to the more common (on both sides) act of crashing a damaged aircraft into an enemy vessel (the details of the *kamikaze* tactics utilized by the Japanese from mid-1944 onward are examined in detail in Chapter Seven of Volume II).

As Royal Navy units began to reach the Pacific Theater of Operations, the basic philosophical differences between the fleets of Great Britain and the United States became rapidly apparent. American ships tended to be more heavily-armed and armored, with the notable exception of aircraft carriers where British designers had built in an armored flight deck for virtually all of the RN carriers while the USN uniformly used wooden flight decks with an armored hangar deck below. The RN believed that this made its ships more battle-worthy, whereas the USN believed that their ships were easier to repair. As events following the Japanese introduction of *kamikaze* demonstrated, there were elements of truth to both positions. The main advantage the USN had over its British ally was in the areas of aircraft designs and underway replenishment. Both of these advantages allowed the USN to maintain a much larger carrier-based air force than the RN, with the American carriers also having a significant advantage in number and quality of aircraft embarked (the poor treatment of the FAA by its RAF cousin in the area of aircraft procurement is outlined in Appendix A). Still, the two navies quickly learned to work together, with the Americans finding the early addition of RAN and RNZN ships of great benefit in the early months of the war. Cooperation at the senior command level was less friendly, with CNO King often regarding the RN to be more of a rival than an asset. Had it not been for the strength of President Roosevelt as Commander in Chief it is possible that King's deep mistrust of all things British may well have caused a serious rift between the two allies.

The July 1943 decision to have the Royal Navy and Commonwealth forces concentrate on the Dutch East Indies and former British possessions of Burma and Malaya also reduced the amount of friction with Admiral King, although the decision did place the Commonwealth forces partially under the command of General Douglas MacArthur depending on their exact deployment. The troops who suffered this misfortune, along with their commanders, would long rue the day.

Possibly the most interesting decision of the entire Pacific Phase was the decision of the Allies to *not* use the atom bomb against Japan. It was, without question, the most controversial decision made in the last year of the Pacific Phase. The decision was driven by intelligence reports smuggled out through neutral Sweden that convinced the Combined Joint Chiefs, PM Churchill and the new President of the US, Harry Truman, that the Germans had concluded that the atom bomb was impossible (the superb disinformation campaign waged by the remnants of the KGB and GRU, both of which had thoroughly penetrated the Manhattan Project against the Nazi nuclear program is brilliantly examined in Patrick Drake's *Stalin's Last Victory*). Knowing this, the decision to keep the Bomb a secret while constructing a stockpile of some size was clearly the correct strategic decision, although the disastrous impact of the decision on the Japanese civilian population has caused much post-war debate.

Unlike the European air war, the American strategic campaign against Japan, if not decisive on its own, unquestionably helped drive Japan to its knees. Along with the massive firebombing of Japanese cities, which resulted in the destruction of every Japanese city with a pre-war population of more than 75,000, there was the mining of the Inland Sea, the Yellow Sea, and the less well-known mining campaign waged from the Aleutians (in dreadful weather and flying conditions) against the sea lanes leading from Vladivostok to the Japanese Home Islands that cut Japan off from its last contact with its European Axis partners. Through all this, the USAAF crushed Japan as an industrial power. When combined with the submarine blockade of Japan, the eventual carrier and tactical air force bombing and strafing effort against Japan's already questionable transportation network, using the B-29, proved itself to be a truly devastating tactic.

It is, of course, the sheer level of success that the blockade and air campaign achieved that makes it so controversial. In the last two decades there have been a number of well-researched books and military simulations that argue that as few as four nuclear weapons would have caused Emperor Hirohito to sue for peace (although most researchers, as well as a recent War Game at the US Naval War College, in which the author participated, indicate that as many as nine weapons would have been required to drive the Japanese to capitulate). Even if the generally accepted nine atom bombs had been needed, this would have resulted in no more than 800,000 direct deaths, with probably twice that in early mortality from radiation effects, or roughly 2.5 million civilian and military deaths. This is well under the estimated 4 million who died in the continued fire bombings, from starvation, exposure, and illness in the Japanese Home Islands (including early mortality from the after-effects of malnutrition and increased infant mortality in the 1946-56 reconstruction period) and among the cut-off Japanese military units before the Japanese Unconditional Surrender on November 11, 1946. In considering the far increased number of casualties in Japan, it is important to remember that it was wartime, and that the only consideration that was proper for Truman at the time was what would reduce Allied casualties in both the Pacific and, later, in the ETO.

"Warm" war and the decision to invade

The period between the defeat of Japan and its subsequent occupation by the Allies (including the remarkable reclamation of the remnants of the Japanese culture during the period of General MacArthur's governance) and the final engagement between the Western Allies and Nazi Germany is best described as a quasi-war punctuated by occasional sharp but brief outbreaks of violence between forward deployed forces.

After the wholesale destruction of the A-4 missile launch sites by American fighter-bombers and the hellishly costly but markedly successful strike by Bomber Command against the German missile facilities, Berlin made a surprising offer to suspend air attacks against Britain and to exchange prisoners to the Anglo-Americans. There was no formal cease-fire offered – the Allied "Unconditional Surrender" mantra, so recently and brutally demonstrated against Japan, was still in place, and there was absolutely no sentiment in Allied capitals or in the Allied electorates for making peace with the Reich – but the end of air attacks was very attractive to the British, and the return of tens of thousands of Allied airmen (and British ground troops, many of whom had been in captivity since the spring of 1940) from German custody was very alluring. After extended negotiations brokered by Swedish and Spanish diplomats, an agreement was reached that allowed any PoW who wished to remain in the country where they were being held to do so, and also provided for the release of any PoW still held in German custody from its six-year-old conquests who wished to come to the West to do so (with the offer to be made by Swedish authorities). Coupled with the release of PoWs was a onetime deal that effectively purchased the freedom of surviving Jews (virtually all of whom were highly decorated German veterans of WWI) for two freighters of raw rubber, and an agreement to cease air attacks against population centers by both sides.

On February 12, 1947, the initial exchange of prisoners began; by the middle of March nearly 275,000 Allied prisoners and 194,000 German, Italian, and other Axis prisoners (virtually all of them airmen) had made the trip from Calais to England or back. Nearly 2,500 Allied prisoners, and close to 13,000 Axis prisoners (more than 11,000 of them from "National" militaries) chose to remain in the land of their former enemies. A total of 2,578 Jews were also released, these being virtually all remaining Jews in Conquered Europe that were known to the Nazis (there were still small Jewish populations in Italy and parts of Hungary that the National governments refused to turn over to their Nazi partners, but these populations were not included in the exchange agreement). The results of the Reich's agreement to trade WWI war heroes for raw materials was to, of course, have profound consequences, far greater than anyone involved at the time believed was possible.

This remarkable transfer of personnel was only possible due to the use of Allied, primarily USN, amphibious landing vessels that had been transferred from the Pacific Theater for the express purpose of making the exchange both possible and rapid. No one in the west truly expected the Reich to completely fulfill the agreement, so time was considered to be of the essence.

Surprisingly, the de facto cease-fire held, at least in the case of air operations, for several years. Combat was generally limited to the North Atlantic and Mediterranean, where Allied antisubmarine forces still waged war with the Kriegsmarine U-boats. The courage of the German submarine crews remains a remarkable story even today. On the wrong side of a technological and cryptographic war (the German penetration of British Merchant Marine codes was revealed via Dutch collaborators to the Allies in late 1944, with a resulting change to full military quality codes for the merchant fleet that blinded the U-Boat force), U-boat crews suffered appalling losses with increasingly little return. Even the introduction of advanced designs like the Type XXI was insufficient to reverse the fortunes of the Kriegsmarine, especially once the Allies began to destroy the supposedly indestructible submarine bases with the specially-designed Grand Slam bomb in late 1944, and the large-scale introduction of the American Type 34 torpedo. Since these "sub pens" were clearly military targets and not located in population centers, even the bomber holiday did not provide them complete safety from air attack (although each Allied strike was very costly and generally responded to by German attacks against British naval and air bases, usually with massive Luftwaffe losses). For over four years, the Sub War was the only ongoing open conflict between the Allies and Axis.

It is unclear how long the limited war would have continued without the intervention of science and what is now generally accepted as a sudden change in Hitler's mental state (although there remains a vocal minority who believe that the change in German policy was not Hitler's idea at all, but that of one or more of his inner circle) that moved the situation from one that was mostly stable, if exceptionally hostile, to the Crusade in Europe.

Forces and equipment

Finally, it is worthwhile to review the two sides, both in equipment and in military philosophy at the time of the final conflict of the Second World War. It is here, in the weapons and methods utilized, that the greatly divergent lessons learned by the two opponents are most clearly seen.

The Reich had been almost unimaginably lucky in the first year of the European Phase, with every action seeming to work perfectly, while every action of the British & French failing against all common sense in Norway and during the Blitzkrieg against France and the Low Countries. This remarkable string of luck continued into the initial drive against the USSR, with the first setback to the Nazi wave of success being caused by an early snow. The notably destructive and vicious fighting that followed in Spring '42 and resulted in the final destruction of the USSR as a European power was also marked by several instances of good fortune, including the success in taking the Crossing at Stalingrad in an engagement that could so easily have gone the other way. The leadership in Berlin never recognized the hand of Chance in any of the successes it had achieved, believing everything to be proof of the superiority of the German Volk and of the National Socialist system. Both of these beliefs were reflected in the design of the Greater German military structure at the time of the Invasion.

German troops were by far the best equipped of all the nominally independent "National Forces" in post-conquest Europe. There is still a degree of argument in military circles regarding the reasoning behind the disparity of equipment, specifically around how much was a conscious decision to hold down the military quality of the other Axis members, including Italy, and how much was simply arrogance on the part of the SS military decision-makers. The differences, in any case, were dramatic.

While the Waffen-SS, which had fully replaced the Heer as the Reich's Wehrmacht ground component by 1948, comprised only 56 of the 235 divisions that defended "Fortress Europe" it operated 47 of the 78 armored divisions on the continent (with an additional 9 of these divisions being under the control of the Luftwaffe) and the various German infantry units were the only fully motorized divisions in Europe (Italy did operate 22 so called "mobile" infantry formations, as well as 9 armored divisions, but each unit only had sufficient transport to move 75% of the total troops in the TOE by truck or tracked vehicle). The remaining ground forces inside the German command structure were mainly basic infantry or fortress troops (a designation that was entirely missing from Allied command structures), with many of the troops trained exclusively to fight from fixed defensive positions. Nearly 70% of the fortress troops lacked personal weapons beyond revolvers as they were artillery or machine gun bunker crews (who the SS high command believed would never need to fight in any role besides servicing heavy weapons and who could not be expected to have any worthwhile fighting skills since they were not German) while many of the pure infantry National units were used as skirmishers in the ongoing low-intensity war along the generally lawless German/Russian frontier.

While the SS armored formations made up only a small fraction of the total European defense force, they made up a significant element of the combat power facing the Allies. The Waffen-SS operated the world's finest tanks, with the Panther Mk III forming the core of its fighting strength. The Mk III was the direct result of the lessons learned by the Heer on the Eastern Front. Heavily armored, reasonably fast at 35kph on gravel roads, and armed with a high-velocity 105mm rifled gun it was, by far, the best tank on the planet. Supported by the heavily-armored panzerwagen SD halftracks and Tiger assault guns, the Mk III was a formidable opponent anywhere in Europe, with the mobility to serve as a striking force wherever needed (the Reich spent years reinforcing bridges continent-wide to allow the movement of the massive tanks and their supporting vehicles).

The Greater German air forces were an interesting mixture of the extremely advanced and "experienced". German interceptors were exceedingly fast and heavily-armed bomber killers, with many carrying cannon as large as 57mm. They were generally larger than their Allied counterparts, but with limited range, being mainly designed as "point interceptors". (The German B&V P.320 held the absolute time to 10,000 meters from standing start climb record until 1961). Germany had also developed a number of "schnell" jet bomber designs that saw use in the on/off air war against the UK and in occasional action as anti-shipping attacks in the Mediterranean Sea. The Luftwaffe also operated a number of ground attack aircraft based on the Fw-190 and the Me-110 designs; these aircraft had been developed in the immediate aftermath of the defeat of the USSR to battle the partisans and remaining Red Army units that had not accepted Molotov's orders. While they were older designs, they had proven themselves in the ground attack role and were expected to soldier on in this vital, if unglamorous, role for years to come. Many of the National air forces operated squadrons of these aircraft, as well as a few home designed fighters/interceptors.

The Kriegsmarine, though the most active of the Reich's armed forces during the Warm War, was also a study in contrast. While its submarines fought an increasingly losing battle in the North Atlantic, it also had, at Hitler's direct orders, constructed a significant surface fleet (it is far from coincidental that this order came down shortly after the death of Admiral Karl Donitz in a British air attack). The surface fleet, with the exception of one cruiser action in the Eastern Mediterranean, had not been battle-tested but was of considerable size with three large carriers, two light carriers, seven 45,000 ton battleships, two Bismarck class BB, two BC, 6 armored cruisers (a unique German design, also known as panzerschiffs), 16 CA, 14 CL, 58 DD and 38 frigates on the rolls. It was, however, a fleet of two parts, with a fleet in the Black Sea consisting of 2 45,000 BB, 2 CVL, 5 CA, 5 CL, 15 DD, and 21 FF with the rest of the fleet in the Baltic Sea.

The construction of the Black Sea force made sense in many ways. Along with the Italian Aegean Sea fleet, it tied down nearly half of the RN and was a serious enough threat that the USN maintained TF 68 (centered on USS *Saratoga*, USS *Enterprise*, USS *Essex*, and all four South Dakota-class BB in 1952) in the Mediterranean throughout most of the Warm War. Ships were relieved on regular, albeit unpredictable, rotation that always kept the US 6th Fleet superior in number to any possible German sortie attempt. In other ways, it was a significant waste of resources, even if most of the labor was supplied by Ukrainian and Polish slave workers. The Royal Navy and, especially, the USN were able to maintain the Allied Mediterranean force without serious strain elsewhere, while the German Black Sea squadron was a substantial drain on experienced German naval personnel and units constructed there were of no use in defending Europe from the Allies.

The entire effort to construct a serious blue-water navy remains one of the main debates surrounding Nazi war planning. What Hitler was actually thinking when he effectively overruled all of his advisors and demanded a "Navy as good as the British have" has never been explained. Had the war ended, and any German Navy had full access to the open sea to train and to "show the flag" a small fleet would have been called for, but in the Warm War Allied forces struck at Kriegsmarine units whenever possible, to the point that German naval pilots were sent to the Crimea for flight training and deck qualification so training operations would not result in an unwanted battle.

The build-up of the surface fleet, much like the dismantling of the German General Staff and Army, is an enduring mystery of National Socialist Germany.

While Germany was building a very powerful armored ground force and strong defensive air force as a result of their experience in 1939-43, the Allies were going in a very different direction. Although Allied ground formations did feature armored divisions, especially in the last few years before the Invasion, neither the US nor British Armies were built around them, both nations favouring lighter formations. This was, of course, a product of the war that the Anglo/Americans had fought, just as the Waffen-SS was the end result of the lessons learned in Europe.

The island-hopping campaign in the Pacific, along with the jungle fighting in Burma and in the Dutch East Indies, had taught the Allies the usefulness of light formations and of the need to be able to construct vehicles that could handle being landed from sea directly against enemy defenders. It is, in hindsight, fortunate that the Japanese armies in Manchuria and China had chosen to fight on, at least for as long as they could, after the fall of the Home Islands. The fighting in Formosa, Manchuria and Korea, while it was against a poorly-supplied and disorganized, if fanatically brave, force, did demonstrate to the Allies that tanks like the Sherman and Crusader were no match for the occasional German-supplied Panther or T-34/85 or for the fearsome, if rarely encountered, 88mm DP gun that was sometimes found in Manchuria. Had the defeat of the Soviet Union not allowed the Reich to ship some weapons to their nominal Japanese ally it is an open question if the Allies would have ever turned away from the "tank destroyers kill tanks, tanks support infantry" mindset that was the US Army's guiding principle through most of the Pacific War. Even with the experience against the German designs in Manchuria, the Allied tanks were not the heavily-armored beasts that the Waffen-SS operated, but they were far better than the Shermans that would otherwise have faced the Nazi forces.

The Allies, especially the Canadian and Australian armies, were early adopters of what later became known as air envelopment. While early helicopters were limited in range and lift, they rapidly proved to be a better way to land troops and light vehicles behind enemy lines as replacements for the despised glider. The helicopter was also ideal for the deployment and supply of small Ranger or Chindit units, a commando-style unit that had become very popular in Burma and then in China and that Allied planners believed would be extremely useful in the liberation of Europe. American Marine units also found the helicopter to be a natural extension of the landing craft, despite the early helicopter's reliability and lifting limitations (one Marine officer is famously quoted as saying that in an attack on a heavily defended enemy position "the damned chopper ride is the most dangerous thing I do all day"). What was not known was how well helicopters would fare in the heavy flak environment that characterized Nazi-dominated Europe.

The Allied air forces had also gone in a different direction than the Luftwaffe. Allied aircraft were almost all designed to be fighters *and* attack aircraft. Fighters virtually all had some sort of bombing capacity that extended to the point where there were few "medium" bombers in the Allied inventories except those left from earlier in the war. Virtually all of those aircraft had been converted to "gunships" sprouting as many as 20 heavy machine guns or cannon that were used against light shipping traffic or in close ground support roles. One result of the mixed-use role of the Allied fighter was that, overall, they were markedly more maneuverable than their Luftwaffe rivals while having greater range, although at the cost of maximum dash speed. The Allies had also long maintained and continued to develop the heavy long-range bomber in much greater numbers than the Luftwaffe. The Luftwaffe had nothing to equal the American B-47, much less the newly accepted B-52.

One area where the Allies had a dominant position was in the atom bomb. While the existence of "The Bomb" had been rumored often enough that many Luftwaffe officers accepted that some such weapon did exist, the German science community was widely split. Thanks to the continued efforts of deep penetration Soviet agents and the actions of resistors among the "loyal" workers in France and across Western Europe, the German nuclear weapons effort had sputtered. Nazi political beliefs helped the Allies in this regard as there existed a deep distrust of "Jewish" sciences and any product of such an unclean source. Unbeknownst to the Allies the Reich had, of course, developed its own "ultimate weapon".

The Allied navies were a vast overmatch for the Kriegsmarine. This is only to be expected, as the American and British shipyards had been producing at wartime levels for more than a decade, and both Allied fleets had massively outnumbered the Kriegsmarine before the war began. The Allied navies included 45 fleet carriers (including 7 of the massive Midway-class angled deck ships), 36 battleships (this, of course, included the old ships of the amphibious fleet Gun Line, which also featured the unusual USN "Cruiser, Large" ships, as well as the more modern "Fast BB"), 110 CVE, 5 CB, 85 CA, 126 CL, and well over 700 destroyers. The amphibious fleet numbered well over 2,000 vessels that deserved the title of "ship" as well as thousands of landing craft that would ferry the Allied armies back to Europe.

With the background now established, it is time to review the events of D-Day themselves.

We begin...

1

The trigger for the move from Warm War to Hot was the infamous 1954 St. Patrick's Day Raids. It is very unfortunate that most of the Luftwaffe records surrounding the planning for the Raids were lost. Insight into the no doubt acrimonious debates that preceded the decision to break the de facto truce between the Reich and the Western Allies would be welcome. The potential success of the Raid, even if it had exceeded the most optimistic expectations in the surviving Luftwaffe documents, seems today to hardly have been worth the effort involved. That is not even to mention the inevitable Allied reaction to the action. Alas, with the lack of records, and the dearth of eyewitnesses to the debates, we are left with only the raids themselves to tell the tale. It is, perhaps, relevant to note that Helmut Goebbels, the eldest son of Hitler's closest confidant Joseph Goebbels, was killed in action aboard U-1632 on his first patrol as a naval officer cadet on January 8, 1954.

The 1954 attacks were, of course, not the first Nazi attempt to attack North America. That distinction goes instead to the Luftwaffe crews who participated in what is now generally called the HMS *Premier* Quail Shoot. The *Premier* was an Ameer-class escort carrier assigned as the flag of an ASW Hunter-Killer Task Force operating in the Denmark Strait in search of U-boats attempting to gain access to the North American coast by moving through the less heavily-patrolled seas north of Iceland. As was typical of her class performing ASW work, her air wing consisted of 12 F4F-4 Wildcats (nee: Matlets) and 6 TBF Avengers, with the Avengers normally carrying depth bombs in place of torpedoes.

On September 27th, 1945, at 10:00 hours, one of *Premier's* escorting destroyers, HMCS *Haida*, reported a very strong airborne radar contact 25 miles to the northeast of the TF. The two-plane Wildcat CAP was immediately sent to investigate, and the carrier launched two more fighters to take their place over the formation. Roughly ten minutes later, Flying Officer Robert Evans VC radioed in to report, "Tally Ho. Angeles 15. A formation of the biggest bloody Hun bombers I have ever seen". Evans had become the first Allied pilot to see one of the Ju-390 "Amerika Bombers"; moments later he became the first Allied pilot to attack a Ju-390.

The Ju-390 was indeed "a bloody big bomber". The aircraft sported twenty defensive machine guns and 20mm cannon, six engines, and, with a wingspan some twenty feet greater than the B-29 bomber and thirty-eight feet greater than the Avro Lancaster, and a range of over 9,000 miles, was the largest operational bomber in the world at the time. Developed in considerable secrecy, the Ju-390 was supposed to "bring the Americans to their knees" by exposing US civilian populations to strategic bombing. While the probability of knocking the US out of the war was remote, the effect of having Americans dying on home soil would have, unquestionably, been dramatic. Unfortunately for the Reich, the Ju-390 was not the right weapon for the job.

The Ju-390 was able to achieve its magnificent range at the cost of performance in other areas, with airspeed being limited to 219 MPH during its long overwater flight and a maximum speed of only of 317 MPH at full wartime emergency power with a service ceiling of only 19,000 feet. The Luftwaffe's operational commanders had been horrified at the prospect of putting any aircraft with that level of performance into a combat situation, but had found themselves overruled by both Göring and Hitler, both of whom were mesmerized by the vision of New York in flames. With the resources of Europe at its disposal, the Reich was able to build up a force of nearly 50 of the huge bombers in relative secrecy (the Allies knowing only the Germans had finally built a true heavy bomber, one that both the Americans and British expected to be used against the UK). It was this huge force that *Premier* had accidentally encountered.

With the Evans contact report, *Premier*'s flight deck exploded into activity. All ready aircraft, including three TBF bombers, were rapidly clawing for altitude in an effort to intercept the Luftwaffe formation. Radio reports were also made to Coastal Command bases in both Halifax and Iceland to warn of what could only be an attack against North America. Even as the Morse message crackled from its transmitters, the carrier's aircraft made contact with the German formation.

The Luftwaffe crews had no idea that they had been found until the first firing pass by F.O. Evans. Following advice he had heard third hand from a captured German ace ("The first thing you must do is kill the tail gunner"), Evans put his first burst into the tail gunner's compartment, killing the Luftwaffe Sergeant manning the position. He then proceeded to concentrate his fire on first the port, then starboard, inboard engines, setting both aflame, again as the German flyer had revealed ("if the inner engine catches fire, it will burn off the wing"). Evans and the second pilot in his element, following Evans' calmly given instructions, repeated this process until both aircraft ran out of ammunition, As the two stubby Grumman aircraft headed back to their ship they left nine burning Junkers (six of them belonging to Evans) spiraling toward the cold Atlantic water. As he headed back to rearm, Evans passed the priceless knowledge from the Luftwaffe bomber killer on to the other fighters heading toward the German aircraft.

With only enough fuel to spend 20 minutes at maximum speed – speed that would be needed to clear the target after the bomb run ahead of avenging enemy aircraft – and still make it home, the German pilots were faced with an impossible choice. Most chose to increase speed and hope for the best. One nine aircraft element of the formation, including three damaged planes, attempted to sacrifice itself by slowing to only 160 knots in the hope of diverting the remaining FAA fighters. This ruse failed, as the fighters continued on to the bombers, leaving the slow formation to the pilots flying the slower, far less well armed TBFs. Two of the final four Ju-390s in the decoy formation fell to the guns of freshly-rearmed F.O. Evans.

By the time the plodding bombers managed to escape the *Premier's* angry brood, thirty-one out of the original forty-six Ju-390s had either been shot down or crippled to the point that they disappeared forever into the cold, cruel North Atlantic mists. Alerted to the enemy's approach, RCAF Mosquitoes, directed by pilots of patrolling Liberators, diverted from their ASW duties to search for the enemy formation, found and destroyed the remaining German aircraft as they flew past Newfoundland's coast. Of the nearly 500 Luftwaffe crewmen who had departed from Norway that late summer evening, only 12 were rescued, one by one of *Premier's* escorting destroyers, HNoMS *Stord*, and the rest by Catalina flying boats out of Conception Bay. FAA losses were two Wildcats and three TBF, along with a total of five aircrew. The battle itself was buried under wartime secrecy for nearly a decade, only becoming public knowledge in 1954 when the, by then, Captain Evans was awarded his richly deserved and long overdue Victoria Cross in the public relations effort following the St. Patrick's Day Raids.

While the German attack of 1945 was defeated, no one in the Canadian or American military or civilian leadership was fooled. The raid would have succeeded, at least insofar as hitting targets in North America, even if the raiders had later been obliterated, as was very likely considering the number of fighter units stationed along the Atlantic coastline from Labrador to the Florida Keys. The reaction was, as noted by CIGS Brooke (later Lord Alanbrooke), classically American in that it locked the barn door after the horse had escaped, much like the robust response to Pearl Harbor had been. The American, and to a lesser extent Canadian, response to this comment was, in effect, "Well, we have a lot more horses in there". Regardless of the timing, the reaction was impressive in scope and endurance. The USN dedicated an entire destroyer flotilla to radar picket duty with additional ground-based radars set along the Atlantic coast as well as in Greenland and Iceland. The introduction of the EB-36 in 1951, with its great loiter time and, for the time, extremely powerful radars, improved and extended long-range warning picket lines far out into the Atlantic. The USAAF also deployed a series of ever more powerfully-armed interceptor aircraft to defend the Continental US and Canada, with the F-89 Scorpion and its Genie missile reaching service in late November of 1953. What the Reich actually knew of these radar barriers and air defenses has long been a matter of some debate, but their presence did not, it seems, noticeably interfere with the Luftwaffe's battle planning.

The German attack plan was remarkably simple, even crude, by comparison to some of the Reich's efforts in the early years of the war. The plan, which was unusually reliant on timing considering the sites of the various attacks, was the first combat action of the Ju-688 super-heavy bomber, an aircraft similar to the American B-36, although with a smaller bomb load and even greater range than the huge USAAF Peacekeeper. The German military had been operating in a practical vacuum since the 1947 bombing pause with no real knowledge of the changes in strategic bombing that had been in progress since 1947. Both the US and Britain had gone to surprising lengths to keep the existence of their pure jet strategic bombers a secret, allowing only scant mention of them into the media, with the American B-36 and B-45 and the British Canberra being the public face of the Allied bomber force. Whether detailed knowledge of the B-47, B-52, and the RAF's "V" bomber series would have altered Luftwaffe operational thought is unknowable, but the Reich's planners advanced into the 1954 bombing under the impression that an aircraft similar to the B-36 was still viewed by the Western Allies as a serious deep penetration threat.

The Reich had spent several years gathering the bomber force that was used on St. Patrick's Day and, by any measure, had developed a considerable force. Nearly 600 of the Ju-688s were involved in the attacks, launching from almost twenty airfields across Europe. Over 400 of these aircraft, in eight separate formations, were destined for the United States. Had the Luftwaffe selected different targets than those that were actually attacked, enormous damage could have been visited onto the American industrial heartland. However, no matter how many staff officers pushed for attacks on Detroit and Chicago and Windsor, attacks that would actually be of consequence to the Allied ability to make war, the Nazi Party powers would not hear of it. Instead the great cities of the Eastern Seaboard, irresistible to the amateur political minds making the actual tactical decisions about the raids, were selected.

Half of the raiders were assigned to New York, with two other groups aimed at Boston and the last two groups meant for Washington DC. Again, for reasons lost in the fog of war and time, the targets for the New York and Boston attacks were not of any military utility at all. Instead, the Luftwaffe was ordered to time their attacks to catch the maximum number of civilians possible by striking Manhattan and downtown Boston at midday (it has long been speculated that Hitler was actually trying to target the famous parades held on the 17th of March in both cities, but in this author's opinion, this is too insane a plan even for the Reich's mad leader).

The aircraft attacking the US left the ground just before sunset on March 16, 1954. Of the 406 aircraft assigned to the mission, 378 were able to actually take off and proceed to North America. Eleven of the assigned aircraft suffered mechanical failures on the ground while seven suffered engine failure while still close enough to their launching points to successfully abort. Surviving Luftwaffe records also indicate that at least 30 bombers fell out of formation during the Atlantic crossing, never to be heard from again. The remaining Ju-688s continued toward the United States.

The first formation, the northernmost, was detected by an EB-36 operating out of Keflavik USAAF base. As soon as the alert was received, additional ships, including two carrier TF, and aircraft began to move into pre-planned defensive positions as air bases and defensive missile and gun positions moved into warning status. In what would be seen as nearly criminal nonchalance today, air base and anti-aircraft unit commanders were authorized to deploy the most secret of systems available to the Allies at their individual discretion. Control of these systems devolved from the President of the United States to Captains and Lieutenants with a single telephone call.

The radar barrier quickly identified seven of the eight attacking formations. Unfortunately, one of the bomber groups was lost in the radar shadow of an Atlantic Storm system and got inside the warning line undetected. What our history, and today's world, would look like if this storm had been offset by 30 or so miles is one of the great "what could have been" questions of our time. The storm, however, was where it was, with the well-known results.

The Luftwaffe forces may have known that they had been detected. The radio operators on the bombers could hardly have missed the sudden dramatic increase in radio traffic, both coded transmissions and, soon, voice transmissions. One can be sure that the crews were preparing for battle, with defensive gun crews making final checks of their control systems, pilots ensuring that crews were on supplemental oxygen in case pressurization was lost, bombardiers arming weapons, and all the manifold other tasks that are part of preparation for battle in the air.

The Ju-688 was, with all due respect to the fabled B-17, a true flying fortress. Unlike the Allies, who had come to believe after years of air combat over Europe that, with the exception of tail guns, defensive armament was a waste of weight on a strategic bomber, the Luftwaffe still believed in defending the bomber with rapid-fire guns. The Ju-688 carried half a dozen four gun remote-controlled turrets, four containing 20mm cannon and the other two armed with huge 35mm autocannon. What this says about the true effectiveness of the bomber box and its defensive fire during the 1940-47 strategic campaign is outside the scope of this work, but the fact that the service that had been forced to face the guns of the 8th Air Force and Bomber Command festooned their most advanced aircraft with defensive guns is nonetheless interesting. It was also, as events were to prove, a waste of effort.

History was, of course, made just after 0800 hours on that March 1954 morning when Major Ed Williams made his radar intercept of Flight 12, consisting of 37 Ju-688 bombers, 350 miles northeast of Boston. At a range of just over five miles, Williams launched one of his two AIR-2 Genie rockets in the direction of Flight 12, known to Williams as Raid One. Williams had just enough time to make his combat break away from the Genie, having lowered his face shield immediately before weapons launch, before the rocket arrived in the vicinity of Flight 12, close enough to trip the proximity trigger in the nose of the weapon. A fraction of a second later the Genie's 1.5kt warhead detonated, marking the first combat use of a nuclear weapon.

The Luftwaffe formation was, unsurprisingly, devastated. Twenty-four of the aircraft were within the 1,000-foot instant kill radius of the weapon and instantly caught fire or suffered structural collapse from the massive overpressure of the detonation. These planes were the lucky ones, with their crews also killed instantly. The remaining 15 aircraft, however, survived the initial blast, although generally with considerable damage. They were also piloted by men who had been instantly and permanently blinded by the sudden, utterly unexpected and totally unimaginable appearance of a second sun less than a half-mile off the nose of their aircraft. A number of other crewmen in the surviving aircraft had also suffered the loss of some or all of their vision. Of the 425 men manning Flight 12, thirty-six managed to escape their aircraft before the planes went out of all semblance of control. Twelve of these men were eventually rescued by USN and USCG patrols.

Between 0810 and 0900 hours, even as air raid sirens sounded up and down the Atlantic coast of North America, six additional Genies were fired at five Luftwaffe formations (one weapon failed to detonate and was lost at sea) with nearly identical results. The nuclear age had dawned in a most spectacular manner, although no one in Germany had any idea that the world had dramatically changed. Still, two German formations remained.

Flight 7, the second of two formations targeted on Washington DC, was not intercepted until it was only 35 miles off the Maryland Coast. This was, in the opinion of the intercept commander, too close for use of a nuclear weapon. Instead, this formation was attacked by two squadrons of F-94 Starfires and a squadron of F-84F Thunderstreaks. As was the case with the doomed Genie targets, Flight 7 was torn to pieces; however, in this case the crews at least understood what was happening. The F-94s were armed with 2.75 inch Mighty Mouse rockets. These had been developed as a longer range alternative to conventional cannon or machine guns, but had, in trials, been something of a disappointment. They had a rather disturbing tendency to spread all over the sky when fired, making them a poor choice for engaging single aircraft. However, when fired en masse by two squadrons of twenty-four aircraft (with each aircraft carrying 48 rockets), the results were devastating. The Mighty Mouse killed 26 of the Ju-688 of Flight 7 and severely damaged three others. The attacks of the Thunderstreaks chopped down eight more bombers, as the Ju-688 gun crews found it nearly impossible to target the 700 mph fighters who flashed through the tatters of the Luftwaffe formation. Despite the best efforts of three full fighter squadrons, five of the Ju-688s made it to the Washington DC area. Two were killed by Nike SAM before they could drop their bombs, but three of the German aircraft managed to drop their payloads on the outskirts of the American capital, killing nearly 200 civilians. None of the Ju-688s made it back to open water before being blotted from the sky.

Flight 5 was the only Luftwaffe formation to manage anything close to a coordinated attack. Having managed to get through the initial radar barrier undetected, it was not located until it was less than 200 miles from New York City. It immediately attracted the attention of no less than 12 fighter squadrons flying everything from elderly P-51s to nine early model F-100 Super Sabers from Wright Patterson airfield in eastern Ohio, as well as F-9 Cougar fighters from the USS *Guadalcanal.* The courage of the Luftwaffe pilots flying through this gauntlet cannot be overestimated, as they had learned of the obliteration of most of their fellows while en-route to the target as one squadron after another reported enemy contact and then dropped off the air. Only eight of the German bombers made it to within sight of New York City, with six of them managing to make a successful bomb run over central Manhattan while a seventh aircraft crashed in lower Manhattan. All told some 18,000 pounds of bombs struck Midtown, causing serious damage and claiming over 800 lives, all but 26 of them civilians. As would be expected, the Ju-688s did not escape the vengeful efforts of the American fighters as they attempted to withdraw.

To put 36 bombs onto Manhattan, and an additional 18 bombs into Georgetown, the Reich had expended 378 aircraft and over 4,000 men.

The Luftwaffe also targeted London as part of the St. Patrick's Day Raids. Here, there was no surprise at all as radar stations along the English coast watched the Luftwaffe formations form up in increasingly alarming numbers. At almost the same moment as Flight 7 was meeting its fate off the Maryland coast, the largest air battle since 1945 began over the English Channel. Here, the RAF and its USAAF allies didn't have the luxury of time or distance to intercept the enemy hundreds of miles out to sea, nor Genie rockets with nuclear warheads to swat the enemy from the skies over the vastness of the open ocean. The British defenders didn't have the advantage of attacking unescorted 400 mph bombers with 700 mph fighters. Here the fighting was done at knife-fighting distances as close to 2,400 aircraft struggled for the upper hand. London was heavily damaged as several hundred German bombers struck at the British capital in the heaviest raid against the city since January of 1946. By the time the last Luftwaffe aircraft retreated behind the flak curtain along the French coast almost nine hours had passed. The toll, both in damage and in aircraft, was enormous. RAF and USAAF fighters claimed 228 kills, while AAA crews claimed an additional 306 Luftwaffe aircraft shot down (post-war records indicate that the actual Luftwaffe losses were between 256 and 292 aircraft) while the RAF had lost 56 fighters along with 19 American aircraft lost.

Even before the last German pilot had been debriefed, Washington and London had made a joint decision to end things in the only way that was certain to work. Europe would have to be invaded; the Reich met and utterly defeated in the field.

2

After the last aircraft left British airspace, and well before the damage results had begun to be tabulated, a serious disagreement arose between Downing St. and the White House regarding the immediate reaction to the German resumption of serious hostilities. While American emotions were aroused by the first truly successful attack on traditional American soil in 140 years, the mood of the British was foul indeed. The capital of their country had once again been shattered, with seven years of reconstruction lost in a single day of battle.

The British were eager, even demanding, to up the ante on the Reich by deploying nuclear weapons against several German population centers while the US was equally resistant to revealing the secret of the Bomb in a manner that would make clear to everyone in the world that such a weapon was possible. None of the decision makers believed that the destruction of even a dozen German cities would end the war; the Nazi state was otherwise too structurally sound for them to crumble that quickly, and enough of the Reich's production was scattered across the rest of the continent that to ensure the crippling of the German economy would require deploying nuclear weapons across Western Europe, killing millions of innocent forced laborers in France, Norway, the Low Countries, and the rest of "Greater Germany". The Americans could see nothing worse than deploying the "Ultimate Weapon" only to find the Reich still standing, bloodied but unbowed. Millions of civilians killed across most of Europe and a defiant Reich still in power and able to pin the dead onto the Allies was the worst of all possible situations, argued Washington. In the end, British heads cooled enough to stand down the six

Vulcans that had already been bombed-up and were waiting for final release.

Still, the Nazi actions had to be responded to quickly and in far greater power than the original attacks. The Allied final battle plan took these requirements into account, as well as several very specific advantages that the West had developed in the seven years of quasi-peace.

Unsurprisingly, the reaction of the Nazi leadership to the St. Patrick's Day raid was euphoric, according to Nazi archives. The Americans had, at long last, felt the pain of war that had been visited on the Volk for almost two decades. The two greatest American cities had been devastated; clearly the minor damage reported by American media was propaganda, 400 bombers would not have caused so little damage as was reported. Just the heroic final dives of the disabled Ju-688 pilots into the American cities would have spread fire and death far beyond the small areas supposedly hit. The British too, after years of Bomber Command destruction of submarine pens and defensive positions that the Reich had allowed to go unavenged, had once again felt the power of the Aryan peoples.

"Spontaneous" street celebrations by residents of every city in Greater Germany and the rest of occupied Europe demonstrated the joy of the Volk and even of the lesser peoples. These celebrations were duly reported to Berlin, as were the lists of "traitors" who failed to show proper enthusiasm at the Luftwaffe's triumph over the Anglo-Americans. Personal journals and diaries kept by residents of the occupied nations, as well as by a surprising number of German citizens, indicate that the true feelings of the average European about the raids were horror and terror. Unlike the Nazi High Command, the average person in the street knew that there would be payment exacted for the Luftwaffe successes; payment that they and their loved ones would make in blood.

Perhaps the most remarkable part of the Nazi High Command's reaction to the March 17th attacks was the non-reaction to the horrific losses inflicted on the Luftwaffe. The Ju-688 long range bomber force, built up over five years of effort, had been, in a military sense, obliterated. Out of an original force of 654 aircraft, only 19 flyable aircraft were available for action on March 20th, 1954. Combat losses in the medium bomber and long-range fighter escort force, including platforms damaged beyond economical repair, were also significant, totaling over 400 aircraft (this figure includes aircraft determined to be useful only as sources for spare parts due to battle damage). According to internal Ministry of Production documents found in Minister Speer's personal files post-war, the raids caused losses that, in ideal circumstances, would take 14 months to make good. The report left unsaid the fact that ideal circumstances were very unlikely to be present post-March 17th.

Instead of the anger that one would reasonably expect to be directed at Luftwaffe chief Göring for the loss of an entire arm of his service, Hitler showered his Reich Minister of Aviation with honors for "breaking the will of the American people" and for "proving, once and for all time", the superiority of German arms.

The hubris of this perspective was soon demonstrated.

3

The Allied response to the St. Patrick Raids, best known by their then codenames of Operation Aries and Operation Roundhand, remain some of the better-known tales of the Final Phase of the European War, with virtual libraries of excellent books that examine them in minute detail; however, in the interest of completeness, we will look at them here. Before we do so, it is worthwhile to recount the Western reaction to the Nazi attacks that resumed the Hot War, mostly because it helps lay to rest, in significant ways, the myth of bombing breaking an enemy's morale.

The day after the attacks, recruiting stations from Labrador to Queensland were deluged by volunteers. This included those in both the UK and the United States, despite the reality that close to 75% of all eligible males in both countries would eventually find themselves conscripted into some level of military service in their lifetime (71% of the males reaching 18 years of age in the US and 73.7% in the UK in calendar year 1948 were called up for at least one year of active training and qualification before their 23rd birthday). These volunteers were not for the reserve or Home Defense components of the military, a common occurrence during the Warm War since it minimized time spent on active duty and far from home, but for full-time active units, with nearly 90% of the Army/Marine volunteers specifying an interest in infantry or armor units (those units most likely to engage in direct combat). Recruiters spent nearly as much time shooing away minors (including, famously, an entire 8th Grade Class in Fredericksburg, VA) as processing applications by eligible volunteers.

Reserve units were inundated by members showing up without orders while factories across the Allied nations began to close down production of civilian products in anticipation of mobilization. The Luftwaffe bombings, rather than cowing the residents of the US or UK, revitalized commitment to victory in a war that had been in a large degree, if not forgotten, marginalized in the minds of most citizens.

It is critical that the modern reader recalls that precision-guided weapons were barely leaving the cradle in 1954, with the ability to literally destroy a single structure in a city block, something that is taken for granted today, being beyond even the dreams of engineers and designers of the time. The reaction of the Allied populations was in line with those earlier in the war by the citizens of all sides. In early 1954 the only exception to this sort of coming together and defiance in the face of attack had been in the final months of the Pacific Phase, when the population of the Home Islands, by then reduced to near-starvation and a pre-industrial state, truly lost all hope and eventually surrendered without a single enemy soldier setting foot on an invasion beach. This reality is important to all that followed the March 1954 resumption of hostilities.

The Allied response to the St. Patrick's Day attacks was, in the purely tactical sense, an interesting study in preparation and military philosophy. During the bombing holiday, as we have seen, the Reich had spent considerable time and effort in creating an improved version of the American B-36 bomber. This decision was, perhaps subconsciously, an admission by Luftwaffe designers and planners that Germany had failed to produce a true heavy bomber during the 1939-47 phase of the war; a failing that had allowed the United Kingdom to survive and even out-produce the Reich during the height of the 1940-41 Blitz and during the later 1943-47 Blitz II. Hitler had, as is well known, blamed that failure on sabotage of the A-4 missile and the destruction of the launch facilities of the A-4 once it was finally brought into action by US naval strike aircraft, but professionals on the Luftwaffe planning staff, perhaps even all the way to Göring, knew that the reasons extended well beyond the destruction of some launching facilities along the North Sea.

It is known that the Luftwaffe was both surprised and seriously concerned by the entrance of the B-36 in the war due to the unprecedented damage caused by that aircraft's huge bomb load and its nearly invulnerable 45,000 foot operating ceiling. Much of the Reich's air defense design was, from 1947 onward, built around defeating aircraft that fit into the B-36 mold: very large, 40,000+ft combat ceiling, with 350 mph top speeds and very heavy defensive armaments. This was almost exactly the design criteria that the Ju-688 filled, and it seems that the Luftwaffe believed that the Allies would continue with what had been a very successful design. The Allies, less from operational security than from tactical utility, had also shown no significant change to the B-36 design prior to the bombing holiday, with even the later "military target" strikes against U-boat pens and other heavily-fortified positions being made by Peacemaker super heavy or Avro Lancaster and Lincoln heavy bombers using specialty bombs like the 12,000 pound Tallboy, 22,000 pound Grand Slam, or the Peacemaker's only 43,000 pound T-12 Cloudmaker bomb. These missions had the unintended effect of confirming the Luftwaffe's preconceptions of what challenges a renewed air war would present.

The Luftwaffe was fairly well prepared to deal with a resumption of the air war that had ended in 1947, despite being the poorer cousin to the Waffen-SS ground forces at budget time (ironically, even within the Luftwaffe, a disproportionate amount of spending went to the hugely expensive Ju-688 very long-range bomber and the Luftwaffe's ground combat units; an affectation of Göring's that Hitler allowed to continue even after the Heer had been displaced by the Waffen-SS ground forces). The Luftwaffe had a series of very fast, albeit short-ranged, point interceptor aircraft, and several early SAM systems that had been built with the expected enemy attackers in mind. What the Luftwaffe lacked were longer ranged, high altitude fighters and, somewhat surprisingly, the radio proximity fuse for its AAA weapons and SAM warheads.

Most, if not all, of the Luftwaffe's shortcomings can be laid directly on the Nazi basic distrust of pure science, such research being seen as both wasteful and of limited use to the state, as well as Hitler's personal love of gimmicks. This was partly due to the failure of the Reich's A-bomb project (effectively sabotaged by the combination of Nazi distrust of "Jewish science" and the remarkable disinformation campaign waged by KGB/GRU agents within the bomb projects themselves) and by the near-simultaneous failure of the "V" weapons to bring about the defeat of the UK. When these dual failures were combined with the Reich's leadership's anti-intellectual perspective, it is perhaps not surprising that cutting edge electronic and other scientific research suffered, especially given the human instinct to re-fight the last war.

The Allies also benefited greatly from Hitler's devotion to the design firm of the Horten Brothers. The Hortens had a long, ultimately failed, fascination with the "Flying Wing" concept, similar to that of American designer Jack Northrop. The flying wing was a seductive design since it, in theory, offered so many advantages over conventional designs which included a vertical stabilizer. The design concept was eventually found to have so many serious stability issues that it was found to be unusable in combat, something that was determined by the US at a cost of nearly $100 million dollars and two air crews, but was not accepted by the Nazi Party for nearly six years and close to RM 2,000 million of investment (well over five times the amount spent by the United States out of a Reich air research and development budget roughly a quarter the size of the US program). The money and manpower used on the Horton Brothers designs set back or eliminated several far more promising, albeit conventional, designs from Focke-Wulf (which had its Ta-183 delayed for nearly four years), Heinkel, Junkers, and Messerschmitt (including the death of the very promising P-1108/I jet bomber project). Had any of these design companies received the support provided to the Horten Brothers Ho X fighter-bomber or Ho XVIII long range bomber between 1945 and 1953, the Allies would have faced a far more capable Luftwaffe. This was, to be sure, not the last time that Hitler's tendency to meddle and almost child-like interest in what can only be described as fantasy projects would greatly aid the Western Allies.

In a nearly perfect counterpoint to the Reich's efforts, the Allies spent far more of their defense dollars on both their air forces and naval systems, with the US Army and its British counterpart being left, if not behind, then surely last among equals. Just as the Reich's early wartime experiences led to a particularly strong belief that ground forces, especially armored formations, were the primary key to victory, the Allied experience led them to the not unreasonable conclusion that aircraft and naval power were critical to success. Fortunately for the Allies, sufficient common sense remained in the Joint War Planning Staff that ground forces were recognized as being irreplaceable in the retaking of the Continent. Had that goal been lost, the results of the Allied war effort could easily have been tragically different.

The Allies had held a generally more offensive stance during the Warm War. Their infrequent, but ongoing, attacks against military targets within Greater Germany and against Reich and Italian naval units, as well as a surprising amount of intelligence smuggled from within the Occupied Zones, had taught them far more about the German defenses than the Germans had learned about the Allies. Allied, especially RCAF, "ferrets" had compiled a massive amount of data on Nazi radar and radio frequencies, while both Resistance and SOE elements had obtained both blueprints and actual physical samples of many of the Reich's air defense systems and weapons. The combination of the signal intelligence, which included decryptions of Reich "secret" communications, Hummit, and Allied technological advances, including some that came as offshoots of "pure science" research at, among other locations, Bell Labs, provided the Allies with a significant strategic advantage.

The initial Allied reaction to the March 17th attacks was two-fold and the result of the heated debate that immediately followed the Luftwaffe attacks.

It was recognized that it would take some time to build sufficient forward-deployed ground units to assault Occupied Europe. The plan to conduct the invasion had, in some form, been in place for close to a decade, although the expected casualty numbers had caused considerable concern in every Allied capital where they were known. The specifics of the plan had altered over the years, but the total number of troops, ships and planes had long been known, to the point that specific reserve battalions had been assigned shipping berths on shipping. Still, as seemingly ready as the plans were, they would take time to bring to fruition as forces gathered from as far away as Malaya and the Philippines to play their role in the assault on Greater Germany. It was also recognized that the Allies, for many reasons, had to strike back against the Reich long before the invasion force could even be considered ready. Once the British government had been dissuaded from its initial nuclear demands, Operation Aries was rapidly accepted by the American civilian leadership, over the objections of senior USAAF planners who felt the losses would be excessive. Operation Roundhand, which had been the USAAF proposal, was also adopted, but in combination with – not in place of – Aries.

Operation Aries, by far the larger of the Allied operations in terms of aircraft deployed, was itself a combination of different existing attack plans from the FAA, RAF, USN, and USAAF, rapidly combined into a massive Blitz against Occupied Europe and Germany itself. Launched from air bases ranging from Iceland to Northern Iran to carriers in the Mediterranean, it involved nearly 1,700 aircraft and close to 50,000 men, including ground crews. Simply put, it was designed to saturate the Reich air defenses and substantially degrade the Luftwaffe and its companion air forces while doing material damage to the Waffen-SS war fighting potential and Reich "leadership elements".

The initial attacks struck far from where the Reich had expected, in the Black Sea and Crimea. The two attacks against the Kriegsmarine bases near Sevastopol and Odessa, conducted by RAF and USAAF bombers, was a stunning surprise to the Luftwaffe, as was the presence of high-performance jet escort fighters nearly 800 miles from the nearest Allied air base. The Luftwaffe defenders were mostly equipped with Me-262E fighters, aircraft that had been top of the line in 1946, that had been redesigned to reach 43,000 feet and carried two wire-guided X-6 AAM with a range of nearly 4 miles and a speed of 700 mph. These aircraft would have been lethal against unescorted B-29 bombers, the last aircraft that had attempted to strike the Crimea in late 1946, and would have even been deadly against the far faster USN AJ-1 carrier-capable deep strike aircraft, but against the faster, far more maneuverable American F-88G escorts (the final version of the famed Voodoo to carry the F-88 series number before the change to the F-101), the German Swallows were virtually helpless as their primary weapons proved to be unable to maintain track on fighters that were actually faster than the missiles themselves. While the Luftwaffe pilots did their best, they only managed to down four of the Voodoos at a cost of 29 Swallows. What happened next was even more of a surprise.

The older RAF Lincolns and slightly newer B-36G aircraft did not proceed to conduct the expected conventional bomb runs. Instead the 36 RAF attacking Sevastopol and 23 USAAF aircraft attacking Odessa launched ASM-N-4 missiles (three from each Lincoln and five from each specially modified B-36) from 30 miles away. The 650 mph active radar guided missiles proved to be nearly impossible for the Luftwaffe anti-aircraft units to engage, especially over Odessa as the departing B-36 launching aircraft each disgorged 6 tons of aluminum foil "window" that reduced radar performance to near zero. The manned portion of the raid worked to perfection, with far lower losses than expected (one B-36 was lost due to an engine fire).

The early ASM-N-4 cruise missiles, unfortunately, did not perform quite as well. The bombers launched over 200 air-to-surface missiles against the two Reich naval bases. Had the missiles worked as designed, the entire Kriegsmarine and Regina Marina fleets in the Black Sea would have been destroyed. Instead, only a total of 9 ships were sunk, with three more damaged, along with some substantial, although unintended, damage to various shore facilities. Tragically, nearly a third of the total missiles fired missed the harbors completely and instead struck the surrounding civilian areas with predictable results.

Nevertheless, the attacks marked the beginning of a very long week for the Reich and its puppets.

4

Allied attacks against French targets were launched within moments of the time that the first bombers left the ground in Northern Iran. Due to differences in the distances involved the French attacks arrived first and were made against far more robust defenses than those in the Crimea. As would be expected, these raids met with varying degrees of success.

Attacks by FAA and USN carrier aircraft against Marseille and Toulon did considerable damage to port facilities and shipping found in the ports, mostly freighters, but at relatively high cost, with total US losses of 32 aircraft and FAA losses of over 40. The losses suffered by the FAA were so serious that they effectively put HMS *Ark Royal* out of action for five weeks while replacements were integrated into her attack squadrons. Attacks by North African-based B-47 bombers against rail yards in southern France were more successful, as both Vichy and Luftwaffe defenses proved to be unable to deal with the remarkably-fast Boeing aircraft attacking from low altitude, especially when supported by jamming aircraft. Similar success resulted from high altitude RAF English Electric Canberra strikes against French defensive positions on Sicily and Norwegian troops based in Sardinia thanks to heavy radio jamming, the liberal use of window, and the presence of RAF Venom escort fighters that proved to be a serious overmatch for the Ta-152 fighters being flown by the French and Norwegian defenders.

The initial attacks against targets in Western France were also successful, although less so than those conducted against the South of France and on other targets in the Mediterranean and Aegean regions. While the stronger Luftwaffe responses in the attacks against Western France caused senior American

8th Air Force commanders to urge caution, especially after the first appearance of heretofore unknown German rocket-powered interceptor designs against a B-36 formation attacking Metz, the British pressed forward with plans to strike against military targets well into Germany. American officers suggested fighter sweeps and focused attacks against Luftwaffe and other "National force" airbases that would reduce the Reich's fighter and interceptor strength before moving against Germany proper; British public outrage over the St. Patrick's Day attacks caused these suggestions to be ignored by the RAF and British civilian leadership. This was to prove a notable error.

On May 8, 1953, the Allies launched a three-pronged attack against the Continent, as well as numerous fighter-bomber strikes against defensive fortifications along the Channel coast. Two of the attacks, one American and the other Canadian, were specifically designed to act as decoys to draw off Luftwaffe assets from interfering with the main RAF strike against the Hamburg docks and rail yards. The two North American strikes, both directed into Central/Eastern France, were bomber-light and fighter-heavy with almost 75% of the aircraft being fighters. The American attack, against railway yards just to the west of the Rhine, was made by 52 B-47 bombers escorted by 163 F-88 Voodoo fighters (nearly every Voodoo in England at the time), while the Canadian raid on munitions works outside of Nancy consisted of 46 Canberra bombers with 135 Saber Mk. 5 fighters as escorts. Even with the extremely impressive escort, both raids suffered losses of over 10% of the bombers sent out. Losses to the Luftwaffe, and especially to French National Air Force, fighters were also heavy, with the Luftwaffe losing nearly 80 fighters and the French, mostly flying late model Fw-190s and Ta-152 against the Canadian jets, losing 174 aircraft (nearly 2 of 3 aircraft sent into battle that morning). The two diversionary strikes succeeded beyond expectations, drawing nearly 600 enemy fighters to them. It was not enough, and, as events demonstrated, the fighter escorts would have been quite useful elsewhere.

The RAF strike, almost 100 Valiants with Hawker Hunter fighters as escorts along with a squadron of RCAF Saber Vs, ran into trouble well before making landfall, with German fighters hitting the formation while still over the North Sea from bases in Southern Norway. While these early attacks were mainly by Me-262 and He-162, neither of which were a match for the RAF escorts, they did have the effect of reducing the fighter escort as the fighters that drove these attackers off were forced to drop their external fuel tanks prior to engagement. Without the external drop tanks, the fighters, especially the shorter-ranged Hunters, lacked the range to escort all the way to Hamburg and back. The attacks continued as the formation continued east, with the result that the bomber formation had only the Sabers left as escort when they reached Hamburg. The 24 RCAF aircraft were simply swamped by the 300+ Luftwaffe fighters that assailed the formation. Had the Germans been ready for a bomber with the performance of the Valiant, the raid would have been an utter disaster. As it was, the RAF formation escaped with relatively light losses numbering only 17 bombers (all from the "low" squadron) and 14 Sabers. Damage to the Hamburg docks was light, while the raid against the marshaling yards did only moderate damage while causing considerable damage to civilian residential areas.

The German response to the RAF strike was a shock to the Allies.

The Allies had, of course, encountered the A-4 rocket before the start of the bombing holiday (as noted earlier, the USMC strike against the A-4 facilities in the Baltic was one of the few true bright spots for the Allies in the Bomber Offensive), and had been prepared to react to attacks by the short-range bombardment rocket once the Warm War returned to Hot. What they had not expected were strikes by the A-9.

The A-9 was the final expression of the Reich's fascination with artillery rockets. More of what we now call an IRBM than an artillery rocket, it had a range of 1,200 kilometers with a 1,000-kilogram warhead. The Waffen-SS Rocket Command began to launch A-9s against the UK before the Valiant formation reached it airbase in England. That first day nearly 100 of the missiles rained down on Britain. It was the beginning of the Rocket Blitz.

The air battles of May 8 established the pattern of the following six months of the war – Allied airstrikes met by Luftwaffe fighters, with A-9 attacks as retaliation. Luftwaffe bomber attacks against Britain more or less ended after June of 1953 due to the ghastly losses inflicted by Allied air defenses, but there was no defense against the A-9 except striking at its launch sites, a difficult target to pinpoint and an even more difficult one to successfully destroy. It was not until information was smuggled out of the General Government region (once known as Poland) that the Allies were able to counteract the A-9.

The destruction of the A-9 manufacturing and development facilities by the USAF, the first large long-range bombing raid made with the support of in-flight refueling, including the longest fighter escort mission to this day, has been the subject of numerous books and several Hollywood films (most notably the 1958 Best Picture-winning, if massively historically inaccurate, *Stratoforts* starring John Wayne and Doris Day) so there is little need to relate the tale here. Possibly even more critical to the success of the Allied effort against the Reich than the destruction of the Syktyvkar manufacturing facilities was the virtual annihilation of the research records and senior developmental staff of the SS Rocket Command, as well as the deaths of most of the skilled (and involuntarily employed Russian) workforce. It was a blow that the Nazi leadership never overcame.

5

Even with the destruction of the Syktyvkar complex and other major German manufacturing facilities across Europe, it was two years before the Anglo-American forces had gained air superiority in the skies above Greater Germany, although the struggle for skies over Inner Germany (the pre-war German nation and pre-war Austria) remained unresolved even longer.

The Allied air forces were doing the lion's share of the work, and reaping with it both the "glory" and the losses. The West's ground forces were training, retraining, and preparing for an invasion that would dwarf anything the world had ever witnessed, even the remarkable five-division assault on Okinawa in late 1944. The Allied navies, meanwhile, found mainly frustration.

The naval forces of the Allied states, especially the United States Navy, had been the undisputed stars of the War with Japan, driving across a third of the planet's face while avenging the shame of Pearl Harbor a hundred-fold. The newsreels of the time were filled with shots of great gray ships destroying the enemy at every turn and the USN, above all other services, had relished the acclaim of the public (and the virtually unlimited shipbuilding budgets that the acclaim supported) and had, against all indications to the contrary, believed that the fleet would be at the forefront of any resolution of the war against the Reich. Instead, except for a series of almost invisible, albeit vital, victories against the U-Boat force, the only clear-cut sea victory in the war's first half-year was by an Australian/Canadian TF centered on HMAS *Melbourne* (an Essex-class ship built to Australian specifications as part of the five-ship 1946 Commonwealth Order) that had caught an Italian flotilla trying to make a dash from the Mediterranean to the somewhat safer confines of the Adriatic. In an 18-hour running fight, the Italians lost three cruisers and a half-dozen destroyers sunk with a fourth heavy cruiser beached to avoid sinking; in exchange the action cost the Australians 11 aircraft and 13 men.

While the Battle of the Capes was the greatest independent victory of Commonwealth forces ever (no American or British ships or aircraft took any part in the main action; although RAF fighters did provide air cover as the Anzac/Canadian units exited the battle area, these fighters never engaged in combat), it was still, effectively, a small unit action compared to the Naval Battle of Iwo Jima. The USN, and to a lesser extent the RN, craved their opportunity to show what real naval power could achieve.

Beyond the desires of the senior naval commanders, the Allies also had very good reason to draw the Kriegsmarine into a major fleet action. It was the best way to destroy it and ensure it did not interfere in any of the amphibious landings that were going to be necessary to reclaim the Continent from the Reich.

This was also the main reason that Oberbefehlshaber der Kriegsmarine, Grand Admiral Erich Raeder, had no desire to meet the Allies in any sort of open water engagement. Unlike the SS men who had taken control of the ground forces and displaced the professional career military officers of the Heer in the process or the Luftwaffe under Göring, the Reich's navy commanders knew that they were facing a much superior enemy and doing so with the wrong tools for the job. Raeder had a total of three carriers available to him, all roughly equal to the British Illustrious-class ships but with the classic "straight-through" deck which prevented simultaneous takeoff and landing operations, to oppose ten times that many Allied carriers (two-thirds of them featuring the angled deck pioneered by the Royal Navy) including seven of the massive, 45,000 ton Midway-class ships that were the pride and joy of the US Navy. Any one of the huge US carriers were capable of engaging all three of Raeder's decks and defeating them. The rest of the Reich's fleet, somewhat to Raeder's disgust, were heavy surface combatants; a ship type that was, in many conditions, nothing but a manned target barge for carrier aviation. The Grand Admiral believed that it was imperative that he waited for the opportunity to employ his battleships when there was, at the least, some chance to survive long enough to do damage to the enemy.

Unfortunately for the Kriegsmarine, Hitler, not Raeder, was the force's Commander-in-Chief, something that Hitler reminded his Fleet Admiral of after one "nein" too many by, to use the USN's slang, "handing him a pail and a shovel and setting him on the beach" and placing an SS officer into Raeder's slot. Hitler made this personnel decision on the 15th of May. The Battle of Iceland occurred exactly six weeks later.

As naval engagements go, the Battle of Iceland was about as one-sided as it is possible for such an action to go. In a sixty-hour period, two American Carrier Battle Groups (a term that had come into popular use post-Pacific War, replacing the Task Force in USN jargon) under the command of Admirals Alfred Pride and Joseph "Jocko" Clark provided a primer on the use of carrier forces to destroy enemy assets. Only one Kriegsmarine strike, from the *Peter Strasser*, was even able to launch before nearly 600 American naval aircraft descended on the Reich fleet, swept aside the 25-aircraft Combat Air Patrol that the Kriegsmarine carriers had aloft, and tore the three swastika-swathed carriers to bits. Over the following two and a half days the German ships were wiped out without mercy, the attacks only ending when the three surviving destroyers, packed with nearly 1,100 survivors of other sinkings, reached friendly air cover near Bergen, Norway. Total US losses were 162, mostly crewmen from USS *O'Brien*, which was sunk by a U-boat while on duty as an outer radar picket and plane guard.

One unfortunate result of the *O'Brien*'s loss was the military's sound, if difficult, decision to withdraw all US forces from rescue operations once all known American survivors had been retrieved. While Clark, who was the senior officer afloat, has been criticized for his heartlessness, his explanation that: "I took an oath to protect the men under my command, not the enemy's. My crews were far more important to me than any other consideration" rang true at the time and still does so today.

Total Kriegsmarine losses, including MIA, have never been fully recorded but are known to exceed 20,000.

6

The actual landings that began the ground phase of the Western/Nazi conflict are the most written about and debated series of amphibious operations in the history of warfare. This is understandable, especially when one looks at the remarkable series of events, the point-counterpoint nature of the landings and Waffen-SS reactions to them, and the almost mind-numbing size of the landings. In the interest of brevity, this work will leave the details to those many superb works while covering the "main events" as they occurred.

The initial Allied landings – those of Operation Otter, the capture of Sardinia; and the near-simultaneous Operation Rover, the invasion of Sicily – are sometimes not included in the "Assault on Europe" histories; but, in the view of the author, both of these operations, along with the closely related Operation Torch, the capture of Corsica, are critical first steps in the Anglo-American return to the Continent. This is especially true in the lessons learned by both sides, and, tragically, in the assumptions that Berlin made based on those lessons.

The Sardinia invasion was one of the rarest of military events: an action that went almost exactly as planned. Operation Otter marked the first combat use of USMC ground forces outside of the Western Hemisphere since 1918, as well as the initial appearance of non-English speaking forces on the Allied side during the Western War in the persons of the 2nd Brazilian Infantry Division. Otter worked as well as it did, in the main, because the Waffen-SS command had discounted an Allied landing on either Corsica or Sardinia, assuming (quite correctly) that any invasion of Italy would be preceded by an invasion of Sicily. What the Waffen-SS commanders had, however, not taken into consideration was the Allied experiences in the Pacific. The Allies, especially the Americans, had developed the invasion of islands to a fine art, and one tends to stay with a strength whenever possible.

The USMC-led assault of Sardinia, along with the follow-up Operation Torch, was the largest military operation ever to fall under the direct operational command of a USMC officer. In this, it was fortunate that the Corps chose perhaps its finest organizational mind, General Randolph M. Pate, to lead the operation. Pate and his planning staff created a five-beach landing strategy, using what came to be known as the "Even Stevens" – the 2nd, 4th and 6th Marine divisions, the 2nd Brazilian Infantry Division, and the US Army's 2nd Armored Division – as the assault forces with the US Army's 22nd Infantry Division (motorized) as the floating reserve. Opposing this substantial force were two light infantry Norwegian "National" brigades, a "militia" division made up of Sardinian natives deemed too old to serve in Italian National Forces and armed with WWI-era rifles, and a single Waffen-SS Panzer Regiment. The Allies were extremely well-informed about the composition and disposition of the enemy forces on Sardinia thanks to information passed by local fishermen (and members of the drafted militia) to Italian-speaking American Intelligence gathering teams drawn from Sardinian-American immigrants.

The Allied landing took place after what, for the USN, was a very brief 16-hour bombardment of the landing beaches. The local Waffen-SS commander made the error of deploying his two battalions in penny packets to all five landing sites rather than holding the forces in reserve to make a coordinated counterattack. Like most of his contemporaries, the Waffen-SS Gruppenführer (Major General) in charge of Sardinia's defenses had no experience in fighting organized units with both artillery and air support, having learned (if the term can be applied) how to command and been blooded in actions against "bandits" in the General Government areas. Based on all available accounts he was also not considered to be a particularly bright light by his superiors, owing his rank, even more than was common in the heavily politicized Waffen-SS ranks, to his family name and the fact that his father had been one of Hitler's earliest supporters. By the time the SS officer and his staff had conceptualized that a USMC RCT would not break and run at the sight of five panzers, it was too late. Those five panzers, along with virtually all of their brethren, had been destroyed, mostly by naval gunfire and air attack, along with their crews and most of the SS force on the island.

Operation Otter, as noted, was perhaps the finest Allied assault of the entire ground war. Pate's forces took less than 800 total casualties in taking all of Sardinia, while capturing the island in less than a month. This result was, of course, greatly aided by the incompetence of the Gruppenführer, who found that his militia melted away as soon as there were no SS stiffeners at their backs and that his Norwegian National forces' light arms were no match for even the fairly light M-26 Pershing tanks operated by the Allied units.

Operation Rover did not fare quite so well.

The Allied landings in Sicily were, unlike Sardinia or Corsica, a joint US-British operation. The Royal Navy provided a good deal of the escort for the landing force and the British Eighth Army, the same force that had met and defeated the lone serious German attempt to invade the Allied Iran/Iraq protectorate regions, provided nearly half the total joint landing force that struck Sicily. One of the first things that Rover revealed was that the American and British forces, while long allied and veterans of countless combined operations in the air and at sea, were not at all used to working with each other on the ground.

In the Pacific Phase, the British ground forces, with the exception of some Canadian and, notably, Australian units, had fought in what is now generally known as South-East Asia while the Americans, along with some Canadian and a majority of the Australian units, had fought across the Pacific sandspit by bloody sandspit. While the American Army had put forces into Burma, they were more symbolic than substantial, and Washington and London had known it. In retrospect, it was unfortunate that a golden opportunity to learn from each other was missed.

Everything from radio code words (including the words used to represent the alphabet) to ration kits was incompatible. While the blame for this has, in large part, been put on the American Commander, General Mark Clark, and his British Deputy (itself a relationship with more than a trace of tension) Field Marshal Bernard Montgomery, the truth is that the blame goes far beyond these two men, all the way to the Combined Chiefs of Staff. The CCS made poor choices in commanders, compounded it by not making the actual command relationship clear, and finally failed to listen to the counsel of the American CNO and the British Lord of the Admiralty (whose forces had gone through their own "separation by a common language" issues early in the conflict). As a result, the "Allied forces" who landed were more competitors than confederates.

Opposing this somewhat fractured enemy was one of the better-equipped National forces in the Greater Reich. The Italians, while not overly eager to fight for the Führer, were much more predisposed to fight for Italian soil against all comers and the three divisions on Sicily were possibly the best drilled and equipped forces in Continental Europe without twin lightning flashes on their uniform tabs, having been drawn from Italian forces across the Reich when it became clear that Sicily was an invasion target. The Italian forces were supported by two divisions of French "SS" troops and a full Waffen-SS Panzer Division. The Panzer division had its full complement of Panther Mk III tanks and Tiger IX assault guns while the Italian Armored division was, for a National force, very well-equipped as well, with Panther Mk I and a smattering of the early version of the Tiger assault gun (the version with the L71 88mm gun) rounding out their TOE. Even the French units were equipped better than the norm, with two battalions of elderly but serviceable Pz Mk IV tanks (interestingly, these were the only tanks in French control anywhere in Europe).

The early hours of the Allied landing went well thanks to a failure of the Abwehr (Military Intelligence) to deduce the destination of the invasion force. The Abwehr had predicted that the forces that invaded Sardinia were destined for Sicily. In this case, the Abwehr commander overruled his subordinates, who were universal in their conviction that the Allies were headed for Sicily, and told Berlin that the forces were reinforcements for Sardinia. It was a fatal error. The same day that the Allied forces landed on the Southern coast of Sicily, Gestapo records indicate that the entire leadership of the Abwehr was placed under arrest. Of the 26 men, and their families, taken into custody only one left any trace (assuming a message carved into the floor of Spandau Prison can be accepted as genuine) and none were ever seen again. The Waffen-SS assumed all duties formerly under the control of the Abwehr and the organization itself ceased to exist.

Despite the element of surprise, and in the face of effective Allied control of the air, the island's defenders fought back with unexpected ferocity and remarkable success. Of the five main landing sites, four were effectively stopped up by the end of the first day. The fifth beachhead made slow but steady progress inland, but at L+ 72 had expanded less than 10 miles inland. The landing near Licata was only saved by the massive firepower of the assembled "gun line", which included the USS *New York,* and Nevada-class battleships with their 14" guns, for the last time. The Italians were stunned to see the bombardment shells from the American (and, to the east, RN) heavies literally destroy their Panthers by tossing them into the air like a child's toy. Had the gun line not been present, it is very possible that the American 1st Infantry Division would have been pushed back into the sea, with all the consequences such a setback would entail.

Just hours after the USN's finest moment off Sicily came its absolute worst. A Regia Marina submarine penetrated the defensive screen of the USS *Saratoga* and put five torpedoes into her hull. Despite the best efforts of her crew and those of her escorts, the "Sara" sank while under tow to Alexandria. The Grand Old Lady of the USN carrier fleet thus joined her sister, the USS *Lexington*, aka the "Lady Lex", on the ocean floor, albeit on the opposite side of the Earth. If it were not for the 350 casualties suffered when the carrier was attacked, her loss in battle would somehow seem to be a blessing since she was destined for the breaker's yard as soon as the first CV-59 class carrier was accepted for service. In any case, if the Italians had hoped that her loss would weaken the Allied effort, they were soon disabused of the notion. The USN had a surprise of its own.

While there has never been a "smoking gun" piece of evidence uncovered to prove it, the belief that the United States Navy, especially the commander of Carrier Battle Group 9, wanted to make a point to the Italians after the loss of *Saratoga* has become so common as to be an axiom. The sudden decision to make the first combat deployment of the BLU-9 fuel-air weapon from USN carrier aircraft less than two days after the ship's loss seems to be too much of a coincidence for there to be no connection. In any case, the results were, simply put, awe-inspiring. They were also tragic.

While common in today's combat environment, the use of the "Propane Popper" was a revolution at the time. The utter destruction of the Waffen-SS armored reserve regiment on Sicily, along with nearly 5,000 troops, by a dozen AD-1 aircraft in under 15 minutes sent shudders up the entire Nazi chain of command clear to the Führer's bedroom. Besides unhinging the entire Italian/SS defensive line in Southern Sicily, the strike convinced the decision makers in Berlin that their information was correct. The Americans had developed a massively effective explosive device, but it was far from a terror weapon that would bring the Reich to its knees. The small chorus of voices warning that the "English" had produced an atom bomb were silenced. The Nazi leaders were now confident that the Allies had thrown the biggest surprise in the bag at them, and they had survived quite nicely.

The Allied ground offensive across Sicily exposed the weakness of both British and American armor tactics and weapons. The American M-26, largely developed based on information from the Soviet/German struggle, proved itself to be no match for the Panther III, and found itself barely the equal of the earlier Panther I; the British Centurion, while somewhat better defended, was also found to be seriously underarmed with its 76mm gun. The American tactic of specialized tank destroyer formations, with tanks deployed to support infantry, was also found to be more than slightly problematic, as was the basic infantry anti-tank weapon, the 60mm bazooka. Only the constant intervention of Allied aircraft prevented the Nazi armor from grinding the ground forces into the dust once the advances left the firing arcs of the gun line. The shocking superiority of the Nazi war machines led to a delay in the main European invasion for almost a full year.

Sicily is also remembered as the site of the first serious heliborne air assault in warfare. The attack by the 82nd "Air Mobile" division, which effectively cut off the retreat of nearly 2/3 of the SS and Italian troops on the island, was preceded by yet another innovation – a series of "flak suppression" attacks against gun emplacements along the entry path of the helicopters by strike aircraft, including additional deployments of the BLU-9.

With the capture of Sicily, along with Sardinia and Corsica, the Reich command knew that the Allies were going to invade Europe via the "Southern Route" of Italy and perhaps the Balkans, and began to move forces from across the continent to meet the threat.

They had a very long wait.

7

The Allied reaction to the unpleasant surprise of their inferiority in tank designs, and the even more pronounced inferiority in infantry anti-tank weapons, is perhaps the most instructive event of the entire final struggle for Europe. It is remarkable, especially to those of us who have become accustomed to the suddenness and extreme violence of current American and Commonwealth military interventions in Asia and Africa, where the Western forces arrive, obliterate their armed opposition and leave after placing an acceptable local leader in control, that the Allies would simply stop all offensive ground operations, save for a series of spoiling actions along the Italian Peninsula that managed to tie down nearly 26 divisions of the Italian National Army and close to six full divisions of Waffen-SS armored/mechanized formation (which will be looked at in some greater depth below), for almost a full year. While the sensitivity to casualties has often been accepted as the main reason for this delay, recently declassified documents from the National Archives indicate that losses were, at best, a secondary concern – not that the elected leadership of all the Allied nations were immune to casualty concerns.

Gold Star Mothers vote; and every politician from the local sheriff to the POTUS knew it.

The minutes of the Combined Chiefs of Staffs meeting, as well as the private papers of the Kennedy Administration, indicate that the main reason for the delay was purely political and focused on the post-war European political landscape. Both London and Washington were (ironically, as events turned out) concerned that, after nearly a generation of Nazi control, the populations of the Occupied countries might view the Allied landing forces as invaders and not liberators. This was a special concern in France, where the Nazis had been supported for nearly a decade by a succession of elected Vichy governments and where the Allies needed the population to be, at a minimum, neutral. With this in mind the Allied command wanted it to appear that the Allied forces were simply superior in every way imaginable to the Waffen-SS, something that the sight of four burned-out M26 tanks surrounding every dead Panther Mk III would not convey. That the Allies were so confident of final victory that such political calculation was already fully formed and a significant part of the actual war planning is almost stunning, given the opposition and the amount of time the Reich had to prepare its defenses.

It is also remarkable that the Allies, especially the United States, were able to re-equip nearly totally their massive ground force with new, or at the least massively upgraded, armored vehicles in only 15 months. The sheer effort would have been beyond the enormous resources of even the United States had the Kriegsmarine still existed as a threat. However, with the end of the threat from the Reich's surface fleet – and despite the impassioned pleas of the USN – naval construction of anything except landing boats and their larger cousins, the LST, virtually stopped, with the material, not to mention the skilled welders and other craftsmen and women, shunted to armored vehicle construction. The results of this effort were, of course, the M47 Sheridan and the M92 Chamberlain.

While British, Canadian, Indian, and South African armies were being reequipped with Centurions mounting the 105mm L7 gun and a modest increase in glacis armor, the Americans (along with their close partners, the Australian Armored forces) had gone far further with the M47. Swallowing a fair amount of pride, the Americans had built the Sheridan around a license-built version of the Royal Armory 105mm weapon being used on the Centurion and an upgraded version of the M26 basic layout that was, to use the words of one American armored veteran, not built but carved out of solid steel ingots. Using the ballistics of captured Panther III 105mm guns as a guide, the Sheridan's front hull and turret armor was proof against the best-known Nazi tank gun at any range over 250 meters. While this level of protection came at the expense of range-sapping weight, and limited the M47 to 29mph, it was a considered to be a reasonable compromise given the Sicily lesson.

The other American tank, the utterly mind-boggling M92 Chamberlain, reflected in many ways the ideals of its primary builder, the Bath Iron Works, a long-time builder of warships. Slow, with a top speed of only 23mph, the M92 was the most powerful and best-defended tank on Earth for nearly three decades until the advent of composite ceramic/steel armor on the British Chieftain II in 1984 and the American M1 in late 1985. The vehicle was covered with almost 9 inches of Category B armor (the same formulation used on heavy cruisers and battleships) and was powered by a 1,200 horsepower version of the Pratt and Whitney R-2000 Twin Wasp air-cooled radial engine. The M92 was armed with a high-velocity 120mm gun, against the M60 (105) and M67 (155mm) SP gun carriages, and the rare (only 350 built) 210mm M71 super SP assault gun; the Chamberlain was so large that it required a modified version of the LST to disgorge it.

While the Allies were rebuilding their armored formations into something to make the Waffen-SS howl, the Italian Peninsula was the site of a series of raids (if the landing of a rump division can be termed a raid) by American and British forces that literally drove the Nazi leadership to distraction. Convinced that the Allied attacks were probes looking for a place to land massive numbers of troops (in the hope of knocking the Italians, and their large army, out of the war), the SS High Command and Luftwaffe moved increasing numbers of irreplaceable units into Italy where they were exposed to devastating air and naval attacks. Perhaps the most successful, and final large scale, of these spoiling attacks was the famed Anzio landings by the 3rd Marine Division.

Anzio, a sleepy fishing village around 80 miles from Rome, was a remarkably poorly-defended point in the Italian fascist defensive screen thanks to the hugely difficult terrain that lay between it and the Italian capital. Rome had long believed, quite correctly, that only a madman would attempt to force the many streams and mountain passes between the seaside and Rome. The Marine landing, and the initial drive inland of nearly 8 miles to a position where Marine artillery observers and SP guns were able to dominate the entire region, gave every impression of being the long-awaited main Allied attack. The resulting SS reaction force was correspondingly large, a full two divisions of SS armor and close to four divisions of Italian mechanized forces (the mechanized elements of almost every division the Italian Army had on the Peninsula).

Unfortunately for the Nazis and their fascist Italian allies, mountain passes, rivers, and streams are obstacles for all military formations that attempt to cross them, regardless of the uniform they wear. While the Luftwaffe and Regia Aeronautica made a serious effort to attack the American lodgment, the Allies had moved nearly a thousand fighter and fighter-bomber aircraft to Sardinia, Sicily, and North Africa with the specific goal of gutting the Axis air power on the Italian Peninsula permanently. With the air wings of six American carriers, including the combat debut of the legendary F-8 Crusader fighter, as backup to the large USAF and RAF formations operating from the land bases, the effort of the already greatly weakened Nazi air offensive was doomed to the failure that eventually befell it. Once shorn of air cover, the Axis armored formations were savaged by air attack and by artillery fire, including naval gunfire support from HMS *Warspite* and the American battleships USS *North Carolina* and USS *Washington*.

The Marine landing at Anzio was so successful that some in the Allied camp, primarily British leaders who had no burning desire to fight a third major campaign in France, pushed for it to become the actual main Allied effort. Thankfully, the folly of fighting across the mountains of the Peninsula, with its resemblance to the killing grounds of southern Okinawa, was clear enough to the decision makers that the suggestion was not adopted. One can only speculate on the outcome of an attempt to fight up the entire Italian Peninsula, across the Italian Alps, and into Germany, and the obvious bloodbath that would have resulted.

Instead, some six weeks after their landing the Marines made an orderly withdrawal from the Anzio area, with the final forces, mainly artillery observers and their security teams, being evacuated by helicopters. In the month-and-a-half engagement the 3rd Marine Division, primarily the 12th Marines, suffered 850 total casualties, including 357 KIA, while the SS and attached Italian units lost nearly 17,000 "unrecoverable losses" (killed, captured or wounded so badly as being incapable of return to service) and suffered the destruction of 1,100 tanks and armored vehicles. The Axis proceeded to build four different, extremely strong, defensive positions that ran the width of the Italian Peninsula in the six months between the withdrawal of the 3rd Marine Division and D-Day.

Anzio was the last warm-up for the main event – the Allied re-entry into the Continent.

8

The Allies had, through a series of increasingly bloody invasions across the Pacific Theater, developed a playbook for invasions. The playbook had stood the Allies in good stead through the invasion of Sicily, but had run into serious difficulties starting with the raids on the Italian Peninsula, with several of the early battalion raids actually being cancelled – although the Waffen-SS leaders never realized that these efforts had been failures, assuming that they were simply more seaborne harassment efforts.

The problem the Allies had encountered was with their preparation of the landing areas. The Pacific had taught the Allies, especially the Marine Corps, that the only thing better than five days of shore bombardment was six days of shore bombardment. When attacking the many island bastions controlled by the Japanese, the Allies had learned to isolate the target, destroy it as completely as possible, then – and only then – put the amphibious troops into harm's way ashore. It was a tactic that had worked perfectly against islands. It was, however, an utter disaster against continental targets where the enemy could move forces from hundreds of miles away in a matter of hours. While these forces were subject to air interdiction, many would get through to the point of attack and upset the correlation of forces. Fortunately, the Allies' delay caused by their rude introduction to modern armored ground combat had allowed them to find what they believed was an answer to the challenge.

In many ways, the Allies' tactic took advantage of the remarkably predictable way that the Waffen-SS reacted. The amphibious raids, even those that were, to the Allies, serious failures, allowed the Allies to build a book on what the Reich's reaction would be to any effort to enter the Continent. As the Allied air forces continued to chew through their Nazi counterparts, and as the Allies found and cut off the remaining supplies of vital materials (including the "capture" of Vladivostok, which sealed the Reich off from any Pacific resources), Allied strategic reconnaissance efforts became both less costly and far more effective. The results paid dividends as the date of the invasion neared.

The Waffen-SS had a notably inflexible tactical playbook, one that the Party Leadership had preached as being *the* reason that even the somewhat decadent Heer had been able to defeat the Soviets "with ease" (left unsaid were the million-plus casualties suffered by the Heer and Reich Allies in defeating and destroying the Red Army). The Party leadership, and by extension the leadership of the Waffen-SS (which was itself a creation of the Party and its unique worldview), accepted as an article of faith that the key to victory was massed armor and relentlessness on the attack by "Aryan" troops. What this meant for the Continent was that the "lower" races were used for fighting from fixed fortifications and serving AAA and heavy weapons while Waffen-SS units were set up to act as fire brigades that would attack any breakthrough. It was Berlin's unshakable belief that the Allies' success in both Sardinia and Sicily as well as the Anglo/American "defeat" at Anzio proved this system to be correct since there had not been sufficient Germanic troops on either island, and that the intervention of heavy SS formations had saved the Italians at Anzio. When Italian military and political leaders had (quite correctly) questioned this perspective, noting that the Anzio attack had never been reinforced by the Americans and seemed to have been some sort of experiment, not a full-out invasion, they had found themselves roundly ignored and ridiculed by their SS "betters" to the point of humiliation. This treatment was to bear bitter fruit for the Reich in the long term.

The Allied tactics were actually very simple when one considers how effective they proved to be. Only an alliance with the overwhelming economic wealth that was available to the Allies, an alliance that was capable of drawing on the raw resources of five continents and nearly 80% of the global manufacturing capacity, would have even dared to consider what the CGCS dubbed "False Peak" (a term borrowed from mountaineering). Only a group of countries that had what can only be termed as the single-minded support of its populations (in large part the result of the St. Patrick Day raids), unlimited self-confidence that came from 15 years of success in combat, and a surprising degree of willingness to act in unconventional ways would have been willing to put False Peak into action. Only an enemy as ideologically trapped and self-deluded as the Reich would have allowed themselves to be taken in by the strategy.

False Peak, when viewed through the prism of 50+ years of hindsight, seems so obvious that it is difficult to imagine that it ever was attempted, much less worked successfully. Yet, unquestionably, it did.

The start of the False Peak operations occurred at the Pas de Calais in the early morning of February 7th, 1957, when the beach fortifications south of the port were struck by 346 B-36 bombers in what was, at the time, the heaviest single air raid ever conducted. A portion of the fortifications covering 120 square miles (10 miles long by 12 miles in depth) was hit with a total of 27,400 1,000 pound bombs. Two hours later, specific strong points were hit by super heavy bombs ranging in weight from 10 to 32 tons. These attacks were followed by fighter-bomber strikes, including the first serious use of napalm against other critical positions. Even as the "INVASION" warning was flashed across the Continent, the second phase of the Pas de Calais operation began.

Out of the darkness loomed what one observer proclaimed to be "every ship in the world", as the Allied gun line approached and opened fire. No less than 12 battleships (4 RN, 8 USN) opened fire on the already-shattered coastline with 14", 15", and 16" gunfire. These ships were soon joined by 17 cruisers and 22 destroyers. SS observers who had survived the initial hail of shells reported that in addition to the bombardment ships there were many "landing ships" approaching the beaches. This confirmation brought the Reich leadership to full alert and they ordered that all heavy guns, including those that had been carefully hidden, be ordered to fire, all possible aircraft be launched, and most critically that three SS divisions be moved from within Germany to the landing zone. Surviving Nazi records indicate that the Führer told his staff that "it is stupid to be predictable". In this, he was quite correct.

When the heavy shore batteries opened fire, revealing the position of those guns that had, incredibly to newspaper reporters and the guns' conscripted crews but unsurprisingly to Allied commanders who had seen how much damage Japanese fortifications in the Pacific had been able to absorb, survived the initial pasting from both air and the sea, the Allies sprang the next of their traps. Using the recently deployed "Big Tim" rockets (a reaction to the difficulties experienced by US forces in silencing gun emplacements on islands like Iwo Jima), with their 1,000 pound SAP and AP bomb warheads, Allied fighters swept over the smoking defenses in attempts to put rockets directly into the heavy gun bunkers. As the Allied fighters worked the defenses over it rapidly became clear to gun crews that to fire was to die, by explosive if fortunate or by fire if unlucky.

As the carefully-husbanded Reich attack aircraft headed to the Pas de Calais they found themselves overwhelmed by hundreds of Allied fighters, including many of the carrier aircraft that had been flown off of land bases as far away as Scotland after having left their home ships the day before. The addition of nearly 600 FAA and USN fighters, particularly the all-conquering F-8, joining with the USAF and RAF aircraft (including the combat debut of the famed English Electric Lightning, although only a single flight of aircraft) provided the Allies with the best correlation of forces to that point in the air war. The result was the "Calais Quail Shoot". At a cost of 38 aircraft lost and 67 damaged, the combined allied forces virtually annihilated the Luftwaffe's jet fighter force in France. The Nazi air force would never again mount a serious challenge to Allied dominance of French airspace. Unmolested and unchallenged, the Allied shelling continued for the rest of the day.

Throughout the night, the Western navies continued to pound on the Calais defenses, increasing the sense of urgency among SS commanders to get mobile forces into position. By dawn, two divisions were moving from bases within France while three more had completed loading and were making their way into France from Germany by rail. The Allied planners in London were somewhat disappointed at this turn of events (surprisingly accurate, near real-time, information was sent back on SS movement by British LRRP teams, American Alamo scout units, and by underground resistance cells that still survived within France) as the Pas de Calais action had been designed to draw at least 8 SS armored divisions forward.

Still, five SS armored divisions was an acceptable set of targets. Reich records are largely missing, but based on BDA (Bomb Damage Assessment) photos and testimony from civilians post war, it seems clear that, in addition to actual vehicle losses that exceeded 80% in the case of 36th SS Panzer and were over 60% across the board, the Waffen-SS divisions caught on the rails suffered nearly 50% casualties in killed and wounded. The losses suffered by 14th SS Panzer and SS Das Reich during their march are more difficult to determine, simply because the two units were reconstituted completely afterwards, but it is striking to note that the senior Das Reich officer whose after action report can be found was a Captain.

As the sun set on February 8th, the "amphibious ships" observed by the SS the previous day suddenly made what, for LSTs, was a sprint towards the beach. As the ships reached within 3,500 yards of the beach, they seemed to burst suddenly into flame, flames that then rushed toward the beach defenses. These ships, far from bearing Marines or other assault troops, were actually LST-R (Landing Ship Tank – Rocket). Each ship, most of them being early versions of the LST design and having doors too narrow to handle the newer Allied tank designs, had been converted to carry almost 300 210mm or 200 240mm rockets (the rockets themselves were an evolution of the Soviet Katyusha design that had been spirited out of the USSR in the days immediately following the Soviet surrender). In the zones struck by the rockets, particularly those treated to a washing by 210mm weapons after a sweep by 240mm warheads, almost nothing remained recognizable, so thorough was the destruction.

The surviving remnants of 14th SS and Das Reich reached the beaches before dawn on February 9th. When they arrived, all they found was smoke, rubble, shell-shocked conscripts and seagulls. The Allied ships were all gone.

False Peak had begun.

The Allies had hoped that the False Peak operations would work once, maybe even twice. They had believed that the German military would wise up to what was happening after only a couple of feints. There is some documentation that Kriegsmarine officers who had survived both the purge of senior professional naval officers *and* the destruction of the German Navy started to urge changes in tactics in the immediate aftermath of Calais and that the few remain Heer senior officers joined them after the Nice operation, but it is clear that the Nazi leaders never accepted that the Allies were leaving voluntarily (this belief was immeasurably aided by the loss of the battle cruiser USS *Guam*, with heavy loss of life, to Luftwaffe ASM guided missiles during the Nice operation).

Instead it is clear from the personal papers of Erich von Manstein (perhaps the best Heer Officer remaining in a senior command position in 1957) that the SS (or, as they are often referred to by Manstein, *scheisskopfen*) only stopped reacting with massive troop movements when the Reich ran out of rolling stock and sufficient undamaged rail trackage to move multiple armored divisions simultaneously.

False Peak is, to this day, a central part of every basic officer course in the English-speaking world. The strategy itself is not the subject of the lesson, rather it is the cost that inflexibility of thought brings to the unwary commander that is stressed.

9

One of the side benefits of the False Peak operations was in the area of psychological warfare. As soon as the smoke cleared enough to allow for clear photography the aftermath of the Calais pounding found its way onto leaflets that were dropped by the millions along the length and breadth of the Atlantic Wall. Created in more than a dozen languages, including German, the leaflets featured the "before and after" shots of every fortification attack. The attacks themselves grew to mythical proportions, with some tales making it all the way to the partisans fighting along the Eastern Frontier. With each retelling the destruction wrought by the Allies grew, the lethality of the attacks doubled, and the effect on morale among the conscripted fortress troops was magnified. By the time of the last operation, near Cherbourg, the mere appearance of heavy Allied warships was enough to cause blind panic among virtually all non-SS forces and even a degree of fear among some of the less elite SS formations. The degree that the Allies knew about this effect was debated in the immediate post-war period, but the way that it came to be known to the CGCS is itself a remarkable story, one worthy of its own volume, but due to space and time restraints we will just touch upon it here.

The Allies had, during the Pacific War, used a variety of methods to obtain intelligence. One of the most effective proved to be the British Long Range Reconnaissance Patrol, better known as LRRP or "Lurps". These were small units, normally not more than 24 men, who went into the jungle and hunted the enemy, or, more famously, tore across sections of China in armored jeeps and lorries, terrifying the Japanese at every turn. American troops performing similar missions went by the generic name of Alamo Scouts (reputedly because any time they were trapped they fought to the last man) or the more conventional Marine Raiders. These units also acted as advisors and liaisons for local resistance and insurgent movements fighting the Japanese. The dizzying array of modern Special Forces units generally track their origins to these two groups (along with the Royal Marine Commando detachments). When faced with the final stage of the war these American and British units had to modify their tactics to the very different environment of urbanized Occupied Europe. That they were largely successful, as is celebrated in numerous books and films, is well known. What is less well known are two other, spectacularly successful and insanely brave units that were instrumental in the gathering of intelligence prior to the Allied landings. There were the Philippine Scouts and the Viet Minh.

How these two Asian units would become the most effective, and far and away most feared, Allied units operating in Occupied Europe will be briefly described in this chapter.

The Philippine islands had passed to American control after the Spanish-American War of 1898. For the islands' native population it was, at least initially, simply a matter of exchanging one colonial overseer for another, a change that was resisted with considerable effort and violence. In the end, however, the Filipino peoples were brought under control by American troops (including men who had learned their trade fighting the Apache in the US Southwest). Over a fairly short time, the Filipinos discovered that the US was a rather different sort of colonial power, one that wanted more than anything else to divest itself of the islands. While the Americans very much wanted to keep control of Subic Bay, one of the great natural anchorages in the Pacific, the interest in the rest of the islands was, at best, weak. By the mid-1930s the American Congress had set into motion a legal process that was meant to provide the Philippines political independence on July 4th, 1945. As part of this effort the American military had begun to train a Philippine military (even though America was still supposed to be the final arbitrator of the islands' defensive needs for years after the end of formal US rule). The Japanese rudely interrupted this process on December 8th, 1941 when they invaded the islands.

The Japanese had expected the Filipino people to welcome them as liberators.

The Japanese were very wrong. They soon found they had a tiger by the tail.

Almost as soon as the formal defense of the islands ended, the Resistance began, under the guidance of Filipino officers and, especially, Philippine Scout Division NCOs. While the occasional American evader could be found with the guerilla bands, in general the Japanese faced fellow Asians fighting for their own homes and families. The Japanese had expected to be able to garrison the islands with no more than two divisions; in practice it took nearly eight divisions, and large parts of every island except Luzon were under Japanese control only on paper. In late 1944, when the United States Army invaded to eject the Japanese, they knew, virtually to the man, exactly where the Japanese were based, how large the troop concentrations were, and what weapons were emplaced where. With this information, and with Philippine Scout units leading American Ranger and Marine Raider units to locations where they were able to interdict and decimate IJA reinforcements, the Americans were able to sweep the Japanese from the islands with surprisingly low losses given the terrain and the number of Japanese troops on the islands. The sole exception was the battle of Manila, where the local Japanese commander chose to fight for the city street by street. The resulting destruction, which ended when the garrison commander and his final few troops were cornered and wiped out by a Scout company, saw the heaviest American and Filipino losses of the entire liberation.

It was with this effort as a backdrop that the United States, to the shock of friend and foe alike, granted the Philippines full independence on July 4th 1947. In doing so, the US kept a promise and gained a highly useful ally.

During the preparation for the Invasion of Occupied Europe, the Philippine Republic sent a small contingent of troops to fight with its former colonial master and current friend. While some historians have tended to overlook this effort or have chosen to lump it in with other "symbolic" contributions from countries like

Korea and Bolivia, this group of specialists had an impact far out of proportion to their numbers.

Led by a 27-year-old Captain, Eduardo Aquino, the Philippines Scout Company provided the Allies with a fearless and utterly ruthless unit of Raiders. Perhaps the ideal example of the men of the Company was their commander. Aquino had been 12 years old when the Japanese invaded his homeland. Within six months, he had gone from being a typical 7th grader to a combat veteran. Before his 16th birthday, Aquino had risen to the leadership of his own guerilla band (and a brevet rank of Lieutenant in the Philippine Scouts) through sheer force of personality and individual ferocity. At 16 he was the unquestioned commander of a unit filled with men twice his age. Tough, brilliant, and resourceful, Aquino was, after two years of intense prep work, the first candidate the Philippine Republic sent to the US Military Academy as a student. A lesser man would have been intimidated by West Point; a weaker man would have taken one of the many chances to rise to insults about his race or size (like many of his countrymen, Aquino stood just five foot, three inches) and found himself out of the Academy for fighting. Aquino was neither intimidated or goaded, not when the reputation of his country was at stake. The insults stopped permanently when, at the start of his Second Classman year, Harry Truman made the President's traditional visit to the banks of the Hudson. The President of the United States took the opportunity to award Cadet (nee Lieutenant, US Army, reserves) Aquino his Medal of Honor.

The Allied command, after more than a little intense debate, decided to deploy the Philippine Scout unit in the exact role that it had been sent to fill. Terrify the enemy. It was a role that the Scouts completed with a frightening sense of professional detachment.

The Allies knew that the Nazis, through their secret police and SS Einsatzgruppen, thoroughly cowed the civilian populations of the occupied countries. A cowed populace was not what the Allies needed. What the Allies needed were SS and National forces that worried about what went bump in the night. In under six months Aquino's men, along with several groups of Alamo Scouts, achieved exactly that goal.

Air-dropped into Normandy and Brittany, the Alamo and Philippine Scout units made the night unsafe for enemy troops; troops who had become so comfortable that they would go into town after dark unarmed and alone. The Nazis' initial reaction, to order reprisals against the local civilians, which had been extremely effective in the past when dealing with local resistance, was an utter failure against the Allied units (one favored tactic was actually to wait for the SS units to be sent out to gather hostages and then ambush the Waffen units on the way to town). When the SS reacted to these ambushes by sending out larger formations, the Scouts would then call in airstrikes on the large columns. Within months SS personnel virtually disappeared from many of the villages of Western France. Once the SS and Gestapo had been forced out, the other Allied Asian secret was unleashed.

Into the gap created by the absence of Nazi troops the Allies sent the S.O.E. (Special Operations Groups). While originally single agents or small two-three man teams, once the German presence and patrolling changed, being left in many cases to French police (many of whom had little love for those in charge of Berlin *or* Paris), the Allies went to the next, far more controversial, part of the plan. Six-to-ten-man (and woman) teams were inserted, mainly by parachute, to build a Resistance infrastructure out of what little was left of the groups that had fought the Reich in 1941 and lost. The S.O.E., while including American and British operatives, was mainly comprised of personnel from French Indochina (primarily today's Viet Nam). Many of them were Vietnamese while others were from French colonial families who had resisted the Japanese and had made what both sides had believed was a short-term common cause alliance against the Japanese invader. Together, with support from both the American and British, they formed what became the Viet Minh. While the Philippine Scouts were experts at jungle warfare and were, by 1955, arguably *the* small unit combat experts in the world, they lacked experience working in urban areas and in organizing resistance "cells"; two things that the Viet Minh excelled at.

While the efforts of the Viet Minh were hampered by both French and Nazi authorities, it is without question that they were a driving force in the Lyon Rebellion and in the prevention of the destruction of port facilities elsewhere in France. Sadly, it was in one of these major successes, at Cherbourg, that both the Scouts (who had slowly withdrawn to the Cherbourg Peninsula to support Operation Maverick) and Viet Minh were nearly destroyed when they came out into the open to protect the port facilities until USMC Raiders could arrive via helicopter assault. Due to unexpectedly effective anti-aircraft defenses, the Marine units were nearly 12 hours late in arriving, reaching the port in time to save around 60% of the wharves and ship offloading equipment, but too late for most of the 2nd and 3rd Company, Republic of Philippine Scouts and for nearly 60 Viet Minh operators who perished with the Resistance cells they had created and trained.

While total losses for both groups seem to be trifling, especially compared to those suffered by the US during Maverick, they represented more than half of the total force sent by the two Asian allies and, to both the Philippines and Viet Nam, when regular operation losses are considered, the virtual elimination of the cream of their armed services.

While both countries have, over the years, proved time and again their resilience as US allies, it is in this little-known period between the initiation of False Peak and Operation Maverick that both countries proved, for all time, their worth as members of the Alliance.

10

With what today's Pentagon calls "battlefield shaping" completed, the Allies now found themselves faced with what Elizabeth II dubbed, during ceremonies commemorating the 20th Anniversary of the Invasions, "Civilization's Moment of Truth". There is no doubt that, had Operations Gravel, Maverick, and Thorn Bush failed, it would have been at least a generation, if not longer, before the Allies would have again attempted to retake the continent from the Nazis, with all the almost unspeakable consequences that would have brought upon humanity.

It has become traditional to deal with the three operations individually, and I will follow this convention as I continue. However, before examining Thorn Bush, it is worth considering the enormity of the overall Fortress Europe operation.

Numbers can be misleading, but in this case tell much of the tale.

SS/Reich/National units loyal to Berlin

Troops: 2,500,000 combat troops (this, of course, includes air defense units and fortress troops as well as Reich forces deployed on the Eastern Frontier and all along the Atlantic/Mediterranean Wall as well as paramilitaries). Because of the forced labor system employed by the Nazis it is impossible to accurately calculate the number of personnel performing support functions, although most studies indicate that the ratio of combat trooper to support across the continent was between 1:10 and 1:12, which seems reasonable given the overall inefficient logistical train of the SS.

Tanks and SP Artillery*: 5,500 (as with the Allies, this is an all-inclusive number of operational vehicles) plus nearly 5,000 damaged or disabled vehicles in various stages of repair/recovery.

Armored personnel carriers and halftracks: 1,250.
Towed Artillery tubes* over 50mm: 3,500.
Combat aircraft (as of the onset of Thorn Bush): Jets: 280, Piston engine: 1,500.
Combat Ships (excluding Submarines): 48 (31 in the Black Sea).
* *This figure does not include mortars or permanently emplaced weapons along the Atlantic Wall.*

Allies (Deployed to the ETO only)

Troops: 3,250,000 (this represents just combat and directly combat related troops like landing craft drivers and combat engineers. Total forces exceeded 23,000,000 when air force formations (including ground support), naval personnel, and logistical/support troops are included).
Tanks and SP Artillery: 17,500.
Armored personnel carriers and halftracks: 11,250 (this includes Amphibious Tractors).
Towed Artillery tubes* over 50mm: 7,500.
Combat aircraft (as of the onset of Thorn Bush): Jets: 7,800, Piston engine: 1,600.
Combat ships (excluding Submarines): 850.
Amphibious ships (including rocket bombardment and "monitors" created from LCT): 860.
Transports and support vessels: 975.
Landing craft (not including Amphibious Tractors or Amphibious Tanks): 2,926.

In addition to the almost unimaginable cornucopia of material available to the Allies, as listed above, there is also the more important matter of the quality of the equipment.

Waffen-SS forces had lost well over half of their modern tanks outside of the Italian Peninsula during the False Peak operations, many of them never getting off the flatcars which were being used for transport. Facing the Allies were a conglomeration of modern vehicles, holdovers from the 1943 Heer, and even vehicles captured during the conquest of Europe. Many of the vehicles in the last two categories had no realistic place on a 1958 battlefield; some were actually obsolescent, if not outright obsolete, at the time of the USSR's surrender. Having entered the renewed Hot War in 1954 with what was the premier armored formations on Earth by the time of the invasions, the Waffen-SS had been reduced to the decidedly inferior in both quantity and quality, although the superb Panther III still represented a serious threat to most Allied armored vehicles. The Allies, as has been related, had actually paused for close to a full year in their war plan to correct the weakness in their armor designs. This did not totally eliminate the M-26 or even the venerable M4 from the Allied TOE, but it did allow any Allied armored formation to approach combat with parity, if not superiority, in forces.

In a similar fashion the Luftwaffe and its National air force "allies" had suffered terribly at the hands of the Allies, virtually from the war's opening day, which saw the long-range strike capacity of the Reich obliterated in an afternoon. Between missions specifically designed to draw Luftwaffe interceptors into killing grounds and effective heavy bombing of targets that the Nazi leadership had been certain were absolutely safe, the Luftwaffe had found itself in a war of attrition that it was doomed to lose. This is perhaps best illustrated by the fact that the number of B52 strategic bombers accepted by the USAF between January of 1954 and July of 1958 exceeded the Reich's TOTAL jet fighter production during the same period. The Allies produced at least a half dozen different fighter designs (F-8, F-11, F-86, F-100, F-88/101, and the Hawker Hunter) in greater quantity that all types of jet aircraft produced in Germany from 1952 to 1958 combined, with just the F-86's 6,500 aircraft production run equalling Germany's total aircraft production (including everything from basic trainers to helicopters to heavy bombers) from 1948-58.

When one looks at the figures above, one is struck by the seemingly incongruous fact that the Allies operated more piston engine-driven aircraft during the invasions than the Luftwaffe. Here too, however, there was a massive difference in quality. While nearly 600 of the Allies' 1,800 aircraft were obsolescent B-29D and Lincoln bombers, the other 1,200 were mainly the AD-1 Skyraider attack aircraft, which many consider to be the finest CAS aircraft ever built, and two other very late WWII designs that never saw action in the Pacific War: the F8F Bearcat and the Sea Fury, both of which operated off of Allied carriers in the CAS role. Luftwaffe fortunes were not as rosy as those of the Allies. While the Luftwaffe did have 75 Ta 152 high altitude piston engine aircraft, most of the propeller-driven aircraft available to the Luftwaffe were carryovers from the early to mid-1940s modified to act in the counterinsurgent role. These aircraft had the potential to be a threat to Allied ground troops, and would have been had the Luftwaffe possessed at least air parity with the Anglo/American air forces; but in the conditions prevailing at the time of the Invasions, where the only Luftwaffe jet fighters outside of pre-war German borders were two scratch squadrons of Me-262 based out of Bergen, Norway, sending any of the Reich's Fw-190 or Me-110 pilots into battle was tantamount to an act of murder.

Balancing these great Allied advantages, at least somewhat, was the fact that continental troops were fighting a defensive campaign, often from fortified positions including the Atlantic Wall. This formidable, effectively unprecedented construct, especially the section facing the English Channel, was as much as 30km in depth, with pillboxes and bunkers sited to provide maximum mutual support. While manned mainly by non-German conscripts there were sufficient "elite" SS overseers mixed into the fortress crews that the choice faced by most conscripts was one of taking a chance of being killed by the Allies and the certainty of being killed by the Nazis. While far from the perfect method of ensuring fighting spirit, the SS system was, as we will see, sometimes brutally effective.

11

Operation Thorn Bush is unquestionably the most criticized of the invasions undertaken to liberate Europe. Many of the operation's most severe critics point, ironically, to its great success as proof that it should never have happened.

Operation Thorn Bush began late on the evening of April 27, 1958, with the largest airborne drop since the abortive attempt to save the USSR from defeat in 1943 by attacking the Channel Islands. To this day, it stands out as the literal textbook example of airborne and airmobile operations. Starting with the air drop of the US 101st Airborne division into areas surrounding the main air assault goal of Bergen airfield in southern Norway, followed by the Canadian/US 1st Special Service Force onto the airfield itself some 20 minutes later, the airborne landing was an utter shock to the SS commander for Southern Norway. Supported by close air support assets (provided by USAF B-26 medium bombers/gunships) that killed any vehicle observed on the roads more than three miles from the airfield, and protected by USN carrier-launched Skyknight night fighters, the 1st SSF took the airbase by 01:30 hours and had cleared the runways within 40 minutes of securing the base. The first RCAF C-124 landed at 03:55 with a cargo of two Ontas anti-tank vehicles. Additional aircraft, including the first combat deployments of the famed C-130 Hercules, carrying additional heavy weapons and vehicles landed every 15 minutes for the rest of the night despite growing defensive AAA. Even with the loss of 43 cargo aircraft to all causes, including six air-to-air collisions (one of which claimed the life of Colonel Robert Posey, the Wing Commander of the 23rd Transportation Wing), by dawn the airbase had been reinforced by some 25 anti-tank vehicles and had received 23

75mm howitzers and 30 120mm mortars to supplement the 60mm and 81mm mortars of the initial airborne forces. Even as the SS commander began to react to the air assault with what was planned to be a regimental-sized attack, the air head suddenly became the least of his worries.

The defenses near Bergen had been one of the False Peak targets. As such, a twenty-kilometer-long portion of the beach fortifications had been the recipient of an average of one 1000 pound bomb every 15 meters. Some 650 16" and 1,822 8" naval bombardment shells, as well as several thousand 210mm and 240mm rockets, had also found final resting places in the craters of the former defensive positions. With the approach of dawn, the shattered remnants of this defensive belt were struck again.

Nearly 700 B-29s, some having begun their mission from as far away as Newfoundland, made bombing runs against the beach, defenses moving parallel to the beaches to minimize the chances of friendly casualties. Despite these precautions, at least one bomb struck LST-R 658, resulting in the loss of the ship with its entire crew. Nevertheless, the vast majority of the 14,000 five hundred pound bombs found their way to the already-damaged fortifications all along the roads inland of the position. As the four-engine bombers cleared the airspace, naval gunfire filled it with steel. The Allies had allocated six fast battleships (the American *Indiana, Iowa, Kentucky, Louisiana* and *Montana* and the HMS *Lion*), 9 cruisers, and 35 destroyers to the gunfire support mission with the stated goal of "chewing through all that cement down to the bedrock underneath".

While the naval vessels did not succeed in this noble goal, they did even more damage to the already shattered defenses. As the conventional gunships ceased firing, the assembled LST-R and LCT-R, nearly 70 of them, added their cargo to the carnage.

Immediately behind them were the first wave of amtracks (amphibious tractors, properly known as LVT-4 and LVT-5: the direct successors to those used by the USMC starting in 1943) carrying men from 2nd and 3rd Battalion, 2nd Marines, which began to churn toward the beach. Soon after they appeared, to the shock of the young marine recruits and the well-practiced disgust of their veteran NCOs, defensive fire began to reach out from the seemingly-shredded fortifications. This was the signal for some of the hundreds of aircraft orbiting the beachhead to move in with rockets, napalm, and gunfire. While some of the attacking aircraft were jets from the carriers standing well off-shore, most were propeller-driven aircraft off the 30 escort carriers cruising just behind the gun line and attack transports. Individual pilots, many armed with Tiny Tim rockets, took aim at previously concealed gun positions or dropped 400-gallon tanks of jellied gasoline on bunkers in hopes of sucking the very air from the beach defenders' lungs.

With the defenders mainly stunned by the ferocity of the bombardment, most of the first wave made it to the beach, with only 12 of the initial 115 amtracks being hit. Losses among the first wave began to increase as the riflemen exited the relative safety of the landing vehicles. As their human cargo dove for cover, the amtracks crabbed around and headed back for their next load of men. A few of the LVTs did not withdraw; these were designed as fire support vehicles with a range of weapons including 105mm howitzers, flamethrowers, and heavy .50 caliber machine guns.

Once ashore the marines began what was, for them, a well-choreographed dance based on knowledge paid for with blood on sandspits across the Pacific Ocean: reduce the strong point with support fire if possible; with grenade, satchel charge, and rifle fire if necessary. Then move forward and repeat, ignoring losses as you advance. As the first wave advanced the rest of the 2nd Marines and part of the 3rd Marines followed in the next wave. To most of the privates, lance corporals, and junior officers, this was their first time in combat; for the rest of the NCOs, more than a few privates, and the more senior officers, it was a return to a job they had hoped never to perform again. As the morning wore on, a rhythm could be felt by both sides. While the defenders, urged on by fanatical SS (both German and "other Aryans"), drew blood, the Americans, now joined by men of the 1st Canadian Infantry division, advanced in a waltz of death. A few men on both sides may have noticed the sound and fury that seemed to be happening far beyond the battlefield, but most were only concerned with the next two or three feet: surviving to cover that ground or to prevent someone from surviving the attempt to cross the same two or three feet.

As men died for inches along the shoreline, the battle was actually being decided miles inland where the 29th and 43rd SS Panzer were moving to relieve the beach defenders.

After being sent first toward the airfield to dislodge the paratroopers there, the Panzers had been pulled back and sent toward the landing zone. SS doctrine was clear: stop the invader at the water's edge and drive them back into the sea. The fact that the Japanese had never managed to achieve this was of no concern to the Party leadership. What was to be expected of Orientals, even against inferior troops like the mongrelized Americans? Aryans, even those weakened by exposure to lesser races, and other whites led by Aryans, were more than capable of defeating the Americans. The Party accepted as an act of faith that no American troops would ever walk on European soil except as prisoners of war.

Every man in the Waffen-SS accepted the Party position. Most had never even considered that a different position was possible; many could not even remember a time when the Führer had not led the Reich. Those older landsers who had childhood memories of the days before the Reich mainly remembered the lack of food, or the chaos, or the whispered words of their parents about money worries that had existed in the days before the Party. A few even dimly remembered the horrors of the Great War, mainly from stories told by parents or older siblings. These older men knew that the time before Hitler had been bad and that the Party had fixed that. They had no desire to see their children or grandchildren live as slaves to the Jews and their American lackeys. It was with this thought that the Panzer divisions drove toward the beach.

Right into a hornet's nest.

The pounding of the SS divisions started as soon as it was fully light and their columns were found by searching aircraft. These first aircraft called in their fellows, and soon nearly 200 fighter-bombers from the Allied carriers were overhead patiently awaiting their turn to attack the advancing Nazis. What few Luftwaffe and Norwegian fighters lifted off to attack the Allied fighter-bombers were intercepted by Combat Air Patrol aircraft well before they could interfere. In short order, thirty-six of the forty-one operational Me-262 available to the Luftwaffe were either destroyed or grounded with battle damage, without having the least impact on the battle. As the first wave of carrier attack aircraft ran low on fuel and munitions, a new group of opponents appeared over the still-advancing armored forces in the form of gunships.

An aircraft modification that had begun in the South West Pacific as an experiment, the gunship had developed into a truly lethal piece of hardware. An aircraft that had been designed as a medium bomber was converted into a strafing platform with as many as 20 heavy machine guns while retaining a decent bomb load. In the years since the end of the Pacific War, the design had been modified, mainly by the replacement of some or all of the .50 caliber machine guns with even more lethal 20mm or 37mm cannon and rockets or napalm canisters replacing the 500 pound bombs used in the Pacific. Working in flights of four, the A-26 and B-26 twin-engine aircraft tore the thin-skinned trucks and personnel carriers of the Panzer divisions to pieces while the armored units found themselves the victim of rocket-driven 500-pound SAP bombs designed for use against warships, with vehicles and men all caught in the greasy flames from napalm drops. 29th SS Panzer found itself cut off and was virtually obliterated in waves of rocket fire, cannons, and pools of napalm.

Despite huge losses that could be tracked by the smoke columns that marked dead wheeled or tracked vehicles, the 43rd SS Panzer had reached within four miles of the inner edge of the fortification belt, less than 17 to the water's edge, when, miraculously, the air attacks stopped. While it is impossible to know, it must have seemed to be a reprieve to the beleaguered Waffen troops as the last aircraft broke way, leaving the sky clear for the first time in hours. It was reprieve measured in minutes.

Without understanding what was happening, the 43rd SS Panzer had been herded from one road to another, constantly under air attack until it had reached Map reference 627, one of five reference points along the possible access corridors to the beachhead. Any of the reference points were a deathtrap, but #627 was the worst. As the column reached the designated point, a series of actions that had not notably changed in half a century began as hoists whined, powder bags were rammed, elevation angles checked, and turrets swung into proper position. When all was ready, it began.

First the USS *Louisiana*, followed some 45 seconds later by her sister USS *Montana*, unleashed her 12-gun broadside toward reference 627. Long before their first shots landed, the gun crews began the laborious reload cycle following a drill that would not have been completely unfamiliar to Admiral Dewey. It is possible, assuming they were looking in the correct direction, that some of the tank commanders may have seen the shapes hurling toward them, so large were the 1,900-pound shells. It was over in less than fifteen minutes. Each ship fired twenty-six broadsides, a total of 312 rounds from each ship, before training their guns in and piping half of each gun crew to chow. In that time, 43rd SS Panzer ceased to exist. When the few survivors emerged from whatever shelter had somehow saved them from the fate of most of their squadmates, they were treated to sights that few men ever see. 50 ton tanks had been thrown through the air and now lay upside down, or on their sides, or in one case where a Panther III had been flipped through the air to land on top of a second panzer.

When the smoke and choking dust cleared, 43rd SS Panzer had been reduced to three operational tanks.

At 14:36 hours local time, the first probing units of 2nd Marines encountered the forward listening posts of the 101st Airborne. This was two hours and twenty-four minutes ahead of schedule.

The first tanks of the Australian 7th Division clanked up to the 1st SSF main perimeter at 06:40 on April 29th.

The Allies' first step back into Europe was complete.

12

While Operation Thorn Bush has entered into the Staff College syllabus mainly as the best real world example of combined amphibious/airborne operations to date, even in the Staff coursework some of the more controversial aspects of the operation are discussed in some depth. These discussions generally fall into three groupings, and all three have their supporters.

The largest, and possibly most reasonable, of the critical views of Thorn Bush has to do with the selection of personnel. All the ground units involved, from the 101st Airborne through the Marine, Canadian, and Australian formations, were very much the cream of the Allied command. The 1st and 3rd Marine divisions were perhaps the premier major amphibious formations in the entire Allied Table of Organization, with the Canadian 1st Infantry and the Australian 7th having earned a lasting reputation during the Formosan operations as hard charging, tough units without a backward step amongst them. It was, or so the criticism goes, unnecessary to devote five of the finest divisions the Allies had at their command to the Norway operation: not when there was still the rest of Europe to be wrested from the Nazis' grip (there is not really much argument concerning the 1st Special Service Force's participation, since the unit had been created in 1956 for the specific task of taking the Bergen facility). This argument has considerable weight, especially when one has the luxury of hindsight.

The Allies could, easily, have replaced the 3rd Marine Division or the 1st Canadian with a National Guard division, and the Australian 7th Armored was, in these circumstances, simply gilding the lily. In fact, it would, according to the critics, have been far better to have used perhaps just the 1st Marine Division, and filled out the rest of the amphibious element with lower quality divisions, be they National Guard or Territorials, or even light infantry troops from one of the Latin American countries. This is, on its face, a compelling argument when one considers the overall resistance encountered by the Allies after exiting the "Wall" fortifications. However, it ignores several realities.

The SS Armored divisions in Southern Norway were a major threat to the beachhead and even more to the airhead. While historically the SS commander sent all of his forces to the beaches, had 29th SS Panzer not been recalled it is possible that, even with air support, the airhead could have been overrun. Had the Reich SS general not waited in order to send both of his divisions out as a single massive fist, it is very likely that the events of Reference 627 would not have destroyed the Waffen-SS force completely. Indeed, an Allied commander faced with the same situation would have done his utmost to wipe the air head out while reinforcing the beach defenses as best he could. Had either – or worse, both – of these possibilities happened, the Allies would have faced the prospect of defeating most of two armored divisions fighting on ground that the units had years of experience moving through. Had this scenario come to pass the critics may well today be arguing that the Allies did not dedicate enough manpower to Thorn Bush.

The critics who claim that there was no need for the Allies to devote two elite Marine divisions to the assault also tend to ignore the reality of it. While the losses suffered in Thorn Bush pale when compared to some other assaults, the reality is that the assault waves took nearly 45% casualties, with the 3rd Battalion, 2nd Marines being effectively wiped out clearing a path through the beach fortifications. These losses sometimes are overshadowed by the speed of the exit from the beaches; nevertheless, it is doubtful that "green" or lower quality troops could have leaned into the face of the firestorm thrown at the Thorn Bush landing elements. While personal comments and recollections are always to be taken with a grain (or more) of salt, it is still worth recalling the comments of Col. Mark Jenning, commander of 2nd Battalion, 3rd Marines, who, being a veteran of the Pacific as well as Thorn

Bush, flatly stated that the first half at Bergen was a bad as the same amount of time on Peleliu. If the colonel was even close to correct, Bergen was no place for 2nd rate troops.

Perhaps the most roundly-criticized use of personnel in the entire Thorn Bush operation is that of reserve pilots in the manning of the transports. Here, the argument goes, the use of "old men" (many of the pilots were well into their 40s, with at least two men documented to have been 50+) was a mistake and their presence accounts for the number of aircraft lost in air-to-air collisions as well as the number lost to AAA. Younger men, the belief goes, would have been sharper: better able to react to the changing conditions. What the critics here fail to take into account is why these "old men" were still flying into a war zone at an age when most military pilots are working at a desk far more often than behind the yoke of an aircraft.

Nearly every pilot in the three air wings (two US, one RCAF) had at least 100 combat missions over the Reich before the Bombing Holiday. They were, if nothing else, the luckiest men the Allies had flying (the RCAF Wing Commander was the only member of his 1940 training class to see the start of the Bombing Holiday), and were generally considered to be the most unflappable flyers in the "business". They were men who had seen everything, most things two or three times, and simply got the job done. The best argument for the use of these refugees from VFW halls is that the air drops were remarkably successful, with nearly 85% of the "sticks" of paratroops being dropped on their predetermined drop zone.

The second major source of criticism for Thorn Bush is that it, in significant ways, simply failed. This is a much more difficult argument to rebut, considering the events of Maverick and Gravel.

The Reich command structure failed to react the way the Allies had expected and planned for. Allied records clearly indicate that there was a huge expectation that the Reich would, at the least, massively reinforce Denmark and all the other False Peak sites. The Allies had prepared a massive ground attack offensive that would further cripple the SS armored formations as soon as the trains began to move. To the Allies' shock, the Reich's only response was an attempt to strike the Norway foothold from the air: even this being a fairly half-hearted attempt three days after the landings, involving less than 100 total aircraft and was not strongly pressed in the face of Allied fighters launched by the score in opposition.

We now know that this general lack of response was because the Reich no longer had the forces available to move at a moment's notice. The Allied False Peak operations, as we have seen, had dealt a body blow to the Waffen-SS and its rapid response capacity. The Allies' prolonged bombing campaign against both rail and road networks had, at least in the short term, deprived the SS of the advantages usually provided to a military organization with internal lines of communication. It was instead the Allies, with their virtually uncontested control of the air and their dominance of the seas (despite the courageous, if generally futile, efforts of the U-Boat force), that had the great advantage in mobility.

The other failure of Thorn Bush was that it had virtually no effect on the population of the Occupied Countries. The Allies had, until Thorn Bush, believed that the conscript armies, especially the fortress troops that "supported" the SS forces, would turn on their Nazi commanders at the first opportunity (something the Allies had seen in Korea and on Formosa). Instead, the French troops who comprised the majority of the National forces deployed by the Reich in Norway fought like banshees even after being cut off and in situations where surrender would not have been suspicious to any outside observer. While today, there are entire sections of libraries crammed with books that discuss the psychological underpinnings of this reaction, the knowledge base of the era simply did not account for this sort of reaction. As a result, within 72 hours of the Thorn Bush landings the instructions provided to Allied troops changed markedly, as "support" became simply support and troops (many whom had already decided to act in this fashion in any case) were told that "anyone in a different uniform, or who doesn't do exactly what you tell them to do, should be considered to be a dedicated Nazi". This instruction, of course, had effects that echo through to our current day.

The final serious argument regarding Thorn Bush is that it was too much of a half measure. Those who take this position are effectively the mirror of the first argument: in their view the Allies should have sent *more* troops to Norway and liberated the entire country, with some even arguing that the Allies should have continued past the border and into Nazi-held Russia. While this is an understandable sentiment, it ignores the manpower and logistical pressures that such an effort would have presented to the Allies and the potential damage that pushing north would have done to Gravel and Maverick.

Overall, despite the criticisms, Thorn Bush was a significant success. It provided the Allied governments with good news, with a demonstration of progress, and thereby bought significant political capital for supporters of the war.

13

The Allies had hoped to follow Operation Thorn Bush with Operation Gravel within a matter of days. As events proceeded, it was closer to two months before the Allies struck next.

Weather over the continent caused several lengthy delays, as the need for good bombing weather and good sea states failed to combine with the right set of tidal conditions. The delay both aided the Allies and caused them difficulties. The delay's greatest assistance was two-fold; first in final instructions and the other in the unending battlefield preparation that marked the Allied way of war.

The Allied armies were quick to pass the hard-won lessons of Thorn Bush on to the forces assembled for Gravel. The revelation that the conscripted European forces would defend their positions with considerable ferocity was a rude shock to Gravel's planners who had expected, and counted on, the conscripts to resist as little as possible, leaving the main enemy as the far less numerous SS formations that were thought to be as much jailers as allies to the National Armies. After questioning of prisoners taken during the Bergen assault, it quickly became clear that there were four distinct groups within the conscripted fortress troops. These groups were:

Devoted Fascists. Based on post-war interrogations it can be said with a fairly strong degree of certainty that nearly a quarter of the non-German forces engaged against the Allies were, remarkably, committed to their own National Party, and, by extension, to the Party in Berlin. This group was heavy with men who had mainly grown up post-occupation, although some were older men well into their thirties who simply believed in the Party's idea of the world. These men would often fight with greater ferocity than their German SS counterparts.

Committed Pan-European Nationalists. Almost completely comprised of men in their teens and twenties, this group was the product of a decade or more of education that taught children in the occupied West that, while things were difficult, the blame lay almost entirely on the heads of the Americans who had come across the Atlantic to attack a peaceful Europe. The rest of the blame went to, in equal measure, the British, who wanted to grow rich on the labor of Europe, and their countries' own leaders in 1939 and 1940 who had been willing to allow the Anglo-Americans to treat France, Denmark, the Netherlands, et al. as little more than colonies and who stupidly stood in the way of the uniting of the continent for their own enrichment (for a thoroughly fascinating study of this phenomenon the excellent *Black is White: The Fantasy of a United Europe, 1940-1959* by Ryss Quirk is highly recommended).

Willing participants. This group comprised roughly 20% of the troops facing the Anglo/Americans and was, in the main, made up of men who were simply convinced that the Reich would win the war. They believed that there was no hope of any other outcome. They had been sent to serve by their home country, and they would do their best to honor their oaths of obedience.

Unwilling victims. Making up nearly a third of the fortress troops, many of these men were considered by the Reich to be near-Aryan, and as such they frequently had better privileges, equipment, and rations than other groups. These men mainly served out of fear for themselves as much as from those in any of the other groups discussed above as well as from the German SS, or more often fear for loved ones at home. The simple fact that virtually all of these men knew that failure to perform to the SS command's standards could mean anything from transfer to the Eastern Frontier (a virtual death sentence), to reduction in rations for their families back home, to the literal disappearance of their loved ones into God knew what terrible fate the Nazis reserved for traitors put the vast majority of this group into a situation where anything short of absolute effort was unthinkable.

Once this situation came into focus in London and Washington, the decision to tell the troops was nearly automatic. From the political leadership to the senior commanders the message was: "Warn the men that all enemy troops are likely to resist to the best of their ability whether they are German SS or other nationalities." The message from the CJSC to their top field commanders was: "The enemy forces in Norway showed little tendency to break off action until overrun. Landing elements in Norway took losses comparable to those troops landing in the Pacific campaign. Alter plans accordingly." This message continued to be distilled until it was given to the ranks by senior NCO. By then the message was short and to the point: "Expect these bastards to fight like the Japs." For a generation who had been largely raised during and immediately after the Pacific War, the real meaning of this statement was clear. The enemy would not surrender, could not be trusted, and the only way to get home alive was to be sure you didn't leave any live ones behind you. This message would reflect on how the rest of the war was fought, by both sides.

While the assault troops and their fellow ground force members were receiving these additional instructions, the Allied air and naval forces continued to maraud along the edges of Fortress Europe. The dramatic difference between the Allied methods and those of the Reich (which had, without exception, made its attacks without any warning at all with only brief pre-attack artillery and air preparations) remains perhaps the most striking tactical split between the adversaries.

Bombing was often done by radar, or with the assistance of pathfinders who would mark targets for the following bomber formations. Radar bombing, while it had progressed markedly since the early 1940s, was still an imprecise science (remembering again that the idea of "smart weapons" was still a decade into the future at the time of the Invasions). However, the Reich had built so many defenses over so large an area that nearly any bomb dropped along the coast that missed water was likely to hit some sort of defensive fortification. To maximize the effectiveness of their very heavy bombers, the Allies adopted a version of the "bomber cell" attack formation (a method used to this day). The bombers would fly, not in a stream that was a hundred miles long and a mile wide, but in formations consisting of five or six aircraft (the USAF favored a six-aircraft double chevron formation while the RAF mainly used a five-aircraft diamond). These formations were found to be especially useful in the case of the RAF Victor, with its 35,000-pound bomb load, and the USAF's B-36 (65,000 pounds) and B-52 (45,000 pounds) bombers, while the smaller, although still substantial, ~20,000 bomb load of the Vulcan, Valiant, and B-47 seemed to be best deployed in slightly larger 10-12 aircraft groups. The older, pure piston engine B-29 and Avro Lincoln were mainly used in mass attacks inside France where they targeted the remnants of the rail network, with special attention given to sections that photo reconnaissance missions indicated were under active repair. These larger formations were always heavily escorted due to the far greater vulnerability of the 1940-era designs. Allied records indicate that in the period between Thorn Bush and Operation Gravel the Allied air forces (including the RCAF and RAAF) dropped nearly 7,000,000 pounds of explosives in what amounted to tactical missions. Overall losses on these missions were quite low, with only around 4% of the newer jet bombers being lost and a higher, but still acceptable, 6.5% loss rate for the older aircraft.

Not included in these figures are the number of B-29s and Lincolns simply written off due to old age or those turned into spare part sources for the remaining force. If these were to be included the loss rate climbs to a more startling 18%. However, this remarkable loss rate need to be considered in light of the fact that Gravel and Maverick were the last hurrahs for the pure piston-powered heavy bomber and that crew losses were still only 6.5%.

Much as the case for the air forces, the USN, RAAN, RCAN, and RN – specifically the battleships, cruisers, and destroyers of these navies – spent the time preceding the Gravel landings pounding enemy defensive positions. Despite some surprisingly vigorous return fire (USS *Colorado* was struck by five 203mm shells in one memorable gun duel with shore batteries), the fleets made the most of the extra time the weather had provided them.

In all, five of the False Peak sites were revisited by the fleet and seven by at least one bombing raid.

Entirely by accident of wind and wave, the Allies had managed to utterly perplex the Reich leadership.

14

The location of the Gravel landings had been a matter of great debate at the highest levels of the Allied command structure since the resumption of the war more than four years earlier. There were, frankly, no good, easy places to attack; nearly two decades and a half of slave labor had seen to that. Virtually every part of the French coast was defended by extremely impressive and well-engineered defenses. In some areas concrete bunkers extended inland for nearly 20 miles; in others the defenses were far shallower, but ended at edge of marshland that was virtually impassable except for a few roads. These roads had heavy fortifications defending them and artillery registered to rake every inch of their straight, exposed surfaces.

One of the finalists for the Gravel landing was the Normandy region. It had a number of good landing beaches and some good ports, including Cherbourg. Unfortunately, it had some serious problems. Beyond the marshes it seemed that there was good country, but Alamo Scouts and LLRP Teams had reported back that the area was littered with dense hedgerows and was alive with sunken roads lined with trees and heavy brush. That intelligence gave pause to anyone who had fought in the jungles of Burma, New Guinea, or Guadalcanal. After speaking directly with several of the Scout teams, Supreme Allied Commander General Matthew Ridgway and his ground force commander, Field Marshall Guy Simonds, decided that the difficulties presented by the closed quarters of the Normandy countryside were too great.

North of the hedgerow country lay Dieppe, site of a disastrous raid in the early war years that still weighed heavily on the Allied command staff (and may well have cost Lord Mountbatten command of all naval forces for the invasions). Further north lay the Pas de Calais, with the enticing port of Calais as a centerpiece. This location was the closest to the British Isles and had been the site of some of the heaviest defenses and strongest Waffen-SS units permanent stations along the coast. Soon after Calais was Dunkirk, and then the Belgian border and the fields of Flanders, a location that awoke entirely different sets of ghosts. South of Normandy was Brest and Brittany; while some of the terrain was attractive, the location also meant the longest possible route across France to Germany. No one in the invasion planning staff had any illusion that every foot gained in Europe would be paid for in blood. All things being equal, the shortest path was the best one.

Eventually, the Allies chose the area just north of Calais and to the north and south of Dunkirk for the primary landings. While a great deal of argument went in favor of feinting at Calais and attacking elsewhere, perhaps into the hedgerows, the final decision was that "the successes of False Peak had robbed the SS leadership of mobility and had allowed the Allies to choose the point of attack without further need for deception" (it remains, even today, a point of conjecture when Ridgway came to this, in retrospect, prescient conclusion). With that statement by General Matthew Ridgway, the die was cast. A million men on the two sides would have their lives altered by the decision.

The Allied attack plan was enormous. The initial assault waves would land on six beaches with the code names (going from north to south): Red, Green, Blue, Archer, Spear, and Rail. Red Beach (2nd and 4th Marine Divisions, 3rd Armored Division) and Green Beach (6th Marine Division, 1st and 29th Infantry Divisions, 5th Armored Brigade), both located to the north of Dunkirk, were assigned to the Americans. Blue (2nd Canadian, 5th Australian Infantry and 8th Australian Armored) and Archer (3rd Canadian Armored, 1st South African, 4th Indian Sikh) were "Commonwealth" beaches with Blue drawing stores with the American units and Archer sharing supply trains with the British. Spear (51st Highland, 53rd Welsh, Guards Armored) and Rail (6th Infantry, 43rd Wessex, 3rd Armored Division) were the two British beaches. For each division tagged for the assault force, there were three waiting either on a ship or in temporary camps in England for transport to the continent as soon as a foothold had been achieved. These forces in turn were the leading edge of a 110-division host that was meant to descend on the Reich.

Landing behind the beaches would be the American 82nd Airborne and 1st Air Cavalry Divisions and the British 1st Parachute Division. It was the mission of these units to capture and hold a series of road and rail bridges until relieved by ground troops. The holding of the bridges against enemy reinforcements was all the more difficult because the airborne troops were to do everything in their power to avoid destroying the bridges so they could be used by advancing Allied armor.

The Allied landing force numbered over 3,000 vessels large enough to be called a ship, including over 350 warships, along with over 2,000 amtracks and more than a thousand landing craft to transport tanks, jeeps, fuel trucks, ambulances, and all the rest of the huge motorized contingent that the Allied armies would need. While none of the navies would risk their precious carriers so close to an enemy shore and in waters as restricted as the English Channel, this did not mean that their aircraft would miss the show.

Overall the Allies had gathered well over 4,000 combat aircraft just in the UK, with most of the RAF and USAF heavy bombers literally moving, some as far away as Iceland, so the shorter-ranged fighters and fighter-bombers had enough elbow room with the specific mission of supporting the invasion. Nearly half of the FAA and USN attack and fighter aircraft were moved from shipboard to land bases, over the occasionally thunderous objections of senior fleet commanders. Flying from runways allowed the carrier planes to carry more fuel or weapons, or both, while letting them play a critical role without risking carriers to attack by enemy submarines or near-suicidal Luftwaffe bombers.

As would be expected in a coalition effort, the Allied command structure was remarkably complex, with command assignments made with nearly as much political concern as command skill (this is not to say that any of the men chosen was anything less than exceptional, merely to indicate the political skills required in

Coalition warfare). While the choice of an American as Supreme Commander was virtually a given due to the sheer volume of men, equipment, and funding that flowed from Washington, the selection of subordinate commanders had been far less clear cut, with highly qualified men available from several countries. In the end, Admiral Sir John David Luce, OBE, was selected as overall naval commander, a position that had nearly gone to Lord Mountbatten (ironically it was Mountbatten's handling of the Dieppe Raid, the same raid where Luce earned his OBE, that caused him to be bypassed for command of the Gravel Naval Operations). Field Marshall Guy Simonds of Canada was selected as overall ground force commander, a decision that was met with considerable initial opposition in London, but was appropriate given the significant contribution of the "Commonwealth" nations to the ground forces; not to mention Simonds's close relationship with General Ridgway, the SACEUR (Supreme Allied Commander, Europe). It is remarkable that despite the differing political leaders involved Ridgway and his command staff worked so well together. Indeed, the main controversy to come out of the Coalition command design was the sheer *lack* of disagreement. Whatever the varied desires of their political masters, the military commanders somehow managed to remain focused on the main mission: defeating the Reich.

One of the controversies that has lasted into the present day is worth touching on here. While the assignment of the beaches has long been a point of conjecture, with conspiracy theories abounding, General Ridgway's personal papers (which the Ridgway family was kind enough to provide the author access to) make clear that the decision was mainly one of logistical ease. There was no decision made at this time regarding which army would be the first to reach Berlin no matter what many contemporary commentators supposed.

15

While nearly all general histories mark June 17th, 1958, as "D-Day" or the beginning of Operation Gravel, in truth the first actions of the operation began at 22:00 hours on June 16th with the by now familiar dull roar of heavy bombers crossing the Channel. The Allies had made so many of the attacks that the initial SS reaction was simply to sound air raid warnings in hopes of minimizing equipment and personnel losses. Even the first ghostly contacts showing ships approaching the French coast caused little comment; obviously the Allies were about to waste several million Reichsmarks worth of munitions in a demonstration of their impotence and fear of attacking the strength of Greater Germany with anything beyond pinpricks.

It was with this rather relaxed viewpoint that the senior SS and Luftwaffe commanders began to receive reports that radar sites had begun to fail all along the northwest quadrant of France and across the Low Countries. While failure of a single radar site was anything but uncommon, as electronics mainly based on vacuum tubes went down with remarkable regularity, it was unusual for several sites to fail simultaneously. Such was the rivalry between the SS and the Luftwaffe that the two commands did not contact the other to discuss the unusual event of having numerous sites fail at once.

The radar sites were, of course, not simply suffering mechanical or communication glitches. They were being systematically destroyed by Allied anti-radar attacks, some featuring the first use of the Shrike missile, and others with bomb or rocket attacks which were the result of months of careful analysis of aerial photos. Three of the control sites considered to be the most crucial were destroyed by LRRP teams that had been inserted into France weeks earlier. Overall, the attacks managed to reduce the effectiveness of the Reich radar network by roughly 70%. Three Allied divisions proceeded to fly right through the holes in that net. While the airdrops of the 82nd Airborne and British 1st Para divisions were mainly remarkable for their overall size, with nearly 20,000 men parachuting into an arc nearly 40 miles in length, the arrival of the 1st Air Cavalry (better known as the 1st Air Cav) represented a radical change in warfare.

While the Allies had used helicopters to land a battalion into a blocking position on Sicily, and some Marine units had leapfrogged over the beach defenses in Thorn Bush, the 1st Air Cav attack was an entirely different matter. Not only were the numbers of men landed (nearly 12,000) vastly greater than in any previous operation, the use of nearly 800 helicopters, including the CH-37 Mojave heavy cargo helicopter, which were able to deliver vehicles and towed artillery directly into the battle zone was a game changer. Even though the helicopters demonstrated a distressing lack of survivability when stuck by even light AAA (85 were lost, roughly a third while inbound to their landing zones), they also allowed the American "airmobile" division to have the mobility of a partly-motorized brigade well behind enemy lines as well as being able to land units fully intact and in something approaching battle formation. The presence of fairly heavy, towed anti-tank weapons and medium artillery in the airborne landing zones was, in many cases, decisive.

The use of helicopters in place of the expected gliders rendered much of the pre-invasion defensive efforts by the Waffen-SS worthless as US and British helicopters landed unhindered in fields that had been scattered with telephone-sized wooden stakes meant to tear landing gliders into splinters. While a few gliders were used, mainly in locations that required an entirely silent approach, the total deployed did not reach 40 aircraft, while all helicopters used in the invasion exceeded 1,000. The inability of the Reich's forces to anticipate the mass use of helicopters has been traced to the very top Luftwaffe commanders, starting with Göring himself. There seems to have been a near hatred for the entire concept of massed helicopters by the former commander of the Flying Circus, something that some biographers have attributed to a desire to see more fighters and bombers produced – something that would have been diluted by a major helicopter program. In any case, the Reich's failure to act, even after the use of helicopters in Sicily, is not out of step with the general tactical inflexibility shown by most SS and Luftwaffe senior officers. It is perhaps fortunate that the same evil mantra that led to the Nazi Party's excesses also reduced its ability to react to change.

While the Allied tactics allowed considerable surprise and also reduced the Reich's anti-aircraft defenses by a noteworthy amount, it did not eliminate them completely. The transport aircraft suffered nearly 9% loss during the opening phase of Gravel, with many of the losses fortunately occurring as the aircraft egressed from the drop zones. The losses were severe and caused difficulties for the Allied forces in the weeks after the initial assault. The surprise also did not provide as much help for the Allied paratroopers as had been expected.

The Reich had long anticipated the use of paratroops in any continental invasion. This had allowed the SS to develop extensive operational plans for dealing with airborne forces, both in passive measures (as noted above in the preparations for dealing with gliders) and in tactical deployments and training for both SS and National forces that were of "high reliability". The Reich's ability to fight when presented with an expected problem, as illustrated on Sicily, were formidable.

The SS troops that were present in the Gravel assault zones were thoroughly professional, blooded units. While their experience was not against well-equipped and organized forces, the simple fact that they were largely combat veterans had profound impacts on their reactions in the early moments of the invasion. The Allied troops were largely "green" with only a small percentage of NCOs and officers having combat experience. Overall the Allied airborne forces were exceptionally well trained and equipped, but they were young, the prevailing wisdom being that airborne operations were a young man's game. This was somewhat less true for the 1st Air Cav units, but overall it was a clash of highly-indoctrinated, semi-experienced troops on one side against well-trained and disciplined but inexperienced men on the other. The resulting combat was, as a result, ferocious in the extreme.

The paratroops began to take losses almost immediately; in many cases well before they actually made it to the ground. SS observers, even in the areas where radar sites had been disabled, found it possible to tell that something strange was happening. The sounds of the low flying piston and turboprop transports was far different from that of the jet bombers and fighter bombers that regularly attacked or overflew the Dunkirk region. Troops were turned out based on the sound itself, with light AAA, especially the dreaded 20mm flak panzer quads, filling the sky with shells. Many of these rounds, fired blind, struck nothing. Some shells inevitably found targets, including men floating down helplessly under canopies, with terrible results. Searchlights probed the skies, exposing other groups of paratroopers to everything from anti-aircraft guns to rifle fire. Once on the ground, other troops stumbled into minefields and other prepared passive anti-personnel systems (it is estimated that nearly 10% of the total paratroop losses were the result of these sorts of weapons).

Once on the ground, the airborne forces had to struggle to organize and move to their objectives. Even in the best of conditions a startling number of paratroopers will sustain injuries simply from landing; in the case of night jumps into unknown terrain this situation is exacerbated. Many of the injured men, with snapped ankles, broken legs and the litany of other disabling injuries that can result from a 14-foot fall (which is what the parachutes of the era provided users at the end of their descent; it is important for the reader to realize that these men were not using the "wing" style sporting rigs seen today), were, by sheer luck of the draw, platoon, company, and in one case, regimental, commanders. Even when not injured, individual "sticks" of paratroops, usually 20 or so men (depending on the aircraft deploying them), had to join up with others at rally points before heading out. This had to be done in near-silence, in pitch darkness, without knowing if the man approaching was a friend or enemy.

Many of the paratroop unit objectives were road or rail bridges, with others having critical road junctures as their destinations (although many of the road junctures were also the final objective of the more heavily-equipped Air Cav units). These sites had to be taken and held, both to prevent the SS from using them to send reinforcements and, ironically, to keep the enemy from destroying them to prevent their use by advancing Allied forces. As the night progressed, small units of American, British, and Canadian troops fought short, intense firefights with SS and National forces with little quarter shown by either side.

One of the major misunderstandings that exist among civilians is that troops are obligated to allow an enemy to surrender. This is not actually the case. While Allied practice was overall to encourage enemy forces to surrender, and to show them good treatment after capture, this is simply not always possible. When it is not possible, be it in the jungles of Burma or the French countryside during an airborne invasion, the resulting combat is especially savage.

By dawn on the 17th, the airborne forces had taken close to ¾ of their objectives. They had, in those same six hours, suffered nearly 35% casualties, with some battalions being reduced to the size of reinforced companies: a fate which befell both the 1st Battalion, Royal Ulster Rifles and 2nd Battalion, 501st Infantry.

Spread in an arc behind the landing beaches, these men now could only dig in and wait for the results of the amphibious landing to be decided.

16

The United States and Great Britain, for all their close cooperation in the Pacific and in the air war over Europe, had never truly become a fully "joint" operating group. The USAAF attacked the Reich during the day, the RAF mostly at night; British and many Commonwealth forces fought across the jungles of Southeast Asia while the Americans, along with much of the Australian and Canadian military, fought a very different war across the expanses of the Pacific on coral island after coral island. The countries cooperated closely at the senior command level, arguably in the most effective manner ever seen for such a partnership, but, although gained against common foes, their experiences were, overall, quite different. Perhaps at no point in the entire European phase were the results of different experiences more on display than during Operation Gravel.

Even though the Allies shared many resources (RN and USN ships were mixed in the gun lines for every beach; RAF, Commonwealth, and US aircraft were on call across the battle front), the actual landing efforts had some remarkable differences. While there have been many articles and papers that discuss the material reasons for the difference in approach to a basic problem, it is still worth reviewing here as we look at the Gravel landings.

The US and US-supported landings on Red, Green, and Blue beaches were the ultimate expression of the combined arms landings that the USMC had developed along with their Australian and Canadian partners, starting at Guadalcanal and evolving during their advance across the Pacific. It was also, in a very real way, an overt display of raw industrial power unlike anything ever seen in warfare. The USN had *nineteen* 16" gun-carrying battleships behind the three beaches (*Colorado,*

North Carolina, and *Washington* were assigned to the southern beaches), along with more than 70 cruisers of various types and 150 destroyers; nearly all of them having come from American shipyards in a ten year period (remarkably, given this incredible display of industrial might, the bulk of the USN's strength, its carrier force, along with nearly 400 destroyers, were not present off Dunkirk's beaches). Over 600 LTS/LSM vessels from the same yards competed for space with swarms of smaller landing boats, amtracks, PT/G boats, and other small craft in the waves. The display alone should have been enough to cause any sane opponent to seek terms, simply based on production capacity on display. Tragically, no sane opponent was available.

The pre-assault preparations were similar to those of Thorn Bush, with the notable addition of several cruisers intentionally shelling the water off the beaches with bombardment shells in a concentrated effort to destroy Oyster pressure mines (which had proved to be a minor, thanks to water depth conditions, but still nasty surprise during the Thorn Bush landings) through hydrostatic shock. While similar to the Thorn Bush (or even False Peak) operations in detail, the scope of the softening effort was far greater. Virtually every heavy bomber available to the Allies on June 17th, including the American B-52 and RAF "V" bombers, took part in the pre-landing bombardment. In all, more than 800 Very Heavy Bombers, many carrying as much as 40,000 pounds of bombs, pummeled the defensive belts defending the sea approaches, with the first raids beginning at virtually the moment the transport aircraft for the Airborne Army cleared the airspace and continuing until dawn. These attacks were followed by a three-hour-long pounding from the massive naval armada crowding the waves. Traffic control was such a serious issue in the restricted waters that a 300-man planning staff had spent months working out the specific details of what ship would be where, virtually minute to minute, during the build-up to the invasion – an achievement all the more remarkable considering the fact that the final assault location was not decided upon until six months before the landings.

The landing on Red Beach (perhaps the most celebrated of all the landings) began at 08:00, some 25 minutes ahead of schedule thanks to a slightly higher than expected wind clearing much of the smoke from the devastated bombardment area. Nearly 400 amtracks made up the initial wave, along with over 100 LCT transporting the initial contribution of heavy armor from the 1st Armored Division. As was to become something of a theme during the morning, nearly as soon as the heavy shelling had ended the beach defenders, mainly Norwegians in this sector, began to return fire; occasionally with startling accuracy considering the hours of tooth-rattling pounding they and their equipment had just received.

American Sumner-class destroyers soon found themselves in gun duels with 88mm and 105mm beach guns while three Des Moines-class cruisers fought it out with a group of four 280mm shore batteries. While so engaged, these ships were less able to interdict the heavy fire from 20mm and 40mm auto cannon as these dual purpose weapons began to engage the landing forces. Marine and USN aircraft, especially the USMC Skyraiders, joined the battle, using rockets and napalm against the very securely dug-in enemy positions. As the landing force crossed the 1,000-yard line, Navy Skyhawks shot across the beaches to deploy fuel-air weapons: not against fortifications directly, but in an effort to detonate some of the masses of mines that the Reich forces had dug-into the beaches. While this dance of death continued over the landing area, the amphibious tractors continued to churn forward, taking losses as they did so. At 200 yards, the gunners in the amtracks finally received authorization to return fire, as much for morale purposes as anything else.

The first amtrack reached Red Beach One just after 08:20, with others, carrying the remnant of the 2nd BATT, 6th Marines, arriving moments later. Slightly to the south, the lead elements of 3rd BATT, 23rd Marines grounded on Red Beach Two with 1st BATT, 25th Marines coming ashore on Red Beach Three. Overall, nearly one in four of the first wave amtracks, along with 35 of the tank-carrying LCTs, were lost during the initial run into the beach. It was a loss level unprecedented in Marine annals.

25% of the landing wave had been killed or rendered combat ineffective before they even reached the beach.

Once ashore, the marines found themselves in a shooting gallery. Despite the heaviest Allied landing preparation ever conducted – from random bombings to radio propaganda – the Norwegian defenders of the beaches poured fire onto the American troops coming ashore while others reached out for the second wave of amtracks headed toward the beach.

Red Beach had rapidly turned into a fight for survival on both sides. Marine fire support amtracks, including a newly-produced variant equipped with a 20mm Gatling cannon in place of the usual 75mm gun, tried to suppress fire coming from reinforced concrete bunkers that spat death at the advancing marines. Army Sheridan tanks attempted to take bunkers under direct fire with their 105mm guns while bunker-mounted 88mm and 100mm anti-tank guns fired back.

By 09:50 the landing force was faced with a shortage of amtracks to land the fourth wave. The Landing Force commander for Red Beach was faced with an unpleasant choice: break off the effort on Red One, where the 6th Marines had been effectively destroyed, in hopes of salvaging the rest of the Red Beach operation or make one more push for the beach using his Corps reserve. Recalled from retirement specifically for this operation, General Puller didn't hesitate. He ordered infantry elements of the 1st Armored to embark onto whatever was available, including the LCVPs that were meant to be used after the beach had been secured to shuttle in supplies.

It was a decision that could have cost the Allies the battle, perhaps even doomed the entire invasion, if it failed. If all of Red Beach had been lost, the American paratroops and most of the 1st Air Cav would have been left to hold for an indefinite period of time in hopes of eventual rescue by the forces landing well to the south on Green or even Blue Beach. Without Red Beach, the Allied position north of Dunkirk Harbor would have been unsupportable, even if the landing on Green and Blue succeeded. The decision was the right one, as results proved, despite the losses suffered by the men advancing to the beach packed into unarmored, open topped LCVP landing craft.

With the help of the aircraft assigned to CAS, especially the heavy bombing and strafing of USAF F-105 fighter-bombers (in their combat debut) and the Marine Skyraiders, the ships of the gun line, and the raw courage of the men on the beaches, by 15:00 the landing forces had secured their D-Day objectives, including linking up with several of the airborne units that had been holding bridges against increasing enemy pressure and were in position to hold the ground they had taken.

Overall, Red Beach was the most expensive day for the US military in its long history; worse even than any of the three days of bloodletting at Gettysburg. Nine men eventually received Medal of Honor citations for their action on Red Beach (7 posthumously). There remains a campaign among veterans of Red Beach to have General Puller (who succumbed to a massive heart attack on July 1, 1958) join these nine recipients.

2nd Marine Division suffered 11,500 total casualties; 4th Marine Division took slightly less than 5,000; and 1st Armored lost two-thirds of its vehicles and took 8,750 total casualties. The 2nd Marine Division was destroyed as a combat formation, as was 1st Armored, with 2nd BATT 6th Marines, which had entered the battle with 947 men capable of duty on June 17th, mustering 86 effectives on June 19th. What was left of the 2nd Division was folded into the 4th Marine Division while 1st Armored Division was eventually withdrawn to the US for reorganization.

Four USN destroyers were lost or beached due to damage from enemy shore batteries. USS *Salem* was in dry dock for a year repairing damage from the 280mm gun of the North Dunkirk battery, and even the battleship USS *South Dakota* had two 5" batteries knocked out by the fire from the Norwegian-manned shore rifles before they were finally silenced.

There has never been a comprehensive list of defender casualties compiled for Red Beach. Many positions were eventually destroyed with satchel charges or cleared by flamethrowers. Many SS and Reich records are missing. However it has been firmly established that on June 1, 1958 there were 16,000 troops, of all nationalities and services, assigned to the Red Beach sector. American forces took 853 prisoners; how many of the remaining men escaped inland or were not present at the time of the assault is unknown.

17

The early moments off of Archer, Spear and Rail beaches differed only in minor details from those off Red, Blue, and Green beaches to the north. There were more ships flying the White Ensign than the Blue Jack, and slightly more aircraft with RAF roundels than White Stars on their fuselage, but the overall preparations were the same: a storm of high explosive and steel.

Even the initial movement of small boats from the gray transports behind the gun line looked the same: amtracks, some LCT with Centurions as cargo instead of the American Sheridan tanks to the north, but then, something very different. Something the British had offered to their American partners but had been, politely, rejected, came into view. The SR.N2.

The introduction of the SR.N2 hovercraft into amphibious warfare was, unbeknownst to anyone, even the Royal Navy, the start of the next great revolution in warfare. The Americans had taken one look at the fragile-looking design and blanched, seeing the loss of platoons at a time when the waterbug-like vessel was hit. The British, however, had seen instead the opportunity to move 50 men or a light armored vehicle at a time from sea to shore at nearly 80 miles an hour as too promising to give up, no matter what the acknowledged experts on amphibious attack from three countries said.

The British had decided to put what they called "Skirmisher" units onto the incredibly fast vessels, units that would reach the beachhead in advance of the other troops and establish themselves, hopefully disabling enough of the enemy bunkers to allow the following main wave to land in relative safety. It was an incredibly bold plan, using some of the best troops in the British military and unproven technology. Remarkably, given the circumstances and the depth of the Reich defenses, in some locations it worked to perfection. This was the case at Spear Beach.

Spear, of all the assault beaches, had been the most thoroughly prepared by the Allies for attack. It had been the third False Peak site and had been perhaps the most heavily-damaged of all the fortifications that had been used to draw the SS reserves to their demise. After the main False Peak operations, it had also been hit during the build-up to the invasion on a regular basis. In addition, it had been the target site for the experimental RAF version of the V-1, with close to 300 of the pulse jet powered, 3,000-pound warhead flying bombs landing in the area over a three-month period (including 125 on D-Day alone). This added attention was undoubtedly one reason that Admiral Samuel Eliot Morison, in his definitive Naval History of the Long War, Volume XIII, described Spear Beach as "the perfect landing", but it was not the only reason, as Morrison went to great length to illustrate in his justly famed work.

The use of the SR.N2 (and small numbers of the even more experimental SR.N3), also played a significant role in the success at Spear. Of the 70 hovercraft used, only two were hit in the initial wave; partly because their great speed made them difficult targets for men who had trained to hit landing boats moving at a tenth of their speed, and partly thanks to that same speed allowing the hovercraft to put men onto the beach before the enemy had time to reach their gun positions following the end of the naval bombardment. Even though 12 of the hovercraft were lost in following waves, as the enemy adapted to their presence, the success at Spear proved the worth of the concept for all time (as can be seen by the RN and USN Landing Craft, Air Cushion (LCAC) and its place of prominence in Royal Marine and USMC operational planning in our current day).

It also speaks to the strength of the Atlantic Wall defenses that the "perfect landing" still suffered almost 5,800 casualties, with fighting so brutal that *three* Victoria Crosses were presented to combatants there (all of them, interestingly, to men from Skirmisher units). When one recalls that only 1,378 Victoria Crosses have been presented since the introduction of the award in 1856 to the present day, the clustering of three awards on Spear Beach is even more remarkable.

If Spear Beach is the example of a perfect landing, and Red Beach an example of pure determination overcoming impossible odds, the remaining Allied landings fall in between these two extremes. The British forces at Rail found the SR.N2 to be notably less effective than at Spear (possibly due to the presence of a Luftwaffe "Hitler Youth" Light Flak regiment among the defenders), but also found the defenses to be somewhat more damaged than the Commonwealth forces at Archer, where the 3rd Transvaal Scottish Regiment was effectively destroyed while taking the bunker complex manned by the 61st SS Hitler Youth (Norwegian) Battalion (a unit that literally died to the last man in its defensive positions). The Commonwealth forces at Blue Beach, and the USMC/ US Army forces on Green beach, were somewhat less severely mauled than those on Red Beach but were still roughly handled; although all landing elements reached their D-day objectives, with some, notably the 5th Australian Infantry Division, reaching their D+2 objectives by sunset on the 17th.

The total losses from the actions on June 17th are, even at 50+ years separation, mind-numbing. Total Allied casualties on all six beaches exceeded 62,000 men, including nearly 13,000 killed in action. SS and fortress troop losses (mainly Norwegian, but also Italian and Romanian) are estimated to have been nearly 45,000, with nearly 70% of that total dead, and less than 7,000 total prisoners taken. To provide perspective, American losses on the 17th of June, 1954, exceed those for any *year* of the 1968-73 Korean Intervention.

18

Hitler's Atlantic Wall had succeeded beyond even his wildest hopes, inflicting losses that were on a scale closer to WWI than anything seen by the Allies since 1939. While the "English" had a toehold on the Continent, the Führer and his brain trust were certain that the decadent Westerners would quickly sue for terms and end the war once and for all now that the cost was so clear to them. Hitler, according to junior officers present at the emergency staff meeting held during the landings, listened to the reports of Allied losses and Allied ships it like he was watching a football match, roaring with pleasure when informed an American light cruiser had been sunk (probably a misidentification of the Sumner-class destroyer USS *Laffey*, which was lost after taking three hits from 280mm shells off Red Beach One). So certain was Hitler of final victory that he had his terms for peace sent to the Reich Embassy in Spain via radio: the easier for them to be presented when the Allies came "hat in hand looking for a way out of their failure". Thanks to the action of the Allied code breakers (and some successful intelligence work in Portugal), the Allied Leadership was able to read the Führer's message before the Reich Ambassador in Madrid received his copy.

It seems likely, although the general dearth of Waffen-SS records makes it impossible to be certain, that Hitler and his minions' misplaced sense of triumph was mainly responsible for the generally sluggish SS response to the landings during the first two or three days of the invasion. It was not until June 21 that the high-flying American U-2 and RAF Canberra photo reconnaissance aircraft brought back evidence of massive mobilization efforts across Germany proper.

The Allied ability, with the remarkable Lockheed and English Electric products and their equally revolutionary optical equipment, to have near real-time intelligence data on Reich movements, not to mention Bomb Damage Assessment (BDA) within mere hours, provided a profound advantage to the Allies throughout the post-St. Patrick's Day phase of the European War. This effect was magnified by the near-total failure of Luftwaffe reconnaissance flights over the UK and Iceland. This great success in the information war is sometimes obscured by the feats of the code breakers, but was no less disruptive to the Reich's war effort and of at least equal value to the Allied command structure: especially once the Baker-Nunn photographic system, with its 25" detail resolution from 72,000', made its debut in early 1956.

While the Luftwaffe was totally unsuccessful in its dogged pursuit of both the U-2 and the Canberra PR.6/7 (according to post-war interrogation of a senior Luftwaffe ground control officer, each attempted intercept of the Allied aircraft cost the Luftwaffe an average of three interceptor aircraft, with one mission, likely by an U-2C based on the flight date, costing the Luftwaffe seven aircraft in addition to the expenditure of a full week's production of EMW D4 SAM), the Allies managed to disable or destroy virtually every Luftwaffe reconnaissance mission from 1957 onwards. While several kills were made by Talos SAM fired from US cruisers on patrol/escort duty in the Channel, and some 14 shoot-downs of the DFS 228 were made by the F-102 squadron based on Iceland for the specific purpose of preventing Luftwaffe photo-gathering, the main nemesis of the Luftwaffe spy planes was the remarkable English Electric Lightning. Most notably, there was the highest recorded interception in history by Group Captain Michael Evans, who tracked down a DFS 228C near Scapa Flow at an astounding 71,560 feet using a pair of Firestreak AAM, a mission that is covered in some depth in Katcher's well researched *RAF vs. the Reich* which covers the entire air war from its 1939 beginnings through the end. In addition to the air-to-air and SAM kills, lower level (i.e. below 60,000 feet) kills were made on numerous occasions by the US Army's 120mm gun/ SCR-584 radar "Skysweeper" gun system and British 3.7" QF batteries. In the case of the AAA kills the Allied advantage in proximity fuse technology was of vital importance, as was the generally better performance of Allied millimeter radars vs. their Reich counterparts.

Despite Berlin's lethargy, the local SS reaction was often very strong and surprisingly effective, given the massive handicaps that the SS Panzer forces labored under. The Allies had managed to firmly establish themselves within the first 18 hours after the landings, pushing over 200,000 men, 29,000 vehicles, and nearly 200 tons of supplies across the Channel on the 17th alone, but the Waffen-SS and French National Army forces fought back with ferocity. The first serious set-piece encounter between the adversaries was just outside the town of Veurne, where 34th SS Panzer had a major base. Despite the severe bombing and shelling in the area, a significant number of the unit's Panther III tanks had survived in their underground bunker/garage. These tanks spearheaded 34th SS Panzer's advance, which was (to the Allies' surprise and great consternation) supported by three Bataillon d'Infanterie of the French National Army fighting in a close and cohesive formation.

The Panzer force ran headlong into 18th Brigade, Australian 8th Armored division, as it drove inland. The Australian force was still somewhat disorganized after fighting through the beach defenses with some battalions having been cobbled together from "orphaned" units, but it was well-equipped with the American Sheridan tank and was overall in roughly equal strength to the SS Panzer force, although with eighty-three tanks compared to the one hundred ten Panthers in the SS formation. The fighting, which took place just as dusk fell (which made intervention by Allied airpower sketchy at best), was remarkable for both its length of engagement as well as for its brutality. The fighting lasted nearly all night, ending only when the remnants of the 34th withdrew in good order before dawn, more out of fear of being caught in the open by Allied airpower than by any loss of morale by the Franco-German formation. The fighting, which had reached the bayonet/entrenching tool level at one point, effectively gutted both formations, although the Australians inflicted considerably more personnel losses on the SS formation than it suffered. Much of the SS personnel losses were taken by the French infantry force, which was on foot and had virtually no armored or artillery support save what was provided by the German forces.

A significant positive from this particular action was the performance of the Sheridan vs. the SS "first team". The US-built tanks proved to be something of an overmatch for the Panther III with the Australians inflicting a 2-1 loss ratio on the Panzer force, and an experimental infrared sighting system that the Australian tanks had installed proved itself to be at least partly effective under real-world conditions.

These positives were seriously outweighed by the willingness of French forces to deploy into a fight that, due to their very limited transport, they could have plausibly avoided without arousing much in the way of SS suspicion. When combined with the heroic resistance of the Norwegian fortress troops on the beaches, the French participation in the engagement, something that was rapidly confirmed at first light and through direct interrogation of "remarkably defiant" French prisoners, was to have serious consequences almost immediately.

Of additional concern, the ability of the SS bunkers to provide shelter for very large numbers of personnel and vehicles, in an area that the Allies had believed to be thoroughly prepared, brought flashbacks of Peleliu and elsewhere to the minds of senior American officers. The thought of having to fight for every yard of ground between the beaches and Berlin was almost impossible to contemplate.

19

Before the first wave of assault troops had reached the shoreline, RAF Lincolns had dropped nearly three million leaflets over Dunkirk, Calais, and the surrounding countryside on the morning of the 17th. Printed in French, German, Norwegian, and Italian (the Allies having somehow completely missed the presence of close to 15,000 Romanian troops along with support staff along this section of the Atlantic Wall), along with slightly different versions in Polish, Russian and Ukrainian, the leaflets directed the residents of the region to leave, as soon as possible, to avoid being caught in the upcoming battle. The BBC and Radio Free Europe also began broadcasting over every available frequency a similar message. Extremely powerful transmitters that had heretofore been kept secret also began to send messages over all known Axis military frequencies, the messages here being a mix of calls for surrender with promises of good treatment and requests for the SS to declare all cities along the French, Belgian, and Dutch coasts to be Open Cities in order to avoid unnecessary civilian casualties.

At 0900 hours the ambassadors of the Allied powers (some 35 countries in all, including countries that were aligned with the Allies but who had no forces committed) presented notes to the Foreign Ministries of Spain, Sweden, and Switzerland, along with the Vatican Secretary of State, asking for their respective governments to convey them to the ambassadors of Belgium, Denmark, Germany, France, Italy, and the Netherlands making the same requests for the declaration of virtually all major cities in the "Occupied Regions of Europe" as Open Cities. The notes gave the Axis Powers 24 hours to remove their troops from these cities, with Allied pledges that troops moving away from these cities into the European interior would not be attacked. These requests were ignored by all the Axis nations, with the responses ranging from polite declines to curt single word refusals.

There has long been debate among historians about the sincerity of the Allied requests. On the surface the requests appear to either be cynical or naïve in the extreme, given the conditions on the continent in June of 1958, but careful review of recently declassified and released minutes of high-level meetings between the various Allied governments reveal a much more complex decision-making process was involved. Not only were the messages meant for domestic consumption (some minutes released by the Australian government in 2008 reveal a surprising amount of Canadian government concern about the reaction of the Quebecois Francophone population to massive French civilian casualties), but they were vital to the maintenance of the anti-Axis bloc. Several South American states virtually demanded that the leaders of the Occupied Countries be given the chance to save their citizens from needless death and destruction in return for continued full support for the war effort. With these countries being supply sources for many vital raw materials, as well as basing for parts of the global Allied anti-U-boat campaign, their governments' concerns had to be addressed, despite what Ridgway described as a "snowball's chance in Hell" of the Axis states conceding so much territory: especially territory with the potential for massive Allied losses.

Even in London and Washington there appears to have been a small and highly influential, although little-known, faction that was willing to go to considerable extremes to avoid "a repeat of the Japanese fiasco". This faction included several members of the President's inner circle, most notably his younger brother John (later an extremely effective five-term Senator from the State of Massachusetts), who, as a US naval officer, had seen the tragedy of Tokyo, with its massive famine and starvation, first-hand while a member of the occupation forces. There were similar concerns within the British War Cabinet as well as the leadership in Canada and Australia; all of them with experience in post-war Japan. In light of these concerns, as well as the remote possibility that one or two cities might actually be cleared, the Allied effort makes far more sense than was the case prior to the opening of the archives.

As events developed it quickly became clear than the Axis militaries were not going to accept the offer, with all road and rail traffic moving into the combat zone, or into secondary defensive positions across France and the Low Countries. Since traffic headed into the combat zones was specifically excluded from the Allied safe conduct offer, these Axis convoys were frequently savaged by marauding Allied fighter-bombers and sea-based gun fire.

It was a combination of these factors that led to the Razing of Dunkirk.

While both General Ridgway and Admiral Luce are sometimes criticized in "revisionist" histories for the operations in and around Dunkirk on June 19 and 20, 1958, it is clear from both contemporary and recently-opened archive records that both men went beyond their orders in an effort to allow civilian evacuation and the hoped-for declaration by the local SS commander of Open City status for Dunkirk. Only when it became clear that the civilians who could or would flee had left the city (the number of civilians forced to remain inside Dunkirk by SS order vs. those who remained voluntarily is still a matter of rather vociferous debate) and that, far from evacuating, the city's defenders were doing whatever possible to strengthen their defensive positions did the Allied High Command give the order to proceed in capturing the city.

Once that order was given, it was incumbent on the field commanders to accomplish their mission with minimal losses to their own troops. This is also something that the revisionists often fail to realize. The main concern of any commander must be the lives of his troops; only after doing all that is possible to preserve them (as the most irreplaceable resource and most precious commodity in the commander's care) can and should any officer give consideration to enemy losses or what has come to be called collateral damage: the destruction of civilian property and deaths of noncombatants. The proper place to lay blame, if blame must be laid anywhere, for the obliteration of Dunkirk is at the feet of the SS High Command in Berlin for their failure to order the withdrawal of troops from the city (although it must be said that defending ports was not something that any military force could have ignored, not on the industrialized battlefield with its vast supply demands).

The capture of Dunkirk was assigned to Commonwealth units that had landed to the north and south of the fishing port on Blue and Archer beaches, specifically the 2nd Canadian Infantry Division and 4th Indian Sikh Infantry. Air support was mainly by RCAF units, with some USMC ground support aircraft, mainly the near-ubiquitous A-1 Skyraiders that had already earned the respect of the Axis ground forces, also making regular appearances. Also assigned to the attack was a rather large percentage of the American gun line: the battleships *Colorado, Illinois, Maine, and Ohio*; heavy cruisers *Salem, Dallas, Seattle, Missoula, Charlotte, San Jose* (all equipped with the "automatic" 8" gun and capable of a prodigious rate of fire), *Los Angeles, Norfolk, Northampton, and Helena*; 15 light cruisers; and 32 destroyers cruising off shore and ready to provide support.

As was common, the first stage of the attack was from the gun line. In what was the first effort of its kind, the early shelling was exclusively against pre-identified anti-aircraft gun positions within a ten-mile arc of Dunkirk proper. The targets, having been found through literally hundreds of hours of painstaking analysis of aerial photographs, had each been assigned a specific target designation with each ship having a list of targets. This part of the attack lasted just over an hour and eliminated roughly 80% of the air defenses in the Dunkirk region (and, not inconsequentially, nearly all of the dual-use 88mm and 128mm high velocity guns assigned to the port's defense). An idea of the intensity of this part of the bombardment can be drawn from the fact that both USS *Dallas* and USS *Seattle* had to withdraw from the gun line and return to port for ammunition replenishment, both ships having expended over 1,300 8" and over 3,000 5" shells during the initial barrage.

With the enemy's ability to defend against air attack effectively eliminated, the CAS aircraft were able to provide nearly uninterrupted support for the advancing ground units. It was support that was desperately needed.

The SS had long realized that any Allied landings would have harbors and ports as major early targets. As such, they had set up strong defensive belts around virtually every port on the continent. While many of these positions had been targeted numerous times during the long preparation for the invasion, significant amounts of the fortification belt were still intact as the Canadian and Indian forces began their advance. Allied aircraft made liberal use of fuel-air weapons, both in attempts to defeat minefields and against specific enemy bunkers, as well as over 50,000 gallons of napalm, helping the ground forces cut through the Axis defenses. Many of the fortifications were manned by non-German troops, mainly Norwegian and French, with some positions on the southern edge of the attack zone being staffed by Romanian troops. The battle for the approaches to the town became a version of the landings themselves, with Allied troops backed by enormous firepower charging into defensive fire from extremely well-sited and strongly-defended bunkers. At sunset on the 19th, the Allied ground forces had taken nearly 1,000 casualties and had advanced less than halfway to the town center.

Throughout the night of the 19th and pre-dawn hours of the 20th, US warships kept up a regular harassing fire on enemy positions and sporadic but intense interdiction fire on likely approaches of enemy reinforcements into the region. It was during these hours of darkness that the Allied forces that had made their way into the dock area properly revealed themselves in an effort to prevent the SS from destroying the port itself and blocking the harbor. Small units, ranging from LLRP and Alamo scouts fighting from occupied buildings to Royal Marine commandos and American Underwater Demolition Teams commandeering blockships to prevent their use, began what was a close-to-suicidal effort to save the Dunkirk facilities for Allied use.

At sunrise, USAF F-105 bombers made heavy bombing strikes against SS gun positions that had been unmasked during the fighting on the 19th. Each of the huge fighter bombers carried more than twice the bomb-load of the American heavy bombers that had pummeled the Reich before the bombing holiday, but dropped their payloads from altitudes as low as 900 feet, with the expected improvement in bombing accuracy. In many ways the Razing of Dunkirk became the Thunderchief's coming out party, with the single squadron of operational aircraft making as many as 12 attacks on the 20th alone.

When the early morning bombings had finished, the controversial elements of the Allied attack began in earnest. With the external fortification belt penetrated, albeit across two rather narrow fronts (each less than 500 yards in width), and with the clock ticking on the forces protecting the port facilities, the Allied approach became one of wholesale devastation. As the ground forces reached the town proper, the SS defenders began what they expected to be a long and very costly (to the attackers) house to house fight for the city streets. It was a tactic that the SS had learned from the Soviets on the Eastern Front, one that had caused great concern during the capture of Stalingrad, and one that the SS expected would cause the Allies as much difficulty as it had caused the 6th Army during the defeat of the USSR. What the SS commander had not accounted for in his planning was the massive difference in firepower and in the number of defenders that existed at Dunkirk. At Stalingrad, the Red Army had, in its eventual failed defense, a near parity in ground troops and reasonable artillery support, albeit in less volume than that available to the 6th Army. At Dunkirk, these conditions did not exist. The SS commander had almost no artillery support, and what was available was subject to near-instantaneous air attack and crushing counter battery fire both from ground force artillery and from the massive gray vessels off the coast. His two battalions in Dunkirk proper (the remainder of his SS division being deployed in the fortifications surrounding the town) were also vastly outnumbered by the Sikh brigade that was the first Commonwealth unit to enter the town, as well as by the Canadians who arrived later that same day from the other direction. Worse, he had not considered what the USN commander in charge of the air and gunfire support was prepared to do to get his UTD teams and the rest of the troops dying in the harbor relieved.

The method of cutting through the SS defenses was simplicity itself. The SS were using the buildings for cover, so the Allies burned and shelled the town to the ground. Any house or building that was used to fire on the advancing troops was hit by at least two, often six, 2,700-pound bombardment shells, followed by either a fuel-air weapon or two 150-gallon napalm canisters. The resulting fires destroyed nearly 90% of the town of Dunkirk and killed close to 80% of the civilian population.

Led by a group of armored bulldozers and amtracks, the Sikhs reached the port itself at 1630 hours, and they then spent the night clearing the piers and warehouses of the port. Despite the best efforts of the units sent to defend the port facilities, 70% of the cranes and other material-handling equipment in the port area were destroyed and a number of blockships were sunk, blocking three of the four piers. Losses among the commando and UDT teams exceeded sixty percent of the men involved.

While the losses to the special warfare units were crippling, as were the losses to the ground forces (which took a total of 2,650 casualties, including 517 killed in action), the Allies had acquired a functional, if badly damaged, port to supplement the cleverly-designed artificial harbors established off Red Beach and near Rail. It was a significant victory, one that would bear much fruit in the weeks to come.

They had also utterly destroyed the first French community of any size they had encountered and killed a staggering number of its residents. This too would gather fruit; however, this harvest would prove to be quite bitter.

20

The ten days after the "liberation" of Dunkirk were generally productive ones for the Allied landing forces. In a remarkable feat of engineering, the Allies managed to get both "Mulberry" harbors in place, cleared enough of the rubble from the streets of the burnt-out shell of Dunkirk (in an engineering effort that was enormously harrowing and hazardous, to the point that the Lt. Commander in charge of the USN Construction Battalion was awarded a Navy Cross for remaining under heavy enemy fire for 14 continuous hours as he directed his armored bulldozers in their tasks), and managed to snake not one, but three 24-inch diameter fuel lines across the Channel and into operation.

The same ten days saw the Allies land upwards of a million and a quarter men and 55,000 tons of supplies into what was a rapidly-expanding beachhead. On July 1st, 1958, the Allies held an area that extended nearly 25 miles inland in some places (with the deepest penetration being to the outskirts of Hazebrouck) and was close to 45 miles wide (with the southern end of the Allied advance just seven miles outside of Calais and the northern end extending towards Oostende, Belgium). The Allied expansion had been far from easy, but the failure of the SS to provide small arms for the fortress troops (almost certainly to prevent any sort of revolt, although the actual performance of these troops during the Allied landings would seem to indicate that such fears were unfounded) made the expansion far easier than would otherwise have been the case. Once SS and National forces were pushed back, the Atlantic Wall positions were found to be reasonably vulnerable when assaulted from the inland direction (also likely a decision made to ease SS takeover in case of a revolt), although

Allied losses in the expansion were anything but trivial in the clearing operations.

Allied attempts to move into Calais were stopped by French National forces with strong SS support. Even with strong support from both air and naval forces, two battalions of the 51st Highlanders were handled very roughly in early assaults. This led Ridgway to decide that Calais was not worth the price, at least in the early days of the campaign. The very heavy resistance by French National forces at Calais reinforced the emerging belief at SACEUR Headquarters that the fighting in France, at least, would be less of liberation than conquest. This belief was reinforced by the relatively easy time Allied forces had when confronting Belgian National forces, where the 12th of the Line regiment folded after what could only be considered an effort sufficient to satisfy honor (and avoid SS reprisals). Other Belgian National units proved to be much less willing to yield, but the Allies chose to believe that the 12th was representative of what would be forthcoming in the country, something that would prove to be somewhat optimistic; but that was unknown at the time.

Overall, the Allied campaign was beginning to resemble what had been expected in the planning stages.

Then it began to rain.

The storm of July 1-5, 1958, was no worse than was common for northwest Europe, but it was severe enough to seriously curtail low-level flying operations. This impacted both the availability of close air support and the effectiveness of the Allied naval gunfire, which now lacked the airborne observation that had greatly assisted in providing accurate fire, especially as the ranges had increased. The Allied armada had already been noticeably reduced, with many of the destroyers and light cruisers having returned to port as the advance outran the range of their weapons, and several of the battleships and monitors having made for port to have their barrel liners replaced. The number of ships on station was still sufficient, but the weather had made them far less effective.

Shorn of their air cover and reduced to mainly their organic artillery (although this was a most impressive array of gun tubes as well), the allied advances slowed from a sprint to a slow walk.

SS and National forces found their efforts to attack Allied formations far more successful when shielded from the hawk-eye of enemy pilots. While the Allied advance continued in some sectors, the weather placed the opponents onto a nearly equal footing for the first time. Local counterattacks by battalion-size SS armored formations managed to inflict serious reversals on advanced units of the 36th Infantry Regiment, which were cut off and briefly pocketed while being subjected to an all-around heavy attack. In what was to become a common event, the SS attacks was broken by the direct intervention of the 26th Tank Destroyer Battalion (heavy) with its recently offloaded Chamberlain tanks. In a July 2 engagement, a company of fourteen Chamberlains engaged four times their number of Panther III from 64th SS Panzer and routed them, with a single tank disabled due to bogie wheel and track damage while destroying twenty-six of the Panthers. One Chamberlain sustained eleven direct hits from the Panther 105mm guns without any full armor penetration. The 120mm gun of the Chamberlain, while having a slightly lower rate of fire than the SS tank, managed at least one through-and-through hit at 500 yards range, with the AP rounds entering through the left front hull armor and exiting through the right rear engine compartment. Several other AP rounds resulted in what the Allied crews began calling "Jack in the Box" kills, with the Panther's turret being blown off the hull by the catastrophic detonation of the Panther's on-board ammunition.

While the dominating performance of the M-92 was a relief to the Allied command (some of whom had questioned the utility of a super-heavy tank), the effect of the lack of air power on ground operations was not. It exposed a weakness that the Allies had not realized existed, even in theory. The discovery was more than slightly disturbing; it had the potential to make the advance across the continent a crawl given the weather conditions that were common across Northern Europe for much of the year. Allied commanders, from senior NCOs up to Generals, had come to rely on the ability to call on Zeus' thunderbolt whenever confronted by a tactical problem, something they had learned over years of training, and would now need to learn how to fight without it "on the job" and while engaged with an enemy fighting on familiar ground, often from prepared positions.

It promised to be a costly education.

21

Axis efforts to dislodge the Allies from their foothold were entirely unsuccessful, even when the weather was very much in the defenders' favor. The damage inflicted by the Allied air forces during the False Peaks operations had reduced the mobility of the SS "fire brigades" to such a large degree that the forward deployed forces were largely on their own, while continued Allied control of the air made even the simplest road march a life-threatening gamble. Even during the early July storms, the SS forces managed to do little more than blunt the Allied advance, and even this success was at heavy cost, with SS losses running nearly double those of the advancing Allied troops. National forces, even the most devoted, quickly developed a fear of Allied artillery that bordered on the pathological thanks to the tender ministrations of the 16" naval cannon that seemed to find any gathering of more than a dozen men at a footbridge an irresistible invitation. Even fanatically-devoted SS troops quickly learned to avoid open ground in daylight because of the risk of bringing on the "steel rain".

Efforts to launch even spoiling air attacks against the Allied forces were almost instantly being called "Kamikaze flights" by Luftwaffe units, with losses reaching close to 80%, even at night, thanks to the Marine Skyknight fighter patrols and the Allied ship-mounted SAMs. The only successes were gained by modernized versions of the Luftwaffe V-1, which had Mach 2 speed during a high altitude approach final dive. When used at night, when the fastest RAF interceptors were far more limited than during the day, and with very short flights from their truck-mounted launchers, the Nazi cruise missiles made life difficult for the masses of service troops that worked around the clock to feed the never-ending hunger of the combat units. A lucky hit on June 28th against the USS *Mt. Hood* destroyed her as well as five other ships, killing nearly 350 men onboard and ashore when the missile's 500-kilogram warhead set off the seven tons of munitions in the *Mt. Hood*'s hold. While spectacular, the damage and losses caused by the explosion were militarily insignificant, although extremely disquieting for the service troops: men whose war was usually marked by long hours of back breaking, but monotonous, work and relatively little danger.

The role of service troops in the Allied invasion of the continent is generally ignored. This is unsurprising because they are the edge of the least discussed, but most important, weapon in any modern army's kit bag: logistics. In the case of the Anglo-American war with the Reich, the matter of logistics is the essential pivot point of the entire war. The Allies, scattered literally around the globe, had to find a way to make use of the vast supply of men and material coming from points as diverse as Mumbai and Chicago; Melbourne, Australia and Melbourne, Florida.

This was the world of the supply officers and their enlisted clerks, the oft-disparaged REMF (Rear Echelon M----- F-----): men who were both hated and envied by the front-line soldiers for the seemingly easy, safe lifestyle they lived and the clean clothes and new boots they wore. What the line trooper often missed was the envy, not to mention awe, which the service troops had for the "line doggies". With the massive mobilization that allowed the Western countries to project more than 100 fighting divisions into Europe, a fairly brutal winnowing of the ranks happened in every group of recruits, with the most physically fit and combat-suited men being shunted into the infantry and armored forces, into the bomber crews, and onto the combat ships. Many other men, most of whom were willing, even eager, to serve in combat were instead shunted into other roles, occasionally based on a special skill (specialists ranging from stenographers to operating room technicians to plumbers were sought after and diverted from the combat specialties, often over the howling protests of the men involved) but often based on what in civilian life were minor issues: issues like serious, but correctable, nearsightedness or hearing loss, that were thought to be serious combat impediments. In earlier wars, the men diverted had included large numbers of otherwise healthy men who happened to have a different shade of skin pigmentation, but by 1958 all the Western militaries had learned that prime combat troops were far too precious a resource to waste based on such trivialities. For the men diverted into the "Service Forces", they found the placement to be close to inescapable. These men were trapped into a war that could be weeks of 18-hour workdays followed by weeks of near inactivity (something that had been especially difficult for troops during the Pacific War, where men were literally left to their own devices on hot, arid coral outcroppings with nothing to do, sometimes for months) with no hope of glory or any activity to break the bland routine. Yet, in a very real sense, the war's result rested on the weary backs of these same men.

They were the wellspring that provided millions of cartridges, bombs, rations, bandages, and every other essential of life to the combat trooper. They were the way that fuel, ammunition, and food made it from the American Midwest to the countryside of northern France. They provided the all-too-rare hot chow that the front line troops yearned for, and provided it while having verbal abuse, often vicious in its inventiveness, piled on them for their "easy" life. They arranged for the greatest of morale boosters, mail from home, to reach the front, connecting to the right soldier or marine despite the way that troops were shunted and shuffled while listening to complaints about how slow the damned mail was. They were the single greatest cog in the military machine that waged war on a global scale. Generally, they were ignored, undecorated, and given as much attention as the crates that they handled. Even among themselves they were considered to be "less" than the front line troops, with little chance to prove themselves as being "warriors".

Yet, remarkably, when circumstances conspired to cause the greatest of disasters, it was proved time and again that heroics were not a matter of combat specialty or military assignment. This was the case in the *Mt. Hood* disaster. In what was as hellish a scene as any that faced Allied troops during the war, REMFs showed that they were anything but the dregs that so many believed them to be. With ammunition burning and exploding all around them, men who had, for any variety of reasons, been moved out of the line of fire proved that they were, in actuality, lions.

Chief Boatswain's Mate Evan Jones made not three, or even four, trips into the flaming hull of the *Mt. Hood* to rescue others. He did it eleven times; the last three after having his left hand mangled by falling debris. For his actions on June 28th, BMC Jones (who was legally blind in his left eye and, therefore, ineligible for a combat slot) received the Medal of Honor. Three other men received Navy Crosses, and two members of the RN received the George Cross for their actions in saving lives and limiting the destruction caused by a single lucky missile hit. These men were just the most outstanding among the heroes of June 28th. If one looks at the number of medals awarded for valor on the 28th, what is striking is that the list has more names than for any action involving a similar group of men on any date in 1958 except June 17th and 18th.

Despite this, the actions of the men of Mulberry "B" are virtually unknown today.

22

The July 1st storm-caused groundings were not a total disaster for the Allies. The five-day enforced pause allowed Allied ground crews to perform much-needed and overdue maintenance on the swarms of warplanes operating from England. The pause also allowed the Allies to at least partially resupply the weapon depots that were rapidly being depleted by the high intensity of the air war.

The Allied invasion consumed almost mind-numbing amounts of material and munitions. Every F-105 fighter-bomber sortie consumed 800-1,200 gallons of jet fuel, while the AD-1 Skyraider CAS aircraft burned 400-600 gallons of Aviation Gasoline (AvGas) on a normal sortie, with both aircraft often expending 10-16 500 pound bombs on a normal mission. When one considers that the USMC alone was operating nearly 400 Skyraiders over France during July of 1958 the scale of the supply needs becomes obvious. Any respite, no matter how brief, in the use of these consumables allowed supply officers at least a moment's sleep.

The delay also allowed the Allies time to unclog the chaos that had enveloped the beach areas. Described by a contemporary as "the result of the entire production output of North America being pushed through a knothole", the massive piles of supplies and personnel threatened to stop the Allied advance in its tracks. With the lessened demand for supply from units that were not in a headlong rush forward, the S-3 commands and their Military Police "traffic cops" managed to reduce the beachhead transport network from a Gordian Knot to a mere "Godawful mess". As "Godawful mess" describes the general state of any massive undertaking, the transition was critical to the overall success of the Allied effort.

While the Allies had attempted to make the best of the weather-caused delay, the Reich found it to be Heaven-sent. Many Panzer units had been immobilized by lack of fuel and other supplies due to Allied depredations. The supplies also generally improved the morale of SS and National Force units; especially those of the National Forces, where some formations had been wavering on collapse after two weeks of near constant pressure.

SS records indicate that the weather delay allowed the Nazis to move as much as 30 days' worth of supplies from depots deep within France to the forward-deployed divisions; along with reinforcements that totaled nearly 11,000 men, roughly half of them SS. The ability to move in daylight hours, even over muddy roads, also allowed the French National Army to relocate what few armored assets were available, as well as moving three infantry divisions north and west (it was the last of these units, 21 ID, that was caught in the open late on July 5th by 23rd Squadron RAF Canberras in the famed "Road of Death" attack).

There remains considerable speculation regarding the reasons that the French National Army forces remained so uniformly loyal to what modern writers have tended to call "the Nazi puppet government" in Paris. Whatever the cause, be it belief in that now-disparaged regime, patriotic fervor, or simple military discipline, it is clear that the French National Army was remarkably disciplined, well led (by French officers, not, as is sometimes speculated, SS commanders), and loyal to their homeland. Had the Reich properly equipped the French forces, even to the level that was permitted to Italian or Hungarian formations, the Allied efforts in the early days of the invasion would have been far more difficult, if not impossible. Instead, the efforts of the French troops, equipped mainly with infantry weapons older than the men using them, and almost no heavy weapons at all, can only be viewed, on many levels, as tragic.

There seemed to have been, even nearly a month after the landings, a sincere belief by the SS High Command and the Reich leadership that a single strong, conventional attack would be sufficient to shatter the Allied position and, quite literally, "drive the Anglo-Saxons into the sea". Whether this belief was a result of pure hubris or perhaps, more kindly, the result of limited information thanks to Allied interdiction of Luftwaffe reconnaissance flights, virtually all SS records and post-war interviews and memoirs (especially that of Field Marshall Erich von Manstein) indicate that it was both widespread and deeply rooted. This belief helps to explain the Battle of Arnèke.

The Arnèke attack was fairly well-planned by the SS, at least when one takes the peculiar belief system that characterized the Nazis. The attack was designed to strike at the "seam" where the southern flank of the 3rd Division (armored) Indian Army and northern flank of the Second Fusiliers (Free Polish) division (assigned to the British 2nd Army) met. Attacking at the juncture of two different commands (something the SS had confirmed by small-scale raids with the specific purpose of capturing prisoners) was a militarily-sound choice, as was attacking near Arnèke, since the location allowed the 19th SS Panzer to make a short road march from its Divisional bunker complex prior to engaging the Allied units. The main reason, however, for the choice of Arnèke was the specific Allied units.

The lunacy of the Nazi philosophy has been discussed earlier in this work, and is well known, with a nearly uncountable numbers of books dedicated to the Nazi system and how such a foul system could come to dominate an entire continent. The repudiation of the Nazi belief system is well beyond the scope of this work; however, it needs to be kept in mind when Arnèke is considered.

The 2nd Fusiliers (Free Polish) was the specific target of the Arnèke offensive. The unit had been identified through prisoner interrogation, something that the SS conducted with considerable relish, and immediately marked as *the* weak point of the Allied line. An entire division of Untermensch seemed to be a golden opportunity to the SS Command. The presence of the 3rd Indian next to it in the Allied line was simply a bonus in the Nazi leadership's minds. The opportunity to attack two "racially inferior" units, rout them, and sunder the American and British armies in one attack was, according to Berlin, potentially a war winner. At the very least it would split the Allied effort in two, making it vulnerable to defeat in detail. In all, the Nazis found Arnèke a perfect opportunity to reverse the course of the war.

Any dispassionate observer would have found Arnèke to be a disastrous location for a major SS attack. The Allied line was within range of the heavy guns of the Allied naval forces, although only the heaviest guns (15" and 16") could reach the location. The region then, as today, was mostly open farmland with no woods or terrain feature to offer cover for attacking forces and the nearest major SS defensive complex was almost 14 miles to the east, putting the offensive at the far edge of the heavy field artillery located there (the decision to attack before the Allied lines had passed through Arnèke was apparently made based on prisoner statements that the 2nd Fusiliers were to be rotated out of the line before Arnèke was assaulted and replaced by the 51st Highlanders). Any trained observer would also have found the 2nd Fusiliers to be a singularly poor choice to assault.

The Free Polish forces were, along with the Polish Government in Exile, almost the only remaining proof that Poland had once existed as a modern, vibrant nation. The 2nd Fusiliers had originally been made up of men who had escaped the Nazi invasion of their homeland when established in 1940. The unit had been nearly destroyed in France during the failed attempt to defeat the Reich's invasion and had been rebuilt from survivors and refugees already in the Canada, the UK, and the US. As the truth of what was happening in Poland (i.e. the General Government Area) came out, more men flocked to the unit and its companion 1st Grenadiers Division. By the time of Gravel most of the 2nd was made up of men who had only the vaguest recollection of Poland, having left the country as toddlers, and more than a few men who had never stood on Polish soil, having been born overseas. The unit was considered by its British sponsors (the UK having provided all equipment and pay to the Free Polish for over a decade) to be exceptionally well-trained and led, with many officers and senior NCOs who had survived the disasters of 1940 as young subalterns or been blooded as part of British campaigns in Malaya or China. American observers thought the Poles to be close to an elite force, with every battalion in constant competition with their fellows for bragging rights. The division's armored regiment consistently scored among the best in gunnery and availability, and admiring inspectors often spoke of "engines you could eat off". Most importantly, the 2nd's troops were not engaged in the same war as their allies: they were engaged in a Holy Crusade against those who had massacred their entire people.

British commanders had expressed some concern regarding the 2nd, mainly fearing that the unit would be unmanageable in combat, so deep was the collective hatred for "the Huns", but the unit had shown no tendency to lose discipline or be overzealous in pursuit of SS units. What the 2nd had demonstrated instead was an almost frightening level of professional detachment to casualties, both their own and the enemies', and an iron discipline.

While the 3rd Indian Armored Division (Tigers) was not on the same level of dedication as the Poles, it was not one of the many reserve divisions that had been activated by all of the major Allied nations as part of the invasion effort. The 3rd Armored was Indian Regular Army. This alone made it part of one of the top combat forces in the world in 1958. Well equipped with Centurion Mk 5 tanks (105mm gunned) and, as was the case with all Regular Indian formations, lavishly provided with artillery. Of all the Allied militaries, only US Regular Army divisions had larger artillery TOE than the Indians. Unfortunately this level of equipment did not always extend to Indian reserve formations. As such, the Tigers were the equal of any unit along the Allied front line on July 11th.

The SS also brought considerable forces to the Arnèke offensive. In addition to the 19th SS Panzer, the SS also assigned the surviving brigade of the 53rd SS Grenadiers (the rest of the 53rd having been destroyed while still entrained during False Peak IV) and the French 6 and 19 ID (the inclusion of 19 ID, a unit that had been earmarked for service in the East, marked the first noteworthy diversion of ground forces from the Eastern Frontier by the SS). The Luftwaffe also committed four squadrons of BV P.209 ground attack aircraft to the effort. The commitment of the precious Blohm and Voss fighter bombers (the Luftwaffe's answer to the US AD-1 Skyraider) that far forward illustrated just how seriously Berlin considered the Arnèke Offensive (Operation Condor).

Condor began just before dawn on July 11, 1958, with a heavy artillery attack on the 2nd Fusiliers' forward positions, including a mass attack by 320mm Nebelwerfer using what the SS called incendiary oil (a somewhat less effective, although still lethal, version of napalm) followed almost immediately by a 12-plane attack by P.209 fighter bombers which inflicted considerable damage on the 3rd Battalion of the Free Poles. It was a very good start to the SS offensive which had achieved total tactical surprise. It was also the high point.

The second wave of Luftwaffe aircraft ran headlong into a dozen F-105s on a strike mission. With the opportunity to collect air-to-air kills, the usually highly-disciplined USAF pilots jettisoned their bomb load and roared into the P.209 formation. Even with a 2:1 advantage in numbers, the dedicated ground attack Luftwaffe aircraft were decimated by the far faster, if less maneuverable, Thunderchiefs. The American fighters collected 14 kills and four damaged for a loss of two F-105s. Had the USAF aircraft been equipped for air combat, with six Sidewinder AAM instead of the two carried while on strike missions, it is possible that none of the Luftwaffe aircraft would have escaped. From the standpoint of the SS, the results could hardly have been worse.

The Luftwaffe commander, operating under instructions to preserve his force, reached the not unreasonable conclusion that the game was up, that the Allies had flooded the area with fighters, and cancelled the last two squadron missions before they ever launched. He then attempted to move his aircraft from harm's way by ordering them to the east. Ironically, by doing so, he lost eight aircraft to RAF Hunters returning from a bomber escort mission. Had the Luftwaffe commander chosen to ignore his orders, the remaining P.209s would have found the sky theirs. It was nearly two hours after the F-105 interception before Allied aircraft arrived over the battle in any sort of number, so complete was the surprise.

In the hours before Allied firepower could be properly brought to bear, the fighting was purely ground force vs. ground force: Nazi vs. Untermensch. The leading SS formation, from 53rd SS Grenadiers, was able to penetrate into the 2nd Fusiliers' rear though a 200-yard wide gap that had been torn in the forward perimeter by the initial concentrated artillery and air attack before being cut off and totally destroyed. There were no prisoners taken from the 53rd SS' 1,350-man force, and SS records indicate that no member of the 53rd returned to SS lines after the attack.

On the northern shoulder of the attack the French 19 ID found itself engaged, then entrapped by heavy artillery and mortar fire: initially from the organic artillery of 17th Horse (the legendary Poona Horse) and then by the Indian divisional artillery park. Even less well-equipped than the regular French formations, 19 ID was left with only 8 Mle 31 81mm and 16 Mle 1935 60mm mortars to counter the 24 155mm and 24 105mm howitzers of the 3rd Indian's Divisional Artillery as well as the SP guns assigned to each infantry battalion. Trapped by the Indian Artillery, 19 ID then found itself attacked by Poona Horse's Centurions and infantry. Only partly trained, and even that training meant to prepare for low-intensity fighting on the Eastern Frontier, 19 ID broke and tried to run. Fortunately, the Poona Horse officers had their troops well in hand, so when many of the 19 ID enlisted men raised their hands in surrender no needless bloodletting occurred (it is important to note that 19 ID was comprised of men that both the SS and Paris thought to be "unreliable" politically, hence its original assignment to the East). Poona Horse counted 1,231 prisoners at the end of July 11th.

On the 2nd Fusiliers front, excepting the portion that had been sundered by the combination of artillery and air attack, the fighting was both heavy and unrelenting, actually reaching the level of hand-to-hand on several occasions. Losses on both sides were in keeping with the ferocity of the engagement, with little quarter given. It is possible, even likely, that the Poles' position would have been overrun if the 6 ID had been able to fully engage early enough in the battle. Unfortunately for the SS, 6 ID had virtually no transport and was limited to the walking speed possible for troops at the end of five days of night marches and daylight hides, and did not reach their jumping off point in full strength by Zero Hour. Even with the late arrival of most of 6 ID, the affair was in doubt until 10:10 hours when HMS *Lion* reached firing position and began to lob 2,000-pound bombardment shells into 19th Panzer's formations. In just over 30 minutes of work, the *Lion*'s gunners unhinged the SS attack, in the process buying enough time for CAS to arrive – including two squadrons of Free Poles flying old, but still deadly, Tempest fighter bombers.

With the arrival of the Allied ground attack aircraft, what had been a very hard fought bit of work turned into a rout. Only the generally-mangled condition of 2nd Fusiliers' command network after most of a day's hard fighting allowed roughly half of the 19th to break contact; and only darkness allowed much of that to make it back to the Divisional defensive bunker complex.

Sunset on July 11th, 1958, found the scoreboard reading Untermensch One, Master Race Nil.

23

The aftermath of Operation Condor is remarkable, not for the military results, although the effective destruction of an Army Corps was a not inconsiderable achievement/loss, but in the manner the results were taken.

The Allied commanders almost immediately (as soon as they completed the so-called "Hot Wash" on July 12th) initiated a series of operational changes designed to ensure that no divisional-sized unit would find itself left with no air cover assigned for emergency call on a bright sunny morning, as had been the case for both the Polish and Indian forces on the morning of the 11th. Immediate efforts were also begun to ensure that, in the polyglot Allied command structure, joining units always had liaison officers who were fluent in their neighbors' language (or at least in English, the de facto language of the Allied forces) so there would be no delay in requesting or receiving support. Both changes were to prove of use as the campaign progressed.

The Allied Tactical Air Forces overall commander, General James Doolittle, perhaps more than any other American officer, acknowledged that the Allied victory was as much a matter of luck as any operational genius or even the courage and tenacity of the 2nd Fusiliers. Luck that the Thunderchief flight literally stumbled over the Luftwaffe attack squadrons as they were moving into attack the Polish formation, luck that *Lion* hadn't been 10 miles further away, and luck that the Luftwaffe had suddenly disappeared as suddenly as it had appeared. Doolittle found that the Allied fighter commanders had, in far too many cases, been assuming that the Luftwaffe would not make a serious appearance, at least not until the Allied lines had moved considerably inland and that, if/when the Reich launched any attack, the Allies would detect the attack long before it happened. This thinking cost the C.O. of the 56th Fighter Group, the group responsible for defending the airspace over Arnèke, his job. He was not the only individual to lose his position due to the action, but he was the most senior Allied officer removed.

While it would have been of little comfort to the 56th's former commander, Operation Condor ended the careers of men with far more gold braid than he possessed in the Reich. The most senior of these was Reichsmarschall Hermann Göring, who SS Commander Himmler managed to paint as the scapegoat for the entire disaster. The political maneuvering that allowed Himmler to effectively cut the man who had once been Hitler's designated successor out of the party's leadership is far beyond the scope of this work, but it represented the first sign of panic among the Nazi senior leadership (for a fascinating study of this element of the Reich's political history, *The Devil's Princes, Leadership in the 3rd Reich* by Guy Lambert, University of Toronto Press, 2001, is highly recommended). Göring's manner of dismissal was responsible for considerable change, not all of it within the Reich.

It is extremely fortunate for the Allies that Göring was not removed in the aftermath of the St. Patrick's Day Raids, given his opiate dependency and his largely successful effort in convincing Hitler that the Luftwaffe was superior in both men and equipment than anything that the Anglo-Americans could field. Göring's confidence in, and championing of, the carefully planted KGB/GRU disinformation concerning the West's A-bomb program was one of the crucial elements in the Reich's failure to discover the remarkably large, although fairly well concealed, American and British parallel and joint weapons programs. Göring's preference for short-range interceptors and relative disdain for extremely long range bombers was also a significant element in the Luftwaffe's overall combat structure.

Göring's replacement, Generaloberst Adolph Galland, was promoted from commander of the Luftwaffe's Fighter Command. An exceptional technical officer, and an acknowledged tactical genius, Galland arrived on the scene too late to re-engineer the Luftwaffe along the lines he had advocated since his promotion to General in 1943, something that was fortunate indeed for the RAF and USAF. Galland also lacked Göring's political power, a situation that effectively hamstrung him in any competition with the SS. This was perhaps best illustrated by Himmler's successful takeover of all Luftwaffe ground formations, including the anti-aircraft forces (with the resultant chaos as SS political appointees rapidly replaced experienced Luftwaffe senior commanders) in the weeks immediately following the failure of Operation Condor. General Galland's lack of political clout was also a strong contributor to the deployment of Luftwaffe resources in the period following Göring's ouster.

Himmler's ability to hang any of the remaining fault for Condor's failure onto the French National Forces and not on the battle plan that he had personally approved and ordered implemented is also noteworthy, not only for the degree of political astuteness it demonstrated, but for its foreshadowing of events to come.

24

The foreign reaction to the Reich's apparent panic over the failure of Operation Condor was initially subtle, although parts of it became public knowledge within weeks of the battle. Perhaps the most damaging to the immediate Nazi war effort was the announcement by Sweden that it would not be renewing iron ore contracts beginning with August shipments to German companies due to better prices being offered for ore by US Steel and a partnership of British Steel firms. While presented as a purely business decision, it was the first of a series of steps taken by Sweden to alter its foreign policy from neutrality with a reluctant preference for the Reich to neutrality with a slight lean toward the West. Despite thunderous threats to Stockholm, Berlin's leader found that their ability to punish the Swedes was extremely limited. Orders to SS units in northern Norway to attack Swedish positions were, in the main, responded to with requests for fuel and other supplies that would allow Panzer units to withdraw from the defensive line being held against the Allies to the north where they could strike against the Swedes. In the rare cases where SS units actually attempted to move against the Swedes as ordered they found themselves targeted by Allied air assets or repulsed by Swedish forces (these short, sharp fights included the combat debut of the Carl Gustav anti-tank weapon by Swedish troops).

While the Swedish action was open for all to see, there were also other, far more subtle activities in Madrid and in Lisbon, where Spanish and Portuguese diplomats found themselves being used as messengers for trial balloons sent by the Fascist governments of Belgium and Denmark, as well as more substantive discussions with the Finnish Government (these Finnish overtures resulted in the August 17 Memorandum of Understanding between

Finland and the Allies which effectively moved the Finns into the status of neutrals, cutting the final reasonably secure overland connection between the Reich and SS forces in Norway).

At the same time as the diplomatic flurry of activity on the Iberian Peninsula, the Apostolic Nuncio to Her Majesty's Government in London presented a letter from the King of Italy to the Prime Minister. The specific contents of this letter are still unknown, having been placed into the British Government Archives for a period of 75 years, but the letter is widely seen as a first halting effort by the Italian Government to begin a dialogue for a negotiated peace. As the Allies had, as early as 1942, proclaimed that any surrender would be accepted only if it was unconditional, it is unclear why the Calallero government (which had succeeded Mussolini upon Il Duce's death following his 1953 heart attack) would have made such a proposal. Perhaps the release of the original letter and the related British Government documents in 2033 will shed light on this curious matter.

The various Allied government were clearly encouraged by these cracks appearing in the edges of "Fortress Europe", although the encouragement was more than counterbalanced by reports from Military Affairs officers in Norway, France, and, to a lesser extent, Belgium. Especially troubling to the Allies was the situation in Norway, where close to half of the country had been "liberated". Despite some displays of celebration, generally by residents in rural communities, the overall mood of the population was, as described by the Australian commander of the Oslo occupation garrison, "resigned". After extended interviews, many of them conducted by American and Australian troops of Norwegian ancestry, the Allied experts found a number of disturbing trends. These included:

Resentment of the Allies because they had "intruded" into what had been a peaceful Norway. This position was held mostly by those under the age of 30 and was neatly bookended by the resentment felt by those over the age of 50 who could not understand how the "British" could have left them to the Germans for as long as they had done.

Anger at the destruction that the Allied invasion had inflicted on their homes, businesses, and neighborhoods was the second most prevalent feeling. The Allied attacks, despite the best efforts of the battle planners, had been hugely destructive, especially when SS or Norwegian National forces had chosen to stand and fight in any built-up area. The Allied commanders, trained to spend as little of their troops' blood as necessary when firepower could do the job with a lower butcher's bill, would, whenever possible, refuse to accept battle in built-up areas and would simply burn or blow up an enemy strong point. While the Norwegian National commanders had quickly learned this and had mainly chosen to do all in their power to reduce civilian casualties, the Waffen-SS commanders had been trained to draw enemy forces into close combat whenever possible, where "superior Aryan morale and courage" would break the enemy's will to fight. While a reasonable lesson from both the Eastern Front battles, especially those of Stalingrad and Leningrad, and from the long-lasting frontier fighting that had raged in the East for well over a decade, it was a tactic that required an enemy to participate, something that the American and Australian commanders who had fought through the ruins of Manila or Seoul against the Japanese had no intention of doing. Allied air and artillery had reduced most of Oslo to scorched rubble, a status that was common across Allied-held Norway. The destruction was in stark contrast to the much less damaging German occupation of 1940, something that Party propaganda stressed time and again.

It was, however, the most common reaction among the Norwegian people that concerned the Allies. There was a combination of fear and a surprising amount of hate toward the Allied troops. Fear that the Allies were killing Norway's sons and hatred when it was known that the Allied troops *had* killed men whom the interviewees personally knew. When one considered the relatively small size of Norway's population, and the number of fortress troops in the Dunkirk region that had been Norwegian, the percentage of the population who knew someone who had died at the hands of "liberators" was stunningly high (various estimates ran as high as 65% in some urban areas). While resentment, even anger, generally fades or can be alleviated by any number of methods, the fear and hatred was not something that could be addressed with any degree of success as long as Norwegian troops were being engaged by Allied troops. With Norwegian troops being common along much of the northern Atlantic Wall all the way to the Danish border, where the fortress troops began to lean heavily to Romanian and Croat, the Allies would be in the business of killing Norwegians for some time to come, especially as the defenders of the beach positions had not shown significant reduction in willingness to fight, even when cornered.

The presence of so many Norwegians in the rest of Europe, dependent on SS forces for food and subject to SS punishment for the misbehavior of their relatives in Norway, was also frequently cited by interrogators as reason for the general lack of cooperation the Allied forces were experiencing. These troops were also the main excuse that Norway's Fascist government gave to the Allies for refusing to order remaining Norwegian National Forces to lay down their arms, even after most of the Government leadership had been captured by the Allies.

With similar results being reported by interrogators from Belgium to Sicily, the Allied leaders began to reconcile themselves to the reality that the flickering hope of a continent-wide collapse of puppet governments due to popular pressure was nothing but a dream.

The war would have to be won with steel and blood, not pamphlets.

25

It was perhaps inevitable that the Allied version of the Irresistible Force would meet the Reich's Immovable Object, and the location of the encounter often seems to be almost poetic when viewed at five decades' distance. At the time, however, neither the 6th Marine Division and 3rd Armored nor the 14th and 33rd SS Panzer Divisions had time for such lyrical musings as the forces engaged near Arras, where the SS had established a major Waffen-SS bunker complex.

Unlike the Atlantic Wall defenses, which were focused on stopping an invader, the SS bunker complexes were designed to give protection to major SS formations and to act as bases from which the surrounding countryside could be kept under control. The complexes ranged in size from overgrown garages to the massive fortifications such as the one near Arras. Initially begun in late 1944, the Arras complex consisted of a series of interconnected bunkers with below-ground access tunnels connecting them to a central citadel. The citadel also, in the case of the Arras location, provided underground, or more properly under concrete, staging for upwards of 300 Panther III tanks, although combat losses and transportation difficulties had reduced the operational panzers at Arras to 185 tracks at the beginning of the battle. The Arras complex was well equipped with tube artillery (up to 210mm), mortars, and the already much-despised Nebelwerfer rocket launchers in various sizes up to 320mm, as well as having been upgraded with substantial AAA defenses ranging all the way to 128mm in size. Arras was also the first SS position equipped with the RPzB.120 wire-guided ATGM encountered by the Allies. Covering close to two square miles, the Arras complex was the largest single SS defensive position in northwestern France, built to allow the Reich to dominate the entire region.

The Americans were, of course, not completely unaware of the existence of the Arras complex. Even today the outlines of the position can be seen in satellite photos of the area, while the reconnaissance photos taken in the lead-up to Gravel clearly showed the positions held by the SS. Alamo Scout units had also been active in the Arras area, and several members of the garrison had been captured and persuaded to provide information on the position. Even with this hard-won information the reality of the complex was only discovered with time.

It was the 2nd Battalion 29th Marines that made the initial approach to the Arras complex. As was the case with most of the USMC formations, it had retained as many amtracks as possible for troop transport and fire support as the battalion advanced inland. Especially prized were the 'tracks equipped with flamethrower mounts or the 20mm Gatling cannon, both of which had proved to be indispensable in defeating defensive bunkers. The 2nd Battalion also had a company of Marine M-26 Pershing tanks in direct support as it moved in on the Arras complex. The battalion was arrayed in the formation that had worked during earlier attacks: rifle platoons forward and arrayed alongside the tracked vehicles to defend the tanks and tracks from enemy troops with what the Allied troops had taken to calling Faussies (the Panzerfaust 350.5, probably the best man-portable anti-tank weapon of the war; capable of destroying any tank in the world at the time, although it was only effective against the American Chamberlain super heavy from the side and rear quarters), with the armored vehicles providing the heavy weapon support for infantry.

29th Marines had been in combat from D-Day and was down below 50% of its original strength, even with replacements taken from the shattered remnants of the 2nd Marine Division folded into its ranks; although 2nd Batt, at 78% strength, was by far the strongest of the regiment's formations. The rifle teams, from the youngest 17-year-old up to the oldest NCO, were veteran, and, more importantly, lucky: survivors of nearly a month of near-continuous combat. Nothing, however – even the horrors of Green Beach One – had prepared 2nd Battalion for what was to come at Arras.

With the usual CAS squadrons overhead, and artillery and heavy mortar fire pounding the obvious strong-points, the marines approached with no more than the usual caution. Experience had taught the marine riflemen when they could expect the SS to open fire; the SS had a book and it fought by that book, or at least it had until Arras. The first Pershing was hit by an RPzB.120 guided missile 1,500 meters away from the forward SS bunkers. This was over half a mile further out than any previous SS anti-tank missile had effectively managed to engage tank-sized targets; in under a minute the entire Pershing company had been destroyed, along with five fire support tracks. As the armored vehicles took their losses, the supporting infantry found itself under very heavy and distressingly-accurate 210mm Nebelwerfer and 120mm mortar fire.

As the circling aircraft of VMF-214 (the Black Sheep of WWII fame) moved in to assist the troops, they were met with heavy light-AAA fire from a number of well-concealed 37mm mounts as well as tracked mobelwagen that were able to roll out of defensive bunkers, engage enemy aircraft, and roll back under cover in time to avoid counter-battery fire. The Black Sheep lost nine of twenty-one aircraft before being driven off by the enemy flak.

In all, the first attack against the Arras complex was an unmitigated disaster. 2nd Batt, 29th Marines suffered 85% losses, including 134 men killed, lost a total of 23 amtracks (leaving the Battalion with only two usable amtracks), and had lost 16 M-26 tanks while gaining no ground at all. It was the most one-sided engagement since the Allied landings (SS losses, based on later prisoner interrogation, numbered less than 30 men), and it was just the beginning.

The Reich, despite the virtually continuous air attacks against known manufacturing sites, had not spent the time since March of 1954 completely idle. At a serious disadvantage in both material access and research and development of certain items, notably transistors and millimeter radars, the Reich had nevertheless made great strides. While it had taken almost 30 months to completely reverse-engineer the Allied transistor technology (based on the many examples salvaged from downed Allied aircraft), it had succeeded in producing its own circuits. The RPzB.120 was the first weapon system that had been produced in quantity with the new transistors; the new electronics allowed the missile to be half the weight of its predecessor while retaining the same sized rocket motor. The combination had proved to be an especially lethal marriage. Other weapons, including improved SAM systems, were also nearing development (and would, in fact, have been already fielded had it not been for destruction of so many manufacturing facilities and so much of the Reich's rail network).

The Arras complex was also an example of the best parts of the Waffen-SS' structure. Every weapon had been pre-registered at various known ranges, making the engagement of advancing enemy forces a matter of simply waiting for the enemy to reach the proper location and laying in extremely accurate and lethal fire. The extensive bunker system, with most bunkers interconnected by below-ground tunnels, and extremely strong blockhouses (some roofs were as much as 6 feet thick, made of reinforced concrete), provided both protection and remarkable mobility for the defenders. According to some legends, the Reich had employed some of the same engineers who had designed and built the Maginot Line in the construction of the SS bunker complexes. While never proved, the underground transport systems of the SS complexes did show very similar design details to the outflanked French defensive positions.

After the blunting of the initial attack, the commander of the 6th Marine Division planned a larger attack, using all of his division, along with 3rd Armored, in a major attack meant to capture one corner of the Arras position. Launched on 19th July, 1958, this attack was a virtual repeat of the 29th Marines' effort but on a grander scale. The Americans had spent several days pounding the SS positions with artillery, including recently-arrived 210mm Multiple Rocket Launchers that fired a total of 12 of the 8" weapons in each salvo, as well as bombing by everything up to B-29 heavy bombers. The attack was a bloody failure that succeeded only in rendering the 6th Marine Division combat ineffective without taking a single significant objective.

With the failure of the Marine assault, Allied Ground Commander Guy Simonds ordered that the effort be taken over by the US 3rd Army under General Creighton Abrams. Built out of the U.S II Corps, the 1st Canadian Infantry Division, and the 6th Australian Armored, 3rd Army was the first full Army Group that the Americans had organized on the continent. Allied overall commander Ridgway also ordered that Allied air forces make the Arras complex a tactical priority. What followed was the largest set-piece battle involving American, Australian and Canadian troops since the First World War.

As the Allies moved forces into position to take the Arras complex, the SS command also began to move forces into the Arras region. The last two fully-undamaged French National Army formations, including the division assigned to the Cherbourg region, an Italian Armored Brigade, and 58th SS Panzer were all ordered into the Arras region. SS records clearly indicate that the entire Nazi leadership, all the way up to Hitler, believed that Arras was the anvil where the Allied effort would be pounded to bits. Over the strenuous objection of new Luftwaffe commander Adolph Galland, the Führer directed that the Reich air forces make a "supreme effort" to support the Arras battle. Luftwaffe units from as far away as Russia were moved to the battle. All of this movement was clearly observed by Allied U-2 and RB-57 flights and relayed to the SACEUR. Arras had quickly become the major fight of the war to date.

One of the first major engagements after the commitment of 3rd Army was between the greatly-reinforced 3rd Armored Brigade and a sortie by 33rd SS Panzer on July 29th. The SS sortie, meant to screen the approach of two French National infantry divisions, quickly devolved into a stand-up fight with an accompanying air battle that was the largest seen over France since 1954. While over 1000 armored vehicles tore into each other near the site of World War I's Vimy Ridge battle, the French Air Force went to its destruction.

Comprised mainly of 1943 and older Luftwaffe designs, the Armee De L'Air, even with the support of three Messerschmitt P.1721 interceptor squadrons (the absolute best remaining fighter squadrons in the Luftwaffe which had been taken from the Berlin defensive assignment), was no match for the nearly 500 jet fighters that eventually took part in the Vimy battle. After two days of round-the-clock air battles (which included the first use of airborne, radar-directed fighter direction by the Americans and their EC-121 Warning Star aircraft), the American and Canadian Air Forces had effectively cleared the sky of Axis aircraft, albeit at a cost of nearly 90 aircraft. French losses were over 300, while the P.1721 squadrons were effectively destroyed in a series of epic engagements with USAF F-101 and RCAF CF-101 squadrons.

With the Axis air threat removed, the Allied ground attack aircraft, especially Canadian B-57 bombers, proceeded to savage the French infantry as they struggled to reach the Arras defenses. Both French divisions were roughly handled, losing nearly a third of their strength, with less than two brigades actually reaching Arras. 33rd SS Panzer lost 42 Panther III and nearly 150 light armored vehicles in the fighting with 3rd Armored and the Allied air forces, with 3rd Armored losing 52 tanks (including 10 to French ground attack aircraft) and a total of 450 men killed and wounded.

The fighting over the next two weeks followed the pattern set on the 29th of July: ongoing Allied tactical victories that had heavy casualties for both sides. It was not until August 11, after five days of heavy bombardment by artillery and rocket launchers directed at SS anti-aircraft sites and at the exit points used by Mobelwagens, that the Allies were able to bring in B-36 bombers carrying 43,000-pound T-12 Cloudmaker bombs capable of penetrating the roof structures of the Arras complex. Even with the super-massive T-12 bombs and use of fuel-air weapons against the blockhouses, it was August 18th before the first American troops managed to enter the heavily-damaged Arras citadel. When they did so, they were engaged by SS troops who proved to be completely unwilling to surrender despite repeated attempts to lure them out with promises of good treatment.

Unwilling to lose any more men, and with Operation Maverick on the horizon, General Simonds ordered that all exits from the complex be sealed by combat engineers using demolition charges and bulldozers. This work done, the Americans left the 45th RCT in place to ensure that no enemy troops broke out of the devastated complex.

The Arras complex battle had effectively stopped the northern wing of the Allied ground offensive for 40 days. No good accounting of Axis losses at Arras has ever been made. It is known that better than 25,000 troops (perhaps as many as 32,000) took part in the defense of the complex. Prisoners taken totaled 2,357, virtually all of them French or Italians. The only SS troops captured were either unconscious or too disabled to fight at the time of their capture. It is presumed that the rest of the defenders perished in the battle.

Some contemporary writers questioned the decision to assault Arras, especially in light of the way that other similar complexes were treated later in the war. These criticisms fail to consider that the Arras battle was where the Allies developed the tactics that were used on other SS sites. While it is true that if one is equipped with a hammer, most problems begin to resemble a nail, the tactics used against Arras should not be viewed as simplistic. Much was learned at Arras, even though the price paid for the education was higher than the Americans would have ever imagined.

26

It has often been stated that the Arras region was one of the pivot points of Europe. This is mainly due to the number of battles that have happened in the city's shadow. None of these many actions, dating back to the 15th Century, or two major European treaties (one of them known under Arras' Dutch name Atrecht) that were signed in the city, had any greater impact that the events of the Summer of 1958.

Arras is where the Allied armies, especially that of the United States, came of age. While it is true that ensuing encounters with the Waffen-SS bunker complexes were handled in a very different manner than the exceptionally bloody affair at Arras, with far less loss of life on the Allied side, the tactics that marked these later actions, namely the usage of truly prodigious amounts of artillery (including the use of 320mm rockets to scatter "instant minefields" that seriously impeded the SS ability to send out sorties from the bunker complex, as well as reducing the effectiveness of the Mobelwagens that had proved so deadly against American fighter bombers at Arras) before the introduction of heavy bombing. The SS bunker complexes are generally credited with delaying the retirement of the B-36 from front line combat use until the end of the war.

The Allied (mainly American, but also employed by the British and Indian ground forces as well) tactics aroused little notice or comment at the time they were employed, but are, today, a source of great debate. These discussions mainly involve the mass use of the cluster bombs that made up the "instant minefields" which proved so effective against the SS and were virtually impossible for either the SS or Allied ordnance disposal teams to clear completely. Even today, more than five decades after the main European battles, the "bomblets" from the cluster bombs are responsible for at least ten civilian deaths each year in France alone (in the author's view, the condemnation of 21st century critics regarding use of bomblets in the European War ignores the "Total War" realities of the late 1950s while relying on 20/20 hindsight).

Nearly as controversial as the use of cluster bombs against the SS bunker sites is General Simonds' plow blade directive. Simonds' decision to simply burn or bury enemy troop positions when the defenders would not surrender has been a point of disagreement from the day it was announced. Critics have long pointed out, with more than a little justification, that the tactic failed in one of its stated goals – SS and National force surrenders did not show any statistically noticeable increase after the announcement (not even after the use of leafleting to inform Axis troops of the policy) – and that some Allied units appeared to resort to the tactic whenever confronted by serious Axis opposition without giving enemy forces the opportunity to even contemplate surrender. The tactic is also criticized for increasing the harshness of enemy resistance and for at least some of the issues Allied troops encountered with civilian population (there are numerous documented cases of Nazi officials using the Allied leaflets for propaganda purposes). Simonds' supporters respond to these criticisms with simple references to the casualty lists: Allied losses far down, and SS losses unknown, but positions taken and ground gained. It is unlikely that the debate will ever truly end.

The most momentous impact of Arras was also one that was completely unknown to the Allies until the end of the war. This was, of course, the September 9th 1958 stroke that felled the very symbol of the Reich, Adolph Hitler, leaving him nearly totally paralyzed and unable to communicate.

While another matter of great debate (at least a dozen well-researched, convincing, and totally incompatible books have been published on the subject just since the turn of the century), it seems clear that the utter defeat at Arras was the trigger of Hitler's medical disaster. Interviews with those who were close to the Führer show a man who had gone from being remarkably confident, even happy much of the time, as late as 1957 to a somewhat more somber leader in the weeks before the Allied landings in Norway, to an individual who displayed what now seems to have been a false euphoria upon the Allied landings at Dunkirk, and then to a brooding shadow of himself as Waffen-SS plans and operations failed. It is clear that Hitler had believed that the Allies would be repelled on the beach and that any small toehold they acquired would be quickly overcome by his SS troops.

The Allied capture of the Dunkirk ports has been said to have astounded Hitler, who, it seems, had never even considered the possibility. The failure of Operation Condor, especially with its critical racial undertones, was enough to push Hitler into dismissing Herman Göring, a man who had been one of his closest advisors for three decades. It also seems to have reawakened Hitler's Parkinson's Disease (or at least caused the symptoms to become far more pronounced). While the observations of those interviewed, most of whom were cooks, chambermaids and the like, need to be taken with some caution, the fact that they are similar (although, critically, not identical) tends to give them somewhat greater weight than might otherwise be the case.

What is clear is that Himmler had virtually guaranteed Hitler that his SS position at Arras was impregnable (Himmler was overheard describing Arras to Hitler as a far stronger Verdun, a place where the American army would be destroyed) and that the Führer had believed his SS commander. Hitler's rage at the fall of Arras was clearly overwhelming, and witnesses to the event state he quite literally collapsed in mid-rant. It is interesting to speculate what might have happened if Hitler had not stroked out at the time; clearly Himmler's days as SS Chief would have been over, and some historians have even postulated that Hitler might have been disgusted with SS failures to the point that he might have put former Heer officers, including Field Marshall Erich von Manstein, Field Marshal Wilhelm List, or General Erwin Rommel in charge of the Waffen-SS forces. This change would have been a dramatic one, with the replacement of mainly political appointees with trained staff officers, but it was not to be.

Himmler was present when Hitler had his seizure, being the recipient of Hitler's rant about Arras. The leader of the Waffen-SS and Gestapo, Himmler had control of two of the three organs needed to take control of the Reich. Thanks to Goebbels' shock at the Führer's collapse, Himmler was able to get the Information Minister's backing as "temporary" Führer until Hitler could recover. By the time the rest of the Nazi Party hierarchy were even able to consider making a move, Himmler had established himself as the de-facto ruler of the Reich.

What followed was one of the more remarkable deceptions in modern history. The world did not learn of Hitler's fall until the end of the war. With Goebbels' help, Himmler stage-managed a series of radio and video broadcasts that seemed to be the Führer, at least to the satisfaction of the listener/viewer. Himmler and Goebbels eliminated anyone they believed would not keep the Führer's condition secret, either liquidating them or sending them to Gestapo concentration camps.

It is almost impossible to say what would have happened had Hitler not been stricken, or what might have happened if Goebbels (or even Göring) had been present in the room when Hitler collapsed. It is difficult to imagine that anyone, even Hitler, could have been worse than Himmler as the Reich's leader beginning on that September day.

27

Maverick is often referred to as "the Forgotten Invasion", and with good reason. Taking place in the immediate aftermath of the Battle of Arras and well away from the established Gravel landing zones, as well as in the shadows of the October Offensive, Maverick is often given short shrift. This is a mistake for any number of reasons, especially considering that Maverick triggered the first civilian uprising in France. The operation also shows the Allied command's ability to adapt quickly to changing circumstances and to take advantage of Axis errors.

The Cherbourg (or Cotentin) Peninsula had long been on the Allies' short list for the re-entry into Europe dating back to 1943. It was fairly close to the British Isles and offered an excellent port, assuming it could be taken reasonably intact. The peninsula, along with the rest of Normandy, had been the runner-up for the location of the Gravel Landings, losing out to Dunkirk mostly due to pre-invasion reconnaissance conducted by LRRP and Philippine Scout units which indicated that it was not conducive to rapid advances because of the hedgerows (massive earthen and fieldstone borders, topped with shrubs and trees) that surrounded most of the fields and pasture lands. In the words of one Scout commander when debriefed about the terrain: "I could hold any one of those fields for a week with three men and a bazooka against a company. Give me a company and I will stop a brigade." Since the commander, as well as numerous others who expressed similar views, had a great deal of experience in disrupting large IJA troop movements with his small guerrilla band, this perspective on terrain had rung quite loudly at SACEUR, tipping the scale to Dunkirk. Even though Normandy had lost out on Gravel, the region offered too many advantages to simply be ignored. Operation Maverick was designed to ensure that it was not.

Maverick also illustrates the tactical flexibility that marked the difference between the Allies and the Reich. While the region was assaulted as planned, the specific landing sites were changed to alternate locations (all of which had been surveyed during the long Warm War period for suitability as landing beaches) based on SS and French Army movements during the Arras battle. The 40-day fight of Arras had seen the SS move 58th SS Panzer, along with the equivalent of a full division of Waffen-SS Panzer Grenadiers and heavy tank battalions, a reinforced Armored Brigade of Italian Army troops, and two full divisions of French Army infantry from the Normandy region to the northwest in what the SS Command had expected to be the battle that defeated the Allied invasion. As we have seen (in Chapter 25), the actual result of this massive troop movement was the destruction or piecemeal defeat of these forces, along with the loss of virtually all the transport that was used to shuttle them into the sausage grinder that was Arras. With the exodus of more than four divisions of the mobile reserve meant to assist the fortress troops in the region (mainly comprised of Danish and Romanian units), the peninsula went from being a "tough nut" to an opportunity not to be missed.

The September 15, 1958 Maverick landing differed little in preparation from the earlier Thorn Bush and Gravel landings, although the use of heavy rockets mounted on converted LSTs was more in evidence based on the results obtained at Dunkirk. More of the naval aircraft used in Maverick were also flown from carriers than had been the case during the previous invasion of Northern France. Overall, the Allied effort was also considerably smaller, consisting of just five divisions plus the 1st Air Cav. Despite this smaller size, the naval gun line was still quite substantial, with 9 BB, a CB, 14 CA, 8 CL, and 42 destroyers supplementing the rocket launchers.

Maverick also featured the *coup de main* that allowed the Allies to capture the port of Cherbourg almost intact. This action, made possible by the success of Viet Minh and LRRP units in developing and energizing a substantial civilian uprising across the city on the evening of September 14th (this effort was greatly aided by the removal of the French Army forces from the Cherbourg region, meaning Frenchmen were not called upon to kill their countrymen in substantial numbers), was accomplished by the 1st and 2nd Marine Raider Battalions who made a pre-dawn helicopter assault on the port itself under the cover of heavy naval gunfire against identified AAA sites (the suppression of these sites was perhaps the critical element of the assault, even with the loss of five helicopters who strayed out of safe passage corridor and were struck by Allied shellfire). Although Marine losses were severe, both in troops and in aircraft (with four of every five helicopters engaged either destroyed outright or deemed beyond repair, it is understandable that there has been no similar assault since Maverick), as were losses among the LRRP and Viet Minh and their French allies, the capture of the port and city were well worth the effort and cost entailed in their capture.

Maverick is also notable in that the majority of the landing force was Indian Army, not American or British. To the shock of the SS commanders (and quiet delight of SACEUR), these Indian forces proved themselves to be just as effective (and heroic) as the Australian, British, Canadian, and American landing forces that had taken part in the Gravel assault in July. Interrogation transcripts of SS officers captured in the attack and in later action on the peninsula are peppered with remarks on the courage and skill shown by these "inferior colored" troops (the irony of calling the units which had overrun their defenses, routed their units, and captured them "inferior" was seemingly lost on the Waffen-SS prisoners).

Maverick was also the first time that some fortress units reacted with anything less than suicidal determination. While many units had to be blasted from their guns, a number of both the Danish and Romanian defenders, especially the latter, took advantage of the Allied promise of good treatment if they surrendered. Even though the voluntary surrenders accounted for less than 20% of enemy defenders, with many others fighting to the last cartridge, the willingness of any of the European units to surrender before they were blasted out of their bunkers was nearly as hopeful a sign to the Allies as the civilian uprising.

These signs were not lost on observers outside of SACEUR, Washington, and London.

28

The remarkably rapid collapse of the Axis forces on the Cotentin Peninsula was a dramatic change from the tooth and nail fighting that had marked the weeks after the Dunkirk landings. At the time the Allies were encouraged by the ease of their advance, but were also cautious, expecting resistance to stiffen at any moment. Today it is clear that the relative lack of French National Army units in the area, far more than any loss of morale among Fascist forces, was behind the unexpected ease of the Allied advance. The surrender of the fortress troops manning the positions on the now cut-off peninsula, left without supply or communication, and with minimal ability to resist outside of their bunkers, was, in large part, also a matter of no choice rather than any vision of the Allies as "liberators". (It is nonetheless interesting to note that the troops who surrendered their positions on the northern side of the Peninsula represented the last Danish units in France, leaving just 5,000 troops holding a portion of the defenses south of Naples to represent Denmark outside of the Danish national borders).

In any case, the capture of the Cotentin Peninsula provided the Allies with a second entry point, and a second port to support their advance. As had been planned, Dunkirk became the primary entry port of American forces and Allied units using American equipment, with Cherbourg becoming the portal where most British and Commonwealth forces entered the Continent. While this was more of an administrative decision than any other (massive amounts of Commonwealth and British supplies and manpower continued to pass through Dunkirk, and the same held true of the US and Cherbourg) the establishment of the second supply base made the expansion of the Allied offensive possible.

It was, in large part, what made the October Offensive (and all that followed) possible.

While the Allied, mainly Indian/British, forces were consolidating the Peninsula, the Allied efforts out of the Dunkirk bridgehead continued unabated. While the weather had begun to cause a substantial number of CAS missions to be aborted, the Allied forces had gradually begun to learn how to make use of artillery, both tube and rocket, as replacements for the "bolts from the blue". The main deficiency in this Allied strategy was the over-reliance on still scarce 280mm rockets to replace aircraft, and as the advance inland continued, naval gunfire instead of the far more available and easier to supply tube artillery by some commanders. Still, the Allied learning curve from mid-July to mid-September was impressive, especially when compared to the rather stolid SS tactical innovations, most of which were meant to reduce destruction by Allied air power in the mistaken belief that all that the Axis troops needed to do was avoid Allied aircraft in order to defeat the increasingly numerous and veteran Allied ground forces.

There were other, far more cynical "innovations" that the SS established as standard practice in the occupied portions of Europe, especially those that fell outside of "Greater Germany". This is perhaps demonstrated nowhere better than the Belgian city of Bruges (Brugge). Renowned before the war for its exquisite 13th century architecture and collection of medieval art, the city was not of particular military importance until the commander of 42nd SS Panzer made it so (the same cannot be said for the nearby port of Zeebrugge, which had been a major U-boat base until being destroyed by RAF bombing).

The Allied, especially American, policy of avoiding street fighting whenever possible was, by late September 1958, clearly established: as was the willingness of Allied commanders to happily spend steel and high explosives in mass quantities in order to reduce combat losses among their troops. As noted, the military importance of Bruges was minimal as it offered no special defensive advantage, nor did it present an unavoidable crossroads for Allied forces. The only way to bring about combat there was to have one side force it upon the other, and that is precisely what the commander of 42nd SS did. The SS commander brought his armored units, as well as three brigades of the Belgian National Army, into the city proper, and, along with most of his mobile artillery, established the city as his main strong point for western Flanders.

The concentration of troops in Bruges was far too large for the American 3rd Army to leave in its rear: the forces needed to keep 42nd SS bottled up simply could not be spared. General Creighton Abrams, commander of the 3rd Army, attempted to get Bruges declared an open city; an offer the SS commander flatly rejected. An attempt by elements of the 89th Infantry Division to push through the city outskirts was comprehensively repulsed with significant losses, confirming that the SS intended to hold the city. It may be that the 42nd's commander sincerely believed that the Americans would attempt to take the city with infantry attacks to minimize damage to the historical sites, slowing the American advance and allowing his troops to inflict maximum casualties in street fighting, something the Waffen-SS had counted on to provide a significant advantage over the Anglo-Americans (captured SS records reviewed post-war indicate that the Reich commanders were, even just two months into the ground war, already experiencing extreme frustration at the Allies' refusal to conform to SS pre-war strategic planning); if so he was to be disappointed. It is also possible that he simply decided that Bruges was a good a place to die as any and that destruction of the city would help turn the Belgian population, and far more importantly the Belgian National Army, which had shown some signs of wavering, firmly against the Americans. The actual truth will probably never be known.

Bruges is seven miles inland. Third Army had the support of TF 77.8 (USS *Iowa*, USS *Wisconsin*, USS *Alabama*, USS *Salem*, USS *Dallas*, USS *Oregon City*, USS *Scranton*, USS *Gary* and 9 destroyers) on the gun line, and had first call on VMA-225 (A1D Skyraiders), VMA-185 (F-8B), 85th, 126th, 33rd (F-100), and 59th (F-105) fighter-bomber wings, as well as medium and heavy bomber assets. This massive amount of non-organic firepower on call was augmented by the artillery assets of IV Corps. The Battle of Bruges lasted for five days. Third Army losses, including the abortive attack by the 89th Division on the first day, totaled 258 (56 KIA). All three brigades of the Belgian Army were destroyed, along with ¾ of 42nd SS Panzer's armored vehicles and roughly half of the division's total personnel. Among the losses were the 42nd's commander and deputy commander, along with all of the unit's senior officers (the senior officer who finally withdrew the remnants of the division was a Captain).

Bruges itself, including the historic area where 42nd SS established its headquarters, was utterly destroyed with heavy casualties among the civilian population. This was in keeping with Führer Order 527 which called for ensuring that no "European cultural treasures" fell into the hands of the Anglo-Americans. This order had been published by Himmler, in Hitler's name, on September 16, 1958. It was the first order of the Himmler Era.

29

The destruction of the 42nd SS Panzer and the Belgian brigades under its control was a disaster for the overall SS defensive strategy for Belgium and the Netherlands. With Allied mastery of the air, the last major SS formation in the country, the SS Wiking division, itself mainly comprised of volunteers from the Netherlands, Norway and Denmark, was effectively trapped in its bunker complex outside of Mechelen. While the Mechelen Complex presented a formidable obstacle, the trapped SS forces within were contained within its perimeter. Outside of the complex the remaining SS forces in the country were mainly scattered remnants of units that had been defeated or destroyed by air attack. While dangerous to individual units, American and Australian losses to ambush by SS rear guard units while in pursuit of the retiring 42nd considerably exceeded those lost in the Battle of Bruges, the Reich forces were incapable of stopping the movement of enemy troops across Belgium. It is unlikely that the surviving elements of the 42nd SS could have made a serious stand, especially against the 9th Australian Armored Division, which had assumed the lead position of 3rd Army after Bruges.

Still, it is, from most military perspectives, exceedingly odd that the survivors of the 42nd SS expended most of their munitions and effort in the wholesale destruction of Belgian cities that had no military value of any kind. This perhaps best illustrated by the decision to dedicate the 42nd SS Pioneer Regiment to the burning of Gent and later Brussels instead of using these skilled engineer units to delay the Allied advance. While SS devotion to strict obedience to the Führer is justly renowned, the willingness of Axis units that were in full retreat to follow orders to destroy culturally important sites and noteworthy artworks, even at the risk of being overrun by advancing Allied forces, is difficult to fathom.

A side effect of the Allied advance across Belgium was the near mass surrender of fortress troops that were cut off from any resupply. Some 11,000 members of these units were captured in a six-day period beginning on October 3, 1958. This sudden increase in prisoners actually caused some delays in the Allied advance as Provost Marshall units were unable to handle the influx without assistance. These PoWs were among the first to be shipped to Canada and the United States (unfortunately, it was while transporting some of these men that the transport S.S. *American Victory* was lost to a submarine-laid mine off the Irish coast with the loss of nearly 600 prisoners and 36 crewmen).

Having advanced, in some cases, as much as 45 miles in a week, 3rd Army paused along a line that ran roughly from Brussels-Mons-Saint Quentin for a brief refit and resupply on October 12th. On October 15th, the Belgian government was overthrown by SOE-supported partisans who called for the return of the Royal Family. Interestingly, SS troops present in the capital did not intervene on the Belgian government's behalf except to provide transport out of the country for surviving members of the Fascist government. With the Mechelen Complex already under heavy, near round-the-clock bombing that effectively neutralized the forces contained there, the provisional Belgian government surrendered unconditionally to the Allies on October 17th (an action that resulted in the so-called Trondheim Massacre when Waffen-SS forces summarily executed 575 Belgian fortress troops in retaliation for their country's "treason against European Civilization" as well as other, smaller group executions in Italy and along the Eastern Frontier).

The surrender of Belgium seems to have caused a near panic in Berlin, far beyond the Finnish actions in August or the Swedish change of stance. It is unclear if the reaction was because of the "communist revolt" that overthrew the Brussels puppet regime or if the realization that the Western Allies were winning the war was brought home to Himmler by the surrender. In either case, the Reich's reaction was immediate and rather dramatic.

SS units were, to the largest extent possible, pulled out of the East and sent, not to the battlefront, but to the abandoned fortifications along the Rhine. This move was accompanied by the call-up of reserve troops as old as 50 years of age. These Heer veterans, many of whom had last held a rifle in 1943, were hastily organized and put under the command of SS officer cadets less than half their age. Other veterans were sent to replace the SS units moving out of the East. These troops were equipped, in many cases, with weapons that had been stored away since the surrender of the USSR, with many of the weapons actually being war booty, including Soviet T-26 and T-34 tanks. These troops were sent, not to fight the ongoing low-intensity war along the frontier, but to keep an eye on the non-Reich conscripts sent to fight and die in the East. So great was the panic that Himmler reactivated a number of retired Heer junior officers to command these new formations, although senior leadership was left in the hands of SS General officers. For reasons never satisfactorily explained (although some documents suggest that the Party had an almost intuitional fear of a military coup led by the General Staff) most of the experienced Heer Generals were not reactivated, even in the case of men who volunteered to fight as common soldiers in defense of the Homeland.

An exception to this general prohibition of bringing back professionally-trained staff officers was the decision to place a particular favorite of Hitler in charge of revitalizing the Rhine defensive fortifications. This officer, General der Panzergruppen Erwin Rommel, a former commander of Hitler's military bodyguard before it was disbanded by the SS, had been a highly successful commander in the Battle of France and had been Hitler's personal choice to oversee construction of the Atlantic Wall. A spry 66-year-old, Rommel was far too old to lead forces in combat but he was, apparently on Albert Speer's direct recommendation, given the responsibility for the Rhine fortification based on his organizational skills as demonstrated in the construction of the Atlantic Wall. Why, after the Allies had managed to breach his Atlantic Wall in under a day on three different occasions (in Norway, at Dunkirk, and on the Cotentin

Peninsula), it was decided that Rommel's hands were the ones into which the final defensive position for the Reich was placed is an open question. This may have been Party cronyism at its best (although Rommel was, by most accounts, something short of a fanatical believer) or it may have been some sort of effort to recapture the magic of the heady days when the Reich's mastery of the continent was unopposed.

On 21 October, Berlin recalled 6th and 15th SS Panzer and 53rd SS Panzergrenadier from Italy, where they had been sent to support Italian forces in repelling the expected invasion of the country, along with 6th Luftwaffe Panzer and 13th Luftwaffe Heavy Anti-aircraft to Germany for "refit pending redeployment". Since these units had not been in any sort of ground fighting since, at the most recent, the Anzio Raid, the labeling of this movement was clearly a face-saving gesture meant to obscure the fact that the SS was running out of units. SS records are, understandably, incomplete, but it seems that by October 21st the SS had been reduced to twenty-one fully-equipped panzer divisions and only four fully-equipped panzer grenadier divisions, which were supplemented by the five remaining Luftwaffe Panzer divisions.

Although it was unknown to the Allies, and not acknowledged by the SS leadership or Himmler in his role of acting Führer, the Reich was no longer capable of defeating the Allies using conventional means. Field Marshall Erich von Manstein's personal diary entry for October 23rd occupies only a single line:

"We have lost the war. The only question is how badly."

On October 24th, the Allies began their Fall Offensive.

30

The failure of Russia to take advantage of the Reich's difficulties has long been a point of often violent debate in the country and remains so to this day. In the Fall of 1958 it puzzled, and then frustrated, the Allied political leadership which had counted on the Red Army, at least the remnants of it that Molotov had under his command, to at least force the SS to keep some top-quality forces along the Eastern frontier. Instead, the Molotov government appeared to ignore all requests from the Allies to act in any meaningful manner, even to cut off the supply of raw materials to the Reich. Some officers in the Allied Combined Staff, disgusted by Molotov's seeming indifference to the effort to defeat the Reich, actually quietly circulated a paper advocating the addition of Russia to the list of enemy powers. Fortunately, cooler heads prevailed and all copies of the paper were successfully retrieved before reaching either the media or, far more critically, the deep-cover KGB (as the NKVD had now become) agents that were still at work in both the US and Great Britain.

The reality was that, far from being indifferent, Molotov wanted nothing more than to re-engage the Nazis. He knew that the only way that Russia would have a seat at the peace table was if the country showed that it was not just another satrap of the Reich. Russia, however, did not have the necessary cohesion to act in any significant manner.

The Russian state was actually in a state of near-civil war and had been since being defeated by the Reich. There were, depending on one's definition, between six and eleven significant competitors to Molotov, all of which had their own supporters in the Red Army and among the KGB. All that kept Molotov in power was the loyalty of five Guards divisions, three of which were based in the provisional Russian Capital of Krasnoyarsk, and one division of GRU troops. The GRU forces were the primary collectors of the ongoing tribute that went West, both materials and slave labor. The Guards divisions loyal to the government were the only forces in Russia that had anything close to a full TOE. Two of the divisions had 80 B-26 tanks and the others had between 60 and 85 B-10 armored cars (the GRU units did operate around two dozen British Fordson armored cars, vehicles that dated back to the early 1920s); although utterly obsolete, these were the only armored vehicles left in the Red Army. As such, they gave Molotov's loyalists an almost insurmountable advantage in the maneuvering for power that was a nonstop part of Russian political life.

The Berlin Treaty had thoroughly defanged the Red Army. Among its many provisions was a requirement that the Soviets/Russians base no military unit larger than a company within 500 kilometers of the new border. The presence of any larger unit would immediately break the Treaty and would be immediately attacked by the Reich. All efforts of the Red Army to move forces forward in the immediate aftermath of the Treaty were found and destroyed by Luftwaffe attacks. By 1953 the Red Army, as it was then constituted, had accepted that it was impossible to move significant forces into the demilitarized zone and concentrated on supplying irregular forces with weapons while simultaneously explaining that, due to the terms of the Treaty, it was impossible for Russia to suppress the frontier bandits. Once outside of the demilitarized zone there were larger Red Army formations, but outside of the units loyal to Molotov none exceeded a brigade, with most formations being regiments or even battalions. In a series of complex movements and shifting loyalties, these units were shuffled across the still massive expanse of Asian Russia as Molotov worked to keep power (and his head on his shoulders).

With the circumstances that existed in 1958, there was no practical hope of Russia providing any aid to the war effort. Unfortunately for Molotov and his country, this perspective of the true state of political affairs in Russia was unknown during the war and has really only been pieced together in the last twenty years.

While Molotov's government had neither the ability nor desire to re-engage the Reich, it was not completely uninvolved in the Allied war effort. Mainly in return for support from the US – which had become the primary source of imported foodstuffs for Russia with the end of the Pacific Phase, a reality that had only become more pronounced as the Warm War progressed to Hot with the US taking control of the Reich enclave surrounding Vladivostok – U.S and British (especially the latter) weapons and military advisors entered Russia either from the south via Iran or from the US-controlled region around Vladivostok, and some information on conditions within the Reich trickled out through NKVD resources within Greater Germany. This information occasionally proved to be intelligence bonanzas, as when they revealed the location of the Luftwaffe's A-9 facilities, as well as giving some sort of insight into the morale of the German population (something that did not make for happy reading at the time in London or Washington).

The British military missions established close relationships with numerous partisan commanders along the "Eastern Frontier" with support for non-Communist groups gradually allowing these forces, many of them "ethnic nationalist" in the view of the Soviets, to become the dominant powers along wide swathes of the frontier and well into the Russian interior. The Molotov government almost howled in protest of the Allied support for these "counter-revolutionary" groups, but found itself in the position of a poor relative relying on a rich aunt for food and shelter and was forced to swallow their anger lest they be cut off.

The Americans, as was their wont, rapidly transformed the region around Vladivostok into something resembling, if not America, then a reasonable imitation. American dollars paid local workers and farmers for labor and provisions Additional roads, railways and airbases sprang up where there had been, quite literally, nothing. In return for one million tons of grain per year, the Molotov government granted permission for the Allies, primarily the USAF, to establish a series of air bases in Siberia.

These bases quickly became connection points in a network for roads and other supply conduits, including a web of fuel pipelines that radically altered the appearance and economy of vast regions of Asian Russia (for an intelligently written, meticulously researched account of the American building effort, Hamilton Richardson's *You want it WHERE?: US airfield construction battalions in WWII* is highly recommended).

Despite the assistance provided by the Soviet government, especially in the area of intelligence, the Allies came to see Krasnoyarsk as nothing more than another minor player on the grand global stage that was the West's war against the Axis. Minor players had little to provide and even less say in the running of the war.

31

The differences in conditions between the Western Allies and the Axis were perhaps never brought into sharper focus than in the days running up to the beginning of the Allied Fall 1958 Offensive. While the Waffen-SS was withdrawing forces from the Italian Peninsula and replacing fairly well-equipped formations on the Eastern Frontier with 45-year-old men who had last been under arms when France had fallen in 1940, the Allied Armies on the continent simply seemed to expand without limit.

The American Army by then had three full Army Groups deployed in Northern France and Belgium, including the famed, if misnamed, 1st South American Corps (actually roughly a division and a half of men from across the continent), all of them lavishly equipped and fully motorized or mechanized. The Canadian 1st Army and Australian 2nd Army combined with three USMC Divisions to create the 15th Army Group, which were nearly as well kitted out as their US Army partners. South of the North Americans and Australians, roughly starting at the outskirts of the still Axis-held port town of Calais (or more properly what was left of that heavily-destroyed port), stood the British 21st and 22nd Army Groups. Not quite as well-supplied as their North American cousins, the British and Commonwealth forces were still close to 90% motorized, even when one included the units of "Free" Poles, Russians, Norwegians and the French Liberation Brigade (recruited from anti-fascists in the French overseas colonies), all of which were mainly supplied with older American and British weapons and heavily reliant on the major Western powers for everything needed to wage war except their own considerable courage and élan.

Lastly, and perhaps most startling, was the robust force that had been assembled on the Cotentin Peninsula. The most powerful formation there was the British II Armored Corps, with its strong tank formation, including a South African brigade, providing the mailed fist that would be used in the breakout across France, but British and Commonwealth forces did not comprise the majority of the Allied forces near Cherbourg. That distinction belonged to the Indian Army, whose ranks had swollen to three Corps in the weeks since the Maverick landings. Indian troops, some arriving directly from the sub-continent, made up nearly 70% of the troops that constituted the 12th Army Group, with an average of a regiment arriving every day. Stunningly, the Indian Army had an additional three Corps of men waiting in India for transport, while tens of thousands of others were being trained for future deployments as needed.

All told, the Allies had moved upwards of 1.75 million troops, close to 7,000 tanks, 9,000 various types of armored carriers, and a stunning 25,000 trucks, jeeps, command cars and other sorts of motorized transports into their ever-expanding bridgeheads to face the Waffen-SS and its total of 750,000 troops and 4,300 tanks (of wildly varying quality). Balancing these numbers somewhat was the fact that the SS forces were fighting a defensive war, with access to many expertly prepared defensive fortifications, and the continued supports of close to 450,000 National Force troops whose governments were still apparently unwavering in their loyalty to the fascist cause.

Both sides had begun the war with years of stockpiled supplies and equipment. Much of that original stock was now gone, expended in the violence that had re-engulfed Europe; a situation that greatly advantaged the Allies, with their massive industrial capacity mainly untouched by enemy attack, compared to the conditions faced by the Reich, with many of its factories, even those relocated far into the new territories, damaged or destroyed by Allied air attacks.

Even the Allies, however, had begun to feel the pinch in materials, to the point that shipping returning from Europe with wounded or prisoners also carried massive amounts of spent brass and discarded or damaged-beyond-repair equipment ranging from tin cups to tanks to feed the enormous appetites of North America's factories. While there was not a "Shell Crisis", bottlenecks did exist, especially in the supply of new weapon types where no stockpile had been accumulated (this was most obvious in the slow trickle of the 280mm bombardment rockets that Allied commanders had begun to use in place of the gradually disappearing option of naval gunfire) or where weapons needed some sort of electronic parts (the availability of AIM-9 missiles was another notable concern to air planners). The lower production pace possible with the newest, most complex aircraft meant their replacement rate was also a fraction of that of their older, albeit far less capable, ancestors, with the result that losses were more seriously felt than in the earlier Bomber Offensive.

The Allies were, however, blessed with large numbers of very capable older designs that had been front line at the beginning of the war, and were, in the balance, still more than capable of completing their missions. This was perhaps best illustrated by the seemingly endless supply of F-86 Saber fighter bombers. The top fighter in early 1954, the F-86 had been surpassed by the F-101 and F-105, but the older jet was still an overmatch for most of the surviving Luftwaffe aircraft, and more than adequate in the ground support role where they were mainly found. The American and Canadian Air forces had entered the war with over 9,000 Sabers of different types; that number had been reduced by around 1,500 aircraft since the start of the war. Still, the 7,000+ remaining F-86s exceeded the combined total aircraft available to the Luftwaffe and its allied air forces (many of the remaining Axis aircraft were 1943-45 vintage Fw-190 and Ta-152 piston engine fighters), something that ensured Allied supremacy in the European skies.

These were the forces available to the combatants when the offensive began.

32

The day of October 24th dawned clear, if cold at 34 degrees Fahrenheit; conditions that provided the Allied air forces increasingly rare unlimited visibility for operations (the only exception was a ground mist that covered part of the Cotentin Peninsula in the early morning). It was what the SS enlisted ranks called "Jager weather", and the Allied fighter-bombers were out in maximum force to take advantage of it. Nearly half of the aircraft were from American National Guard squadrons, flying everything from F-8B fighters that had seen their first European skies in the days immediately preceding the Bombing Holiday to early-model F-86 and P-80 jets. Even with the addition of these American reserve squadrons and a half-dozen freshly arrived Indian Air Force squadrons equipped with Gloster Meteors (the first fruits of Gloster's Indian expansion plant), the overall coverage was less than during any of the Allied invasions. The Allies had chosen to attack on a series of fronts, the goal being to overwhelm the defenders remaining west of the German border.

Third Army, as the lead element of US 14th Army Group, was tasked with capturing Antwerp, Amsterdam, Brussels, much of the Netherlands, and cutting off the SS forces in the Jutland Peninsula before wheeling south into northwestern Germany. The US 15th Army Group, with the Canadian 1st Army as its van, would split away from the 14th near Brussels and proceed east with Liege as the initial objective; Aachen had already been designated as its entry point into Germany. The US 11th Army Group would be the reserve formation for both of these spearheads, and would then pass through the 14th for a drive across the northern German plain that would end, hopefully, in Berlin, although American planners had contingencies in place to continue east as far as Warsaw should the Nazi leadership fall back in that direction instead of making a stand in Berlin as expected.

The British/Commonwealth 21st and 22nd Army Groups were scheduled to break out of the area around Calais along a slightly southeast axis to Lorraine, before re-orientating due east to the German city of Stuttgart, moving on to Dresden and then heading towards Berlin. The 12th Army Group, centered on the British 1st Armored Division and Indian II Corps, would drive out of the neck of the Cotentin Peninsula along the 21st's flank, take Paris, and move to the Swiss border. Once there it would refit and move through Czechoslovakia into Austria.

The Allies' offensive anticipated that the remaining Axis powers (a group in which the Allies now included France, based on the ongoing resistance by the French National Army) would surrender with the destruction of Germany. If this failed to occur, the Allied planners had constructed a series of options that would end with France, Italy, and Romania overrun.

The decision to make Berlin a mainly American objective was controversial at the time and has remained so to this day. General Ridgway's personal journals hint at the political pressure he received to arrange for an "Allied force" to take the city. Ridgway, to his credit, resisted all pressure, to the point of offering his resignation, to any political changes to the operational planning. His mission was to destroy the Third Reich, crush its army, and extract unconditional surrender from its criminal leadership while holding Allied losses to as low a level as possible. Nothing would be allowed to interfere with this ultimate goal.

While the Allied planners had set cities as the objectives for each Army Group, the planners, looking to hold down Allied casualties to the maximum extent possible, had also decided that the cities themselves would not be entered if defended unless such an assault was unavoidable. Cities would be bypassed and cut off, much as the islands in the Pacific had been, with a force left behind to ensure that no enemy forces sallied forth to attack supply lines. The forces ringing the cities would be artillery heavy and would spend most days gradually shelling the cities into rubble until the end of the war or until either city and/or country surrendered. It was expected that few cities would actually attempt to become fortresses; Reich propaganda had already shown what the Allies did to fortress cities, while Allied propaganda had emphasized the relatively low damage to Cherbourg where local forces did not force the Allies to raze the city.

The first clue that the Allies had that things were not quite as expected came when the 29th Infantry, leading Third Army, encountered the Waffen-SS Mechelen Complex near Brussels. While the complex had been the subject of heavy bombing, the Allies fully expected that it would be necessary to detach a full division to keep the complex surrounded while it was reduced from the air. Instead, recon elements of the 29th encountered much lighter resistance than expected, with only around one emplacement in five firing, and most of these were returning fire at a volume far below that expected. When the 29th was detached, its commander was instructed to launch probes into the defenses while the rest of the 3rd Army advanced toward Antwerp and Brussels.

On the early morning of the 26th, as elements of Third Army entered the burning husks of Brussels and the destroyed city center of Antwerp, 1st Battalion 29th, under strong air cover, advanced against the Mechelen Complex. Within two hours they had gained entry; within four they had almost half the complex under control, the rest of the complex being protected by both heavily defended positions and intentionally collapsed corridors. Captured defenders were found to be Austrian conscripts with virtually no training. These prisoners readily informed their interrogators that their battalion had been in the complex for only a week, and there were only two companies of Waffen-SS troops within the tunnels. It was clear that the conscripts were far more frightened of the SS troops than the Americans because "those German fellows are quite mad".

The Reich had begun its long retreat.

33

The Allies were at first surprised, then encouraged by the suddenly reduced resistance by SS forces. This sense of elation lasted less than three days, to be replaced by puzzlement.

This was after the spearhead of the British 6th Armored Division had sprinted almost 20 miles on the 24th of October, making the single greatest one-day advance since the invasion, with almost no resistance. On the 27th, expecting to continue this advance against a broken opponent, the Northamptonshire Yeomanry Regiment set off at first light when they encountered a carefully-sited ambush, consisting of a half-dozen Panther IIIs in hull-down defilade and four of the fearsome 128mm DP guns that the Allies had previously only encountered in fixed fortifications and SS bunker complexes, in a wooded area near Riqueval.

Showing considerable discipline, the SS forces waited until the Yeomanry had closed to within 300 meters of the wood line before opening fire. In minutes the regiment had lost fourteen Centurions as well as eleven Bren Gun (Universal) carriers and eight Kangaroo APC (the Kangaroo, a development of a vehicle first created by Australian forces in Manchuria, used an older model tank chassis as a base for a remarkably versatile vehicle) to SS tank guns, 128mm guns, and Panzerfausts. Simply put, the Northamptonshire Yeomanry ceased to exist, taking over 85% casualties, with the 6th Armored advance stopped dead in its tracks. The balance of the day was spent combing out SS troopers from spider holes and out of tree stands, a costly task mainly assigned to the Royal Hussars who suffered some twelve KIA and 25 WIA before the small woods were declared secured. The eventual destruction of the four 128mm guns, their prime movers, and four of the six Panthers (three killed by RAF Hawker

Hunters as the tanks attempted to withdraw) was a poor payment on account.

The ambush outside of Riqueval was only the first of a series of similar costly fights between carefully hidden SS rearguard units and Allied forces across the entire Allied line of advance. Units would make huge gains, then suddenly, seemingly at random, find themselves in fights for their lives at the edge of a wooded area, on the main road leading through a village, or at a river ford. Allied losses multiplied, while losses to SS and French National units were far smaller, despite the fanatical nature of the fighting by these rear-guard units. This tactic of flexible defense centering on small, almost suicidal, units was an utter surprise to the Allied High Command: the first tactical surprise that the Waffen-SS, who before the October offensive had been almost embarrassingly easy to predict, had managed to spring on the Allied armies. Soon, the sprint out of the bridgeheads slowed to a slow walk, one punctuated by irregular, but at times overwhelming, violence.

This change in SS tactics has long been a subject of debate.. There has never been a "smoking gun" command document found that indicates that the withdrawing Waffen units were specifically ordered to change to the delaying tactics. Instead it seems to have been a case of "institutional memory" shared by SS officers and senior enlisted men who had fought in the closing days of the Barbarossa Campaign against the USSR, with these long-term veterans taking lessons learned from their communist enemy and turning them against the Allied spearheads. It marked an ominous change in SS behavior.

As puzzling to the Allies as the sudden appearance of the new rearguard tactics being employed by the SS was the irregularity of its application. For every SS platoon that fought to the death at a river ford, there was another that did nothing to actively oppose the advancing invaders, instead spending their efforts on almost random destruction. The poisoning of wells, destruction of bridges, and even the intentional demolition of stone structures to use as roadblocks all made perfect military sense to General Simonds and his Corps commanders. What made no sense to them at all was the use of demolition charges, fuel, and manpower to shatter statues, burn tapestries, defile churches, and execute village and town leaders, sometimes even the massacre of the entire population of small villages by retreating Waffen-SS units. The Allied senior command found itself confronted by an enemy who had, it seemed, gone completely mad, killing and burning almost at random.

This is perhaps best illustrated by the well-known mining of the Netherlands dikes. While this act did cause some discomfort to the advancing American Army, the devotion of close to an entire SS Panzer Grenadier division to the flooding of an almost totally unresisting region defies understanding, even decades after the senseless war crime. It has been speculated that the Nazis believed that the American Army would simply stop its attacks to aid the Dutch population. If this was the case – and no evidence that this was a consideration in the mining effort has ever been found – the Reich was to be sadly disappointed. While the Allies did provide considerable aid to the Dutch population, the effort was not allowed to delay the advance of 3rd Army by even an hour.

By November 14th, when the first of a series of winter storms swept across Northwest Europe, the Allies had settled into a steady, if costly advance that brought it ever closer to the Reich's borders.

Little did the commanders and politicians in London and Washington understand just how grave the war had already become.

34

The Allied surprise at the Waffen-SS withdrawal is indicative of the general limits of intelligence gathering during the final phase of the war. While able to read almost all Axis codes in near real-time and having almost unlimited ability to collect photographic images thanks to the U-2, the Allies still lacked the knowledge of day-to-day circumstances within Germany that would have so greatly eased their effort to defeat the Reich.

While some information was gleaned from prisoners recently arrived at the front, and through the efforts of diplomats in neutral states, along with some true nuggets that came through the Molotov government, Washington and London had no idea about the overall mood of the average Reich citizen. Before considering the events following the Allied October Offensive, a review of conditions in the Reich is worthwhile.

Modern readers, even casual students of 20th century history, often fail to realize the remarkably high standard of living enjoyed by the average German in the early 1950s.

After the end of the Allied bombing offensive in 1947, Inner Germany rapidly recovered from the remarkably widespread damage that RAF Lancasters and USAAF B-17 and 29s had visited on Germany. Fully half the conscripted labor provided by the Molotov government in 1948-52 was employed (in 20 hour days) on the reconstruction of German cities and infrastructure, with the result being fully rebuilt cities rising phoenix-like from the ashes of the Allied 1940-47 bombings. German citizens who did not fall afoul of the Gestapo, which to most Germans had become more of a bogeyman than an actual threat as dissent (and dissenters) disappeared from daily life, enjoyed full employment, seven weeks of paid vacation (ten weeks in the case of Party members) subsidized by the Reich Government, and free medical and dental care. The Reichsmark was the most powerful currency on the continent, allowing German travelers incredible purchasing power on their regular trips to France, Italy and the rest of Occupied Europe, and the Mark's strength continued into the neutral states of Portugal, Spain, Sweden, and Switzerland, where luxury items, including some products from the West unavailable within Occupied Europe, could be secured for the trip home. Through these shopping adventures the average Reich citizen was able to keep themselves well-supplied with otherwise-embargoed consumer goods, ranging from exotic spices from the East – and other foodstuffs, including oranges from Florida and avocados from California – to inexpensive appliances, with the Mark's buying power allowing the average hausfrau in Berlin to enjoy luxuries virtually unknown outside any other city in Europe except to the ruling elite. Even the average American family did not enjoy the leisure time, easy work life, and buying power that were common across Inner Germany.

The Reich citizen was constantly reminded of how good their life was by the Party-controlled media. Be it radio, films, or the new television, the media showed constant reminders of the innate superiority of the Aryan Race to all others. Cleverly written "news" programs and films showed the seething unrest rampant across the US, massive food riots in England, and open civil war across India. None of these were true, but with no independent source of information the Reich citizens did not know this. What they did know was that the Americans were gangsters, the British brutal colonizers, and that the Allied armies were gathered from the scum of the Earth. No Reich citizen doubted, even for a moment, that barbarism would descend on the entire world if the shining light of National Socialism was extinguished.

This life was surprisingly uninterrupted by the reigniting of the Hot War, at least for the first two years. Allied efforts to avoid civilian casualties, coupled with the Reich's decision to move much of their military-industrial production out of German cities and into the General Government areas, meant that, contrary to fears, German cities were not returned to rubble. Even military deaths were not far out of proportion to those suffered in the constant strife along the Eastern frontier. The only difference was more Party members found themselves receiving the telegram announcing the glorious sacrifice of a loved one in the name of the Führer as losses mounted in the air war (where many offspring of Party families had secured appointments in the far more glamorous Luftwaffe instead of the Waffen-SS). This seemingly easy war was brought to a close with the beginning of the Allied False Peak campaign.

False Peak strikes on rail transport resulted in more German civilian deaths, not to mention the massive increase in Waffen-SS casualties. For the first time since 1943, wounded young men, many with missing limbs, became a common sight in German cities. With the losses due to the Allied operations mounting, the call to colors came to ever-younger men, until most male students were mustered into the Waffen-SS within days of leaving secondary school. The reality of the war was also brought home as men who had completed their compulsory terms were recalled to duty.

Initially, these reservists were kept close to home, many serving in Luftwaffe AAA units within easy travel of their homes. This changed as the naval artillery of the RN and USN combined with the Allied air forces to chew one SS division after the next into pieces. Soon the younger reservists were headed to the frontline, with their places taken by girls from the Hitler Youth and recovered wounded who were no longer capable of full combat duty. By the time of the October Offensive there were few families within the Reich that did not have at least one family member directly in harm's way; frequently a house would have three, sometimes more, occupants who were absent from the table at dinner time.

Even with this, even with the ever increasing number of Allied air attacks and the absence of Luftwaffe aircraft in the skies, nearly everyone within the Reich still believed that the war was being won. News programs told of the destruction of entire fleets of enemy shipping by the Kriegsmarine, the elimination of hundreds of enemy aircraft in every attack, and the obliteration of enemy ground forces on every front.

Sacrifices had to be made: diversion of electricity to war industries, reduction – first in selection, then in quality, and even in quantity – of clothing, or appliances, and finally food, all made sense. Victory was never easy or without struggle, but it was also inevitable. Defeatists were to be reported to the authorities as traitors to the Volk, wreckers who would bring the mongrelized Armies of the West into the Fatherland out of their cowardice. This was the message that came from the media, the pulpit, and from teachers in school. After a quarter-century of Party rule, the average German simply accepted these statements as fact.

While some residents of the Occupied Countries had begun to realize that the Party had lied, that their local fascist leaders were actually the enemy, this had not occurred to one Reich citizen in fifty, with the few doubters mainly to be found in the new parts of the Reich (Austria, Sudetenland Germans, etc.) where the memories of the days before the Führer were not quite as bitter as within Deutschland. Even where the stray thought had bubbled up it was kept utterly secret. Allowing it to do otherwise resulted in denouncement by a neighbor, a knock on the door, and, if lucky, a quick bullet in the back of the head.

Germany was united behind the Party, either through devotion or fear. It would take more than a few bombs to change that.

35

The Reich had, of course, not suffered strategic surprise with the opening of the October Offensive, although surprise was achieved on the tactical level; especially by the British 21st Army Group, which had managed through carefully designed "failures in signals security" to convince local SS leaders that the main initial attack would come along the southern end of 21st Army Group's lines, where it would be supported by forces out of the Cotentin Peninsula rather than from the region just south of Calais as actually happened. There were simply too many SS and Gestapo agents left behind Allied lines, too many local citizens who, either for pay or out of dedication to the Fascist cause, were willing to pass messages through the Allied lines, and far too much radio traffic to hide the massing of the forces within the Allied lodgements. The way that Himmler and his deputies used the knowledge allows a window into the mindset of the German leaders' perspective, one that is especially interesting now that the morale of the average Reich citizen has been discussed.

Beginning on October 11, 1958, units of fortress troops all along the remnants of the Atlantic Wall began to receive movement orders. These forces, representing more than 60% of the men manning the surviving fortifications, were mostly withdrawn from the French Mediterranean coast, Italy, and the Balkan coastline. These troops, along with most of the Reich forces remaining in Norway, were moved by both rail and truck, generally at night in hopes of avoiding the ever-present threat of Allied air attack, into Germany and Austria proper. Once they arrived, these troops were either installed into existing fortifications along the Rhine or put to work extending the defensive belt that protected Inner Germany. While a few trains or truck convoys were attacked, with the usual bloody results, most were not. This was, in large part, due to the Allied air forces' need to prepare the battlefield and provide support for the ever-expanding ground forces while still maintaining the pressure on Axis (increasingly purely German) industrial sites. Train and truck convoys headed away from the war zone were simply not as high on the target lists as those moving toward the front lines or railways that were known to be supplying raw materials to the SS armaments factories. By the end of October, more than 125,000 men had been relocated. Remarkably, many of them had positions ready for their arrival.

One of the Allies' major errors in the fall of 1958 was underestimating the speed with which General Rommel could construct defenses. Provided with over 350,000 laborers, roughly half of them Russian slave workers (along with 50,000 other forced laborers moved from the General Government regions), Rommel could improve/rebuild nearly 20 miles of the border each day. SS requisition parties stripped France, Denmark, and Holland of building materials, along with many skilled tradesmen, and funneled all of it into Rommel's vast construction project. By early November the Inner German defensive perimeter, which had been mainly overgrown with weeds at the beginning of September, had been transformed into the strongest non-coastal fortification belt on Earth, with additional bunkers and tank traps appearing almost hourly.

Ridgway and his commanders, well-supplied with aerial photos of the work, made conscious decisions to allow the work to mainly continue unmolested, unwilling to be diverted from their offensive plans by "a bunch of poor bastards with shovels". The Allied air commanders were told that they should designate the construction work as a target of opportunity for aircraft returning from missions with unexpended ordnance, but that no specific attacks should be planned. Whether air power would have been able to stop the construction is an open question, but it is, however, beyond doubt that regular heavy attacks would have greatly retarded the work, albeit at heavy cost to the laborers.

It is interesting to note that the slave workers sent to work on the defenses, and thus mainly under the supervision of Rommel and several other recalled Heer officers, suffered a death rate far below that common across the Reich. There is even evidence that Rommel diverted supplies from regular civilian sources to increase the rations of "his" workers. This may account for the impressive construction effort put forth by the Rhine fort workers.

The Reich's recall of reserves has been noted earlier, but it is worth repeating here. Most of the transferred fortress troops were placed under the watchful command of Hitler Youth leaders, many of them as young as 15, who are almost universally described as "utter fanatics" by the foreign troops they commanded. These young men, some barely more than boys, were given the power of life and death over troops more than twice their age. It is often said that there is nothing more frightening than a teenager with an automatic weapon; this is even truer when the teen is a brainwashed madman. Though almost no records survive, it is estimated that over 5,000 foreign troops were summarily executed by their high school-aged commanders for offenses as minor as oversleeping.

While the main construction effort was underway along the Rhine, Himmler also had a "Final Redoubt" in the Alps revamped and provisioned (located along the Inner German border with the Austrian State). Himmler ordered that a complete duplicate of the Berlin command complex be created in the Redoubt so that it would be possible for "the Führer" to fight on even if Berlin was over-run. While his government was proclaiming that the Reich would stand for a thousand years, he was preparing a final bolt hole for himself. He had very good reason to do so.

On November 2nd, 1958, having been informed that the Alps complex was fully ready, Himmler issued Führer Order 720 to his Victory Forces as the first step in launching the Reich's counteroffensive.

36

As noted previously, Himmler committed his "Victory" forces to action on the 2nd of November 1958. The specific date has been a matter of great debate since the end of the war, but recent document discoveries in the archives of the French military have made this date as certain as the day of the St. Patrick's Day Raid or of D-Day. This, at last, proved the fallacy of the "Rome Myth".

After several months of negotiations, mainly held in Lisbon at the Portuguese Foreign Ministry building and in Madrid at the Presidential Palace, the Italian Government (without a trace of irony on either side) tendered its Unconditional Surrender to the "United Nations" on December 5th 1958. The announcement was followed almost immediately by arrival of heli-borne American and Brazilian forces just north of Rome (some units actually arrived while the press conference announcing the capitulation in London was still in Q and A), where they assumed blocking positions to ensure that SS forces did not attempt to retake the Italian capital. That this was an entirely unnecessary effort was not clear for some days; we now know that there were no Waffen-SS mobile forces within 200 kilometers of Rome on December 5, 1958. Within days, the Italian military had been almost entirely demobilized except for units along the country's heretofore friendly border with the Reich. It was these units, ironically supported by Allied airpower operating out of Sardinia, that blunted the attempt by the 57th SS Panzer Grenadiers to enter and occupy Italy before additional Allied forces (mainly Indian units diverted while transiting the Suez Canal and Red Sea, along with 3rd Brigade, 12th ANZAC Infantry Division which was moved from its garrison in Syria) arrived to reinforce the Brazilian/USMC forces already in country.

The Italian "Unconditional Surrender" was remarkable mainly for the generous terms granted to the Italian state. The peace deal effectively made Italy a junior member of the Allies under a "transitional government" nominally led by King Umberto II (the fascist government was immediately taken into Allied custody, and the true ruler of Italy was Lord Louis Mountbatten, the uncle of the British monarch and the Allied officer designated as military governor). Whether this arrangement would have worked absent the Reich's actions in the days following Italy's "treachery" is a very good question, albeit one that can never be properly answered.

It is unsurprising that, in the wake of Italy's dramatic departure from the Axis, Gestapo units, which had long been present in the background of all the "Axis" countries except Italy, became very visible; displacing, in most cases, the personal security detachments responsible for the wellbeing of each country's leadership and the leadership members' families. This ended the immediate threat of any further defections, although post-war records conclusively demonstrate that the only remaining occupied state in discussions with the Allies had been Denmark (the Allies having already entered the Netherlands, crushing the Dutch National forces in the process, made the discussions that had been underway with The Hague moot). Nevertheless, the deployment of Gestapo teams (elite Waffen-SS troops in all but name) by the Reich demonstrated exactly who controlled Europe.

If the remaining fascist satellite states had known what was about to be visited upon them, one can only wonder if even Gestapo killers would have been sufficient to keep them in line.

37

Himmler's order to deploy his "Victory" forces has long been the subject of intense debate within both military staff colleges and university Poli-Sci departments. Whether the de facto leader of the Third Reich believed that his country could defeat the far more powerful Allied forces on the battlefield has never been clear, nor is there much hope of ever reaching a definitive answer. It is, however, a virtual certainty that Himmler, like virtually all Nazi Party leaders at the time, firmly believed that the "Aryan Race" was morally and genetically superior to any other on Earth, and that the Reich could therefore turn defeat into victory by sheer will. This mindset is the only possible answer to the "Why?" that has haunted the West for nearly three full generations.

While the Allied nations had managed to harness the power of the atom, turning it into a weapon of massive devastation as well as an energy source beyond any other, had made great strides in electronics and had even created the early computer age, and could brag of a host of other scientific achievements, the Axis states had not been left entirely at the starting gate. The Allies had been rudely shocked by Luftwaffe weapons like the Fi 103 and A4 and by the early Type XXIV U-boats, but the Reich's greatest achievements were almost as great of a mystery to the Allies as nuclear weapons were to the Axis.

Reports of revolutionary German chemical weapons had managed to make their way to the West, almost entirely through the efforts of agents working for what had once been the Soviet Union, including small samples of several of the nerve agents that the Reich had developed. Western scientists had been impressed by the agents, although their actual utility on the battlefield was far from certain, at least in the minds of senior Allied officers.

The Allies also knew, in broad strokes, of the Imperial Japanese Army's efforts in biological warfare, but again thought it to be of very little use on the battlefield.

In these beliefs, as the Reich demonstrated, the Western leaders were both right and wrong.

What the Allied leadership had failed to realize was the amount of practical experimental evidence that the Reich had managed to acquire regarding the effects of both chemical and biological weapons. With a morally vacant leadership that was already engaged in the wholesale murder of entire ethnic groups, it was easy for Nazi researchers to extend their efforts in biochemical warfare far beyond the laboratory. The samples that had been carefully analyzed in American, Canadian, and British research centers had been gathered by GRU officers in the aftermath of small scale attacks using the agents along the Eastern frontier. The effectiveness of different distribution systems had been carefully documented, as had the tactical impact of the new chemicals on the battlefield. At least the Allies had some inkling of these efforts, although the scale of the testing, much of it in the General Government area, was not understood by Allied planners.

Even less understood by the Allies was the knowledge gained by the Reich in over a decade of utterly ghastly experiments that the Party, in a perversion of language almost as extreme as the perversion of the acts themselves, labeled "medical research". The details of these experiments are well beyond the scope of this work, but that they were useful to the Reich in planning the December Counteroffensive is quite clear (for an excellent, if sobering, review of the Nazi experiments, David Andersen's definitive work *The Devil's Apprentice: Josef Mengele and His Mad Quest for Knowledge* is highly recommended).

Contrary to the beliefs best typified by the "Rome myth", the Reich counter-offensive did not begin on December 11th, 1958, in reaction to the Italian surrender. It began on November 26th, just outside the French town of Coutances. It was here that the first smallpox-contaminated articles were left along the roadside. The decision to use dolls and other toys as the bait was both brilliant and evil in the extreme, as was the decision to spread typhus-infested vermin across the region. The Coutances area had fallen to Indian forces just days earlier, and the region was rife with refugees from the fighting. Over the next ten days, Allied medical officers were horrified to see a veritably Biblical series of plagues explode across Normandy. Allied medical units found themselves overrun with ill civilians, and rumors that the diseases were being brought into the region by the "foreigners" (interestingly, these tales were mostly not spread by Nazi agents but by local citizens) began. This belief was strengthened by the fact that almost no Allied troops fell ill, something that local citizens found to be "proof" that the Indian troops were carriers of the diseases while being immune to them. No volume of explanation that the troops were not falling ill simply because they had been vaccinated would suffice. Even the breakout of similar epidemics in the area controlled by 21st Army Group did nothing to reduce the surge of xenophobia. The only region mostly immune to the rumors was in the Low Countries, where Reich destruction of the North Sea dikes and subsequent flooding was given the blame for the epidemic outbreak.

What made things worse for the Allies was that the situation played perfectly into the propaganda that the Fascist governments had spread since the resumption of the Hot War. After hearing that the "enemy" would bring disease and destruction to their homes, spread by "mongrel races" for better than four years, the sudden appearance of numerous deadly illnesses, many unknown in the region for years, that coincided with the arrival of "Asians", it was easy for French civilians to put one and one together and come up with five. What had until then been a somewhat cautious perspective to the Allied advance rapidly became overtly suspicious and hostile. By the first week of December, many sick French civilians were fleeing from the Allied lines rather than seeking out assistance from the admittedly harried Indian and British medical units. This, of course, allowed the epidemics to spread ever wider, a situation that was exacerbated by the shocking number of unburied dead bodies in the areas beyond Allied control. Within Allied lines, most military efforts were reduced to the digging of mass graves, providing the maximum medical support to the populace, and dealing with a sudden low-level, but bothersome, insurgency movement

The sudden epidemics across France were suspicious to the Allies, but since the illnesses had no real military utility there was much doubt expressed when Reich involvement was first suggested. As the locations of the outbreaks grew, the chance of coincidence in their origin shrank, although naysayers remained. It was not until the Isle of Wight smallpox case was reported on December 10th that it was universally accepted in Western capitals that the Nazi regime had, for some inexplicable reason, contaminated portions of France, and were attempting to contaminate Britain, with highly infectious and quite lethal, although medically controllable, diseases.

What the Allied leaders did not understand, and was not clear until after the war, was that the Reich had fully expected that their efforts would indeed devastate Allied ground troops. The Nazis, not entirely unreasonably, had assumed that most of the troops of non-Anglo/American origin would not have received full vaccination regimens and that their formations would lack adequate medical staffing to deal with the epidemics which would surely sweep through their ranks. The Party gave scant concern to the welfare of most of the National forces and large segments of the civilian populations in the occupied countries, considering them to be little more than animated machinery, and assumed that the same would hold true for their enemies. Indeed, there is some evidence that Himmler was more surprised by the massive medical effort that the Allies made to help the local population than he was that the Allies had bothered to provide sufficient medical support to their "slave troops". This remarkably brutal worldview may provide one of the best windows into the depravity that was the Third Reich.

The overt phase of the Nazi counteroffensive was, while not a strategic surprise (Allied air reconnaissance had noted sufficient movement that there was little question that something was in the offing), quite well organized, especially when one considers the complexity of the operational plan and the crippling disadvantage that the SS had to work under.

Despite being under nearly constant observation from the air, the Reich forces managed to conceal the primary axis of their attack, move nearly 125,000 men, nearly half of them freshly recalled reservists, and considerable amounts of equipment into place (albeit with murderous losses to air attacks that claimed nearly 20% of the force while still in movement), and achieve tactical surprise. The SS effort was aided by the typical December weather over northwest Europe, which reduced daylight flying hours and dramatically limited visibility even during the remaining daylight. Allied efforts to use both radar and primitive thermal sensors to penetrate cloud cover were mainly failures, although the few successes provided considerable useful intelligence and accounted for much of the 20% losses suffered by the SS during movement.

The SS was also aided by the failure of Allied analysts to pick up on some indicators that might have allowed proper reinforcement along the SS axis of attack. The greatest of the failures was, of course, the "ox cart gap". Criticism of failures by Allied photo analysts to recognize the marked increase of draft animals in photos as being highly indicative of an army on the march can, to a degree, be forgiven or at least explained by cultural expectations. No large Allied formation would have even imagined making a serious movement using horse-drawn supply wagons and artillery; that was something for a different era, or so the basic belief at SACEUR went. Yet this was exactly what the SS did, achieving well over half of its movement with draft animals, including the movement of most light and medium artillery pieces using this ancient, yet effective, method (interestingly, the SS fully expected the large increase in draft animals to be noticed, to the point that considerable effort was expended in moving decoy herds in other areas behind the front and scattering various farming implements near supply dumps).

The attack itself, which began well before dawn on December 16th, took place near the "seam" between the US 15th Army Group and the Commonwealth 21st Army Group somewhat south of the Belgian capital. Designed to be a double envelopment, the attack plan recalled the heady days of 1941 and Barbarossa (considerable evidence exists that many retired Heer officers, as well as the few remaining senior staff officers who were on active duty with the Waffen-SS, were consulted regarding the attack overview, if not directly involved with the actual attack plan), but without the veritable sea of reserves that were available to the Heer when it entered Russia. The plan was to split the Allied forces by nationality and inflict maximum casualties on American ground forces while holding the British forces at bay.

An interesting part of the plan is that the Nazi leadership believed, even at this late date, that it was possible to drive the Americans out of the war by inflicting losses, thereby leaving the Reich facing only the British (with Himmler believing that he had checkmated the 'English'). It is remarkable that any nation's leaders could cling to a fantasy for nearly three decades, but it seems that the Nazis managed to do so. History shows just how severe the misread was.

The SS opened its attack with a brief, if surprisingly powerful, artillery barrage against the famed 5th Marine regiment. While the Marines were scrambling for cover, the SS unleashed its Nebelwerfer rocket batteries, with the first rounds fired at 06:35 local time. It was the first time that the "screaming Mimis" were used in their intended role since the invasion. All Allied troops had landed with a gas mask and two "gap pencil" injectors; they were among the first items that every infantryman discarded after crossing the beach. Within five minutes almost the entire strength of 2nd Batt. 5th Marines were dead; the first Allied combat deaths from nerve gas. They soon had a great deal of company as additional Nebelwerfer batteries opened up along a four-mile wide front. By 08:00 the 5th Marine front simply collapsed, and with it, the southern flank of the 15th Army Group. As the sun came up, the Luftwaffe made its first large-scale appearance since D-Day, increasing the disorder behind the Allied lines.

Specially-equipped units of 32nd SS Panzer rapidly punched through the disrupted 5th Marine lines and headed into the Allied rear area, rapidly spreading panic among the rear area service forces. The Allied response was almost immediate, if initially unorganized.

Contrary to the expectations of the SS leadership, there was no massive flight by the American troops even in the face of the sudden attack. After the initial, understandable, panic, American rear area troops, supported by units of the 62nd Highlanders which were moved from the neighboring 21st Army Group, began to show commendable resistance to the advancing 32nd SS. At the same time, Allied air assets began to pour into the area from as far away as Iceland.

Himmler's 'Victory Offensive' was underway.

38

The SS command was, if nothing else, observant. They had expected that the Allies would surge to the point of the breakthrough, especially with all the tactical airpower that it could muster. The Allies performed exactly to expectations. The air defenses for the British Isles were virtually abandoned in the rush to stop the SS onslaught.

At 10:00 hours local, in response to a code word transmitted three hours previously, six type XXXII U-boats surfaced in the English Channel fifteen miles off the British coast. The six subs were the survivors of an 18-boat squadron that had left Bremen on November 26th. The remaining subs had fallen victim to mines, patrolling RN warships and aircraft, and various mechanical difficulties en route to their patrol area. The subs had been specifically forbidden to attack any enemy vessel or take any action that would expose their existence to the Allies before completing their primary mission.

The Type XXXII U-boat was the next logical step in submarine design as a weapon system. While the American navy had followed the path of improving the existing breed by marrying the limitless power of the atom to the stealth that a submarine provided, thereby creating the ultimate hunter, the Kriegsmarine had gone in a different direction, and chosen to make a more versatile killer. Each of the U-boats carried six short-range A-12 ballistic missiles, with a maximum range of 120 miles, in their greatly lengthened sail. The A-12 was given an initial launch by compressed air sufficient to push the missile sixty feet into the air, at which point the missile's solid rocket booster would fire, accelerating the missile to 1,800 MPH and a height of roughly 250,000 feet before tipping over and making a terminal dive.

There was virtually no defense against the missile itself thanks to its great speed, small warhead size, and a short window of exposure between missile launch and arrival at the target.

Primitive by modern standards, the A-12 lacked any sort of sophisticated guidance system and had a payload of only 450 kilograms. The A-12 had similar performance to the US Army's MGM-3, but it entered service a full two years before the Lance missile was ready for production. It had been designed specifically to carry a cluster bomb unit warhead, with each bomblet containing 1.5 liters of Tabun nerve gas. While a finicky weapon, the rocket's warhead could, under ideal conditions, spread Tabun over a four-square kilometer area (an area smaller than the circular probability of impact point for the weapon itself). A true "area" weapon, it was the first of what are now called Weapons of Mass Destruction (or Terror) to be used in combat.

The German plan was to attack Allied air bases, ports, and supply depots across the Channel Coast of England and Scotland, along with a separate strike against USAF bases in Iceland. Unfortunately for the Reich, the two U-boats tasked with the Iceland attack were lost en route by unknown causes, along with ten of their sisters. The remaining boats still represented a significant strike force, although the goal of crippling the Allied air forces was lost along with the twelve submarines. This fact was, however, unknown to Himmler and his advisors due to the strict radio silence imposed on the U-boat crews.

The Kriegsmarine boats all had the same orders. They had taken submerged positions near known locations (mainly RN navigation buoys, but also some easily identified coastline landmarks) and awaited the code word that would launch the attack. Once the order was received the subs surfaced and began the process of launching their missiles, something that took at least five minutes (or an eternity to the sub crews as they bobbed exposed and defenseless within view of the enemy coast). One boat, the U-3357, had the almost unimaginably bad luck to surface directly in the path of an RAF Canberra returning from a strike mission over Belgium and was promptly chopped to pieces by the aircraft's 20mm cannon. The other five subs were far more fortunate and managed to successfully launch a total of 21 A-12 missiles (four weapons failed to launch, and five failed to ignite after a successful initial launch). In no case did the total flight time exceed 10 minutes from launch to target.

It was at this point that random chance began to enter the situation. One missile intended for the Edinburgh docks failed to have proper warhead separation, with the entire weapon ending up in a marsh, causing a high level of localized toxicity but no direct human casualties, while the second weapon went long by nearly five miles, hitting the village of Burntisland on the far side of the bay. Here the warhead performed almost perfectly, resulting in the death of more than 800 residents of the small municipality. The remaining three missiles from U-3365 (one having failed to launch) were supposed to hit a USAF base near Dumbarton; instead all three released their warhead over northern Glasgow, resulting in the deaths of 2,652 civilians.

All four successful launches from U-3352 reached their intended target, the RAF station at Blyton, which was shared by the RAF and the 558th Bombardment Group (B-66s). Here casualties were almost all military personnel and proved to be crippling for the 558th, which lost nearly half of its ground echelon, including flight line mechanics. The five missiles meant for Plymouth managed to hit virtually nothing, mainly killing farm animals and a few unlucky herdsmen. U-3351 had the fewest successful launches, with just three missiles performing as designed, but all three reached their target: RAF Brenzett (Ivychurch), home of three CAF F-86 squadrons. The missiles caught 28 aircraft on the ground while being refueled and rearmed, resulting in the loss of 22 pilots and most of the unit's ground support staff.

It fell to U-3361 to make the "glamor" strike: the attack on London. Supposedly ordered as retaliation for RAF strikes on Berlin in the war's opening weeks, it seems that this strike was meant to drive the British from the war, much as the SS attack against 15th Army Group was designed to cause the United States to blink. Considering the history of London's residents' reaction to air raids, Himmler's confidence that the use of Tabun would be enough to break the spirit of the entire British Empire can be best described as misplaced. Still, one can only imagine that the Nazi leader would have been delighted at the casualties caused by the attack. Almost 11,000 Londoners died in the missile attack, which dispersed almost 3,500 pounds of nerve gas across most of the British capital; casualties included three members of Her Majesty's Government, the seniormost being the Chancellor of the Exchequer, who was killed, along with his senior deputy, by a piece of a missile body when it crashed to Earth.

Remarkably, the Reich's surprises on that day had not yet ended. The Fi 362 (the direct descendant of the V-1 and bigger brother of the missiles that had nearly destroyed one of the Mulberries in June) had been designed for use as a "stand-off" missile for the Ju-688 and other large Luftwaffe bombers, but the virtual annihilation of the Luftwaffe bomber force had forced the designers to come up with an alternate use for the missile. With some effort (and the addition of an unmanned pulse jet "mother" aircraft that bore a striking resemblance to the V-1 and lofted the missile to 22,000 feet), Fieseler engineers had saved the Fi 362 from oblivion, inventing the cruise missile in the process. Liquid fueled, the Fi 362 had a range of over 250 miles and could reach a top speed of Mach 3.5 at 58,000 feet (but not if it was fired at maximum range). Originally meant to carry a 2,000-kilogram conventional warhead, the weapon was instead equipped with a larger version of the CBU dispenser used on the A-12. An exceptionally difficult weapon to manufacture, the Luftwaffe had only managed to acquire sixteen of the missiles before the Fieseler Company's Ukrainian factory (and most of Fieseler's design staff) had been destroyed by a B-52 attack in January of 1958. The December attacks were the weapon's combat debut.

The pettiness of the Nazi leadership, as well as their remarkable lack of strategic vision, may have reached its zenith with the targeting of the Fi 362 missiles. A remarkable weapon, in many ways years ahead of its Allied counterparts, the missiles should have been used only against the most valuable of targets. Instead, at the direct orders of the acting Führer, only six Fi 362 were targeted against useful military targets (three at Bristol Docks, and the remaining three at bases in Berkshire, including Combermere

Barracks), with the remaining ten weapons being targeted against Genoa, Florence, and Rome (there is some evidence indicating that all that spared the already devastated Belgian capital of Brussels from a nerve gas attack was difficulties in arranging to transport the Fieselers to Northern Europe in time to make the attack on 12 December; these were the weapons that eventually targeted southern England).

The Fi 362 missiles were supposed to be launched at the same time as the A-12s from the Channel. Due to an error in communication, the ground launches were made almost twelve minutes after the A-12 strikes. This brief delay allowed USS *Boston*, which had just gone to General Quarters in the wake of the multiple missile attacks, to make the sole interception of a Fi 362 on December 12th with a Talos missile. Of the remaining fifteen Fi 362s (five fired from Brest, four fired from outside Nice, and six, all directed against Rome, fired from a hastily-built launch site on the Croatian coast), eleven reached their general target area and distributed their payload. Both missiles targeted at Milan struck near the city center, resulting in 13,000 civilian casualties, while one of the two missiles directed at Florence reached close to the city center and scattered its bomblets there (the second missile directed at Florence struck the edge of the urban area), with both missiles accounting for over 5,000 casualties. The six missiles fired at Rome scattered devastation across central Italy, with only two of the warheads reaching Rome proper. Italian civilian casualties from the missiles fired from the Balkans exceeded 19,000.

It is, of course, the six missiles that were launched at England that were to have the greatest impact on the war. Five of these weapons made landfall over England, with two of three reaching their general aimpoint near Bristol's busy port facilities. These two weapons caused some five thousand total casualties (thankfully much of the nerve agent was swept away by rainfall before it could reach most of the civilian population's air raid shelters). The remaining three missiles, all targeted at Berkshire military installations, all missed their primary targets: two scattered their bomblets over farmland, while the third, of course, killed HRH Charles, the ten-year-old Prince of Wales, HRH Anne, the

Princess Royal, and Queen Elizabeth, The Queen Mother, who were in residence at Windsor Castle when the attack took place.

The missile that killed the sovereign's son (and heir), daughter, and mother, was by all evidence not meant to kill members of the Royal Family. Even the Nazi leadership was not so detached from reality as to intentionally attack two of the most famous children in the English-speaking world and their much-loved grandmother intentionally. It seems that the actual target was the barracks of the Household Division and the roughly 5,000 men based there. Whatever the intention, the results were simply a catastrophe of the highest order for the Third Reich.

39

The initial Allied reaction to the massive chemical attack by Germany was, understandably, shock. The 'Chemical Weapon Ban' had been the one major "laws of war" agreements that had come out of World War One that had, in general, been observed during the entire European Phase of the War, and had even been observed by the Japanese Empire despite that unfortunate nation's overall disdain for internationally accepted behavior during the Pacific Phase. Worse, the Nazis had used the weapons not just against troops in the field, but against civilian populations in what the Allies assumed to be an indiscriminate manner.

Following the shock was a closely related feeling of horror. As bad as the virtual obliteration of the entire 5th Marine Regiment, along with most of the 1st Battalion 8th Marines (a casualty list that eventually included POTUS Kennedy's youngest brother Captain Edward Kennedy as well as Michael Morrison, the eldest son of actor John Wayne, although the death of the youngest Kennedy brother was not confirmed for nearly a week after the attacks), might have appeared, it was the images of some of the better than 50,000 civilians who died in the attacks that caused the greatest reaction by audiences around the world. The utter feeling of revulsion towards the Nazis, and by extension every resident of an Axis country, while quite understandable, also provided the Allied civilian leadership with a political blank check. Indeed, it has only been in the last 20 years that any level of criticism of the Allied reaction to the "December Massacre" has made its way into public debate.

Ironically, Himmler's offensive came remarkably close to achieving its main goal of splitting the Allies, although not in the manner the acting Führer or his advisors imagined. While the specifics of the debate are still unavailable (three separate FOI requests by the author for access to the US Government's archives on the matter were refused on the grounds of "National Security" and all UK records are sealed under the National Secrets Act and unavailable until 2135) it is known that the American suggestions of restraint were met with something close to apoplectic rage by the Prime Minister, who (according to witnesses) had to be physically restrained from bodily throwing Secretary of State Fulbright out of his office when a "cooling off period" was recommended. At no point in the last 70 years was the famed "special relationship" closer to divorce than the morning of December 13th, 1958.

It was, by all accounts, the former British Prime Minister Winston Churchill (who was in North America, making one of his regular visits as Her Majesty's Special Representative/ Ambassador Without Portfolio to Washington and Ottawa) who tipped the scales in Britain's favor within the Kennedy Administration. Churchill, as he had for two decades and three Administrations, masterfully presented HM Government's position to the American President. Joe Kennedy, and perhaps more importantly his brother Jack, were known to be massively impressed by Churchill and the role he had played in shepherding England through the dark days after the Fall of France (something that was said to greatly upset their father, the former US Ambassador to the Court of St. James), and were predisposed to be receptive to the former Prime Minister's arguments.

Churchill's job was greatly eased by the Reich's actions in the immediate aftermath of the attacks. Rather than even feign contrition for the deaths of the young Prince of Wales and his even younger sister, the Princess Royal, Himmler allowed himself to be broadcast on German television stating that their deaths, and the deaths of the other victims of the nerve gas attacks, were entirely the fault of the British and American governments, that the only way to avoid even more damaging and widespread attacks was for the Allies to withdraw from Europe entirely and for the "traitorous cowards who betrayed Italy" to be handed over to the Reich for trial and execution. This was, of course, the same broadcast where Joseph Goebbels announced that the Allied nations would be expected to pay, in gold, a thirty billion pound indemnity to the Reich for damages caused since March of 1954, payable over a period of 10 years, as part of the price of obtaining the Reich's agreement to end hostilities (other requirements included the end of the naval blockade, return of all Axis nation colonies in Africa and Asia to the control of "Greater Germany", and below-market access to a long list of commodities for a twenty year period "to make good the improper treatment of the Third Reich by the English speaking nations"). Coming just 18 hours after the attacks, the speeches were effectively a demand for Allied Surrender.

It fell to President Kennedy to give the Allied response.

> *The United Nations call upon the German Government to:*
>
> *Eliminate for all time the authority and influence of those who have deceived and misled the people of Germany into embarking on world conquest.*
>
> *Order and ensure that all German and allied military forces be completely and immediately disarmed.*
>
> *In return, Germany shall be permitted to maintain such industries as will sustain her economy and permit the exaction of just reparations in kind.*
>
> *We call upon the government of Germany to proclaim now the unconditional surrender of all German and allied armed forces and to provide proper and adequate assurances of their good faith in such action. The alternative for Germany is prompt and utter destruction.*
>
> *Failure to accept these requirements in their entirety by Noon, Berlin Time, December 16th, 1958 will result in the unleashing of destructive forces upon Germany and her Allied states such as the world has never witnessed.*

The die had been cast.

40

The Allied response began well before the deadline on bases within 30 miles of London and as far away as North America. The somber (and often enraged) aircrews were each given a flyer when entering the briefing rooms that the crews immediately began to call the "Get out of Jail Free Card". The flyer informed the men that the operation about to be briefed involved direct attacks against civilian targets that were certain to involve non-combatant fatalities. The flyers also stated that the Judge Advocate General of their respective service branch had ruled that the operation conformed to all existing international and national laws (the validity of this pronouncement remains a subject of intense debate to this day) and constituted a valid order. The flyer finished with a unique option: "Any crewmember who believes that their personal moral code prohibits taking part in this operation may request to be excluded from this mission. Any such request will be honored and will have NO IMPACT on the crewmember's military career" (A full reproduction of this flyer can be found in appendix B). A similar, although differently worded, document was also provided to members of ship's companies (also reproduced in appendix B).

The flyers had been proposed by members of the US military well before the December attacks, dating back to the wake of the Pacific Phase. That such a document had even been seriously discussed, much less produced in bulk, is perhaps the most revealing window into the collective military psyche of the Allies after the reduction of Japan. Senior mission planners had anticipated that as much as a third of aircrews might opt out of attacks against civilian targets; however, in the wake of the Sarin and Tabun attacks against London, the opt-out rate was below

1%. Revulsion, it seemed, had its limitations. One can only wonder how many of the RAF crews later reconsidered their decision.

The overall strike was, from a purely organizational perspective, brilliant. It combined strikes by disparate types of aircraft spread across three continents and warships in two separate bodies of water into a single massive attack which struck across all of Continental Europe within a 90-minute period. Even considering that the basic outline of the plan had been in place for several years and regularly updated, the success of the plan is a testament to the professionalism of the men and women who designed it.

Interestingly, it was not a Reich city that was the first to feel the wrath of the Allies: that unfortunate distinction belongs to Brest. At 04:12 hours local time USS *New Hampshire*, sailing 8 miles off the coast of France, fired two ranging shots from her Number 1 turret. These were followed at 04:14 hours by a single W-23 special munition from the # 1 gun of her Number 2 turret, and then followed 1:30 later by a second round fired from the #3 gun of the same turret. Flight time was 65 seconds, with the first weapon detonating nominally at 4,900 feet over Bellvue (the calculated origin point of the Fi 362s that had wreaked havoc in Bristol and Berkshire) and the second weapon detonating approximately 300 yards east of the first weapon. The Luftwaffe unit responsible for the launch was literally obliterated in this counter strike. Unfortunately, the launch site was just a half a kilometer from the residential districts of Brest; the site selection a result of Luftwaffe observations regarding Allied targeting of residential areas.

The detonation of the weapons devastated Brest, with the main destructive agent being fire. An estimated 29,000 individuals died within 30 minutes of the weapon's detonation. It was just the beginning.

USAF F-105 fighter-bombers struck at SS Bunker complexes outside of Paris and Saint-Etienne in France and Bremen and Kiel within Germany proper. These strikes, flown at virtual rooftop height in near-total darkness, were supported by very heavy jamming and chaff (interestingly, the actual bombing was done by two-man fighter-bombers, with jamming support and chaff delivery provided by a squadron of B-47 bombers, four bombers supporting each two-plane F-105 element). The German cities of Bonn, Frankfurt am Main, and Hamburg were all directly targeted by USAF bombers (the latter two cities by pairs of B-58 supersonic bombers) with each city receiving two bombs; Bonn and Cologne were each destroyed by two AMG-28 supersonic stand-off missiles launched from B-52 bombers over the Baltic Sea. At virtually the same time as the USAF strikes, US Navy Vigilantes (four of which had been specifically assigned to USS *Coral Sea* to conduct any "special munitions assignments") struck at the primary SS command complex for southern France in the city of Aix-en-Provence and the SS bunker complex just outside of Nice. Overall US losses were five aircraft (one escort F-101, two F-105, one B-47 and one B-58), none of them still carrying a nuclear weapon when lost.

French fatalities from the strikes were mercifully low, at just under 180,000, mainly due to the concentration on SS positions located several miles outside of the closest cities. German losses, especially in Hamburg and Cologne, were far higher, with Cologne's weapon alone estimated to have claimed 177,000 lives solely from immediate weapon effects. Even with the relatively low casualty figures suffered in the French strikes, the combined, long-term casualties from the American strikes have been estimated at between 1.5 and 2.5 million people. Remarkably, the Americans were, in many ways, just the opening act.

The British decision to strike Germany with every weapon at its disposal has been controversial from the day it was made. While it is easy to look back at the events with half a century of perspective and say that Whitehall went too far, one needs to recall that more than 20,000 civilian residents of Britain (including the Prince of Wales) had been killed less than four days earlier, with tens of thousands of others injured (many of these permanently disabled, although this was not known to British leaders at the time). Given these realities the dramatic (over)reaction of the UK is far easier to understand.

RAF strikes included nuclear strikes against SS bunker complexes near Bourges and Strasbourg and direct population strikes at Stuttgart and Munich. The vast majority of the RAF effort, however, was dedicated to "Operation Whirlwind".

The need for massed formations was one reason that the RAF strikes against Nuremberg and Berlin were the final events in the Allied 90-minute dance of destruction over Europe. German air defenses and civil defenses were in utter ruins by the time the first Vulcans and their CF-101 fighter escorts reached their targets. In all, the Vulcans and Victors dropped over 300,000 pounds of anthrax-laden bombs over metropolitan Berlin and Nuremberg and almost 400,000 anthrax-laced "cattle cake" bomblets over the agricultural areas outside of Munich.

The RAF nuclear strikes were responsible for an estimated 90,000 French civilian casualties and nearly 600,000 German civilian deaths. The total casualties from the anthrax strikes have yet to be calculated, the process being complicated by the continuing deaths in the contaminated regions of what were once the Reich's centers of power and food production.

Collectively the Allied attacks resulted in well over three million human deaths from a single morning's work.

This foul task completed, the Allies waited for the Reich to simply collapse. Unfortunately, to the horror of many in the Allied command structure, the critics who had questioned if even a dozen burned-out cities would be enough to force the Reich to surrender had been correct. A few million bodies were not going to be sufficient to eliminate the Third Reich.

On December 23rd two B-58s destroyed the Kriegsmarine base at Sevastopol in the General Government Area, while RAF Vulcans struck the Piesteritz GmbH Chemical Works on the outskirts of Lutherstadt Wittenberg, Bayer AG chemical works near Leverkusen, and the Hoechst AG works outside of Hoechst (where, ironically, refugees from the December 19th Frankfurt strike had gone for "safety"). US Navy A-5 strike bombers attacked what was believed to be the base of the Luftwaffe unit that had attacked Milan. This targeting was, unfortunately, in error, and the site destroyed was under the control of the French National Air Force. The actual launch site was roughly a dozen miles inland from the attack's target location. It is believed that the Luftwaffe forces responsible for the Milan/Florence attacks escaped this raid, which did, however, destroy over 40% of Nice and killed in excess of 65,000 residents of the city.

On December 27th, the Swedish Foreign Minister delivered separate letters to the U.S and British Ambassadors from the Governments of Denmark, France, and Romania. Both the Romanian and Danish letters were, effectively, surrenders, in that they pledged that their national forces would not oppose Allied forces once their territories had been entered. The letters from both countries stated that "for obvious reasons" no public announcement of their capitulation would be forthcoming. The French government's letter, unlike those from the other Occupied States, was defiant and was signed by the French Vice-President as the President was unavailable (having been executed by Gestapo agents the previous day, something not known to the Allies until much later).

From Germany itself came no communication at all.

Further efforts would be needed.

41

It is hard to determine who was more stunned by the Anglo-American public unveiling of the atom bomb – the Axis leadership, the leadership of the United Nation countries what had not been party to what has to be counted as one of the few truly "secret" weapons of modern times, or the civilian populations of the UK and US. What is clear, however, is that no one was more shocked by the Reich's decision to continue on in the face of what, to this day, is considered to be the "ultimate weapon" than the same men who had, with great reluctance in many cases, released the pale horse upon the Earth. While the British leadership had demanded a robust response to the nerve gas attacks against England, and had even, despite strenuous protests from the Americans, made good on the threat that had been issued by PM Churchill regarding retaliation in case of German use of chemical weapons against the UK, it is clear (despite the enduring inaccessibility of the official records) that no one in Her Majesty's Government imagined that the Nazis would do anything except rapidly collapse in the hours after the December 16th attacks.

What the American and British leadership had failed to understand was that, in many ways, all a nuclear weapon does is make a bigger boom than more conventional bombs (this was particularly true from the Nazis' perspective, given the near total absence of information regarding the effects of fallout available to the Reich). Each of the cities destroyed in the attacks of December 16th and 23rd had been mostly demolished by Allied bombers between 1940 and the beginning of the 1947 Bombing Holiday. The RAF/USAAF bombing offensive of the 1940s had killed over 900,000 civilian Reich citizens while maiming or orphaning many times that number (some estimates put the total toll, including casualties in the Occupied Countries, at well over one million dead) while destroying 1,300 years of Germanic cultural treasures. Seeing major cities immolated by "English" bombers was nothing new.

Even more critically, the Nazi leadership, from Himmler down, had grown almost immune to shock at huge casualty figures. These were men who had, with ghastly efficiency, virtually obliterated the entire Jewish and Roma population of Europe (save those few survivors given refuge in Italy, Finland, and the neutral countries), depopulated Poland and much of Western Ukraine, and had routinely worked between 700,000 and 2,000,000 slave laborers to death annually beginning in 1942. There is no documentary evidence that any of the Party's leaders ever lost a moment's sleep over the killing of at least 50,000,000 human beings. Considering these disturbing facts, the ability of the Nazi leadership to remain unperturbed by two or three million deaths from the Allied counterstrikes is much less of a surprise.

What was also not fully understood by the Allied leadership was that the Reich had, with the events of December 16th, effectively shot its bolt. Unlike the Allies, especially the US, who had, even by modern standards, a frighteningly large inventory of nuclear weapons and the ability to produce more on an industrial scale (indeed, American bomb builders produced 15 nuclear weapons in December of 1958; of these, nine were manufactured after the Nazi nerve gas attack), the Reich leadership had gambled everything on single massive strike that had utilized virtually the Reich's entire long-range strategic inventory. While considerable amounts of nerve agent remained available, the Reich had only regular attack aircraft, artillery shells, and chemical mortar rounds left to carry them. These weapons posed a serious risk to Allied front line troops and to civilians in the still-occupied portions of western Europe, but the chances of a second successful attack against British population centers were, at best, dismal. Had this been understood by SACEUR Ridgway and his Air and Ground deputies or by the political leadership of the de facto nuclear powers (Australia, Canada, Great Britain, and the United States) it is possible, even likely, that the attacks of December

23rd would not have occurred, or if they did proceed, would have been somewhat less general in nature.

While the reaction of the Party leadership to the overwhelming Allied response to the December Massacre is, after analysis, not especially shocking, the rather blasé acceptance of the situation by the average German is. What is frankly incomprehensible to this day is how little the support for the Party was shaken in the first days after the Allied attacks. This is, in part, thanks to the remarkably effective media campaign waged by Joseph Goebbels in the immediate aftermath of the attacks and to the ability of the Gestapo to stifle any sort of rumors, at least initially. However, even after the true nature and horrific power of the Allied nuclear strikes became widely known, a stunning percentage of Reich citizens seem to have accepted the attacks as just another part of fighting a war that they were certain the Reich would win. Analyzing this reaction goes far beyond the scope of this volume. Indeed it is beyond the scope of an entire book, but that it existed, and deeply, is without question. This almost blind belief in the Führer (who was, by this time, in what is now known as a persistent vegetative state and kept alive with the assistance of a ventilator) and his ability to save the Volk was to bear the bitterest of fruits.

(For those readers wishing to delve into the physiology of this phenomenon, the difficult to find, but meticulously researched and written *Hitler's Aura, the Beguiling of a Nation* by Professor Adrian Nguyen Ph.D, MD published by University of California Press is recommended as a starting point.)

42

Often overshadowed by the truly apocalyptic events that coincide with it, the actual combat surrounding the rupturing of the Allied front on December 12th represents some of the most dramatic and insightful actions of the entire land campaign. Featuring as they do the one great role reversal of the entire war, with the Waffen-SS in full attack mode and the Allies scrambling to defend against a shattering reversal, the actions allow one to contrast the differences between the two opponents with each assuming the other's usual role.

When looking at the Waffen-SS attack, both in its plan and its execution, it becomes rapidly apparent that the Allies were quite fortunate that their battlefield preparations were as effective as they were in crippling the SS ability to mount immediate counter-attacks against any of the beachheads. The SS in attack was an utterly different creature to the same forces on the defensive.

On defense, the SS relied on strategies that were effectively unaltered from 1941 and that relied almost exclusively on the enemy both being willing to play according to the German rulebook and being casualty-averse. When these conditions did not exist, particularly in the absence of Luftwaffe support, SS doctrine left their formations vulnerable to overwhelming firepower and the enemy's ability to maneuver almost unopposed away from designated "fortresses". Frontline SS units, when cut-off from support that usually was fatally dependent on Reich ability to rapidly move forces across interior lines of communication via rail, were quickly reduced to a series of immensely savage, fanatically-fought yet inevitably futile "to the last cartridge" defensive stands. These were so predictable that Allied planners, just a few months into the land war, had begun to factor them into operational plans, to the degree that offensive plans were timed to allow concentration of air assets to crush the expected final "turtle shell" defensive position that SS forces seemed to consider the only option when a major position was about to be lost. It seems to have never occurred to the SS High Command that this mentality allowed the Allies to use tactics that had been perfected during the bloody advance across the Pacific against another utterly fanatical, immensely brave, but ultimately annihilated opponent.

On the offensive, however, the Waffen-SS troops were, if not breathtakingly innovative, both aggressive and adaptive. After breaking through the 5th Marine lines the 7th SS Panzer, 32nd SS Panzer, 47th SS Panzer Grenadier, and 7th Luftwaffe divisions made a rapid advance that put their lead elements almost 12 miles into the American rear areas before Allied resistance even began to coalesce into something approaching a reasonable speed bump. At the same time 47th SS Panzer Grenadier and 7th Luftwaffe Grenadier altered their initial line of attack and tore into the now-anchorless flanks of the 8th Australian Armored Division, rolling up the 2/26 Queensland Battalion and driving into the 2/30 Tasmanian Battalion as the 27th Brigade found itself utterly outflanked and outnumbered on the order of 9:1. With the Luftwaffe throwing almost its entire remaining strength into the air, the American and RAAF units assigned to provide air cover for the 2nd Marine Division and the adjoining Australians found themselves outnumbered and fighting for their own survival, entirely incapable of altering conditions on the ground.

By 11:30 hours the Axis forces had pushed close to 500 tanks and assault guns into the ever-widening gap and had begun to overrun Marine and Australian divisional headquarters areas. The overrunning of 2nd Marine Division's HQ led, of course, to the infamous Halle Massacre when the 2nd Medical Battalion's facility was, inexplicably, targeted by SS Aufklärungs Battalion 32 and left a smoking ruin despite the clear Red Cross markings that adorned every tent and structure. Despite the heroic efforts of the support troops in the area, many armed only with .45 pistols, the SS units killed over 250 bed cases and better than 90 trained medical personnel.

Allied troops, most of whom had never been in combat, showed admirable courage when faced with the battle-hardened and ruthless SS troopers, with warehouse troops quite literally pulling weapons out of their shipping crates and putting them into action. The overall wisdom of the Marine and Australian practice of requiring all troops, including service forces, to maintain qualification on the full range of small arms was shown time and again as small, scattered handfuls of truck drivers, bakers, cooks, medical orderlies, and clerks made surprisingly effective stands against the Reich's premier ground troops.

It was here, when thrown onto the defensive, that the differences between the Waffen-SS, with its rigid discipline and single-minded devotion to structure, and the troops fielded by the Western democracies became obvious. Rather than blindly follow some series of standing drilled instructions, the Allied troops, starting from the lowest private soldier up through the enlisted ranks to the NCO and junior officer levels, innovated, adapted, and overcame the massive disadvantages placed upon them by circumstances. Expected to either surrender en masse or to run in blind panic, instead the service forces, be they Australian ranch hands, Marines (with the "every Marine a rifleman" tradition as their guide), Navy warehouse workers, or English truck drivers who wanted to be home abed, did neither, fighting like lions with whatever fell to hand, from rifles to spades. Slowly, surprisingly, the SS formations began to bog down as the sun set and Allied defenses began to react with a sense of coordination and direction.

By the early hours of December 18th, the Allied air forces had regained control of the skies, although rain greatly reduced the ability of the air forces to assist the troops along the battlefront. The SS offensive, having driven a five-mile-wide, twelve-mile-deep pocket into the Allied lines, was slowed as ready stores of fuel began to run low and second wave units began to find themselves under attack by British 21st Army Group units pulled out of rest areas and American 53rd Armored (NG) battalions diverted from being en route to the northern flank of the Allied advance.

After the devastating blows dealt by Allied nuclear weapons, even the SS military command realized that there was no chance that the land offensive would achieve its goal of fracturing the American will to fight and a general withdrawal of the Panzer forces in the pocket was ordered on December 29th. It appears that this order was transmitted without the knowledge or permission of Himmler, since the officers responsible for it were sacked, demoted, and sent to the Eastern Frontier. By this time, however, the withdrawal was well underway and far too advanced to reverse.

Of the 650 tanks and assault guns and close to 110,000 men sent forward on the offensive's opening day, fewer than 45,000 men and only 225 armored vehicles escaped the Nivelles Pocket and made their way back to the Rhine. Allied losses during the two-week campaign, mainly American and Australian, but including British, Canadian, and Polish troops, were 21,856 killed in action over the two-week battle, 32,000 plus wounded (this includes 11,826 gas victims who were permanently disabled by lingering neurological effects that were to hound them for the rest of their lives) and 7,682 captured/missing in action.

Overall more than 75,000 men died in the land battle (with many of the SS losses occurring when cut-off units chose to fight to the death rather than surrender), a number that fades into insignificance when compared to the 3,500,000 civilians who died during the same two weeks.

43

Even before the Himmler Offensive ground to a halt, Christmas 1958 had become a nightmare across the Inner Reich. The massive Anglo-American nuclear retaliation strikes had, in a few hours, ripped the heart out of much of Germany's infrastructure and had incinerated most of the Reich's largest population centers, and had resulted in what many scholars believe was, to that point, the deadliest single day in human history. Many within the Reich had begun to secretly believe that the war was lost. The nuclear strikes, as horrific as they were, were shortly put into perspective by the tidal wave that was Operation Whirlwind.

It is difficult for a modern Western reader to conceptualize the nightmare of an invisible, undetectable, and unstoppable plague that simply appears and strikes without warning or any sort of readily-visible pattern. The modern outbreaks of AIDS or the various "potential pandemics" that seem to appear in the news on a quarterly basis cannot begin to compare with the horrors of the 1959 anthrax outbreak.

While the disease was far from unknown, being endemic across Eurasia, it was also rare in humans (although Nazi extermination camps had recorded several outbreaks) and tended to be found mainly in rural areas, with those in the sheep and wool industries being the most common victims. Whirlwind broke this centuries-old pattern in the most dramatic manner while managing to, at least initially, disguise the actual cause of the outbreak. Within five days of the Whirlwind attacks, dairy farmers in Bavaria began to see a sudden uptick in animal deaths that began as a worrisome blip before becoming an endless pile of dead cattle and, within a couple of days, sheep, goats and horses. Deer carcasses also began to appear along country roads and game trails, followed, ominously, by foxes, dogs, and even the occasional bear. The first fatal human case of gastric anthrax is believed to have been reported on December 26th by Reich medical authorities in Munich. By January 8th deaths from the gastric version of the disease were being reported across the breadth of Germany and among senior Reich officials in France, including the death of France's Education Minister, Alain Poher, on January 11th, five days after he had dined at the Reich Embassy in Paris. By the 15th of January, for the first time since the Party came to power, there were serious food shortages across Inner Germany as the authorities forbade the sale of any fresh meat or raw produce, leaving the public only canned or dried alternatives. The relative shortage of these supplies resulted in the mass confiscation of canned and dried food supplies from warehouses across Occupied Europe in a manner so obvious that virtually no one living in a European city or town with a distribution facility was able to miss it. This effort also spread the food shortage across the Greater Reich, resulting in increased unrest that French National Police and the Gestapo were not entirely able to suppress (ironically, much of this food never reached Germany proper as its transport was subject to the usual savage Allied air attacks on anything that moved on Europe's roads or rails, with the undamaged portions of the loads finding their way into the black markets that sprang up despite the secret police's best efforts).

Even the ever-lengthening death toll due to tainted foodstuffs, mostly meat, were suddenly and dramatically dwarfed by the outbreaks of both cutaneous and, ominously, pulmonary anthrax in the Berlin/Nuremberg region beginning on January 4th. While a few cases had been reported prior to the 4th, most were initially misdiagnosed as other, run of the mill respiratory infections. It seems certain today that the three-day bout of unseasonably warm weather that Berlin enjoyed starting on December 27th was the event that triggered the mass outbreaks beginning on January 4, 1959, as those mild days encouraged Berliners to get out of their homes and move around the heavily-contaminated streets to run errands and prepare for New Year's festivities.

What made the Berlin outbreak all the worse is that the Party had either not realized or had kept deeply secret that the Berlin bombing attacks were anything other than a regular RAF attack (records on the events are understandably patchy). It seems incredible in hindsight that Himmler and his cronies would have believed for even an instant that the Allies would intentionally spare the Reich's capital from atomic devastation unless something even worse was in the offing, but much evidence points in that direction. This includes pages from Goebbels' personal papers where comments are found indicating that the Party senior leadership believed that the "English" lacked the courage to kill the Reich's leadership lest they be caught in a war without end against the Aryan peoples. Whether these statements were a matter of whistling past the graveyard or sincere beliefs, it does seem that the RAF decision to mix conventional HE and incendiary weapons in with the anthrax-laden aircraft succeeded in concealing the true severity of the attack until the spores had had time to begin their work.

When Berliners began to realize that there was, indeed, something seriously wrong, their first natural instinct was to flee the city. They quickly found, to their considerable terror, that transport out of the metro region was not available at any price. Trains were allowed to bring in supplies, but no passenger traffic was allowed out. Autobahn traffic was, as was always the case in the Reich, carefully regulated, and even those who had managed to collect enough ration certificates to buy fuel for their private vehicles found the stock "temporarily unavailable due to pressing needs at the Front", an explanation that ensured that no one would dare challenge it in fear of being seen as "defeatist". Similarly, those brave, or frightened, enough to attempt to walk out of the city in the dead of winter were quickly stopped by Gestapo patrols and either turned around with the sternest of warnings or simply disappeared as so many opponents of the Party had been in the decades before. Without any sort of public announcement ever being made, everyone in the region realized that they were under house arrest, and the house was on fire. Even for orderly, committed Nazis, it was too much to be borne.

The January 13th Buch Riots were the first major display of public unrest in the Reich since Hitler had assumed full power. The Party reaction was exactly what one would have expected from a group that worked at least a million people to death every year for a decade. The Nazi leadership utilized Einsatzgruppen units rushed into the Buch borough of the Reich capital from the General Government areas to first contain the riots and then deal with the rioters. The rioters, mainly terrified seniors and hausfraus who were as much demanding food as escape, were in no way prepared to deal with the mailed fist of the Party's goon squad, while the Einsatzgruppen units appeared to relish the opportunity to deal with the spoiled civilians who had been living high while the troopers had been clearing an entire nation of its native population. The number killed in the riots has never been even remotely established, although it is known to have exceeded 1,000 (based on orphanage registration records for February and March of 1959), but the total toll is obscured by the anthrax fatalities that coincided with the riots.

Berlin's medical facilities were utterly overwhelmed by anthrax cases by January 7th (records do not indicate any admissions for injuries due to the Buch Riots; undoubtedly this is creative bookkeeping on the part of hospital administrators, but even had the riot victims been properly identified their numbers would have been less than a ripple in the tsunami that struck the medical system). Even with some effort on the part of the Party to divert medical resources of the Waffen-SS medical corps, which itself was hard pressed to deal with the carnage of the Himmler Offensive, antibiotic medications were exhausted in Berlin and Nuremberg in under a week, with even those lucky enough to receive treatment finding results to be, at best, mixed.

The current medical treatments which allow close to 100% recovery from anthrax infection, assuming very early treatment upon exposure, did not exist anywhere in the world in 1959, and the sulfa-based drugs preferred by Reich medical professionals were simply not equal to the task. Allied medical officers had access to recently-discovered antibiotics like Tetracycline and Vancomycin that were literally so new that they had not even appeared in peer-reviewed journals, but no such magic bullets were available in Berlin (despite some revisionist statements to the contrary, a review of the global stocks of both drugs in January 1959 will show that, even if it had been desired, the Allies' entire supply of these medications would not have been able to dent the Berlin outbreak).

It is estimated that roughly nine percent of Berlin's population died between December 1958 and June of 1959 due to Whirlwind, with the figure for the Inner Reich as a whole being around five percent. Both figures are, at best, educated guesses that must be utilized with extreme caution.

Berlin was not fully evacuated until after the end of the war.

44

The reaction of SS forces in the field, and even those of some of the French National "elite" forces, to the collapse of the Himmler Offensive and the Allied counter strikes was remarkable; all the more so since it seems, by all accounts, to have been largely spontaneous. The first sign that things would be radically different was seen on December 20th, when a four-plane flight of RAAF Canberras came under attack by eight Ta-152 piston engine fighters near Freiburg.

The appearance of enemy fighters was, in itself, something of a surprise, since the Luftwaffe had long ceased challenging the small CAS strike packages that the Allies had in the air on a nearly continuous basis, preferring to husband resources for use against either Allied ground formations or against RAF/USAF deep strike efforts. The use of the propeller-driven aircraft against Allied jets was also unusual, although not unheard of, especially in the case of the Ta-152, which had sufficient speed to occasionally surprise jet bombers if they were using an "economy" throttle setting and make a single firing pass before the jets could accelerate and break contact. What was unusual was that seven of the eight Luftwaffe aircraft attempted to ram the Australian aircraft, with five of them succeeding, resulting in the loss of three Canberras and the damaging of the fourth. A second similar attack, this time by utterly obsolete Me-163 rocket interceptors against a flight of 8 USAF B-66 bombers striking at SS supply lines near Munster, which destroyed three of the Allied planes, was reported a few hours later. By the end of December 21st there were some twenty-seven reports of similar ramming attacks across the entire Theater of Operations.

Initially believed by LeMay to be a snap reaction to the dramatic revelation of the Allies' nuclear capacity, one that would end once it became clear that every Allied aircraft was not toting its own miniature sun, the tactic did not end on December 23rd or even a week later. Instead, if anything, the attacks increased in ferocity, with everything from the Luftwaffe's premier interceptor, the B&V P.320, to elderly Me-262s to advanced trainers hurling themselves at the Allied attackers in what almost instantly were called "KamiNazi" suicide strikes.

Allied combat aircraft losses, which had fallen to a level that was actually below the non-combat operational loss rate (mainly due to the weather conditions prevailing in a European winter), soared to 1955 levels as mission planners scrambled to come up with a counter to the new Luftwaffe tactics. Much as their USN counterparts had done in 1944, the Combined Air Staff found itself hoping the Reich ran out of either madmen or airplanes.

It was, however, when the SS retreat from the Nivelles Pocket began that the Allies were fully confronted with the changes that the previous month had wrought. While the SS offensive had been clearly and comprehensively defeated despite the use of chemical and biological weapons (with the Allies responding with massive escalation in turn), the spirit of the SS troops was anything but broken, something that became clear on January 4, 1959, near Lier, Belgium. It was here that 3rd Platoon, Charlie Company, found itself under attack by eight individuals in civilian clothing who ran out a wooded area bordering the road, threw themselves under moving vehicles as they passed and detonated satchel charges. The attack destroyed two armored cars, two jeeps, and three 6x6 supply trucks (the remain two attackers were killed by their intended targets' wheels before they could set off their charges). After the survivors of the attack expended several thousand rounds of ammunition raking the surrounding woods, searchers found the tattered remains of the attackers' Waffen-SS kit in what had likely been a neat stack before the application of .30 caliber machine gun fire, along with identity papers and "dog tags" (identification discs) on the three bodies that had not been totally destroyed by the explosions. This was the beginning of what quickly became a running fight of almost unspeakable brutality.

Allied troops, even those who had faced the Imperial Japanese Army in its death throes, were stunned at the almost joyous way that SS troops and fascist youth group members (some as young as 12) would throw themselves into the path of advancing Allied vehicles or run out of hiding places ranging from ditches to church doorways into groups of Allied troops and simply blow themselves, and their surroundings, to bits. Unlike their experiences in the Pacific, Allied commanders found that many of the suicide attackers were civilians and, to make matters worse, adolescents. Most, but not all, of the "Banzai Bunnies", as these youths came to be known among American front line troops (a term found to be more acceptable among senior commanders than the "F%^&*%^ Fools" that had been another of the early labels for these attackers), were from families that were dedicated fascists and that had wholeheartedly bought into the Nazi education system and embraced Party goals. Some of the attackers, particularly in France, were self-described "European Patriots" who wanted nothing to do with the "dirty English" and their foreign ideas.

One can only speculate if this same sort of reaction would have been present in the Low Countries and Norway if the Allies had not already almost entirely overrun the major population centers of both regions before the Nivelles Offensive. It is noteworthy that there were almost no serious insurgent incidents in Normandy or the Calais region, which had already fallen under Allied control before the Nazi introduction of biological agents onto the battlefield, unlike the areas cleared after December 1, 1958.

The appearance of these suicide squads had a vast, nearly instantaneous effect on the Allied war efforts. The number of PoWs being taken dropped by 70%; calls for air attacks – even on small villages – skyrocketed, as did complaints from local civilian leaders regarding ill-treatment by Allied troops as front line units lost the ability to discern the sheep from the goats.

A common complaint was that Allied troops would require all males to strip to their undergarments before allowing them to approach roadblocks and would require *all* civilians to remove everything from baskets, carts, or wagons so they could be inspected before allowing passage. Interestingly, even at the height of this paranoia, Allied commanders strictly forbade troops from requiring female civilians to disrobe. It is possible, even today, to determine almost exactly where the front line was on January 4th, 1959, simply by mentioning the Liberation.

45

The Allied Armies' pursuit of the fleeing Waffen-SS has been described as a series of fox hunts, with the occasional Bengal Tiger being substituted for the fox at random intervals. Some of the British/Indian formations breaking out of the Cotentin recorded advances of as many as 60 miles in a single day, with the 17/7th Rajput Regiment, operating as the lead element of the 32nd Indian Armored Division, vaulting forward 168 miles between January 9 and 12, 1959, only halting when it ran too far ahead of its supply train to continue it headlong advance. It was not always that easy, with the Indian 20th Infantry Division 4/3 Madras battalion running into a very well-laid Troupes de Marine blocking force ambush east of Vendee on January 15th that resulted in the battalion being virtually wiped out.

In the north, the American 14th Army Group had reached the mouth of the Rhine, having finally cleared all remaining SS resistance from Rotterdam's approaches after remarkably heavy fighting against Romanian fortress troops and an iron-hard core of SS "stay-behind" units who most often literally fought to the last man. The fighting had cost the USN three destroyers and the near-sinking of USS *Oregon City* by a U-boat-laid mine (while the cruiser survived, minus 45 feet of her bow, she was never repaired and was decommissioned and scrapped in 1963). At this point the Americans also drew to a halt, in this case to allow time for the arrival of LSTs carrying the amtracks needed to cross the Rhine and the other major waterways that General Rommel's work parties had strongly fortified. The Americans also found themselves in something of a quandary since the main targets of the northern advance, Bremen and Hamburg, were still considered to be too "hot" for long-time troop exposure. Since this included the areas where prevailing winds had driven the fallout plume, Allied commanders were being forced to make what were the first of a series of "no-win" decisions.

The contaminated regions were far too large to simply bypass, and SS forces could readily concentrate in the radiation shadows of the nuclear attacks and cause severe disruption for Allied supply lines. While "hot" in a relative sense, most of the area was no longer so radioactive as to cause short term onset of illness, meaning that the Reich could use the region without any regard for conditions and, more critically, that Allied forces could transit the area and even establish short-term residence in the regions, albeit with an elevated risk of illnesses like leukemia and some sorts of cancer in the future ten to twenty years. The debate regarding these dangers quickly passed out of the hands of the field commanders, with only the briefest stop at SACEUR before reaching senior civilian policy-making levels. The final decision to send Allied troops through these regions, while probably the correct one from the perspective of leaders trying to end the war before another, perhaps more serious, nerve-gas attack was made against civilians in the UK (or America, although this seems to have been mainly left unsaid lest the discussion of it leak to the public), remains controversial to this day.

While almost all records of the discussions surrounding the decision remain inaccessible to researchers, recent FOI efforts have managed to get some records, mainly from the archives of the US Public Health Service Commissioned Corps, into the public record. These recently released files reveal some of the most heated exchanges that the author has ever read in the official minutes of a high-level US Agency meeting. Perhaps the most shocking are the statements attributed to the US Surgeon General, Luther Terry, in which he accuses the President, Joe Kennedy Jr., of intending to murder "thousands of our own men". Even Edmund Morris, President Kennedy's biographer, has stated that these FOI revelations demand further examination, although efforts to have Congress require the release of additional records have, to date, gone nowhere. Until a comprehensive release of records occurs, the decision to send troops through the numerous contaminated regions, which has been conservatively estimated to have resulted in the early deaths of at least 15,000 former servicemen in the US alone, will remain the single most disputed policy decision of the 20th century.

The Waffen-SS, as it began what rapidly became a headlong retreat to the Rhine, began to implement Führer Order 527 with ever-increasing gusto. Originally the order had ensured that the SS troops destroyed historically-significant structures and famous items of public art that could not be literally unbolted and carted off as the SS withdrew, the better to ensure that the Allies were deprived of the benefits attendant to "European Civilization", but during the retreat this interpretation expanded astronomically. In addition to the ongoing desecration of historical artifacts, SS units began to burn entire villages for no other reason than to destroy the (in some cases nearly new) buildings. SS units also began to destroy whatever stocks of grain and agricultural products that they could not readily arrange to be sent to the Inner Reich; this included livestock and preserved meats, although most ready supplies of foodstuffs were simply stolen and taken back beyond the Rhine. Waffen-SS engineers also ensured that water supplies, treatment plants, power generation facilities, and hospitals were either destroyed or damaged beyond ready repair. As they withdrew, the SS left a ruined landscape, often with additional contamination by biological weapons (the Tularemia outbreak that virtually halted the 21st Army Group for almost two weeks is believed to have been the direct result of one of these contamination efforts).

Possibly the most critical of the SS depredations occurred when the Eguzon Dam, located on the Creuse River and a major source of electricity for the Limousin region, was destroyed on January 19th, 1959, despite being off any of the primary axes of Allied advance. It seems that it was this action that broke the camel's back, since the French Uprising began with 48 hours of the dam's destruction.

While most Americans think immediately of the Lyon Rebellion as being the major event of what was more of a short-lived French Civil War than a true rebellion against the occupying

Germans, it was actually just the most successful event of its kind, despite its tragic end. The destruction of the Eguzon Dam set off near-spontaneous rioting across France (including, it is often forgotten, in some of the areas under Allied control) as the French people finally reached their breaking point; a breaking point that was the direct result of an especially brutal war being fought across their homeland.

The rebellion was, of course, doomed to ultimate failure since there was no leadership, no coordination with the Allied forces (again the Lyon Committee being the exception thanks to its Viet Minh and SOE supporters), and no unified goal. Some of the rebels wanted to clear France of all foreign influence; some were long time Resisters who could not allow the Boche to continue to rape their homeland; some were simply townsfolk who were unable to see how they would survive the coming months without food or heat. The majority of the Paris government seems to have been against the rebels, despite many of the eventual survivors of the Fascist regime proclaiming themselves to be secret opponents of the ruling party, although a few men were clearly and openly ready to see all foreigners out of France and others seem to have been legitimate members of the Resistance who had worked to reduce the damage to the French people by their occupiers.

The suddenness of the uprising caught both the SS and French security forces by surprise, with many of the early gun battles featuring local police fighting National Security officers and some National Army units. As the rioters and resistance units gained strength, some units of the National Army either shot their officers or joined them in fighting the ill-defined enemy (in some areas as much as 40% of the troops joined the Rising). The relatively small number of Resisters in the Allied Controlled Zones were generally handled with minimal force, although there were a number of deaths when suspected human bombers failed to follow repeated orders to halt. Most of these deaths were in the Cotentin region, where distrust of the Allies was already at a very high level thanks to the serious pandemics spread by the SS. This was, of course, not the case when hardline French Fascist or

Waffen-SS units were confronted by crowds mainly armed with rocks and barrel staves.

Lyon was the last major rebel stronghold to fall, with the resistance there collapsing on February 5th. This was after a detachment of French National Security Department commandos, aided directly by several Nebelwerfer rocket batteries on loan from the 9th Luftwaffe Panzer Division, launched almost seven tons of Sarin into the city between January 30th and February 2nd. It was estimated by Allied medical units that over 60,000 residents of Lyon, where the population had swollen to better than 400,000 as the survivors of other recaptured cities streamed into the "Free City of Lyon" as the Fascist Government's troops reasserted control of the countryside, either died in the gas attacks or at the hands of French secret police units after Lyon fell.

Only the arrival of the 267th Indian Armored Brigade at the outskirts of Lyon on February 23rd, following a heroic drive across 230 miles of strongly enemy held territory by the Indian III Corps, stopped the secret police's bloodbath.

It was this diversion of III Corps, in a futile effort to save Lyon, that gave the SS enough time to raze Paris.

46

In ways that the Reich had never envisioned, their use of bioweapons, suicide squads, and scorched earth tactics did slow the Allied advance. Given the conditions prevailing in the Reich by February of 1959, it is questionable if delaying the Allied entrance into the Inner Reich was actually a wise decision, at least when the welfare of the average Reich resident is factored in. While the Allies worked on tactics to overcome human bombs and worked to prevent the death of millions of often uncooperative noncombatants, the average Reich resident found their daily calorie intake reduced to below 1400 as the impact of Whirlwind on food stocks conspired with the need to keep troops in the field supplied and fighting to impose real want on the German people for the first time in 30 years.

The Nazi Party's decision to destroy Europe rather than allow the "English" to have it has been compared to a petulant child throwing a tantrum, but a closer comparison would be the divorced husband who attempts to hide his assets and then ruins everything he can touch rather than let his spouse have it. A child doesn't really understand what they are doing is wrong, while the estranged husband does know and simply doesn't care; indeed, he wants to cause the maximum amount of damage out of simple spite. Some action that was taken, such as the destruction of the Lourdes Grotto and the adjoining St. Mary's Church, cannot be explained in any other manner. The Nazis knew exactly what they were doing in destroying the cultural legacy of a millennium as the great artworks of thousands of artists, architects, engineers and stonemasons burned or disappeared in the dust of explosions, and all evidence is that the forces dedicated to the work did so with considerable zeal. While those who proclaim that Order

571 represents the Nazis' "true crime against humanity" are almost unimaginably narrow in their views, they are correct in highlighting the obliteration of much of the "beauty" that had been bequeathed to future generations and the impact that such actions had on humanity as a whole. As deplorable as the cultural impacts were, what was truly the Nazis' most severe offense against the occupied portions of Europe had little to do with the arts.

As already discussed, the SS effectively destroyed the economy and farmlands of the Netherlands by destroying the dike systems that kept the North Sea and the major rivers flowing into it at bay. The effect of the salt water flooding, especially when mixed with chemical contamination from flooded industrial regions, is something that has not been fully eradicated to this day. The destruction of water delivery systems and treatment facilities in France and Denmark, while little discussed, had enormous ramifications on the populations of the regions served by these facilities. When coupled with the ongoing efforts of Reich bio-weapon units to contaminate as much of the ceded ground as possible with a witch's brew of bacteria and viruses, it is fairly easy to understand why so many of the large urban centers experienced severe pandemics that killed or crippled many of the residents.

In rural areas, the Nazi effort – often aided by local fascists who fully expected that they would be rewarded by the Party after the "invaders" were defeated – to poison wells and other groundwater resources did much to ensure both famine and the spread of disease, while the bioweapon units (many of them Einsatzgruppen veterans who had taken part in the initial slaughter of Europe's Jewish population and were recalled to active duty to act as "muscle" for the Party scientists who oversaw the spreading of the bio-agents) added crop blights, including a few that had been selected for use as they were resistant to commonly-used preventatives, to the human plagues that had been used starting in Normandy and along the Allied line of advance across Western France.

Field Marshal Sir Richard McCreery, 1st Viscount McCreery, VC, in his memoir, stated that 22nd Army Group was delayed in its advance to the Rhine by nearly seven weeks due the diversion of resources by his command to humanitarian efforts in an attempt to limit the impact of Reich destructive practices. He further states that his decisions in this area, or more correctly the reasons for his reduced rate of advance, were questioned by Ground Force Commander Simonds as well as SACEUR Ridgway (something that is confirmed in General Ridgway's personal papers), to which he responded: "Gentlemen, I will be damned if I will let these people die in the name of a schedule. We are not our opponents; we cannot act like them." Apparently both of his seniors agreed with him, as they approved the diversion of additional rations as well as medical personnel and supplies to civilian relief efforts, not just in Sir Richard's Operational Area, but across the entirety of the Allied Zone of Control.

There was some considerable friction between Ridgway and his US Ground Force commander (and close personal friend), General Maxwell Taylor, concerning this policy, with Taylor arguing that the best way to deal with the situation was to defeat the Reich. Taylor's position is something that has been largely, and in the author's belief correctly, attributed to the fact that most American units were in areas that suffered less at the hands of the SS (Belgium and Holland) than the far larger French countryside. Belgium had been overrun by U.S forces nearly entirely before the first bioweapon attacks, and the conditions in the Netherlands, although serious, were more easily handled than those in the French interior thanks to the ready accessibility of the region by US naval vessels whose presence allowed easier resupply of Taylor's forces as well as a very substantial additional medical resource from the medical staffs of the warships offshore. Taylor also had the advantage of having the shortest distance to advance, something partly offset by also facing some of the Waffen-SS' best formations and most formidable defenses. In the end, however, Taylor, once he had had his say, bent to the task with enthusiasm, with his staff engineering a logistical pathway that sent roughly 400 trucks of supplies to the south every 12 hours.

It has been estimated that the entire Allied effort may have saved as many as half of the potential victims of the SS effort between December 1, 1958 and February 28, 1959 (roughly four million people) from eventual starvation or death from illness.

Unfortunately, while the Allies worked to save those already impacted, the SS continued its efforts to undo fifty generations of European progress as it fell back to the Rhine and Germany proper, only stopping when a line 50 kilometers from the Inner Reich frontier was reached, lest the Fatherland be contaminated.

The citizens of the Reich were to learn that many things in nature do not obey lines on a map.

47

The delays caused by the Nazi biological attacks and the heroic efforts of the Indian III Corps to relieve Lyon allowed the Reich to complete or greatly advance several projects that were to have a serious impact on the war. The most militarily significant of these was Rommel's effective completion of the Rhine defensive line.

While vastly weaker than the Atlantic Wall, the Rommel Line had several advantages that the formidable Channel defenses lacked. The Allies were not able to make use of their awesome naval artillery assets against the fortifications, denying them a toolkit that had crushed wide sections of the defenses along the coast of both Norway and France. Waffen-SS and Volksturm units were also able to make most movement between bases at night without needing to shelter during the day in the often vain hope of avoiding Allied air attack, reducing the "easy kills" that had so greatly reduced SS forces in Belgium and France as they attempted to react to the False Peak operations and to the landings themselves. Lastly, there was the incalculable advantage of troops defending their own homes. As fanatical as the SS had been from the moment of the invasion, the thought of untermensch troops setting foot on the sacred soil of the Fatherland raised their determination exponentially. This was also the case for the reserves that allowed a vast increase in SS numbers.

The Volksturm (literally People's Storm) was a significant threat to Allied operations. The units moved to the Rhine were primarily made up of men who were under the age of 40. Most of these reservists were very current in training and well-equipped; many of them were drawn from previously "reserved" jobs that the Party had determined to be critical to the war effort, including ordinary police units, skilled technicians, and mid- and even upper-level Party officials and members of the Party senior leadership's personal staff (including Himmler's gardener) that had previously been sacrosanct. In addition to the active reservists, most of whom had served in the Waffen-SS during their active service, there were older inactive reserve units, staffed with men as old as 65 and drawn from local communities, a few of whom had first carried arms for the Kaiser during the Great War and many who had been part of the Heer's victorious sweep across Europe between 1939 and 1943. While these older men were far more limited in endurance and training, they had also never tasted defeat and were fighting not just to defend the Fatherland but their individual homes.

These older reservists were joined by Hitler Youth battalions, meant to consist of 16 and 17-year-olds, but often having a significant cadre of 15 and even 14-year-old boys in the ranks (there is also at least one documented case of a 12-year-old boy serving in a Hitler Youth battalion, a formation that included both of his living brothers). The older of these teens were possibly the most fanatical element in the Reich, having spent their teens in a nation at war receiving ever more strident lectures on the evil that was "the English". Mixing the utter dedication of the thoroughly indoctrinated with the sense of personal invulnerability and immortality that characterizes the young, these Hitler youth formations have been described as the most fanatical forces fielded since the Spartans (an equally good indicator of what these formations offered is the observation that "there is nothing on this Earth more frightening than a child with a machine gun").

While the Reich moved its past and future into the Rhine defenses, the Party leaders sent the darkest of their nightmares into France to bring Order 571 to its greatest visible peak. The effort spent to dispatch three Einsatzgruppen brigades from the continued "Germanization" of the East, across the Inner Reich, and into France while transport was desperately needed to move rations into the stricken regions of the Reich speaks volumes about the lunacy of Himmler and his minions. The willingness of Himmler to waste almost 12,000 men on what amounted to a massive act of vandalism, even six decades later, simply boggles the mind.

While one of Einsatzgruppen brigades spread across France east of the Meuse and continued with the retail destruction of infrastructure and historically significant structures and objects, the other two brigades, with Fallschirm-Panzer Division 2 (the last full-sized conventional German Division west of the Meuse by 18 February) providing security and heavy combat power in support, moved into the Paris area and proceeded to utterly destroy the entire region.

Fortunately for the people of the Ile de France, the commander of 2 Luftwaffe insisted both on warning the civilian population in the region that they had to evacuate, and, more importantly, that the Einsatzgruppen commanders wait 48 hours after the evacuation order to begin their work. One can only imagine the results if the Luftwaffe commander had not extended this warning to the millions of civilians in the region and had left them to the SD forces' mercy. Why Major General Hanns-Horst von Necker, commander of the Luftwaffe forces, chose to act in the way that he did will never be known for certain, as he was killed in an RAAF air strike on his withdrawing command on March 4, 1959, but some evidence exists that he was following the orders of Luftwaffe commander Adolph Galland (a serious risk if true, as the SS had assumed overall command of all Luftwaffe ground formations some weeks earlier). General von Necker also had sound military reasons to evacuate, as the prospect of having to fight block to block, even against poorly-armed French police and National forces, would have been enormously costly in both time and blood. With the evacuation, most of these potential enemies were fully occupied in aiding in the mass evacuation.

While unwilling to defy von Necker and his Panther IIIs, the SD units did not sit idly by while the 48 hours given for evacuation ran. Structures were either destroyed or rigged for demolition, water distribution facilities were wrecked, and anyone showing even the slightest sign of resistance was simply shot out of hand, even in the presence of Luftwaffe personnel (von

Necker's protection apparently not extending to what the SD liked to call "bandits").

As soon as the ordained 48 hours of grace had passed, the Einsatzgruppen took to the streets in earnest, as von Necker's units withdrew to perimeter security positions. This was a death sentence for tens of thousands of civilians who had been either unwilling or unable to evacuate as SD teams began their depredations. Gas mains were uncapped or opened with explosives to aid in the spread of arson fires; landmarks, along with almost every structure in Paris and Orleans predating 1800, were demolished, often while live television coverage of the activity was broadcast back to the Reich (and, not entirely accidentally, to the rest of France and Great Britain). Film crews made permanent records of the destruction of Notre Dame and the rest of Ile de la Cite's structures, the Arc de Triomphe and Tomb of the Unknown Soldier, the Louvre (with the infamous barbarity of Venus de Milo being blown into gravel being a particular low point, one that was rebroadcast by Reich television for weeks) and, of course, the toppling and subsequent chopping up of the Eiffel Tower. Film records were also made of the obliteration of other public works and arts across France. The destruction of the Palace at Versailles, which had been the headquarters for the Reich Minister to France, was captured by another motion picture film crew, the better to save the event for future viewing.

When the SD had completed the destruction, an orgy of violence that took the better part of a week, Paris, Versailles, Orleans, and the surrounding areas were effectively erased from the map of France. The final actions of the SD were to contaminate the entire department with every biological agent the Reich had at its disposal, poison the Seine for 50 kilometers on either side of Paris, fill cisterns with mustard gas, and thoroughly mine the rubble with both conventional bombs and nerve gas shells rigged to explode if disturbed. The SD also left behind well over 75,000 civilian casualties and several hundred thousand refugees who had to fend for themselves in a ruined, contaminated, and poisoned landscape.

As the Einsatzgruppen withdrew toward the Reich, they paused at Reims and repeated the process used in Paris to obliterate the historic coronation site of French kings and what had been one of the most famed cathedrals in Europe. Unlike von Necker's heavy formations, the SD columns mainly escaped to the east with minimal losses.

48

While somewhat outside the main focus of this work, the reaction of the rump USSR (or more properly, Molotov's government) to the momentous actions taking place in the West offers an interesting counterpoint to the massive battles in the West.

Limited by the Berlin Treaty to a maximum force of 100,000 troops, no modern tanks to speak of and no air force, along with numerous additional limitations on weapons and fortifications, and with 3,000 Reich "Peace Observers" having free access across the entire country to ensure that the treaty limits were observed to the letter, the Molotov government had very little to work with in the way of military power. Even worse was the limitations placed on Red Army movements toward Greater Germany, which were severely limited by a treaty that quite intentionally ensured that any Soviet force that moved to the West would be overmatched (and likely as not destroyed) by "partisan" units fighting the SS in European Russia. Even when Red Army forces were not simply set upon and killed by guerilla forces they were usually surrounded and forced to surrender by one band or another whose hatred of the Nazis was nearly matched, if not exceeded, by their hatred for Molotov, or Communism, or occasionally each other. Once forced into surrender the Red Army units would be stripped of useful equipment, sometimes down to their boots and greatcoats, and sent back on foot into Molotov-controlled territory.

With virtually no way to deploy even a brigade to fight the much-depleted SS formations fighting along the frontier, Molotov was hard pressed to find any way to demonstrate to the Allies that the USSR was still a worthwhile partner. When the Allies crossed the nuclear threshold, displaying a capacity that was even more effective than most in the Soviet science community had expected, Molotov decided that he had to play the only cards left to him.

Soviet "reparations" were due by the 10th of every month. This entailed the transfer of specific quantities of oil, various raw materials and metal ores, finished goods (usually military clothing or the simple striped uniforms that forced laborers were required to wear), and 100,000 "guest laborers". Generally, the reparations were sent throughout the month as there was insufficient transport to move it all in a few days' time. By January 10th, 1959, the Soviet payment was far short of the required amount. Soviet officials, all the way up to Molotov himself, stated that severe winter conditions had caused the delay. When Reich Peace Observers confirmed that the winter seemed to be more severe than normal, Berlin was unconcerned; the delayed arrival of the monthly quota had happened several times since the end of the war and a standard penalty of an additional 20% of the monthly quota had been established, with the penalty due in the following month. It was not until late January that Party officials began to grow seriously concerned as the February shipments, especially of ores and slave laborers, had not begun to materialize. Pointed messages were dispatched to Krasnoyarsk warning that failure to meet treaty quotas would result in "noteworthy actions" to ensure compliance.

On February 10th, 1959, Soviet shipments were nearly 80% below quotas. Continued Soviet protests blaming unusually severe weather began to sound increasingly hollow to the Party leadership, who demanded the shipments be delivered without further delay (the weather was, ironically, one of the worst winter months ever recorded in Russia). Reich officials stated that until the full shipment quotas, including a 50% penalty for non-performance, were received, no guest workers would be allowed to return to the rump Soviet state. This statement was almost a literal death sentence for the 15% or so of the forced laborers who had survived their five-year visit. Despite this, Molotov, who like most Allied political leaders couldn't imagine that the Reich could possibly survive another month of fighting, failed to order the gathered materials and selected workers to be sent to the Reich. It was an act of defiance that was impossible to misinterpret.

On March 1st, when it became obvious that the March shipment would amount to almost nothing, Himmler requested a face to face meeting with Molotov with Himmler personally guaranteeing Molotov's safety. To put Molotov further at ease, Himmler proposed that the meeting take place under the auspices of the Swiss Foreign ministry. Reluctantly, Molotov agreed to the proposed meeting, perhaps because it was the first time in years that any foreign leader, including his supposed allies, had actually treated him as anything even close to an equal. It was under these circumstances that Molotov flew to Switzerland on March 8, 1959.

When Molotov arrived, he was surprised to learn that the usually pathologically punctual Germans had not yet landed. He was informed by the Swiss Foreign Minister that Himmler had been delayed by enemy air activity over Berlin and would not arrive until March 9th. As a consolation, Molotov was invited to dinner with the Foreign Minister, a meal that, according to witnesses, he devoured like a man who had not seen food in a month.

March 9th was reasonably clear and surprisingly warm day for early March in Central Russia, with temperatures reaching the low 50s. The troops of the 25th and 39th Guard Motor Rifle divisions were taking advantage of the weather to do much needed maintenance to the roads and buildings of their base that had, as was always the case, suffered greatly from the harsh winter conditions. Radar stations near Krasnoyarsk noted unusual traffic, but without an air force were unable to dispatch any interceptors to identify the unknown aircraft. A few of the operators speculated that the aircraft might be either American or British bombers that had received battle damage and were trying to find any safe place to land. While unusual, an American B-36 had landed at Krasnoyarsk 14 months earlier, so it was not an improbable explanation. Unfortunately, it was wrong.

The Ju-688s approaching Krasnoyarsk were ten of the dozen survivors remaining in the Luftwaffe. Completely obsolete in the

West, where Allied fighters, radar-aimed AAA, and SAMs made them nothing but particularly oversized targets, they were death incarnate over the nearly-demilitarized Soviet capital. Eight of the aircraft headed for the Guard's base while two proceeded into the heart of Krasnoyarsk. Each bomber was carrying 20,000 kilos of "special" bombs. The crews had no idea what the bombs contained, only that they had been told not to leave their pressurized compartments under any circumstances and that they should leave their bomb bay doors open after the raid for at least 30 minutes during the return flight before re-entering Reich territory.

Utterly unopposed, save for some ineffectual 75mm flak that lacked the range to reach the bombers' altitude and which only opened fire after the attack had begun, the Luftwaffe crews attacking the Red Army base broke the extremely tight formation that they had maintained en route to the target area for a specific formation that they had been ordered to assume "in order to maximize the effective coverage of the target" while flying at an indicated 300 KPH. At exactly 10:37 hours local time the lead bombardier hit his release toggle, with all other aircraft in the formation following suit within five seconds. The aircraft then accelerated to full speed and broke away from their target in a surprisingly elegant maneuver for such a large aircraft. When the simple pressure sensors in the falling bomb's tails indicated that they had reached 1,500 meters, pins which had been secured in place by safety wires while being carried to the target withdrew from drogue parachute packs and the bombs' descent rate was reduced by some 80%. At 300 meters altitude, a second simple pressure sensor was triggered and the nerve gas-laden bomblets within the bomb casings were released. Of the 464 bombs, only 22 failed to perform as designed. Losses in the 25th and 39th Guard divisions exceeded 85%.

While their brethren were eliminating two-thirds of Molotov's best, and most loyal, troops, the last two Ju-688s made their attack against Krasnoyarsk's Government District. This attack killed roughly half of Molotov's governing officials and many of their families, including three of Molotov's great-grandchildren.

When Molotov arrived at the Swiss Foreign Minster's Offices at 11:00 hours on March 9th he was not ushered into a meeting with Himmler. Instead, he was handed a note by the profoundly unhappy Foreign Minister, who also informed him that Herr Himmler would not be coming after all. The Minister also was the first to inform Molotov of the general outline of what had happened earlier at Krasnoyarsk, based on information received from the Swiss Charge's mission.

The note itself was the soul of brevity: "Russia will provide 150% of the Berlin Treaty quotas for the next two years before being allowed to resume original Treaty obligations. Failure to do so will result in much larger attacks than those of today."

All the Luftwaffe aircraft returned to base without incident.

49

Viewed in a vacuum, the March 12, 1959, USAF nuclear strikes against the three suspected air bases that launched the Krasnoyarsk Raid is often seen as a rather severe case of overbombing, or of using a sledgehammer to kill a single ant. There would be a great deal of truth to this viewpoint if the reason for the strike was simply to eliminate a dozen Ju-688 bombers; in actuality the destruction of the bombers was simply a bonus (although one of the Krasnoyarsk aircraft actually survived the war intact, having been on a recon mission at the time of the strikes, the Ju-688 force was eliminated by the attacks. Interested readers can now actually see this aircraft, tail number #8765692, in fully-restored form at the USAF Museum located at Wright-Patterson AFB in Ohio).

The real reason for the strikes was well worth the expenditure of six 1.2 megaton bombs, even though this reason has only become clear in the last decade or so. While the USAF attack has long been seen as an Allied effort to show Russia that it was not forgotten, this has now been clearly shown to not be the basis for the attack.

By the time the American Hound Dog missiles had finished their dramatic flights, Russia had, as a political entity, ceased to exist. While Molotov's immediate family escaped the post-attack disorders by seeking shelter in the US and British Embassies and Molotov himself was given sanctuary by the Swiss Government until conditions "permitted his safe return", the same was not true for the rest of his political power structure. Most of its bureaucrats and, in many cases, their families, found themselves victims of mob justice as the fragile veneer of organization and legality that marked Molotov's reign shattered. To say that the situation in Krasnoyarsk descended into bedlam is an understatement.

American records show that no fewer than sixteen different groups presented themselves at the gate of the US Embassy as being the new "Russian" "Soviet", and/or "Emergency" Government in the weeks immediately following the attacks (British Embassy records show *seventeen* claimants, only three of which also appear on the US lists). Fortunately, none of the rivals for power were suicidal, and no efforts were made to attack any of the foreign legations except those of the Third Reich, France, and Romania. All of these Axis legations were overrun by rioters. Although Canadian Embassy guards managed to evacuate most of the Romanian Embassy staff before the compound itself was burned down, the French and Reich Embassies, both of which were larger and in a different section of Krasnoyarsk than the Romanian embassy, were taken with almost complete loss of life. The attack against the Reich compound included what were almost certainly Guards division troops in civilian attire and the use of heavy weapons on both sides (an excellent recounting of these dark days in Krasnoyarsk can be found in Sir Charles Jensen's *Doing Her Majesty's Bidding*. Sir Charles' autobiography covers his entire illustrious career, from his days as a junior functionary in Molotov's Russia to his days as Governor General of Canada).

While Washington and London were helpless to prevent much of Asian Russia from falling into open civil war, other diplomatic endeavors proved to be more fruitful. In the wake of the televised destruction of Paris and the incontrovertible evidence that the Reich was conducting on-going biological warfare across France, long-standing efforts to get Spain and Portugal to break off relations with the Third Reich finally bore fruit as both nations recalled their diplomatic delegations on March 18th. Somewhat surprisingly, the Party allowed both of these complete delegations, as well as those of Turkey, Sweden, Switzerland and The Holy See, to embark onto a special ferry that took the diplomats and their families, along with a number of "employees" (mainly Jews who had been sheltered in the legations for years), to Sweden. The reason for this remarkably civilized act by the Nazis has long been debated, although most signs point to some sort of forlorn hope that by acting within internationally accepted rules and behaviors in this area Germany might somehow escape full retribution. In any case, by March 26th, the only diplomats remaining in the Reich were from the other Axis states, a single Charge representing the Swiss and another from the Vatican.

On April 2nd, 1959, Portugal and Spain declared war on the Third Reich.

On April 3rd, 1959, after years of effort by the Allies (and, it seems increasingly certain, a closed-door meeting between the Prime Minister and Secretary of State Fulbright where Fulbright is reputed to have flatly stated "We will remember who our friends were, who our enemies are, and who stood by while evil reigned"), Turkey declared war on the Third Reich and its allies.

More than any other nation in history, the Third Reich stood alone.

50

The Turkish declaration of war allowed the British government to initiate Operation Crossroad. Designed to cut off the retreat of SS forces into the General Government area, Crossroad was not just the brainchild of the CIGS, it was perhaps the most "Commonwealth" operation of the War since the Japanese had spectacularly brought the United States into the conflict at the end of 1941.

Crossroad was not seen fondly in Washington or at SACEUR, where the belief that the focus of any actions should be exclusively to hasten the break into German Territory and the rapid conclusion to the war. It is actually an open question if the Americans, and to a lesser extent the Australian and Canadian governments, would have approved the actual implementation of Crossroad if the Molotov Government had not utterly collapsed after the March 9th Raid. The lack of anything even resembling a unified government in Russia allowed the CIGS the opening needed to get consensus for the operation.

While the primary purpose of Crossroad was the one presented for UN concurrence, there was a second goal that was nearly as much desired by Whitehall, namely supporting a few favored partisan groups that London deeply preferred as post-war rulers in the Ukraine and European Russia. While the American political leadership suspected this to be the case, in the aftermath of March 9th the US also had no residual obligation to support what had once been the USSR and therefore chose to ignore the signs that indicated that London was already working to alter the post-war map despite American insistence that local self-determination would be the driving force of any changes in the post-war map.

Crossroad began with the movement of the assault force into the Black Sea, with the first ships moving through the Bosporus on April 23. This movement was, of course, utterly impossible to conceal and became known in Berlin within a few hours. An attempt by Luftwaffe units to interfere was soundly defeated by RAF, RCAF, and FAA units that had been deployed in Turkey within 48 hours of the Turkish declaration of war. No Luftwaffe aircraft managed to even reach their launch point before being blotted from the skies, and Luftwaffe records indicate that only three of the 52 aircraft sent on the raid reached home. The state of the Luftwaffe at this point in the war is indicated by the inclusion of 18 Fw-190F-8/U3 torpedo bombers and 8 Fw-190D-9 as part of the strike package, all of which seem to have been moved from ground attack squadron service along the Eastern Frontier. This was the sole attempt of the Luftwaffe to use manned aircraft to interfere, although some 30 jet-powered cruise missiles were launched from Bulgarian territory, with each missile causing near-panic in Turkish government offices in the not altogether unreasonable fear that they were carrying chemical weapons. None of the missiles proved to be carrying that particularly lethal cargo, and none managed to interfere with the passage of Allied shipping.

The passage of the Allied fleet, which included some 8 CV and 28 ships mounting guns over 203mm, was in clear violation of the Montreux Convention, especially considering that each of the carriers and battleships exceeded the total tonnage limitations placed on the transit of foreign vessels through the Strait at any one time, with several of the battleships displacing more than three times the individual vessel limitations for non-Black Sea origin warships. Reich protests regarding this Treaty violation were met with stony silence from Ankara and with howls of laughter when they were presented to the British Legation in Bern. The willingness of the Turks to violate the Convention was an early indicator of exactly how the post-war world would develop.

The Allied invasion fleet itself was centered on all five Malta-class CVA operated by the Royal Navy, along with HMS *Eagle* and the Essex class HMAS *Melbourne* and HMCS *Warrior*. The Australian and Canadian ships both operated primarily USN-sourced aircraft, with the A4 Skyhawk being the primary light strike aircraft while F-8 Crusaders provided fighter protection. All the fleet carriers also carried at least one squadron of the ubiquitous AD-1 Skyraider for close air support. Crossroad also marked the combat debut of both the De Havilland Sea Vixen and the Supermarine Scimitar. While the Sea Vixen proved to be an exceptional aircraft, the Scimitar proved to be something of a mechanic's nightmare, with many of its innovative systems proving to be a bit too advanced for field service. While the Scimitar's maintenance issues limited its utility, it was only present in full squadron numbers on *Eagle* and HMS *Africa*. Along with the eight attack carriers, the Allied flotilla also included some 28 light and escort carriers whose primary function was the provision of close air support. While the USN provided two battleships (USS *South Dakota* and USS *Alabama*) and eleven heavy cruisers to the gun line, along with a good number of LCT(R) and LST(R), and nearly two-thirds of the attack transports, the vast majority of the assault support force was provided by the Royal Navy.

The Allied landing, which had been expected to be at least as difficult as that of the Cotentin Peninsula, proved to be nearly bloodless. While there were a series of well-sited fortifications along the landing beaches south of Odessa, they proved to be lightly-manned – mainly by Bulgarian conscripts and some German reservists who had last seen action during Operation Barbarossa. This was the first verification by the Allies of intelligence reports that most Axis forces had been withdrawn to the Inner Reich frontiers. Having been ready to take several thousand losses to establish themselves on the beaches, the commander of the invasion force was pleasantly surprised when total losses on D-Day amounted to less than 500 KIA and under 2,000 casualties in total.

Even more surprising was the near absence of any organized SS resistance as the Crossroad force advanced inland. While the personnel of the 10th Armored Division quickly developed respect for the "those old bastards in the grey uni's" and their ability to set ambushes, there simply were not enough of the old Heer veterans around to stop the progress of the British IV Corps. The primary limiting factor on the speed of the Allied advance was supplies, especially of fuel. The few surviving Kriegsmarine U-boats in the Black Sea (survivors of five years of regular Allied air attacks on Axis naval bases) proved themselves to be a menace, with 23 cargo ships sunk, until they were eventually either hunted down at sea or destroyed when they returned to base to rearm.

Even with the difficulty of operating at the end of a considerable supply line, Crossroad units had advanced well into the General Government by late May (this advance was greatly aided by the Bulgarian decision to change sides on May 5th, 1959, which considerably improved the Allies' logistical situation). More critically, the British forces managed to establish reasonably secure communication lines with the Ukrainian National Army (London's long-preferred partisan group in Southern Ukraine) and the Russian Patriotic Front. This made these two groups the de facto governments for much of what had once been the southern region of the Soviet Union. With RAF, and gradual USAF, support, mainly consisting of the elimination of all Luftwaffe presence south of Warsaw, both partisan groups began to make inroads against the "SS" forces (mainly consisting of conscripts sent East due to political reliability concerns and 50-year-old Heer veterans) along the Eastern Frontier. Inevitably, the advancing partisan units often took vengeance on the "SS" for nearly two decades of repression as they advanced. While Allied military advisors (around 60% British, but including Viet Minh and Philippine Scout elements) did what they could to limit the bloodletting, there were few prisoners taken by partisan units.

SS reaction to Operation Crossroad was almost nil. Understandably, the Reich's attention was focused on the West.

51

There remains some debate regarding the unrest that overcame France in the wake of Paris' televised obliteration. While it was clearly an uprising against the retreating SS, it was much more than just a reaction to a retreating invader. There was nearly as much resistance shown to the Allied armies advancing across France as against the withdrawing SS, as well as a multi-level civil war and brutal fighting for sheer survival among the French people.

The Allied effort to move forward, already delayed by the massive medical effort combating the Reich bioweapon attacks, was further delayed as two different SS "stay-behind" units began to operate, usually without any command connection between the differing groups. These were the infamous Werewolf "A" and "B" detachments. While the "A" detachments continued the suicidal human bomb and car bomb attacks against Allied positions, with hospitals and dressing stations being a particular magnet for human bombs as efforts in 22nd Army Group focused increasingly on aid to civilians, the "B" detachments waged a far more subtle and corrosive campaign.

Very little is actually known about the specific orders given to the B Detachments beyond the obvious "Dress in captured Allied uniforms, speak English, commit wholesale acts of barbarity against civilians and leave plenty of witnesses to spread the word of what the 'English' were doing". It is estimated that there were some 5,000 men (and a few women) assigned to "B" Detachments across France in the wake of the failed Himmler Offensive, some of whom were never accounted for post-war. While a large percentage of the "B" attacks were crude and obviously, even to isolated rural residents, actually the work of Reich (and in a few cases French Secret Police) forces, enough were well done to spread utter distrust of British (and to a far lesser extent American) troops across the width of 22nd Army Group's line of advance. As tales of rape, murder and other atrocities spread across occupied France the only civilians that the advancing British units encountered were those so ill or wracked by hunger that the certainty of death by doing nothing overcame the fear of the unknown.

While never entirely eradicated, Viscount McCreery's order eventually greatly reduced the "B" Detachments by assigning their elimination to the troops of the 5th Gurkha Rifles. This move allowed 22nd Army Group to move forward while suffering far less harassment than had been the case when the imposters were roving about unchecked. McCreery's order was controversial at the time, and remains so to this day since it was effectively a hunting license for his Nepalese troops to find and "eliminate" spies dressed in British uniforms. Finding themselves hunted relentlessly by the 5th Rifles, some "B" Detachment units attempted, generally unsuccessfully, to surrender. Despite the effectiveness of the solution, by the time the impostors had been overcome nearly a third of France was unsafe for unarmed Allied troops (and in many areas for armed individuals or groups below squad sized).

The greatest long-term damage done to the French Nation was, however, the result of the civil war and food shortages that held sway in areas not yet overrun by the Allied advance but where the SS had largely abandoned. Scores that went back generations were settled, as often as not with makeshift weapons or bare hands, as order (along with most food and potable water) virtually disappeared in both urban and rural areas along with the retreating SS. While French civilian officials were sometimes able to retain some sense of authority and order, in many areas the authorities were hard-pressed to save their own loved ones from starvation and thirst in the wake of SS well poisonings and destruction of reservoirs and water systems. Reich poisonings were so effective that in some areas Allied troops had to have potable water shipped to them along with fuel and ammunition

(Allied records indicate that nearly 125 miles of the Meuse River was "rendered lifeless" by withdrawing Reich units).

The collapse of the already-tattered French National Army into roughly a dozen factions, each proclaiming allegiance to a different general or politician, allowed many of the Einsatzgruppen formations to escape French vengeance as they withdrew into Inner Germany as the thirst for revenge was forgotten in the imaginary chase for control of France that consumed the nation's leadership. The "disloyal", starting with individuals insufficiently dedicated to pushing out the "invaders" (a term used interchangeably for both Allied and Reich forces in some cases), followed by those who were seen as being too close to the rapidly-departing Nazis, followed then by supporters of the wrong French faction as conditions changed, found their lives to be controlled by the slightest twist of fate. The number of those killed in these various purges will likely never be fully known, nor will the number who died simply for being in the wrong place at the wrong time. What is known is that the damage done to French society by the retreating Nazis, subsequent breakdown of civil authority, and resulting anarchy has not been fully repaired to this day.

Between food shortages, lack of water, illness and civil strife, France was virtually destroyed as a modern nation. On April 14th, 1959, the last significant Reich formation withdrew behind the "Rommel Line", with long-range Allied artillery chasing it across the river.

On April 16th, 1959, concerted Allied air attacks began against portions of the Rommel Line.

52

The true foolishness of the Luftwaffe suicide tactics was quite literally hammered home by the 8th and 14th US Air Forces as the real preparation for the crossing of the Rhine began. While the initial attacks had come as a shock and had cost the Allies many aircraft and some very valuable men, the Allies had both the aircraft and, realistically, the manpower to spare. The Luftwaffe had neither, and following the initial shock, the Allies – especially the USAF's 14th Air Force, with its specialization in tactical operations – took advantage of that fact.

By early March the Luftwaffe had nearly shot its bolt, having lost 80% of its already vastly-diminished strength, leaving a few of the remarkably powerful Focke-Wulf P-366.67 fighters and around 150 Fw-190 and Me-410 ground attack aircraft to oppose the thousands of Allied attackers.

Arguably the best fighter flown by any of the combatants during the war, production versions of the Raubvogel did not begin to reach the Luftwaffe until late February 1959. Production of the twin-tailed, Mach 2.7 interceptor was severely curtailed by material shortage and a highly-focused Allied air strike, featuring some 62 deep penetrator versions of the BLU 15, on the underground complex where the aircraft was produced. While the Allies had rushed pre-production versions of the F-4 Phantom into the field to attempt to counter the Raubvogel, and had moved EE Lightning squadrons close to the front line to try to deal with P-336.67 movement over liberated Europe, it remains an open question if these countermeasures would have been enough to stop the Raubvogel if the Luftwaffe had been able to field 500 of the aircraft instead of the 75 that made it into operation. Recently declassified USAF documents reveal that the

Air Force began a crash program in late January 1959 to modify the A-11 Oxcart as a possible counter to the Raubvogel. These declassified (and heavily redacted) documents do not reveal if this aircraft, which would have been a Mach 3.2+ interceptor if built, was ever test flown or even completed. Numerous FOI requests for additional information have been met with stony silence. In the end, 75 superb aircraft had no chance against the Allied aerial juggernaut.

The pounding of the major strong-points of the Rommel Line was a round-the-clock celebration of Allied logistical genius. Well over one thousand miles of railroad trackage was laid to reduce the need for truck fuel to transport munitions and vehicles forward, as were eight 32-inch underground pipelines for the movement of vehicle and aircraft fuel to the battle front. While the manpower available to the Allies to complete this work staggers the mind, nearly as much as the $3 billion cost of the work, it remains a remarkable achievement in construction, one that paid dividends for decades. With the transportation hub in place, the famed "Factories of Freedom" were hard-pressed to keep up with the ability to move material across the Atlantic Ocean, Indian Ocean, and through the Panama Canal to the fighting men nearing the Rhine. Just the US 12th Army Group required a *minimum* of 12,000 *tons* of supplies each day it was engaged in combat, or 8,000 tons while at rest. When one realizes that the 12th was just one of seven Allied Army Groups in Europe, the true dimension of the Allied effort becomes clear, as does the reason that for every combat soldier the Allied armies used there were eleven men in support functions, as well as the jobs provided to thousands of civilians across the liberated zones (the Allies had actually hoped to employ over a million civilians in direct support positions – cooking, cleaning, translation, etc. – as they advanced, but the reality on the ground reduced this number by around 85%).

The dismantling of the Rommel Line forts rapidly established a routine, with Allied tube artillery and rocket artillery (mainly 240mm, but also a few of the monstrous 380mm systems with their complex loading systems and 120-man crews) delivering what the SS quickly dubbed "Devil's Rain" during the night and Allied air attacks taking over during the day while most of the gunners slept or performed maintenance tasks, save a few batteries kept on alert in case counter-battery fire was needed (a task usually left to a battalion of 240mm launchers in each division). The Allies pounded against more than two dozen pieces of the Line, although they had no intention of attack against each targeted section, and demonstrated with commando raids against others to keep the SS from concentrating its rapidly swelling ranks in a few sectors.

The Allied air attacks were mainly conducted by fighter-bombers, although at least one section of the line was treated to a 40-plane B-36 attack each day that deposited 1,400 tons of high explosive over a five-mile front and others were hit by BLU-15 FAE weapons dropped by C-130 transport aircraft as the air defenses were gradually pulverized.

On April 20th, 1959, the reequipped and rededicated Italian 22nd and 23rd Infantry Divisions, supported by the 2nd New South Wales Armored Division, began attacks against the SS Alps defenses. Designed to draw Reich manpower and attention rather than achieve a serious breakthrough, the offensive nonetheless managed to capture two passes into Austria, although at serious cost. Occurring three days before the British Black Sea landing, the Italian Offensive succeeded in effectively freezing the SS southern command in place, preventing it from reinforcing to the East or moving units to the Rhine – a situation that continued for nearly the rest of the war.

The Allied preparations continued until May 9th, 1959, when Operation Chainsaw began.

53

The Allies had expected that the German practice of scorched earth would at least begin to subside once they crossed the "traditional" German border and entered the Inner Reich. This had of course not been the case, as flame and explosions continued to obliterate the work of centuries. The only difference was that, in the main, the civilian populations of the abandoned regions were evacuated in what became a close to headlong flight as the land border defenses of the Reich were penetrated with surprising ease by Allied formations, often with nothing more than brief, albeit hard-fought, skirmishes with local reserve formations, many of whom hadn't seen active combat service since 1940 and who were frequently equipped with virtually the same weapons as they had carried when they had taken part in Fall Gelb. The encounters with the middle-aged (and older) Landsers were something of an education for the Allied units, as they encountered troops who fought well in small units, were led by NCOs and "junior" officers (in rank, if not in age), and who fought until defeat was inevitable and then surrendered honorably. More than one Allied battalion commander's battle diary includes comments remarking on how fortunate they had been to not encounter these men during their prime, or even in their current condition but with up to date weapons and training. In many ways, these battles were the simultaneous rebirth and death of the Heer.

With the exception of these local reserve formations that were left behind by the SS to protect their farms and shops, mainly to act as "speedbumps" in an effort to buy time, the rest of the Reich's remaining military assets were either behind the Rommel Line or headed there as quickly as possible once they had pushed civilians out of the many towns located in far western Germany.

Advancing Allied scout units began to see a disturbing pattern as they cautiously searched for enemy blocking units. In village after village, the cavalry units found destruction and dead civilians who had clearly committed suicide rather than be captured, as well as groups of dead civilians who had equally clearly been murdered.

While it was initially believed that these victims were slave laborers, it turned out that many of the dead were locals who had not wanted to leave their homes, preferring Allied occupation to flight, or who did not wish to leave without their kin among the local reserve units. This position was seen as outright treason by SS and Gestapo personnel, who would then ensure that the 'traitors' were properly handled before the area was evacuated. It was the first time the Allies had encountered this sort of behavior since the conquest of Formosa in 1946, and it left many of the younger Allied troops both shaken and outraged. A war that had already become something close to a crusade on both sides was pushed to new levels of ferocity.

Operation Chainsaw opened with the first use of nuclear weapons in direct support of ground operations, as no fewer than five of the remaining "fortresses" that had survived all previous attempts to silence them found themselves the subject of F-105 strikes. The attacks against the Konigswinter, Leverkusen, Niederheid, Duisberg, and Wessel strong points, all of which were hit by two ground burst weapons delivered at 06:30 and then 12:00 hours, were literally glaringly obvious indicators of where the Allied forces were planning to cross – something that the troops on both sides understood, and that Berlin had been waiting for as the indicator of where they should send their few remaining reserves. Reports by stay-behind agents who told of large numbers of amphibious tractors and enemy troops moving toward Leverkusen and Duisberg gave Himmler even more proof of where "the English will meet their demise", as Propaganda Minister Goebbels had begun to refer to the Allied effort to cross the Rhine.

All along the Rommel Line, men on both sides knew the moment had come, knew that they would be involved.

They were all wrong.

After extended movement and demonstration, including the launching of three regimental-sized assaults across the river on May 10th, the Allies launched their main assault out of the Netherlands, with the 12th and 15th Army Groups making their main attack near Bremerhaven on May 11th with the support of the US Navy's gun line. After a difficult initial wave, where 1/3 Marines suffered nearly 50% losses, the Allies firmly established themselves on the Bremerhaven side of the river. With almost 800 aircraft providing air support, both from land bases and off carriers, by sunset the entire 1st Marine Division was over the river. By daybreak on May 12th, combat engineers from the 1st Canadian Army and 23rd SeaBees battalion had established four ribbon bridges to support the bridgehead, with four additional bridges, two being established by the Australian 2nd Army, nearing completion. Sunset of the 12th saw the entire 15th Army Group's combat formations across the river and driving to the east.

In what was a first, the civilian government of Bremerhaven sent a delegation to meet with the commander of the 1st Marine division and surrendered the city to him without conditions. The Commander of Canadian 1st Army received a similar visit from the "ruling council of Wilhelmshaven" that requested that the municipality be declared an Open City, pledging full cooperation with Allied military authorities. Immensely relieved by the prospect of not having to oversee the reduction of the cities to rubble by the guns of the Allied gun line, both Allied officers accepted the surrenders and sent Provost Marshal units to finalize details.

The Reich's attempt to retake Bremerhaven is mainly noteworthy for details of its failure. The American nuclear submarine USS *Pike* became the first nuclear-powered warship to sink an enemy vessel as she collected not one, but two Type XXXIV U-boats that had sortied from Kiel to attack the invaders. *Pike* located and sank both U-boats solely with her sonar, finding them while they were near the surface snorkeling and using their diesel engines. It was the first of what would eventually be many examples of the enormous advantage that nuclear power provided submarines so equipped. The Bremerhaven action was also the first (and so far only) time that a nuclear depth charge was used in anger, as USS *Farragut* used her ASROC launcher to deliver a Mark 17 depth bomb (ten KT yield) against a target that surviving KM records indicate was the U-2753 at a range of some 7,000 yards. In all, some 11 U-boats were lost in KM attempts to intervene in Chainsaw, with only one Allied ship (USS *Sullivans*, which lost some 35 feet of her bow) being hit.

The Reich's last major defensive line had been breached.

54

The Allied end-run around the laboriously-constructed Rommel Line placed the Waffen-SS command into a trap of their own creation. The SS leadership had put everything available into the Rhine defenses in the vain hope of at least forcing the Allies to stop short of the Reich's core. Now those forces, including nearly all the surviving SS Panzer tanks and SP guns, were trapped along the Rhine floodplain and subject to constant air attack and shelling. Despite losses inflicted by Luftwaffe SAM and antiaircraft positions (which were themselves then subjected to murderous air attack and, if in range, 280mm rocket barrages), Allied pilots found their missions to more resemble fox or pheasant hunting than anything else, as aircraft lazily circled waiting to pounce on any "game" that was flushed or tried to flee.

The post-war USAF Strategic Bombing Survey (Volume III) credits ground attack aircraft with the destruction of some 350 tanks and SP guns, nearly 200 other tracked vehicles, and well over 1,000 trucks/passenger vehicles during the period between May 14 and June 2, 1959. While this figure must be considered with some care, it is also important to note that kills were only credited when gun camera footage showed catastrophic damage or when advancing Allied forces overran destroyed enemy columns.

The relentless shelling and air attacks against the defensive works of the Rommel Line, especially in areas of the line that were never selected for eventual crossing attempts, has long been a matter of some debate. In the wake of the 40th Anniversary of Gravel and the celebratory events marking the "Liberation of Europe", something of a cottage industry has developed around the publishing of revisionist histories and television documentaries that question if Ridgway and Simonds were not themselves guilty of atrocities in the manner that these "forlornly isolated and beaten men" (as one Dutch documentary styled the fortress troops) were "slaughtered".

These revisionists are, of course, ignoring the military reality that existed during May and June of 1959, and the simple fact that the SS had, even without counting the foreign fortress troops, almost 40,000 German reservists manning the 150-mile-long Rommel Line. These men, along with a portion of the "foreign' troops (some of whom were, despite the characterizations, not draftees who were forced to serve the Reich but members of the Waffen-SS "Outlander" divisions who had withdrawn along with their SS brothers) presented a clear and ongoing danger to the Allied advance. It is noteworthy that even after many of the fortifications had been turned and were totally surrounded, the German and "Aryan" Outlanders fought literally to the last man rather than surrender their doomed positions (something that continued even in the wake of June 17th). It is understandable that Belgian, Dutch, Norwegian, and even French authors seek to downplay the willingness of their grandfathers and uncles to fight on for the Reich to the very end, but it is unfortunate that so many of them, like their American and British brethren, choose to twist facts while doing so.

The rapid advance of both 12th and 15th Army Groups following their crossing of the Weser caused true panic among the Nazi leadership, perhaps for the first time since the Party had come to power in 1933. Literal warehouses of documents related to the "Final Solution" (a phrase that itself was nearly obliterated along with the files), actions taken in the clearing of the General Government areas, and files related to the pacification of Europe were put to the torch across the Reich in hopes of denying the future the truth (an effort that failed mainly due to the almost unbelievable volume of records, in addition to the number of personal photographs, home movies, and souvenirs in private hands across the Reich).

While records were destroyed within the Reich, Party officials outside of German borders began to seek a way out. The Reich Ambassador to Switzerland presented himself and his family to the Foreign Ministry requesting political asylum on May 17th, with his counterpart domiciled at the Holy See following suit two days later. The Reich representative in Sweden was pre-empted in his attempt when the Swedish Government declared him and most of his Staff persona non grata on May 20th, ordering some 95% of the Embassy staff to leave Sweden within 48 hours "for activities contrary to their diplomatic status". This left the Reich Ambassador to Tibet as the senior active Party official outside of Germany.

Ahead of the rapidly-advancing Allied troops went the "Handbill Bombing Offensive", as heavily escorted B-29s and C-130s dropped the first wave of what was eventually be 300,000,000 leaflets (nearly half the available printing presses in Italy, Portugal, Spain, Turkey, and the United Kingdom were used to produce this blizzard of propaganda). The leaflets were simple, promising good treatment, medical attention, and food to anyone who presented them to the advancing Allied troops in a very specific manner. Unfortunately, thanks to the large number of suicide bombers already encountered, the requirements were such that most Germans simply refused to follow them until starvation was setting in (men had to stop 200 meters from Allied troops and disrobe completely, women had to disrobe to what was effectively swimming attire before being permitted through checkpoints).

What was generally obeyed was the Allied edict to stay off the streets and to instantly obey orders to halt (this may be partly due to this sort of requirement being commonly issued by the Gestapo). German civilians as young as 10 years of age who failed to follow this particular order were often shot out of hand, especially as stories (some of them actually true) spread among the ranks about "little kids with satchel charges" blowing up trucks when G.I.s slowed to give them K Rations or candy. While the number of juveniles who were killed in this manner has never been satisfactorily established, it is noteworthy that long-term psychological issues regarding the action ranks, to this day, as the primary PTSD issue reported by veterans of the European Liberation Campaign.

While 15th Army Group was driving to the south, the US 12th Army Group drove directly to the east in an effort to cut off the Danish Peninsula from the Reich. Since Germany was, by this point, getting nearly 35% of its total food supply from this region of northern Germany and Denmark, the 12th advance was also seen, correctly, as the more dangerous of the two Allied lines of advance (something that did not change even after the British 22nd Army Group crossed the Rhine north of Duisburg on May 19 in Operation Cobra). In the van of 12th Army Group was the American 3rd Army, which found itself opposed by what remains the oddest hodgepodge of equipment ever seen on a battlefield.

SS and reserve units, mostly dispatched in small scratch units entirely insufficient to stop the hard-charging 24th Infantry Division (Mechanized), deployed with, in one case, a company of 1917 vintage Renault FT light tanks and even earlier vintage FK 96 77mm guns straight out of the museum and a variety of other captured, obsolete, or in the case of a few Char B tanks, captured *and* obsolete equipment. Allied records indicate that reserve units mostly comprised of "old bastards" often gave good, even impressive efforts with this mixed bag of equipment, while regular Waffen-SS units would fight manically but be easily brushed aside when similarly outfitted. How much of this was due to the reserve forces fighting for their own nearby homes and families and how much of it was due to SS demoralization is impossible to determine, but the combat diary of General Creighton Abrams, the 3rd Army commander, makes a point of observing on several occasions that he was glad he hadn't had to fight the local militia when they were twenty years old since they were "a pretty clever bunch".

The highlight of 24th Mech's advance was certainly the famous Battle of Bad Oldesloe. This engagement marked the one and only combat action of the Pz. VIII Maus. Apparently a vanity project of Hitler and his favorite designer Ferdinand Porsche, the Maus remains the heaviest land combat vehicle ever fielded at 207 standard tons (188,000 kg). Armed with both a 128mm and 75mm high velocity gun it, has been speculated that the vehicle was actually meant to be a mobile pillbox meant to fight from a prepared position (something that seems reasonable given its outrageous weight and 7 mph top speed), although the lack of records or design notes makes this impossible to prove definitively. What *is* easily proved by the record of the engagement is that the Pz. VIII should never have left the factory, much less have had 21 units produced (with eleven of these being built after 1955). With a hull measuring a stunning 34 feet in length and having a turret that towered 13 feet from the ground, the vehicle was literally "as big as a house". It was also just about as easy to target. While its front armor proved to be immune even to the Chamberlain's 120mm AP round, the same could not be said for the side or rear armor (another indication that the tank was never really meant to engage in mobile combat), which was incapable of stopping the Sheridan's 105mm AP rounds, much less the Chamberlain's mighty 120. The vehicle's turret transverse system also proved to be insufficient to rotate with sufficient speed to track the 30 mph Sheridan, which was illustrated on several occasions during the action. Twelve of the huge SS vehicles were destroyed by 24th Mech tanks, at a cost of two Sheridans, with the remaining nine falling victim to air-delivered napalm and 11.5" rockets (a weapon originally designed to defeat battleship and heavy cruiser armor).

It took the 12th eleven days to effectively cut the peninsula off from Inner Germany (something of an anticlimax since the Danes had surrendered three days previously, on May 20th), by which time the Allies had three separate Army Groups in addition to the 12th on German soil. Having achieved its initial objective, the Group paused to resupply before moving on to the east.

On May 25th, Adolph Hitler's heart stopped beating, allowing his body to join his long-deceased brain.

It was not the kind of thing that even the Gestapo could keep quiet for long.

55

The source of the news of Hitler's death has never been identified, although most speculation centers on the five medical orderlies who were assigned to him to ensure that he (or rather the ventilator that kept him alive) was tended to 24 hours per day. None of these men survived the war, so it was never possible for Allied investigators to speak to them on the subject.

While word had gradually filtered out that the Führer was ill, perhaps even gravely ill, in the months following Hitler's July 1958 stroke, there seems to have never been any concern that he would actually die, at least among the rank and file Reich citizen. Perhaps this was due to the fact that close to half of the Reich's population could never remember a different Führer, could never remember a time before National Socialism, and that these individuals simply could not conceptualize a world without the "Beloved Führer" guiding the Volk. The reality of Hitler's death struck these people like a thunderbolt.

It has been firmly established at more than 10,000 Germans committed suicide in the 96 hours following the official confirmation of Hitler's death on June 4th, 1959 (some estimates go as high as 40,000, but with the other events of that same period it is impossible to establish that these deaths were self-inflicted). Hundreds of thousands poured into the streets of Berlin on June 7th, 1959, to attend the funeral ceremony (with millions of other Germans denied entry to the capital to attend due to the total quarantine), an event that the Allied High Command ensured was not interrupted, to the point that the Allies discontinued their heavy jamming of Reich television signals during the event. This decision was quite controversial at the time (the commanding officer of the RAF Bomber Command's 823 Group resigned his post after his request to obliterate the site of the memorial with a nuclear weapon was denied) and has remained a bone of contention in some circles to this day. While some critics are of the opinion that a successful attack on the service would have broken the Reich's will to resist, as well as killing off the Nazi hierarchy at a stroke, the SACEUR leadership at the time believed that an attack would have had the opposite effect of setting the Reich population's resistance in stone, an opinion supported by the civilian leadership in both the US and UK.

This show of "respect for the feeling of the German people" ended within minutes of the conclusion of the service, with the Allies managing to wrest control of the Reich airwaves for more than 10 minutes during which a carefully designed message was broadcast directly to 90% of the homes in the unconquered (primarily central and eastern) portions of the Fatherland as well as a second, slightly different message that was transmitted into what had once been Poland for the consumption of the "settlers" residing there. While Goebbels's deputies were able to jam the Allied message after 10-15 minutes, that the Allies had broken through at all is an indication of just how severely Hitler's passing had impacted the men and women on duty (there are many first-person reports regarding individuals fainting or being overcome with emotion during the services, even when watching them from home).

Reaction to Hitler's death by Waffen-SS units seems to have been closely related to how junior officers handled the news. In units where platoon leaders kept their heads, the reaction was similar to that of US troops to the death of FDR – sadness tempered by the desire to get the job done in his memory. In units where the platoon officers lost their composure, this rapidly spread to the troops, with the result being either near total loss of combat effectiveness or the altogether too common decision by the unit commanders to simply charge the nearest enemy position to "make the enemy pay" for causing the Führer's death. Perhaps the best known of these incidents was the one that overtook the III and IV battalions of the 1st SS Panzer, whose 1,800 men, with 35 Panther III tanks as support, made a headlong attack against the 7th Australian Armored Division near Hanover on June 8th. The attack, which began at 07:00 in full daylight under clear blue skies, was a slaughter of the first order as the presence of so many troops moving in the open, in broad daylight, drew Allied aircraft like moths to a porch light. By 09:30 the attack had ended. Australian losses were 22 dead, 72 wounded, with the loss of two Sheridans (one to a human bomb). SS losses were virtually 100%, with all 35 tanks destroyed and 1693 dead (a number at their own hand to avoid capture) and only 107 taken prisoner, nearly all of whom were either unconscious or otherwise so disabled by their wounds as to be unable to resist. As had by then become standard practice, these wounded were treated and then placed immediately into a secure holding facility rather than being left in the ordinary common wards (something that the Allies had quickly found to be unnecessary when dealing with reserve formation PoWs as these Heer veterans were simply glad that they were not shot after capture).

While the Hanover attack was the largest, and best documented (thanks to the presence of a newsreel camera team with the 7th), it was far from the only one. Virtually every significant Allied formation in Germany or Austria reported attacks ranging in size from squads up to a full battalion. In no case were these human wave attacks successful, illustrating the enormous firepower that even a simple infantry platoon could deliver thanks to the magazine-fed combat rifle and the proliferation of light machine guns into ever smaller units.

By June of 1959 every American platoon included a three machine gun section of 9 men armed with the M-52 (an Americanized version of the superb German MG-42), consisting of three gunners and six ammunition carriers, all of whom were trained to act as assistant gunners. This effectively gave every infantry squad the firepower of a Pacific War rifle platoon.

By 12th June, it was clear that German civilian morale was collapsing as town after town simply surrendered at the first sight of an allied unit.

Unfortunately, Nazi Party leaders and many of the remaining Waffen-SS formations had no intention of going quietly.

56

With defeat staring them in the face, the Reich leadership was faced with a stark set of choices ranging from bad to instantly fatal:

A. The leadership could throw itself on the debatable mercy of the Allies, who had been fighting the Reich for two decades, seen the appalling cruelty of those in charge, and had proof that the Reich had: 1) unleashed a series of lethal bio-weapons on civilians; 2) murdered well over 40 million people (the now widely accepted total of 90-95 million was not calculated until the early 1980s) on the basis of their race; and 3) had seen Nazi chemical weapons kill thousands of civilians, including members of Her Majesty's immediate family.

B. The Reich could fight on, in a battle that was clearly and unquestionably lost, at appalling cost in Aryan lives and in a nation where disease was rampant as all the plagues spread by the SS came home to roost. From surviving records, it is clear that, unlike Hitler, who had an unreasoned belief in final victory up to the moment of his stroke, none of the Party leaders had the slightest illusion by late April of 1959 that the Reich could win the war.

C. They could attempt to disappear or try to find sanctuary in a neutral country. The only neutral close enough to reach without running an Allied gauntlet was Switzerland. The Swiss had, on May 13th, closed their borders to all entry, citing the need to quarantine themselves in view of "the unusual number of illnesses currently present in the rest of Europe". The various expatriate German communities around the world had long since washed their hands of the Nazis (as often as not to ensure their own positions in their adopted countries), leaving few, if any, places for the Party leadership to run.

D. Death at their own hand. This option at least allowed the individual the choice of method.

Unsurprisingly, the Party leadership chose all of the above with predictable results.

Göring, who had never really gotten over being replaced as the leader of his beloved Luftwaffe, took poison the same day the 21st Army Group crossed the Rhine. Persistent rumors exist that he took this course after receiving word that any attempt to reach Argentina and the substantial German population there would result in, at best, his being handed over to Argentine authorities. Since an Argentine division was an active part of the 12th Army Group's advance into central Germany, the consequences of such a turnover were clear. If the rest of the Party brass had made the same choice, many innocents would have been spared, especially in the Ruhr Valley city of Essen.

Essen, in a war marked by horror, stands out for sheer needlessness. The Allies had not selected Essen as a target for the retaliatory nuclear strikes, and the city hosted one of the major state-sponsored medical offices in Germany. Both factors had led to the city being flooded with refugees and those seeking to escape Pandora's revenge on the Reich.

Krupp AG had major facilities on the outskirts of the Essen; these had been the subject of rather intensive Allied conventional bombing and were mainly out of production. Unfortunately, the Reich also established a below-ground chemical production center, run by Krupp, some five miles west-northwest of Essen which had become the primary production center for chemical weapons after the obliteration of the Piesteritz GmbH Chemical Works by a British nuclear weapon. This was unknown to RAF mission planners, who believed the recently-detected underground factory was being used to manufacture small arms and scheduled it to be bombed on June 14th. The raid, conducted by twelve Vulcan bombers equipped with specially-designed, ground-penetrating "earthquake" ten-ton bombs was virtually unopposed save by some local 88mm manually-aimed anti-aircraft guns. Four of the twelve bombs found their way into the man-made cavern holding the chemical works, each leaving a 45-foot hole in the roof. One weapon detonated near the storage facilities, rupturing numerous pipes and creating a shock wave that caused containment failures on five 8,000 liter tanks, four of which were full and contained Sarin, with the fifth being nearly empty of the weapon. Prevailing winds did the rest. With over 74,000 casualties, including 18,000 fatalities, Essen remains the deadliest nerve gas release in history. Over 90% of the casualties were refugees; two-thirds of these were women and children. The Essen release was not discovered until Canadian troops entered the area on June 19th, by which time there was virtually nothing that could be done for the victims. Survivors of the release suffer from debilitating nerve damage to this day. None of the Vulcans sustained any damage, and all returned to base without incident.

Himmler's order, published on June 9th, instructing that any town which attempted to surrender to advancing UN forces was to be razed by Waffen-SS forces, has long been cited as the triggering event of the June 17th Mutiny. This ignores the statements of those credited with starting and leading the Mutiny, especially Field Marshall Erich von Manstein and General Adolph Galland, both of whom maintained that the Mutiny resulted from Hitler's death and the personal oath of obedience that all Reich officers had sworn to the Führer in the late 1930s. While it is difficult to believe that a spoken oath was sufficient to keep thousands of Heer veterans from acting against the Nazis, it is clear that Hitler's death was the Mutiny's spark (it seems likely that the mutineers did not act until Hitler was out of the picture to enhance the chances of success).

Whatever the reason, the insurrection spread quickly among former Heer officers and senior NCOs – the troops that formed the backbone of the Reich's reserve formations. Waffen-SS officers, many of them barely out of their teens, found their troops utterly unwilling to obey orders; at least, the lucky ones did. Those less fortunate, or those who had managed to make enemies of the Landsers they commanded, were often shot out of hand. Australian postwar studies indicate that up to 30% of SS officers in command of reserve units were killed by the men under their command.

The virtual collapse of the Reich reserve force, which included numerous firefights within units as the 14 and 15 year-old Hitler Youth who had been placed under arms as the Allies approached fought with their "Uncles", allowed Allied formations to make rapid advances, with the 2nd Indian Armored reaching Vienna on June 22nd (Vienna's current position as one of the most picturesque cities in the world is entirely due to the Mutiny, as it was the local reserve unit that virtually wiped out the Einsatzgruppen unit sent to destroy local cultural icons).

By June 27th, Allied troops controlled over 80% of German territory. The remaining Nazi-controlled zones were within the more heavily contaminated Anthrax Zones.

The Allied solution to the difficulties presented by these "No Go" regions remains controversial to this day.

57

While limited today to historians, the debate over the Allies' choices starting on July 4th, 1959, once evoked passions sufficient to start bar brawls. Today the brawls are generally confined to academic works and the occasional popular history book, but at the time the choices literally altered and ended careers.

It all began on that remarkably hot Saturday morning with the appearance of a light SS staff car displaying several white flags approaching the listening posts of 29th Marines near Havelberg, Germany. After a series of radio calls, Major Bruce Williamson, the deputy commander of 2nd Batt/29th, arrived on scene with three LVT-5 amtracks. Williamson found a sizable part of his Fox company on high alert, all focused on two enlisted SS troopers, an Untersturmführer (2nd Lt.), and a remarkably arrogant Oberführer (Senior Colonel/Brigadier), all of whom were waiting outside of their vehicle. After military formalities were exchanged (with the SS officers in full dress uniforms and Williamson and his aide in well-worn Marine BDUs), Oberführer Strauss informed the astonished Americans that he was bearing a peace proposal and requested that he be transported to the proper authorities. Within three hours, Strauss was face to face with General William Westmoreland, the recently promoted commander of 15th Army Group. Finally satisfied that his message was being treated with its due respect, Strauss handed over the documents which Himmler had personally entrusted to his care.

Himmler's so-called "Peace with Honor" has long been seen as proof that the SS leader had lost all contact with reality. The document called upon the Allies to:

Agree to an immediate cease-fire.

Cease all aggression against the peaceful people of the Third Reich.

Recognize the Himmler Government as the sole legitimate leader of the Reich.

Withdraw all Allied troops to the 1933 Western borders of the old German Republic and from "New Germania" to the East as far as the "internationally recognized border with the USSR as it had existed on March 17th 1954".

Give formal recognition of Reich treaties with the USSR which were in effect on March 17th, 1954.

Provide immediate medical supplies to relieve the "many diseases that the English and Americans have set loose on the peaceful German people".

In return the Reich would:

Renounce claims to all territories located to the West of the internationally recognized Reich borders as of September 1, 1939.

Guarantee that no further U-boat attacks would occur.

Investigate and prosecute, when appropriate, Reich troops and officials who had violated international treaties regarding treatment of Prisoners of War captured after January 1st 1950.

Agree to talks aimed at ensuring a lasting European peace, based on the input of the peoples of the "European community".

Renounce, in the interest of a lasting peace, its altogether justifiable claims for reparations for the destruction caused by the aggression of the United Kingdom and its Allies as they existed on October 1st 1940.

In short, Himmler's offer required the Allies to accept, permanently, all Reich conquests in the East and to agree that no international or military tribunal would take any sort of action against Reich officials or troops. It was the sort of peace offer that might have been acceptable in 1942, or even 1944 (had the Allies not have already announced their "Unconditional Surrender" policy), but with Allied troops within 50 miles of the center of Berlin it was madness.

All Allied Army Group commanders had been issued standing orders regarding the acceptance of cease-fire offers. These were specific in that the Army Group commander could accept a complete ceasefire on all fronts only if it included an unconditional surrender offer. Smaller cease-fires could be afforded "in the interest of humanity", but that was the limit of a field commander's authority. Since Himmler's offer was anything but an unconditional surrender, Westmoreland sent it (reluctantly) to SACEUR, resending it 30 minutes later (legend has it that Ridgway, when presented with the first message, said "this is either garbled beyond belief or Bill's drunk, get a confirmation of which it is"). Within an hour of the second message's arrival, the text was in front of the British Prime Minister and POTUS. The call between Washington and London to discuss the matter lasted less than five minutes.

The Allied response was simple. "Offer refused. The only acceptable offer is Unconditional Surrender."

Himmler's attempt to keep power post-war had failed.

The Allied Supreme Council took three days to come up with a reply to the Himmler Message.

Sent over with the signatures of the representatives of all the powers facing the Reich, the message stated:

The United Nations hereby make the following demands on the leadership of the German Reich.

Immediate unconditional surrender of all military forces.

Immediate unconditional surrender to Allied Authorities of all members of the German Reich leadership.

Immediate release of all Allied Prisoners of War.

Immediate release of all foreigners from German Reich prisons, labor camps and work centers.

Failure to comply with these demands by Noon, Berlin Time, on July 10th, 1959, will be construed as a rejection by the German nation.

Rejection of these demands will carry the most severe of consequences for the German People and for the leadership of the German Reich.

The message was sent via the Holy See and through the Reich Ambassador to Tibet on July 8th, 1959.

No reply was ever received.

58

At the same time as the Allies sent their formal demands to the Reich's leadership, they also virtually papered all of unoccupied Germany and the General Government areas with leaflets repeating the same demands. One significant difference in the leaflets was an assurance that civilian populations would be treated in accordance with all terms of the Geneva Convention, a statement that would also be broadcast across the breadth of the country. Following the rejection of the ultimatum by Berlin, the Allied dropped a second five million leaflets (an act that disrupted newspaper delivery across Britain for two days due to paper and press shortages) with the following stark message:

To the Citizens and residents of the Third Reich:

Your leaders having ignored our Ultimatum of July 8th, we offer you individually the following opportunity:

Any civilian presenting themselves to Allied forces by Sunset on July 12th, 1959, will be properly treated, given medical treatment if necessary, and food and shelter. Individuals wishing to accept this offer should bring this leaflet to the nearest Allied forces. Follow ALL direction given by Allied troops. Failure to follow ALL instructions may result in the use of lethal force.

If you choose to decline this humanitarian offer be aware of the following:

Any movement observed in territory not under Allied control as of Sunset on July 12th, 1959, will be subject to attack by Allied air, ground, or naval forces.

Any residential center, be it a village, town, or city, that resists Allied troops may be totally destroyed without further notice as of Sunset on July 12th 1959.

All facilities capable of being used to support Waffen-SS or Reich local reserve forces are subject to attack by any and all weapons within Allied control. This includes agricultural production and transport.

Any person found in possession of a weapon but not in uniform will not be provided the protection due to belligerents under the applicable Conventions. Any person or persons found to be sheltering a spy or saboteur will be likewise considered to be a spy or saboteur.

The distribution of these leaflets produced a single primary reaction among German civilians: utter panic. In several towns near the Allied front lines, open battles broke out in the streets between those attempting to flee and those who saw them as traitors. In other locations the panic took a form that the Allies had not even considered possible, with mass murder-suicides on a scale unseen since the final defeat of Japan (some estimates of the dead from these mainly family group acts exceed 70,000; a not unreasonable figure given the enormous size of many German families, where six children were considered to be a modest brood). While many of these cases were seemingly voluntary, at least by those old enough to understand (some 20,000 victims were under the age of seven), there is also indisputable evidence that at least five villages were wiped out by SS troops aided by local Hitler Youth with the younger perpetrators then taking their own lives. In defense of the Allies, this phenomenon was not discovered until after resistance collapsed in the regions affected. In other areas, mainly those furthest from the Allied lines, the civilian population largely seems to have accepted that they were doomed and gone about their regular activities.

The leaflets also unleashed a firestorm within Allied military circles, especially once the rules of engagement putting them into effect were released by the Combined Chiefs of Staff. Often called the "Tokyo protocol" or the "Oxcart directive", the rules called upon Allied air, naval and ground units to "disrupt ALL enemy movement, be it by foot, animal transport, motor traffic, rail, or air" without warning or consideration for "collateral damage" (the first known use of the term by Anglo-American planners). The orders were nothing short of a hunting license issued to well over 2 million Allied troops and airmen in Europe.

The first casualty of the new orders was the newly-appointed US Chief of Naval Operations, Fleet Admiral Joseph "Jocko" Clark, who submitted his retirement papers simultaneously with the broadcast of the Rules of Engagement. His retirement letter, which included the now famous "I cannot be a party to another massacre of innocents; once in any man's lifetime is all that can be borne", and his subsequent memoirs have long been viewed as examples of honorable protest in the face of impossible choices. In short order, Clark's resignation was followed by that of the Assistant Commandant of the US Marine Corps, the Secretary of the Army, and the First Lord of the Admiralty. What all of these men, and most of the close to two dozen other military and civilian senior leaders who followed their lead, had in common was service in Japan immediately after the Capitulation.

While the number of resignations or refusals to follow orders on moral grounds by the lower ranks was far from crippling to the war effort, it remains striking that virtually all of these cases came from men who had served in immediate post-war Japan. This was seen, at the time, as a unique form of "battle fatigue" (and based on today's understanding of Post-Traumatic Stress Disorder, it is probable that many of the cases were PTSD-related), and to the credit of SACEUR General Ridgway none of the men (or six Army nurses) involved had any corrective action taken against them. All American personnel were sent home to the US to complete their term of enlistment and were, if cleared by medical personnel, allowed to continue their military service in non-combat branches (actions by other nations varied slightly, but no national force was willing to publicly go against SACEUR at this point of the war).

The Allies actually extended their deadline by a full day in order to ensure that the maximum number of civilians were allowed to escape the firestorm to come. Just before sunrise on July 14th, the Allied air forces began their work. The target was Magdeburg.

Located just outside the "Berlin Contamination Zone", Magdeburg's population had swollen from its normal 200,000 to nearly 300,000 with refugees from the Contamination Zone and those seeking to escape the rapidly advancing Allies. Australian forces had been fired upon when approaching the city and radio calls to surrender had been ignored. The USAF therefore chose it as an example of what the Allies could do, even without resorting to nuclear weapons. The 14th was nearly perfect bombing weather, with an unlimited ceiling and very low winds. Nevertheless, the Australians, on the advice of RAAF CAS observers, pulled back nearly four miles from the visible city limits in the hours before the attack. The troops then dug in and waited for what was expected to be "a bloody big show". This belief was an understatement.

At 05:43 hours local time the first three-plane cell of B-52 bombers dropped their payload on the eastern edge of the city. Each aircraft was loaded with sixty 750-pound bombs for a total of 45,000 pounds per aircraft (something of an overload, but with the relatively short distance to target, and the availability of 15,000 foot runways, the mission proved to be well within the Boeing's capabilities) and the carefully-configured three-plane formation ensured the best possible coverage for the combined 180 bombs dropped by the formation. Exactly three minutes behind the first cell was a second, which dropped its bombs exactly three minutes after the lead group. The eleventh bomber cell was offset 800 meters to the east of the first stream's flight path and its bombs were once against aimed at the eastern edge of Magdeburg, with the 22nd cell starting the next tunnel of destruction. This procession continued for two hours until 120 aircraft had dropped along the same corridor. This process created a continuous wave of destruction that rolled through what had, until 05:42 that morning, been the capital of Saxony-Anhalt. A second wave of bombers, scheduled to begin its attacks at 13:00 hours, was cancelled when BDA observers over flying the city at 11:55 reported that there were "no remaining discernible target markers available". The city had been pulverized beyond any recognition as a site of human habitation. Five B-52s suffered some sort of mechanical failure during the attack, with one being forced to crash land at the recently reopened Paris airport. This aircraft, which had to be written off due to the damage it received when it ran out of runway, was the only loss suffered by the bomber force. Luftwaffe losses were all eight fighters that appeared to challenge the nearly 100 Allied fighters protecting the bomber force.

Deaths in Magdeburg have never been firmly established, partly due to the number of refugees in the city who were untraceable, but mainly due to the utterly destroyed condition of the city. The Commander of 1st Battalion, Royal Australian Regiment's battle diary describes conditions in Magdeburg on the morning of July 16th as "resembling a freshly plowed field, if the field in question had previously consisted of bricks, concrete and wood." In places, the debris, none of it larger than a man's fist, was measured as being 8 feet deep, with no identifiable structures remaining intact. Australian forces eventually counted 37,659 civilian survivors who were moved to temporary camps.

It was the start.

It was far from the finish.

59

Amid the truly tragic events that marked the death throes of the Third Reich and that odd political movement that was modern fascism, there was the occasional moment of farce. Perhaps the most extreme of these happened in the aftermath of the Magdeburg Raid.

With the Allies having made Magdeburg their intentional counterpart to the Reich's televised destruction of Paris, to the inclusion of major television and newspaper figures being allowed onto each of the first six bombers, including the still-famous segment with Walter Cronkite reacting with almost child-like exhilaration to the sudden leap upward of *Alaska's Wrath* (the lead aircraft of the Magdeburg mission) as it released its payload, the media of the world broadcast the mission and its aftermath within hours of the attack. With the destruction of the Reich National Broadcasting transmitters, even those Reich citizens who had any sort of television or radio access were also "treated" to the almost casual obliteration of one of the Reich's largest remaining population centers, complete with German narration. Considering the willful media blitz, it was probably inevitable that some unexpected reactions would result.

What was not expected, however, was the accidental comedy that came out of the East. On July 18th, 1959, three groups claiming to represent the USSR delivered documents to the Allied Charge's offices stating that they were repudiating the Reich/Soviet peace agreement and were declaring war on the Third Reich. Two other groups, one of which no one in the West had ever heard of, followed suit on July 20th. A sixth "Provisional Soviet" provided a press release to the BBC on July 21st claiming that all the other groups were frauds and called upon the US to withdraw from "sovereign Soviet territory" and for the Allies as a whole to cease support for the "counter-revolutionary bandits" in the western portions of the Soviet Union.

What had been (until the disasters of 1942-43) a major part of the anti-fascist Alliance was now the subject of lounge comedians and the butt of Bob Hope's jokes on his 1959 USO tour.

The elimination of the USSR, one of the Third Reich's main war goals, was accomplished even as the Nazi Party itself was on its deathbed.

On July 19th, Field Marshal Rudolf Schmidt, the commander of all Reich reserve forces, and, with the apparent isolation of the Party leadership in Berlin, the de facto governor of the entire General Government area, surrendered to the Allies in the person of Creighton Abrams, Commander, 12th Army Group. Through sheer chance, the surrender took place at the Headquarters of the 1st Argentinean Infantry Division, a unit that had just rotated into the van of the 12th Army Group the day before. Using his unquestionable authority (Schmidt had been named commander of all Reserve forces by Hitler himself immediately before being put out to pasture along with the rest of the senior Heer leadership, an appointment that had, for reasons known only to Hitler, never been rescinded), Schmidt was able to achieve something that Manstein had been unable to accomplish in the West: have the youngsters of the Hitler Youth lay down their arms without massive German-on-German casualties.

With the total collapse of resistance in the East, save that of a few fanatical SS units that refused to recognize Schmidt's authority, Third Army scouts linked up with advanced elements of the 12th Gurkha Rifles near what had once been the Polish/Ukrainian border on August 14th, 1959. With this link up completed, the War in the East effectively came to an end, to be replaced almost immediately by low-level warfare between the surviving Slavs in the region and the German "settlers". As the occupying powers, it was up to the Allies to protect all the civilians, and German POWs, in the region. This was, of course, far easier said than done, as revenge killings and revenge for the revenge bloodshed continued despite what, by all accounts, was a sincere effort by Allied forces (primarily American in Poland and Commonwealth to the south and east) to keep a lid on things.

The Allied efforts were complicated by the presence of thousands of heavily-indoctrinated Hitler Youth and Waffen-SS veterans who could simply not bear the shame of having lost the war. While many of these young men (and more than a few women and girls from the BDM ranks) chose to take their own lives, often with their prized Hitler-Jugend-Fahrtenmesser as the tool of choice, a few chose instead to fight on as "werewolves". It was the action of this small minority that led to the most well-known massacre of the Occupation.

The records clearly indicate that the settlement of New Hamburg was one of the more troublesome in all of Northern Poland. Allied Provost Marshall records list no fewer than 52 incidents between its occupation on August 3rd and the events of October 17th, including two murders of American troops that were conclusively tied to the settlement by physical evidence and the murder of at least seven Polish civilians, including a district councilman. While in no way excusing the massacre which followed, the record does, perhaps, explain it.

The American method of securing settlements like New Hamburg was remarkably simple, and usually effective in reducing violence. The Americans simply bought every weapon that was presented to them, no questions asked, regardless of who brought them forward. Since there was almost no way to obtain Occupation Scrip besides working directly for the Allies (which was, in turn, the only way to obtain anything beyond the bare necessities of life, especially tobacco), the chance to get what was six months' supply of tobacco or real coffee in return for a broken Mauser or a pound of sugar for a bayonet was a serious incentive. At night, American troops would patrol the perimeter of German settlements to ensure that there was no entry of local residents looking for revenge.

On October 17th, the Platoon assigned to duty at New Hamburg was from the Kansas National Guard. Unlike previous guard units, Easy Platoon had suffered a KIA (almost certainly at the hands of a New Hamburg "werewolf"). In retrospect, it was a serious lapse in judgment to assign this platoon to the curfew watch. Each four-hour watch roster required five five-man teams to secure the perimeter (two men in a jeep mounting a .50 cal machine gun and three riflemen), with the rest of the platoon acting as a reaction team in case of a disturbance. The midnight to 04:00 watch on October 17th had two teams assigned to the same sector, leaving a section of the settlement wall unpatrolled. This was done intentionally, as the later General Court Martial of Captain Neil Massey proved, with the intent of allowing two members of the local Polish community to enter the settlement and perform a beating on a former death-camp guard who lived in the settlement.

What happened is, of course, well known. Ten members of a local underground cell, all of whom had lost at least one parent to reprisal killings during Nazi rule, entered the settlement, rousted pre-selected victims from their beds, and executed them while their families were forced to watch. In all, 17 German settlers, ten of them ex-Einsatzgruppen commandos, and seven Auschwitz guards were killed, and some thirty homes burned to the ground before the group attempted to make its escape. None of the murderers managed to escape, since the arson that accompanied their other crimes brought out the reaction force which engaged them in the light of parachute flares. Seven of the intruders were killed, the others captured. In the investigation that followed, Capt. Massey took full responsibility for the event, although it is unlikely that the scheduling error could have escaped either the platoon sergeant or the squad leaders of the assigned teams; none of them were even questioned in the face of Massey's statements.

The Court found Massey guilty of dereliction of duty and sentenced him to two months' confinement to his company area, loss of 60 days' pay, and reduction in rank to 2nd Lieutenant. This sentence has long been a source of debate, since the Court ordered the terms to begin immediately and Massey's unit was, at the time, preparing to rotate out of theater and had been isolated from contact with outsiders for 21 days, starting the day before sentencing, as part of the quarantine put in place to prevent the transmission of illness from Europe to the US. The movement back to the US took Massey's unit eight days from arrival at the embarkation point to arrival in New York. The unit was then placed into isolation barracks on Ellis Island for three weeks before being shipped back to Kansas by train, a process that took two days. Once it reached Fort Riley the unit was subjected to a final battery of medical tests, debriefs, and equipment return. Massey's platoon, save Massey himself, was given 30 days leave on January 12, 1960. Lt. Massey was released from confinement to the company area and given 30 days leave on January 13, 1960. Massey was not discharged from the National Guard as a result of his conviction, and on the strength of the entire service record, including two Bronze Stars with "V" attachment and a Purple Heart with two Oak Leaf Clusters, he was promoted to 1st Lieutenant on August 6, 1960. Massey retired from the National Guard as a full Colonel. It is speculated that the conviction for New Hamburg cost him a General's Star.

Since it had been badly damaged in the October 17th attack, the settlement of New Hamburg was evacuated on October 24th, 1959, and the residents returned to Germany. The rest of the settlement subsequently burned down in unknown circumstances.

60

While the Allied successes in the East allowed them to "liberate" massive amounts of territory from Reich control, they did little to advance the end of the war. To end things, the Allies had to deal with both the last fanatical hard core of the Waffen-SS – and with an even more serious opponent, this one of their own making.

The 1,000 Year Reich had, in its 26th year, been compressed to two small ovals centered on Berlin and Nuremberg. Both areas were extensively contaminated with anthrax to the point that neither the US nor UK would risk troops (either their own or those under their overall command) in them. At the same time, the Nazi Party leadership, having been driven back into Berlin by the Allied advance on all fronts, seemed to take a perverse pride in braving the seething caldron of disease that surrounded the Reich capital. The leadership, especially Joseph Goebbels, made regular broadcasts daring the Allies to come and face the Reich in Berlin. The Allies attempted to stop these surprisingly effective propaganda broadcasts with air attacks on transmitter sites, but the resourceful Goebbels always managed to find a way to erect more (although the strength of the broadcasts weakened with each relocation, the broadcasts continued virtually until the end of the Reich).

With their options limited, the Allies focused on actions which would make the contaminated areas unlivable while consistently bombarding those within the region with promises of comfort and safety if they would surrender. As time passed an increasingly large trickle of civilians, eventually joined by some SS troops, came out to the Allied lines (which by late August had come to resemble permanent bases, including semi-permanent corrugated metal structures, many of which are still in use today) and surrendered. Those who didn't endured some of the worst conditions of the entire war.

Allied air forces owned the skies – it is estimated that by September 1st the entire Luftwaffe totaled less than 20 operational aircraft – and struck at anything that moved (in the grim humor common in war, pilots began to name their aircraft things like "Horse Hunter" and started to paint animal drawn wagons on the sides of their planes to indicate "kills"). As had been the case 15 years earlier during the blockade of Japan, anything with wheels became a legitimate target. After more than five years of doing everything possible to avoid civilian casualties, Allied planners had reached the point that a handcart loaded with firewood was seen to be an "enemy economic asset". As brutal as this warfare was, it was about to become, somewhat unintentionally, far worse.

On August 28th, 1959, twelve C-123 Provider aircraft from the Texas National Guard began Operation Scythe. The aircraft, modified as "crop dusters", were targeted on apple orchards on the edge of the Nuremberg "no go" zone. Each aircraft carried 2,500 gallons of the herbicide Tordon (better known as "Agent White"), a commercially-available stump and sapling killer used by American farmers and foresters to control unwanted growth in limited areas. Two days later, the same aircraft sprayed what had been tentatively identified as freshly-sown winter wheat fields outside of Berlin with a mixture of Agent White and Agent Orange. Escorted by both fighters and ground attack aircraft in case any opposition was encountered, the C-123 spraying missions continued on every day that weather allowed. By mid-October the number of spraying aircraft had expanded to 192, allowing the spraying of virtually the entire area still under Nazi control.

The results of Operation Scythe were devastating. Food production, already greatly impacted by lack of both animal and human workers thanks to anthrax and other disease, virtually ceased on a commercial level. As the spraying missions expanded, so did the famine. By the time Scythe was suspended for the winter in early November, Allied air operation planners bragged that there was not a piece of open ground the size of burial plot that had not been "treated" anywhere in unoccupied Germany. This level of coverage meant that even small personal gardens and city park-based communal gardens were usually exposed to at least one, often three or more, spraying visits over the end of summer and into the fall harvest season. The immediate impact of the defoliant missions was huge. The later impacts due to dioxin contamination of the herbicides (something never envisioned or known by Allied planners) continue to echo down the years to this day, making Operation Scythe one of the most hotly-debated operations of the entire Second World War.

By late December, the Germans stumbling into Allied lines to surrender began to look more like skeletons with skin stretched over them than human beings. These pitiful scarecrows told stories detailing the suffering within the Reich pockets that horrified Allied intelligence officers. As word of these interviews inevitably spread through the military and civilian chain of command, protests began to rise at the reluctantly-accepted strategy of starving the enemy into submission. This unrest began to show up in the civilian media with predictable reaction from those who had seen the horrors of Japan first hand years before. Something had to change.

Unwilling to alter the "Unconditional Surrender" policy, especially since it would almost certainly mean allowing the remaining Party leadership to escape the noose, Washington finally, reluctantly, acceded to a plan first brought forward by the British in late October.

On January 15, 1960, Operation Digger began. With massive air and artillery support, the First Polish Corps began its attack into the Berlin Hot Zone. Consisting of the Free Polish Army, two brigades of Ukrainian troops that had been recruited in the recently-liberated Ukraine, and the Maccabees Division (mainly Jews recruited from the British Mandate of Palestine, along with volunteers from existing Commonwealth formations, the US flatly refusing to allow any of its troops, volunteer or not, to be exposed to the dangers of the Hot Zone), the all-volunteer force entered combat with a fanaticism usually reserved for Holy Wars. Although every man in the First Polish Corps had been vaccinated for any disease that had a vaccine available, and all were taking prophylactic doses of antibiotics, the danger to the troops was still extreme. Volunteers were told that their chances of survival were below 50%. Such was the hatred against the Nazis, especially in the Jewish population in Palestine, that the number of volunteers exceeded the available slots by a third (British recruiters in Palestine reported turning away men in their 80s and boys barely old enough to see over the recruiter's desk).

Operation Digger featured some of the most vicious fighting in modern times, with virtually no quarter asked or given. SS strong points were obliterated by massed air attack, generally using fuel air weapons and/or napalm, or by long range artillery (Allied heavy guns and 240mm rocket batteries ringed the Hot Zones virtually wheel to wheel as the weapons used to conquer a continent concentrated on two small regions). The dividing line between combatant and non-combatant, already blurred, ceased to exist on both sides of the conflict as medical personnel and civilians were caught up in the cauldron of combat. As was once noted about warfare in North America between irregular forces during the Anglo-French wars: "Things were done, none were spared". Allied troops who went too far were dealt with by field court martial without being sent to the rear. Waffen-SS troops were generally shot out of hand, with no opportunity to surrender. It was war stripped of any sort of concern for the enemy.

It lasted for seven weeks.

On March 9th, 1960, the Commander of the 1st Polish Corps General Stefan Rowecki (a truly remarkable individual who fought the initial Nazi invasion of Poland, escaped Reich custody in 1943, made his way across Nazi lines into the Soviet DMZ and wound up in Britain having effectively traveled around the world to get there, where he joined the Free Polish Army in 1945) declared Berlin secured. Shortly thereafter, the remains of Himmler were found, as were the bodies of Joseph Goebbels, his wife, and their daughter Holdine (apparently murdered by her father). Goebbels's two youngest daughters, Hedwig and Heidrun, were found nearby having escaped their parent's desire to "save them from a world without National Socialism". Goebbels's two youngest children were the only two of the seven siblings to survive the war. Both his stepson and son died in action, his eldest daughter died in a 1958 Allied air attack, and daughters Helga and Hilegard succumbed to Anthrax in the Fall of 1959.

With the loss of Berlin, the garrison commander of the Nuremberg Pocket accepted the inevitable and surrendered to British forces on March 12th, 1960.

After 7,499 days, the European portion of the Second World War was over.

61

One of the great misunderstandings by average citizens in the US, UK, and much of the West is that because the last Nazi redoubt surrendered on March 15, 1960, that date marks the end of the dying in Europe. Nothing could be further from the truth.

In the nine months remaining in 1960, Allied battle deaths (primarily American, Commonwealth, and Indian) exceeded 1,000, with German deaths being at least twenty times that number (with some historians putting the total closer to 100 times the Allied figure).

The wide variance in German deaths estimates is due to a number of factors, some of them due to different ways of gathering and analyzing statistics; some, however, are frankly political in nature as revisionism has taken its toll. Allies troops fought mainly small unit actions across Germany and Austria, usually, but not always, in rural areas far from the more reasonable (and shattered) city leaders. Allied reactions to these Werewolf units were uniformly harsh and, by design, exceptionally disproportionate.

After one attack on an American Civil Affairs unit that killed three men as they passed through a part of the Black Forest, USAF bombers burned some fifty square miles of the wooded areas on both sides of the road to ash and followed the destruction with heavy application of Agent White to ensure that no stumps or saplings survived to restart growth. Whether because the attack killed the insurgents or simply because the robust response was an unmistakable message to all in the region, attacks in the Black Forest dropped to virtually nothing. The reaction of other Allied units when confronted by insurgents was not quite as massive, however, with commanders being given an entirely free hand in rural areas where "collateral damage" was unlikely and dramatic shows of force were the rule, not the exception.

The much rarer cases of urban attacks were handled in a uniform manner. Allied units would withdraw from the town, taking with them their medical personnel, medications, and field kitchens, and place the community under a 23-hour curfew for a week to ten days (or until the insurgents were identified and turned over to Allied authorities). With the medical and food supply conditions prevalent across what had once been the Inner Reich, the withdrawal of Allied support meant instant hunger and significant increases in serious illness. Deprived of the "sea in which they swam" (to paraphrase the failed Chinese Communist revolutionary Mao Tse-Tung) the Werewolves became increasingly ineffective in the months following the surrender, but even as they were destroyed they were responsible for over 100 KIA every month from March to October of 1960.

Allied and German civilian losses in Germany and Austria were dwarfed by the bloodshed in the East, where the end of the war was more of a signal to settle old scores and take revenge than the cause for any celebration. The remnant of Poland's prewar population turned on those who had collaborated with the conqueror and on the conquerors themselves. The US Army was forced to deploy three full divisions across Poland and the western part of the Ukraine simply to keep bloodshed to a minimum, with the Commonwealth needing close to five full divisions to keep a lid on Eastern Europe.

SACEUR carefully and quite intentionally delayed the return of the Free Polish Army to its homeland by putting the 1st Polish Corps in charge of the evacuation of *all* residents from the Berlin and Nuremberg Pockets, a task that lasted several months. To the immense credit of General Rowecki and his men, they performed this thankless task with what can only be called remarkable professionalism given the conditions that surrounded them.

Despite their close contact with a civilian population that loathed them, and that they loathed in return, war crimes or simply acts of revenge by Rowecki's men were far lower than that found among other Allied units. This may, in part, be due to the extraordinary powers the Polish Government-in-Exile afforded Rowecki when it came to field discipline.

Even in the West, Allied troops were not completely safe from attack. French fascist insurgents, who blamed the Allies for the fate that that had befallen their country, were an irregular threat, but one serious enough that most Allied troops had very little contact with French civilians outside of the initial landing zones and Normandy. The resulting separation meant that Allied attitudes toward France did not change to the same degree that was the case in Norway, Belgium, and even in Italy. The attitude was critical in the change over to civilian rule.

The decisions made by the Allies (actually almost entirely by London and Washington) regarding who was placed "temporarily" in control of the European states liberated at enormous human cost – and how – remain a subject of vigorous debate to this day.

In the West, the choices were somewhat easier, thanks to the "Governments-in-Exile" that had fled ahead of the advancing Wehrmacht (although the legitimacy of a leadership which had not set foot in the territory they were to rule for two decades was more than somewhat shaky). After a considerable debate (perhaps the largest disagreement between the UK and US since the decisions surrounding Whirlwind), the White House prevailed in imposing the "Right of Self Determination" over all territory that had been under "Fascist Occupation or Allied Protection" on January 1, 1950. This phraseology allowed Washington to exclude most of Asia from Self Determination, something that the US was utterly opposed to for Japan (where American Civil Affair units were gradually making headway in the creation of Modern Japan, with its vibrant, sometimes chaotic democracy). The British managed to alter the original American proposal to allow the "Allied Protecting Power" to determine exactly what territory comprised each area voting on self-determination, and to hold off elections until Allied Civil Affair teams certified that the voting population was "de-Nazified sufficiently to ensure true free and fair elections". What this phrase actually meant was a source of irritation in the generally remarkably close relationship that has long marked "Atomic Four" interactions in the post-war world, especially in Washington, where many believed (with more than some justification) that they had been "outfoxed by the damned Brits again".

Nevertheless, by late 1960, civilian rule had nominally returned to Belgium, Denmark, Italy, Greece, Luxembourg, the Netherlands, Norway, and Poland (the Polish situation in 1960 and its resolution is far beyond the scope of this work. Although numerous excellent books are available that chronicle the fascinating reconstruction of the country, David Leland's exceptional *From the Ashes, Poland 1960-1995* is not to be missed by anyone interested in a single-volume history on the subject).

In the East, the situation was far more difficult, with no easily-transferable exiled bureaucracy available to implant, and with fascist governments still in nominal control, albeit at the whim of Commonwealth troops. Again the efforts in the East are far beyond this work, or any single work, with each country's struggles to find their way in the post-war world deserving separate close examination. This being said, a few words concerning the end of 20th Century Europe's other totalitarian empire are called for, for clarification if nothing else.

With the end of the Reich, all of the many claimants to leadership of the "USSR" demanded recognition of their claims to one version or another of the territory controlled by the Soviet Union on June 19, 1941. The Allies (mainly the UK, with the US very much in the background) simply ignored all of these demands and claims. In part it was a desire by Whitehall to ensure that the specter of communism not be allowed to return in any significant way; mainly, however, it related to the British government's overriding desire to ensure that no single continental power would again threaten the British Isles and require the spilling of oceans of British blood to set things right. Twice in one century, for both the US and especially the UK, was enough.

This overarching goal was what resulted in the independence of the Baltic States long before any sort of vote on the matter, the establishment of East and West Ukraine, the creation of the Belarussian Republic, and, most importantly, the recognition of the Russian Tsarist Republic (a constitutional monarchy built along English lines with Tsar Andrei Alexandrovich as the titular, albeit virtually powerless, sovereign). Supported by both Commonwealth troops and, more importantly, by the leaders of the two most powerful partisan bands in Russia, the Tsarist Russian Republic was rapidly recognized by virtually the entire Alliance – or, as it was increasingly called, the United Nations – as the legitimate government of what had been Nazi-Occupied European Russia. The loud protests of the many claimants to the mantle of the Soviet Union fell on deaf ears, and feeble threats of military action from groups that counted anywhere between 1,500 and three thousand militia fighters (and as many as 22 BT-26 tanks) as their entire army against the two British and two Canadian divisions and a New Zealand Armored Brigade were treated as the ineffectual ranting that they were.

While statistics can sometimes be misleading, those concerning what is globally referred to as the Second World War are stunning and a brief list seems appropriate at this time:

190,000,000: Total dead

155,000,000: Civilian dead (including 62 million from the USSR, 29 million Poles, 21 million Chinese, 13.5 million "German", 9.5 million Japanese, 8 million from the "Southern Resource Area", 5 Million from "Western Europe")

35,000,000: Military dead (includes 9 million Red Army, 11.5 million Wehrmacht/Waffen-SS, 6 million Japanese military, 5 million Nationalist Chinese)

71,000,000: Total deaths suffered by the Soviet Union (mostly due to forced labor and starvation)

85%: Percentage of Pre-war Polish population killed or unaccounted for by war's end

97.5%: Percentage of pre-war European Jewish individuals liquidated by the Reich

$3,800,000,000,000: Economic damage (measured in 1960 US Dollars)

2,175,000,000,000: US share of total Economic Impact

147,000,000: Troops who performed military duties between 1/1/1937 and 3/15/1961

400,000,000: Number of civilians left homeless/displaced for at least seven days due to military action (this amounts to roughly one person in five alive during the war)

No actions or activities by the human race, before or since, have approached any of these figures. One can only pray nothing ever does.

Afterword

The genesis of this project was a desire to look at the utter insanity that Nazi Germany had planned for Europe after gaining final victory. The decision to present that as the preface to one volume of an imaginary history of the war, was, in the main, done to improve the readability and also provide reasonable break points in the essay. The conclusion of the "Preface" was initially meant to be the end of the project. Fate, as it is wont to do, intervened, and a number of people who had read the original work encouraged me to "complete the project". The rest is (alternate) history.

There are portions of the work that have been strongly debated by some early readers. Many of these relate to the manner that the Soviet Union is defeated. It is quite difficult to actually find a likely way for Hitler's legions to be victorious against the Soviet Union that works in the "real world"; the manner I chose is, I believe, one of the more possible, albeit still extremely unlikely (a danger common to alternate histories, as history often really dislikes change). The other source of debate by early readers is in the timing and use of nuclear weapons. The decision to delay use seemed completely in keeping with what is effectively a serious case of collective PTSD that afflicts those who had a hand in the alternate defeat of Imperial Japan by blockade and starvation. The societies of what came to be known as the "Western Allies" in our world, even when waging "total war", have an aversion to causing the sort of intentional suffering that victory by blockade would cause. The reluctance to return to mass slaughter, even in war, would, in my opinion, color any decisions regarding use of the Bomb in future conflicts (much as is the case today, where no nuclear weapon has been used since August of 1945, a condition that one can only pray continues indefinitely).

Lastly, a word of thanks to those brave men and women of our world's "United Nations" who defeated the scourge of fascism at enormous cost of blood and treasure. Their unblinking, enormous sacrifices are the sole reason that this book is pure fiction. Be they members of the Red Army, or Australian "diggers", or Indian Army troops, or American service(wo)men, they saved our world.

All non-historic persons in this work are purely fictional and any resemblance to actual persons is entirely coincidental.

Sea Lion Press

Sea Lion Press is the world's first publishing house dedicated to alternate history. For our full catalogue, visit **sealionpress.co.uk**.

Lightning Source UK Ltd.
Milton Keynes UK
UKHW01f2044230518
323110UK00001B/4/P

9 781976 423239